DREAM MATES

JANE HANDLER

Dream Mates

Book Two: Into the Parallel Omegaverse

Jane Handler

For everyone who sometimes feels like they just don't fit.
Maybe you're just in the wrong world...

About This Story

Welcome back to the parallel omegaverse! *Dream Mates* is a why-choose, non-shifting omegaverse, fated-mate, portal romance and is Book Two of a trilogy. If you have not read Book One, *Dream Girl*, you're going to want to read that first. Like Book One, this ends on a cliff-hanger. But I promise that there is a happily-ever-after in *Dream Pack,* Book Three. This is a 'why-choose' romance, so Grace gets her HEA with multiple people, and her story is ultimately m/m/m/m/f/m.

Grace is from our world and falls into another. Wes lives in a *parallel universe* that's similar to ours. While some things are the same, there are *many* differences, given everything evolved a little differently. This has affected everything from physical places to laws and technology.

The biggest difference of all is that alphas, betas, omegas, and many other designations exist. Each designation has specific characteristics. Alphas are larger, faster, with better senses and are often leaders. Betas make up most of the population and are your average, ordinary people. Omegas are nurturers, and often physically smaller. They are the most physically compatible with alphas and are sought after as mates. Mate bonds between an alpha and omega are as legally binding as marriage.

Many people live in packs, which have the legal rights of families, no matter what designations comprise them. There are also plenty of couples and throuples. Same-sex and polyamorous relationships are legal and accepted in this world.

While this story and world aren't particularly dark, some of the characters do have darker pasts. As a teen, Grace suffered physical and mental abuse at the hands of her religious mother and church. While there are no flashbacks, she does go into more detail about what happened to her than in Book One. Brennan, too, had some significant mental health struggles, and details them a little more in this story. Other characters have also had their own struggles, and/or have suffered the loss of family members or partners. There's some family drama, including gaslighting and bullying. There are a couple of scenes involving physical violence, and there's some scenes at a medical testing facility. There are brief references to past genocide and child trafficking. This book has no cheating, or third-act break-ups, and while there's some women causing drama, it's not to steal Grace's guys.

This book is meant for adult readers. There are graphic spice scenes, some of which include multiple partners and the crossing of swords. This book contains bonding, knotting, praise, oral, group scenes, heat scenes, dp, dvp, rope play, soft daddy doms, and other spicy things.

Enjoy your return to the Parallel Omegaverse. Because dreams aren't real–until they are.

Note for those joining us from the HockeyVerse: Yes, we meet Verity and company in this book. This trilogy takes place before Finding the Forward.

Chapter One

Wes

"Grace!" I took off down the street as the strange, black, unmarked car drove away.

They were taking her. I didn't know who or why, just that someone was taking my Grace, *my mate*, away from me. Fear shot through me as I ran after the car, chest shaking.

No. I'd just gotten her back. They wouldn't take her away from me. They couldn't. I wasn't about to fail to protect her again.

The car disappeared from my sight. Shit. I stopped, putting my hands on my thighs, bending over to catch my breath. My heart shattered. *Grace.*

No. That was okay. Obviously, I wasn't as fast as a car. But I'd find her. This time I'd fucking find her and get her back. I wouldn't abandon her to some awful fate again.

Fumbling for my phone, I opened the tracking app and watched as her location *disappeared.*

Shit. Did they take her phone?

Grace's panic shot through our bond along with nausea.

Then...

Nothing?

Nothing.

Just emptiness where she'd been just a moment before.

Shit.

"No." A growl ripped from my throat as I sank to the ground in defeat. No location. No bond.

Not again. Bile rose in my throat.

Evan caught up to me, face contorted in pain. "I... I can't feel her. She was so scared and suddenly, she wasn't there. She's not..."

It came out like a sob as panic and dread shot through our bond, his lemonade scent going burnt with fear.

The bottom dropped out of my belly. Oh, I hoped not.

Our bond wasn't strong. That was it. It had to be. She wasn't gone; our bond was still weak because of Grace's concussion. Yeah, I'd go with that.

Still, I couldn't bear that Evan, my omega, my mate, was in pain. I wrapped my arms around his giant form, pulling him to me.

"What the fuck is going on? That car had no plates." Brennan joined us, panting from exertion. His blue eyes gleamed with worry and confusion as he brushed his black hair back with his hand.

"Grace." My voice broke as I held onto Evan like he was a lifeline.

Grace. Grace was gone with some unnamed guy in a dark suit. One thing the movies had taught me was that nothing good ever came from unnamed guys in dark suits.

A sob ripped from Evan's throat, defeat radiating off him. For a moment we stood there, holding each other in the middle of the road.

Grace.

"Let's go back to the house. I need to know what just happened." Brennan put his arms around both of us, voice low, but alpha-firm. His pine scent filled with concern.

"Back to the house? I... I can't feel her. She's gone from my phone. We have to get her. I can't..." Panic gripped my chest.

Didn't he understand? I couldn't let her face some awful fate alone again like when her mother sent her to that horrible wilderness camp when she was a teenager.

"Hold it together, Wes. You're an alpha. Hold it to-fuck-ing-gether. Let's go back to the house and re-group. For fuck's sake, you're not even wearing shoes," Brennan growled, the slightest bit of alpha dominance in his voice.

True.

The three of us walked back to the house, Evan sobbing. Wave after wave of anguish rolled off my sweet, giant, omega mate.

When we got home, Riley stood in the living room, laptop open, yelling at Spencer.

"Agent Asshole said that he'd bring her back. They'll realize she's innocent and *bring her back*. And in the meantime, I will fucking find them." Her light brown hands sat on her hips, as her heavily-lined brown eyes squinted at him.

"Ri, I am sorry to say this, but they're not going to bring her back. Jett, get off the phone. Calling the police isn't going to help." Spencer paced the living room, one olive hand raking his dark hair, which held a hint of grey.

"Will someone tell me what the fuck is going on? Who took Grace and what do you mean they're not bringing her back?" Brennan demanded, turning on the air filter on the wall. The air was bitter with the smell of burnt leather and sour anise.

I froze at Spencer's words, because if anyone knew what was happening it would be our resident mad-genius.

"They're not bringing her back? Spence, what do you fucking know? I can't feel her. She's not dead, right? Just unconscious?" My voice shook.

"Is this the whole Omega Protection Program thing? Are they throwing her back in?" Jett joined us, dark hair pulled back in a ponytail. He got out his phone.

"What are you talking about?" I clawed at my chest as if doing so would make me feel her. It was like I was nineteen again, when I finally realized that she was never coming back to my dreams.

"I need to know what just fucking happened." Evan returned to the living room, pushing the entire bar cart.

Spencer took a deep breath, leaning against the back of one of the chairs. "That man was clearly from what I always thought of as the Temporal Police. I'm guessing they took her because she's not supposed to be here. That's what they do—ensure that the ban on interdimensional travel is enforced. She's gone from our phones because they probably went to whatever parallel world that they take people to. That could be why you don't feel her."

"Oh fuck. The people running the simulation? You knew they'd take her and *didn't tell us*?" Riley punched Spencer in the arm, scowling.

"No. I just knew it was a possibility. Especially since we still have no idea how she got here." Spencer bowed his head, his brown and gray eyes filling with sadness, scent turning salty.

"Ri, you know that she's from another world?" Evan handed me a glass of bourbon.

She knew? I'd thought only Evan, Spencer, and I knew about Grace's interdimensional-traveler status.

"Um, yeah." Riley rolled her brown eyes. "How do you even know who they are? Since I'm guessing they're some super-secret agency? How could you do this to us? You're an alpha; you're supposed to protect her. I thought you cared about her." She started punching Spencer again, tears streaming down her face, smearing her makeup.

"You knew someone would *come and take her*?" I stared at my packmate, my friend, my boss, too angry and upset to move.

Spencer gently took her pummeling fists and held them, pulling her to his chest. "I do care about her. So very much. I didn't know if they'd come and if they did, there's nothing we can do to stop them."

"Wes, she told us this. That was why he didn't want her to research how to get home or any of her old theories." Evan nestled into my arms, sadness coming through the bond.

"I didn't want Grace to draw attention to herself. Those theories are dangerous." Spencer shook his head.

"I didn't realize that there's some actual agency that could come and take her. How do you even know this?" I countered, holding my omega tighter so that I didn't punch my packmate.

"What the fuck is going on?" Brennan roared with enough dominance that we all stopped. His pine scent flared with anger as alpha pheromones filled the room.

Spencer sighed and sat on the couch with Riley.

"We know about Grace's fake identity," Jett started, holding on to his husband. "Bren had a PI investigate her. Why was she in the Omega Protection Program—was it because of her mom? But why would they take her back *now*? Who do I need to call? I'll pull in every favor I can."

While that was nice, it wasn't going to help. An agency. There was some actual agency keeping parallel world travel a secret. Grace had mentioned it, but I just brushed it off.

Mostly because I wanted her to stay here with me. So, I didn't listen. And they *took her*.

I turned to Brennan, anger rising inside me. "You had her investigated?"

"I have to protect the pack. It's literally my job as head alpha. She was hiding something. I needed to know what. Once we were told she was part of the Omega Protection Program, we let it go. We figured that if she didn't tell us in her own time, we'd broach it eventually." Brennan took a long drink of bourbon, hand shaking slightly.

"Of course she's hiding something, you asshole." Riley glared. "You're all assholes. Wait, someone knows my records are fake? Evan, I thought you made calls? Fucking shit, I need to protect myself because I'm not going to prison because Bren has trust issues."

"Riley made the records?" I knew Riley was *good* but...

"Um, yeah, because I'm the best." She bent over her laptop, her black-polished fingers starting to type at a rapid pace.

"Shit. Part of me wants to be mad because you're not supposed to break the law anymore, but part of me is really proud that you can create government records. That's some skill right there," I admitted, draining my bourbon. While I could easily hack the government, I wasn't sure I could do *that*.

"I did make calls," Evan replied. "That's why there's Omega Protection Program fingerprints all over Grace's files. I was trying to make it as real as possible, especially with everyone poking around and us needing to legitimize her so that she could have a life here with us."

"Ri, you can make fake government records?" Brennan asked, brow furrowing.

"Be proud, fucker." Riley didn't look up from her laptop.

"Grace isn't part of the Omega Protection Program. We created her record because she didn't have one, then I looped it in to cover our asses. That's why the Eastside station and the Center couldn't find her initially. It wasn't the glitch; it's because she doesn't exist here. The glitch just worked to our advantage and bought me time." Evan sighed and buried his face in my shoulder.

My arms wrapped around him. "Grace isn't from here. We needed to make her exist so that she could stay. Shit, how do I even tell this story?"

It sounded weird when I said it out loud.

"Short version. Grace dreamt of Wes for her whole life. They got married. Her shitty mom made her forget him by hurting her. After that, Grace no longer dream-traveled and thought Wes wasn't real. Wes couldn't find her because she existed in another world which he couldn't get to. One day she woke up on a bench and *poof*, she's in this world and Wes is real, and they are reunited in person, and fall back in love. There, told it," Riley retorted, still typing.

Brennan poured himself another drink, brows furrowing. "What?"

"While we were going to tell you, we hadn't gotten there yet. Grace was terrified that she'd say the wrong thing and be put on a psych hold–which happened when she was in high school." I continued to hold Evan to me. "That's why she wasn't doing individual therapy with the Center even though she desperately needs to deal with her abandonment issues. She was afraid that she'd let it slip that she's from a parallel world and things would go sideways."

"Even now, she's afraid. Going to work terrifies her because of all the tiny differences between our worlds," Evan added. "When she says weird things or doesn't get into specifics, it's because she truly grew up elsewhere. When she doesn't get a reference, it's because her world has different things."

"Grace is what now?" Jett stared at us, brown eyes full of questions. With a sigh the beta police officer poured himself a glass of bourbon.

"Many, many worlds exist. Some quite similar from ours, some vastly different," Spencer explained. "Grace is from a world that, from what I understand, is not dissimilar from ours, though with one main difference—and many, many smaller ones."

"When Grace was a kid, she decided that she was going to use string theory to figure out how to get here, to our world, to me, so that we could be together in real life and not just in our dreams," I added. "But it sort of became just a side project after her mom made her forget me. It wasn't what she was doing for work, and her research wasn't anywhere near actually being able to *travel* to another world. She's pretty sure that's not how she got here. Not that she remembers how she got here or the events leading up to it."

"Which is why they're going to *let her come back to us.* She didn't break interdimensional law, it was just an accident or something," Riley insisted.

Spence put his head in his hands. "Oh, how I hope they will. But travel between worlds is *illegal.* At least from this one. I hope that it's different where she's from. But we're going to have to come to terms with the fact that we'll probably never see her again. She's gone. There's nothing we could have done to stop them. We're lucky that they let us live. I half-expected him to explode the house on the way out since we shouldn't know about them or other worlds."

He *what?*

Brennan rubbed his chin, his look somewhere between apprehension and disbelief. "You're trying to tell me that Grace is from *another universe?* That man dragged her back to where she came from?"

"Not where she came from. She's probably in interdimensional prison for breaking the law, if she's not already dead. I don't know much about the Temporal Police. But their rules are very strict." Spencer didn't look up, his scent salty. After all, he loved her, too.

"She's not dead. Don't you dare say that," Riley spat. "She's going to be questioned and brought back."

"I hope you're right." Spencer's voice broke.

I nodded, heart thumping. "You're right. Grace didn't do anything wrong. She probably got caught in an experiment at work and was brought here by accident. They found her, she'll give her statement, and then, you know her, she'll convince them to let her return here and stay with us."

It was ridiculous. But I had to cling to something.

"I'm really confused. Grace is from another world? But she's also your mate, right? What?" Jett took a swig of his drink and squeezed Brennan's hand.

"Scent matches can see their mates in dreams, you fuckhead. Sometimes even before they get their designation. Have you *not* seen those movies?" Riley was still on her computer.

Jett's eyebrows rose. "Through dimensions? That seems really mean, for you to find your mate but not be able to get to them, if parallel world travel isn't normal wherever you are."

"That's what Grace said. But like I said, when we were kids, she was going to become a string theorist and figure it out so that we could be together." I raked my dark blond hair with my hand.

Brennan gave me a hard look. "Start at the beginning. Because I still don't know what the fuck is going on."

I grabbed the bottle and refilled my glass, sitting down in a chair, pulling Evan to my lap.

"It wasn't my whole life. Just seven years. I was twelve–it wasn't that long after we'd moved to Rockland. I had a dream where I was sitting on a bench, drawing, in the park near my house on the Eastside–the same park that she was found at. Anyway, I went there a lot, so it wasn't that weird to dream of it. There was this blond girl on the swings. She walked up to me and told me that she was going to marry me." I closed my eyes, remembering. Her pink dress, her smile, her audacity.

Slowly, I told them everything. How night after night she came back. The adventures we had. How we confided in each other. How we slowly realized that we were both real, just in other worlds—and that we were in love. About the helplessness I felt when the trouble started and that bonding with her was one last act of desperation to keep her safe. That failing as an alpha to protect my mate had broken me so badly that I left my university and enlisted in the Army because I was afraid that if I didn't do something drastic temporarily, that I would do something drastic permanently.

"So, you can imagine my thoughts, when years later, I walk into my living room, and see her sitting on the couch with Jett and Evan." My hands fisted as I struggled to keep it together.

"That is really romantic, and sad." Riley closed her laptop.

"How do you know that this is your Grace? I remember the pictures you drew of her, but how do we know that she's yours if there are other worlds?" Brennan poured himself another drink.

"Unless there's another Grace Ellington with my bite under her boob, I'm sure she's mine. I just got her back and now she's gone. She's probably so scared. I'm a shitty alpha." My head rested on Evan's shoulder, and I tried to ground myself in his lemonade scent.

"You're not a shitty alpha. You did everything you could. This is extenuating and all we can do is hope that they realize she's not some world-hopping evil genius and let her come home to us." Evan started to purr to calm me down.

Brennan shook his head and looked at Spencer. "You all believe this?"

"I knew from the moment I smelled her that she wasn't from here," Spencer replied.

"Fuck, that conversation in the kitchen." Brennan rubbed his temples.

"Yeah, we didn't tell Spence. He figured it out," Evan said.

"She told me. Out of all of you she loves me best." Riley checked her phone and stood just as there was a knock on the door.

We all froze.

"It's just pizza. I'm still hungry. Evan, I got you garlic twists because you're weird and don't like pizza." Riley got the pizza and put it on the coffee table, moving her laptop.

"Why didn't you tell me where she was from? We're not supposed to have secrets from each other. Especially one that can bring danger to the pack." Hurt dripped from Brennan's voice.

I leaned over and grabbed a slice of pizza, mostly because I needed something to do. "We were planning on it. We just hadn't yet. Mostly because the trust between you and Grace isn't there. You called a thug to scare her. You yelled at her over playing the piano. Also, you're not familiar with the scientific theories behind parallel world travel like we are."

"You put the pack in danger." His voice rose. Jett put a hand on his arm, and he sighed. "But I understand her fear."

"Her world is enough like ours that basic things are the same. Food, languages, motorcycles, math. But what's that big difference you said?" Jett asked. "Because I can understand her when she speaks Mandarin even if the dialect is a little strange."

"Her world lacks magic dicks." Evan grabbed a garlic twist.

"What?" Jett laughed.

"Knots. That's what she calls alpha knots," Evan explained.

"Her world doesn't have designations. At least not like ours–and no bonds," I added. "Also, polyamory isn't accepted as widely as it is here. Heterosexuality, not bi- and pansexuality, is the norm, and packs are a completely unfamiliar concept. Most families in her world have one or two parents. But yeah, that would be why she can ride a motorcycle and recite *Pi* to a million places but knows no popular songs or movies."

Brennan's brow furrowed as he took a piece of pizza. "She's not even a gamma? What else did she lie about?"

"She *is* a gamma. She also *bonded* with us. I don't know how it all works in her world, but you can check her medical record and see for yourself," Evan explained as he grabbed a garlic twist.

"Grace really didn't lie about anything. She doesn't like lying. She was scant on details, but I think you can understand why. Bren, she was scared. I was just so fucking happy to have her back that I didn't always pay attention to how weird everything must be for her and how afraid she was." I should have. We were supposed to take care of each other.

"How do you know about this anyway, Spencer? The laws and Temporal Police?" Brennan asked.

"My father was engaged in research using qubits to map the fifth and sixth dimensions. He stumbled onto the existence of parallel worlds. I was there when the Temporal Police arrested him and his research partner and dragged them off for breaking interdimensional law. I was fourteen. I hid when I saw what was happening. I got out right before they exploded the super collider to hide what had been found." Spencer's voice broke and he looked away.

"Spence, *that's* how your dad died? I knew it was a work accident, but fuck." Evan got off my lap and joined Spencer, putting his arms around his best friend. He started to purr, the calmness coating us.

"My father and Dr. K didn't die in the explosion. They were brought to wherever the Temporal Police bring their lawbreakers. My research yielded little, other than that trying to get them back would be dangerous and fruitless. Given that my father never returned, and my mother stopped feeling him through their bond, I assume that he's dead. I hope you understand why I never told you. The Temporal Police didn't know that I saw them, and I worried about the ramifications." Spencer rested his head on Evan's shoulder.

"That's why you were obsessed with parallel worlds for a while when you were in high school," Evan breathed.

Spencer nodded. "Indeed. I wanted to see if there was any hope of getting them back. That was also why I told Grace that I wouldn't stop her from wanting to go home, but being able to do it–especially reliably–would break the law, and it would be best for her to stay here with us."

"Spence, I'm so sorry about your dad." This all made so much more sense now. My heart broke for him–to see your dad get taken away like that? Horrifying.

"I knew Grace was from another world because at the beginning she smelled a bit like them," Spencer added. "Parallel world travel has a smell. Well, it's not the travel itself, it's the specific neutrons that cling to you for a time."

"Neutrons. She smelled like neutrons." Brennan rubbed his head. "Shit. I don't even know what to do. Given this is some secret agency I'm guessing we can't make calls. We can't report her missing. But she is and people will miss her and there will be consequences. Fuck."

"There's nothing we can do but wait and hope." Spencer sighed. "At least the police investigation is closed. I can delay her job for a couple weeks. Mrs. Beekman thinks we're going on vacation. That will give us time to weave a story."

We'd need one. Mrs. Beekman, Grace's advocate from the Omega Center, would get fierce if Grace simply stopped answering her and showing up for appointments.

"Time might work differently." Riley took another piece of piz-za. "We should all set our phones to alert us when she gets back, since she had her phone in her pocket. Spencer, you should stay here when they go to the cabin. Send the door camera to your phone so when they bring her back you'll know she's here if you're out."

Spencer nodded. "That sounds like a good idea. I can think of many excuses to stay behind without alerting anyone that anything is amiss–which is exactly what we need to do. I can try to do more research, make more calls, but we can't get our hopes up."

"We can't lose hope, either," Riley said.

"We can't let anyone know that she's missing until we know how to handle this or we'll end up in jail. Fuck." Brennan put his head in his hands.

We didn't need that, either. I was pretty sure that Brennan's mom wasn't going to help us this time.

"I don't even know who to call. Secret interdimensional agencies are above my pay-grade," Jett added, leaning into Brennan's larger form.

"Riley will go to her sister's, we'll go to the cabin as planned. Spence, you don't have to stay here alone at the house. But given we'll be pretty indisposed, it will be your job to figure out a cover story. Eventually Mrs. Beekman will call, and we don't need to be investigated for Grace's disappearance," Brennan directed.

Anger swirled inside me. "That's the plan? We're not going after her? We're just going to wait and hope she shows up? We're going to still go to the cabin? That's a stupid idea."

"Where would we go, Wes?" Brennan retorted. "I get that you're upset–"

"She's my mate!" I shouted.

"So is Evan and he fucking needs you, too. I won't let you abandon him during his heat when there's literally no place to go to and get her back," Brennan yelled, filling the air with pine, trying to assert his dominance over me.

I stood and growled. "I can't just sit and do nothing."

"The moment we know *how* to get her back we will. But if people know she's missing, it will be a fucking nightmare, and you'll probably go to jail," Brennan snapped. "We have to handle our shit. She's not the only one in the pack, so alpha up and help me keep the fucking pack together while Spencer figures out what's going on and how to get her back."

"That's a little optimistic but I'll do what I can," Spencer said. He pulled Evan closer. "Hey, Evan, it's okay." He started to purr to calm him down.

I wasn't sure I'd ever heard Spencer purr.

Something ripped through my bond. A pained expression clouded Evan's face as he doubled over in pain.

"Alpha," he croaked, as his omega perfume filled the air.

Brennan ran over to him. "He's warm. Jett and I will get him upstairs. Wes, get your shit together."

Evan looked stricken as they helped him up the stairs, muttering soothing things as he whimpered.

"Wes, go and take care of Evan. He needs you. I'll do what I can to find Grace. There is nothing you can do about her, so focus on him," Spencer assured.

"She'll kick your ass if you abandon him when he needs you. As will I. Don't worry about me, Spence and I will play video games." Riley took another bite of pizza.

My chest shook. "This is just so much like when they took her to wilderness camp. I couldn't find her. They were hurting her, and I couldn't protect her."

That was the place that finally broke her. Us.

Spence put an arm around me. "I know this hurts. But it's not your fault. You didn't fail her. You *can't* fall apart. I'll handle getting Riley to the airport tonight. Go take care of Evan."

It smelled like it was just a spike. But Evan's heat was only days away, and emotional news could cause his heat to arrive early.

While I was worried about Grace, Brennan and Spencer were right. I had another mate, and I couldn't abandon him since we didn't know where she was and had no reliable way to find her.

Grace would understand. Wouldn't she?

I finished my bourbon and hugged Riley, then went upstairs to find Evan. The weight of the loss of Grace made every step seem like a marathon. Part of me still wanted to rage after her—or curl into a ball. But I could feel Evan's need through the bond. Not to mention, he was upset about her being taken, too.

The Temporal Police. Shit.

Even though we had no idea how Grace got here or if it was illegal, they'd taken her from us. Not feeling her, not knowing what was happening, not knowing where she was, was destroying me inside.

As much as I wanted to be optimistic, I had to come to terms with the fact that she was gone.

Gone. Once again, Grace was lost to me. Once again, I couldn't do anything about it.

My soul felt raw and angry. I knew I'd be gutted if she ever left me again.

I just never thought that it would happen like this.

Chapter Two

Grace

Agent Weigmier gave me another push into the courtroom as everyone stared at me, sending chills up my spine.

I took a deep breath as my memories continued to return to me. *3.1415926535.*

Shit. I knew what this was and why I was here. Fear tangled around me as I recalled the last time I saw the familiar people near the front of the court room. The ones shooting me angry looks, probably mad that I was here.

Professor Jaffey, as well as my boss at Rydor Corp, and two of my co-workers were the ones I'd seen selling weapons to people from another world one night late at work. They're the ones who plunged me into this whole mess.

Before that night, parallel worlds were just a theory on my laptop. A theory that Professor Jaffey had deemed unworthy of being anything but a hobby.

Which had been wrong. Just like I'd been wrong about her. She'd been a second mom to me. But it was really just a ruse so that one day she could throw me under a bus.

Now here I was, testifying against *her*.

The judge, in her red robe, gave us an annoyed look. "What is the meaning of this interruption?"

"The prosecution would like to call Dr. Grace Ellington, from world 1218, to the stand," the woman behind me said–the one that had chastised Agent Weigmier for cutting it so close.

I approached the judge, who gestured for me to take the stand. A number of people eyed me curiously. Taking another deep breath, I continued to recite *Pi. 8979323846.*

Memory bubbles continued to pop, everything becoming clearer. I hadn't been wrenched from Wes and everyone, because I was in *trouble*. It wasn't because I'd broken interdimensional law.

Agent Weigmier had retrieved me because I was a *witness*.

A key witness that the defense didn't want taking the stand. One that had been *hidden* so no one would hurt me. Because my testimony was key and the defense tried to get rid of me.

My heart squeezed. No, my beloved professor hadn't just set me up to take the fall, but had tried to kill me when that plan failed so that I couldn't testify.

"How could you?" Professor Jaffey had muttered to me that night, her blue eyes narrowing. "I gave you a chance. I gave you everything."

My former mentor, the one who'd persuaded me to pursue a PhD in math and guided me through the process, looked like she wanted to strangle me. Her dark blonde hair, with a hint of grey, was up in a bun and she was dressed in a suit. She looked respectable, likable, and trustworthy.

Once, I'd thought precisely that.

Like I had a choice to testify against you. I'd almost ended up on the defense bench with them.

Or instead of them.

Me not testifying against them had never been an option open to me. I took another deep breath. Yes, I could do this. I had to. *So I can go back to Wes.* That's the one good thing that came from this mess. I'd somehow gotten to *him*.

After a couple of confirmation questions, the prosecution–which was led by the Temporal Authority–asked me about the night Enforcement raided Rydor Corp for violations of the Parallel World Travel and Trade Embargo for Class IV worlds.

Bit by bit, I told the judge what I'd seen that night at Rydor Corp, the defense company where I'd worked during and after my PhD. I'd accidentally wrecked a colleague's research. To make it up to them, because they were mad at me, I'd been staying late after work to fix it. I'd gone to the vending machines for a snack and ended up seeing things I shouldn't have.

Because I could be a real dumbass sometimes, I got closer...

...and had gotten caught.

Those memories I'd had, of running in the foggy dark, of fences and guns and men with badges? They had been of *that* night. The night that I'd seen my favorite professor engaging in a transaction with military officers in uniforms I'd never seen. She, my boss, and a few others had been moving crates of weapons through some strange device that made them *disappear.*

I ran, was caught, they'd hurt me. Right after that, we were raided by the Temporal Authority Enforcement–or, what Spencer called the *Temporal Police.* Enforcement was the department responsible for investigating unauthorized movement between worlds. I'd been brought in with my colleagues, interrogated, imprisoned, and generally terrified.

Especially when my side project about traveling to parallel worlds was used against me. Professor Jaffey tried to pin their entire interdimensional smuggling operation on *me,* to make *me* the mastermind of the operation in order to save herself.

They'd known that selling our weapons to another world was illegal–though they'd tried to plead that they'd only known that *people* going back and forth was prohibited. Their interdimensional mapping project was a cover for their smuggling ring.

That was why I hadn't been put on that project like I'd hoped. Why I'd been told that my parallel world project wasn't viable for funding, just something for fun.

Her plan all along had been to use me as a scapegoat if things went wrong.

The prosecution finished their questions, and the defense took their turn, making me cry, as they painted me as an unstable liar who should be on meds. They used records from my teenage years to prove that I really could be a mastermind, not just building a device to enable parallel world travel, but orchestrating contact with a parallel universe to smuggle weapons.

"Her disappearance only solidifies her guilt. She was supposed to be in protective custody with the others, and she *disappeared.* The only one who'd be able to do that would be the one behind this, the one with the connections," the defense stated.

Another sob ripped from my throat as I wished that Wes was here to hold me. I'd been so lonely after graduation. Some of my colleagues were my friends, but most had gone on to other places and projects. I'd worked long hours and often been isolated from the few friends I had. Probably on purpose.

A secretive loner made a better mastermind.

No one would miss me if anything happened to me, either. I had no significant other, no mother, and had gone no contact with my family, other than the occasional text from the people I'd grown up calling *dad* and *grandma.*

Apparently I also made a good mastermind because my calculations for parallel world travel were *close*.

"If she's the mastermind and disappeared, then why would she reappear just in time to testify?" the judge asked the defense, her look skeptical.

"Enforcement found her, obviously. Either that or she wanted to make sure they were imprisoned so that she could stay free," the defense pressed, giving me a scathing look.

"If I could interject," the prosecution said, "the witness is *not* on trial here. She didn't disappear. She was placed elsewhere for her own safety after an attempt on her life when there was a breach in protocol regarding protective custody. She returned because we asked her to."

I shuddered, remembering that *breach*.

What I didn't precisely recall was how I ended up on the park bench in Wes' world with amnesia.

"An attempt she probably staged," the defense countered. His eyes focused on me. "Where have you been hiding, Dr. Ellington?"

Don't trust anyone. Don't mention where you were, Agent Weigmier had whispered to me before he pushed me into the courtroom.

"With all due respect, where I was is of no consequence, since I'm not the mastermind of this project. I was in protective custody because Professor Jaffey tried to kill me. Just like she killed the others." My heart wrenched at the thought.

I hadn't been the only witness that the Temporal Authority had brought in from my world to testify.

"There's no record of additional protective custody for this witness," the defense stated, reviewing a tablet.

"Well, yes, considering what happened to the others," the prosecution added. "We have a full brain map of the events in question. It proves that Dr. Ellington isn't the mastermind and what she says is true. Not that she's the one on trial, as I would like to remind the defense."

The defense froze. "You got authorization for a brain map?"

I didn't even know what that was, and I had no memory of that. Though my head twitched, as if recalling the process. It didn't sound fun. Their technology was so beyond anything we had.

The prosecution tapped on her tablet. "Your honor, we're sending you the permits and scans."

The judge nodded. "We'll take a recess so I can examine this evidence and decide whether it's admissible."

Professor Jaffey lunged at me. "You bitch. If it wasn't for me you'd be teaching kindergarten in your small town, married to some abusive, religious, asshole while popping out a kid every two years."

Uniformed guards held her back.

Tears streamed down my face as Agent Weigmier led me out of the courtroom. I remembered how good Professor Jaffey had been to me. How helpful and patient she'd been as I worked through my childhood trauma to get to the point where I *could* disobey my mother and reclaim the childhood love of math that I'd been forced to forget.

I first met Professor Jaffey when she taught a special seminar at my university in undergrad. My love of math had been truly rekindled, along with my hopes of getting my PhD. She'd taken an interest in me and encouraged me to apply to the university that she was going to be teaching at–even if it meant making my parents mad and moving to the other side of the country.

My doctoral program had been hard without family support. I'd been massively underfunded by the university and had to work and take out loans. But she'd invited me to her house for dinner, paid me to babysit her kids, and got me a teaching assistant position.

When she'd formed a partnership with Rydor Corp, I'd been honored to assist with her research, and then be hired after graduation—even if it wasn't the project I'd wanted, and the pay wasn't that great. Especially because I never got the opportunities to research, present, and publish like many of the others had.

Seeing her engage in illegal activity had confused me. It was the opposite of everything I'd come to know about her. But I'd given her the benefit of the doubt.

Hearing her accuse me of being behind it had broken me.

Her trying to murder me had destroyed me.

Chapter Three

Grace

While the judge went over the evidence, I sat in a small locked room, alone, with a weird sandwich and something that tasted like carbonated iced coffee. Even though my stomach was rumbling, I wasn't interested in the strange food that tasted wrong.

Fear sat heavily in my belly taking up any and all available space. While I understood I was a witness, I still had no idea what was happening.

Also, the defense's lawyers had been *mean* to me, even though their literal job was to get their clients off free. The best way would be to blame it on me.

Poor me. Literally *poor me.* The main reason I'd been so underpaid at Rydor Corp was because money could be a huge motivator to commit crime.

Hoping the room had no cameras, I removed my phone from my pocket. No bars, no signal—just like last time. I set mine to battery saver, since even if they had a compatible charger, they weren't going to let me use it.

In the notes section, I started writing down everything I remembered in case they made me forget again. Video or audio would be faster but would take more battery.

Obviously the Temporal Authority made me forget what happened, then remember. I wasn't sure if it was the shot in the neck or the weird little bottle of juice. I also had no idea how I could understand everyone–and they could understand me. That wasn't something they ever explained.

I still didn't quite remember everything.

However, I did recall that the Temporal Authority was obsessed with secrecy. Which I understood. But did they really have to leave me in another world unable to remember *my own name* or that they were coming back for me?

Writing everything down would also help me work it out in my head.

After I'd gotten a lot of my memories down, no one had come for me. I had to pee. How *was* this all going to go? When I finished testifying, would they take me back to Wes? Drop me back in the world I grew up in? Try me for some other crime?

I'd asked so many questions when they took me, trying to get answers, mostly out of professional curiosity. After all, parallel worlds weren't just real but there was a reliable way to move through them, and a governing organization to police it all.

While I got zero access to things like equations, or the machines they used, I had learned travel was very regulated and entirely illegal in my class of world. But, the discovery of parallel worlds, or how to travel through them, wasn't inherently illegal. Depending on how I handled it, had I managed to find a way to actually travel to Wes' world, I might not have immediately been arrested or punished.

I'd been informed that because of my contact with the Temporal Authority, I'd never be able to engage in my side project or adjacent research. There were also a whole lot of rules, and no one would let me anywhere near them.

Oh, I should write down everything I knew about the Temporal Authority for Spencer, to add to his own knowledge.

Wait. If the discovery of parallel worlds wasn't inherently illegal, then why did the Temporal Enforcers take Spencer's dad then blow up the super collider to destroy his lab?

Maybe Agent Weigmier would tell me. If one good thing came of this it would be being able to let Spencer know why his dad was taken and what happened to him.

If they let me return.

Please, please, please let me return to Wes.

A sob ripped from my throat as I started to cry. I was drained. Scared. What if I never got to see Wes and everyone again?

Wes. He was probably beside himself. While he tried to hide it, I knew that he felt awful for never being able to find me back when we were teenagers. That failing to protect me went against his protective alpha instincts. That knowing I was being hurt, and not being able to stop it, had made indelible marks on his soul.

Evan would be hurt, and so would Riley, because they let me in. Spencer was probably just sad—and thought I was dead.

Oh god, Spencer probably told everyone about everything and that I was dead. That would be his thought, and he'd share it with the group.

If only I could let them know I wasn't. Damnit. Brennan would be pissed at me. I hid this from him. I'd lied. I'd brought harm to the pack. Just when the two of us were making headway, this had to happen.

More sobs wracked my chest. I set my head on my arms and slumped over the table, crying myself to sleep.

The door opened, and I sat up, eyes crusty, bladder ready to explode. My back ached from the unnatural sleeping position. How long had I been asleep?

"You're upset." Agent Weigmier slipped in, still in that severe black suit. He was an unassuming man, of an average height and build, with brown hair, brown eyes, and forgettable features.

Which was probably the point.

He looked tired. But I had no idea what time it was or what all he did here.

"Of course I am. I don't know what's going on or what's going to happen to me after the trial." My chest shook as I remembered my fears of never seeing Wes and Evan again.

"We'll discuss that later, pending the outcome of the trial. But it will be according to protocol." He stood in front of me.

"Which is? I get it. I'm from some backwater world that doesn't get to know anything about your laws, but don't I have rights? I didn't even know you were coming. I thought I'd broken a law, and you were here to kill me." A sob escaped my throat, which was raw from crying.

He frowned, voice lowering, as he shook his head. "Not here."

I stood. "Fine. I need to pee."

His eyes focused on the uneaten food on the table. "You didn't like your food?"

"I was too nervous to eat, but I could use something now. Maybe something hot? How long was I asleep? When can I go home?" I prodded, anxious to be done with this. "Can I tell the guys I'm okay? I don't want them to worry."

That's what ate at me the most.

"The evidence has been accepted. We need to speak before you meet the judge." He put the hat he'd used before to help obscure my identity back on my head.

Agent Weigmier led me down the hall to the restroom.

"I'll wait here. Be quick. Talk to no one." He leaned against the wall.

I went to the restroom and ran a hand through my short blonde hair. I was going to meet the judge? Great. It would be nice if I knew more about temporal due process.

My T-shirt dress was wrinkled. My sandal wasn't mine, it was Riley's and covered in silver spikes. It wasn't quite the same height as the removable walking cast on my broken foot, which made walking a little lopsided. Also, this had been my indoor boot. Now it was gross from walking all over wherever I was.

While I knew that I was in a Temporal Authority complex, I didn't know what world I was in, if this was the main facility, or much of anything. It hadn't been for lack of trying on my part. You'd think that someone would want to answer my questions. *Nope.*

I came back out and he was waiting. Agent Weigmier had only been assigned to my case about the time someone had tried to kill me.

He glanced at my injured wrist, which was in a little removable wrist brace and my walking cast. "Are those from your previous injuries or are they new?"

"New." I trotted to keep up because his legs were long, and well, I had a broken foot.

"Do they hurt?"

"A bit. If you have ibuprofen, it would be much appreciated." They ached. I ached.

My heart ached.

He nodded. "I can provide a mild pain reliever. I'd rather keep you out of the infirmary. We still need to minimize contact."

"You said that to me before." I frowned, trying to remember all the blurry bits.

"Yes." His expression was impassive.

I really wanted answers, but the hall wasn't the place to ask them.

It felt like he intentionally took me down backstairs and used janky elevators and turned down halls needlessly. Though if it was to confuse me or protect me I couldn't say.

We finally ended up in a small office. There was a couch, a table, a desk, some chairs. It looked almost film noir–if film noir had gone paperless.

"Sit. Please don't leave. This is for your own safety. I'll get food and come back. We have much to discuss. Drinks are in the cooling unit." He left, and I could hear the door lock.

I got a bottle of what I hoped was water out of the mini fridge and plopped down on the couch. In novels, it was never good when the heroine ran off when told to stay put, so I was going to stay.

Also, I wanted those answers.

And, well, I might have testified, but that didn't mean I was finished–or that the danger was over. Yep, better off staying here. Especially if anyone still wanted to kill me. Taking out my phone, I tried to write down more things.

Something brushed my ankle, and I looked down.

A black kitty looked up at me with big blue eyes, ones that sparkled with intelligence. He had a blue collar with a little crystal on it.

"Hi, Kitty. You are absolutely some sort of shapeshifter, aren't you?" It was in the sharpness of his face, the pointiness of his ears.

Then again, I was in an interdimensional police station that served thousands of worlds, occupied by all sorts of people. Kitties could be different on other worlds. Did worlds with elves or faeries exist? He was absolutely a fae cat.

The cat jumped up on the couch and headbutted me.

"Do you want scratches?" I scratched behind his ears. "Hopefully, I'm not offending you or binding me to faerie or anything. I'm just a humble mathematician from a Class IV world, and I know nothing of the universe."

Looking up at me, the cat gave something that was very close to a laugh.

"Can I take you home with me?" I asked the cat. "We have no pets. I think we need a cat. But if I get chickens you can't eat them."

The cat meowed and rested his head on my thigh. I tried to pet the cat with one hand and continue writing with the other.

When the door clicked, I shoved my phone back in my dress pocket.

Agent Weigmier came in with two containers. "What do you think you're doing?"

His tone made me jump.

"I was just petting the cat? Do I not pet the cat?" I looked at the kitty. "You're absolutely a shapeshifter, right? Your name is Eugine, and you work in shipping, and you snuck in here to take a nap?"

"I was talking to him. And no, he's not a shapeshifter, and he shouldn't be in here." Agent Weigmier glared at him. "Escaped again, huh?"

Kitty gave him a very innocent look and meowed.

"Awww. I think I'm going to take you home." I gave Agent Weigmier a sly look.

He sighed. "Please don't. Here is your food. Please don't feed him, he has food allergies."

Yeah, he wasn't an ordinary kitty was he?

Handing one container to me along with some silverware, he set his down. With a sigh, he did something on his tablet.

"Thank you. Can I let my guys know that I'm okay? They're going to think I'm dead." Inside the container there was scrambled eggs, fried potatoes, and some sort of sausages. That would work.

He shook his head as he sat down with his container. "No. They shouldn't even know that I was there, but there was no time. We had a very small window in which to retrieve you if we were to keep anyone from knowing where you were and still planned on you taking the stand."

That made sense. I'd seen a few of those movies.

"Will I get to go back to them? I'd like to stay there." If they made me return to my own realm, I'd be shattered. There was nothing left for me there. I took a sip of the drink, which while clear, was fruity, then gave the kitty a pat.

"It depends on the results of the trials." Again, there was nothing in his face or voice to give me additional information. He was probably amazing at poker.

My fork full of potatoes stopped halfway to my mouth. "Trials? As in plural?"

"Yes. There were two worlds involved, so there are two trials. You are only a minor witness in the other trial, which is currently already in process, so you need not be here for long. They are simple, straightforward trials—two worlds and property. It wasn't like it was an elaborate multi-world person-smuggling operation." He took a bite of his sausage.

"I see." I had to do this all over? My heart pounded at the idea of being up on the stand again.

"I trust that Fade found you in the park as agreed. I disliked simply thrusting you into that world with nothing set up, especially with you needing medical care. But we had no time, and I couldn't risk them finding you again, and we needed to minimize contact."

He took another bite of food, his voice bland as if talking about the weather instead of giving me vital information.

"You knew about Fade. And the park." I had no recollection of telling anyone about that. But, that meant Agent Weigmier leaving me in that world had been intentional. Huh.

"It was most ideal that you had that agreement in place. Putting you in regular protection wasn't safe enough. I normally have no contact with that class of world, so me trying to locate him would arouse suspicion. It was imperative that no one knew where I was placing you for your own protection." He took a sip of his drink.

"Fade, Wes, found me. He was there at the house. Please, let me go back to him. *Please.*" It was half-sob, half-whine, especially as I recalled Wes chasing after the car and the look on his face.

I'd been placed with Wes on purpose. Did that mean I could go back?

Kitty meowed and headbutted me again. I rubbed his head, taking the offered comfort.

"I'm happy to have been able to reunite you with your husband," he said. "You are spoiling him."

"He's a kitty. They like pets. How do you even know all this?" I frowned, as I took a sip of the drink that was not water.

"It's my job." Agent Weigmier shrugged and started on his eggs.

"You left me on the bench but came to their house. How did you find *me?*" I looked at my hands. "Do I have a tracking chip?"

He shook his head. "No. Because they could hack the system and find you."

"You're secretive. Are you psychic?" If I wasn't mistaken there were different types of worlds. Some even had psychics, or supernaturals, and an assortment of variations–like alphas and magic dicks. Wes' world probably wasn't even the only one like that.

"You already know too much." He met my gaze.

"That's a *yes.*" I frowned. "Violation of privacy much?"

Brain map. Had he been the one to read my brain, and maybe gotten Wes and the park out of there?

"It was an emergency, you consented, and everything not relevant was erased, with the exception of what I needed to know to protect you," Agent Weigmier explained as he continued to eat.

That was a lot to digest. But it saved my life–and reunited me with Wes.

"You once mentioned wanting to work here. Is that still something you wish for?" he added.

"No. I'd like to go back to Wes–Fade. Please. I beg you." My chest shook. "I won't continue my research. I have a new project. One that doesn't involve anything you said I couldn't study."

"If those from your world are found innocent and set free, then you'll immediately be put into formal protection. You'll be given a new identity and hidden in a new world. It will not be your world of origin or your world of residence. You won't be allowed contact with them. Your old identity will be marked as deceased and you may remember very little depending on the judge's orders," he informed me

"No," It came out as a strangled cry. I'd rather die than be forced to live a new life in some other world unable to remember them.

His look went pained. "Calm yourself. Do you need me to recite equations with you?"

I took a deep breath, trying to push away my impending panic. *3.14159265359*

Kitty started kneading biscuits on my thigh like he was trying to comfort me.

"You are such a good kitty," I told him. "I'm okay. I just want to go back to Wes. Do you really think they'll be set free?"

"No. If they're found guilty, the standard witness protocol for your type of world is to mind-wipe you of everything regarding the trial and the Authority and send you home. I will do my best to ensure that you are sent back to your husband. But there are things to consider." Agent Weigmier set his empty box on the table.

"Like if someone still wants to kill me and the fact he's in a different world and I'm sure that's not legal?" I prodded, my food no longer that appetizing, not that it had tasted much better than what I'd had previously.

"If you wish to stay with your husband I'll try my best," he promised.

I finished my drink. "Yeah, I wish that. But can you please try not to leave me unable to remember my own name this time? That got awkward."

"Oh. That wasn't the intention. You are very small. You must have gotten too much. Per protocol you weren't supposed to remember anything about the trial. I also apologize for any anguish my abrupt retrieval of you caused you, your husband, and family. They clearly care for you," he added.

"I appreciate it. Being reunited with him..." Tears pricked my eyes, as I set my half-eaten food on the table as the idea I might never see Wes again tore me in half.

What would be worse, loving him and being torn away? Or never having known he was real?

No. The past two months had been worth it. Still, the idea that I'd broken their hearts by leaving suddenly wounded me.

"Just discovering parallel words doesn't necessarily mean you go to jail, right?" I asked, wanting to clarify something.

"No, of course not. Innocent discovery can be a building block to transitioning classes of worlds. Had you actually accomplished it, someone would have come to educate you and assess your world. It's those who don't heed or misuse that are punished."

I frowned. Should I ask? I didn't want to put Spencer in danger. But when else would I have the chance to discover what happened to his dad?

"Yeah, I'm not telling you how I know because I want to protect everyone, but… I… I know of someone, two someones, taken by the Temporal Authority years ago. Would I be able to know the exact nature of their charges and how long is left on their sentences?" I asked, hoping that I hadn't made everything worse.

"Do you know their name and world of origin?" he asked, going to his desk.

"Dr. Thanukos and Dr. Katsopolis, both from Fade's world."

He tapped on his weird little tablet and looked up at me. "They were part of a very complex multi-world person-smuggling ring. Both were given life sentences, though it looks like Dr. Katsopolis passed a few years back." He typed more. "Dr. Thanukos might be released on dotage."

"If that means you let old people out for good behavior, I'll take him. I'll be responsible for him. I promise." My chest constricted. Spencer's dad was alive.

Though poor Mrs. K, never getting to see her wife again.

"Person smuggling? Like they were selling people from one world to another?" I couldn't see someone who raised Spencer doing that. But then I still had problems visualizing Professor Jaffey smuggling *weapons*.

"No. They were moving vulnerable populations to safety. But there are rules. You can't just bring people from one world to another without permission, even if it's for the better, especially across types or classes of worlds. Most parties had been warned multiple times and told how to appeal. I wasn't here then, but it was a bit of a mess and cleanup is still in place. Every action has a reaction—when it comes to movement between worlds the smallest thing can be catastrophic." He gave me a look. "I shouldn't even tell you this much. I'm guessing he means something to someone in your life."

They were helping people to freedom? Or perhaps moving people from a dying world to another? Now that I could see. I could also understand how that could be problematic even if they were saving lives.

Not that they should put people in jail for helping others. Though that was probably only a fraction of the story. Still, Spencer's dad was *alive.*

"Can I see Dr. Thanukos? Please? Or send him a note?" Just to let him know that Spencer missed him, loved him, and had grown into an amazing man.

"Absolutely not." He kept tapping, then his head tilted. "We need to see the judge soon."

"Then what? More trials?" I sighed, just wanting a nap and a hug. At least I had a nice kitty to pet. His fur was so soft.

"Indeed. You probably won't have to take the stand again for this one, but there is the other trial. You will be kept isolated both for your own safety and if you want any chance to return to your husband." Agent Weigmier gave me a warning look. "Understood?"

"Yes. I'll do whatever it takes to get back to Wes. What do I tell the judge? Sorry, Kitty." I removed the cat from my lap and stood, wishing I had a hairbrush and some clean clothes.

"As little as possible. But be truthful. She'll know if you lie. Don't tell her where you were, don't mention your husband and family, don't elaborate. Just stick to the facts. Change." He held out a bag.

"Thanks." I took it.

His eyes focused on the cat. "Stay here. If they have to chase you down again, they'll be quite annoyed."

The cat glared at him then started cleaning himself.

Agent Weigmier sighed. "Also, please spray yourself well. Apparently you smell like alpha bait. If you wish to go home, we need to avoid nosy alphas."

"Yeah, I'll do that," I agreed. The last thing we needed was for some alpha interfering, thinking it was for my own good.

All I wanted was to get this over with so that I could go home to mine.

Chapter Four

Spencer

"Spencer, have you been here all night?" Mrs. Katsopolis scolded, coming into my office, with a cursory knock on the open door.

Light streamed through the windows of my office, and I lifted my head off my desk. A glance at my phone showed no calls, no texts, no alerts.

At least not the ones that I yearned for.

"Why? I have nowhere else to go." It came out more bitter than intended. Grace had been taken Friday night, and it was now Tuesday morning. I was losing hope. If she was found innocent, surely she'd have been returned to us by now.

Which meant that like my father and Dr. K, she'd been tried and prosecuted, and I'd never see her again. The prospect broke my already fragile heart.

"Spencer, you're supposed to be on vacation. I don't know what happened, but you should go home—or somewhere." She approached my desk.

My beta assistant looked fresh and crisp in her sensible dress with her understated accessories. Her grey hair was neatly curled.

"I need to wait here." I promised Riley that I'd stay in town. Otherwise, I'd be far from here, and drunk off my ass.

Mostly likely Grace was dead. Once again, someone I loved had died needlessly.

And I couldn't stop it.

"In your *office?*" She scowled. "Put on a fresh shirt. I'll get you coffee and some breakfast."

With that, she left, closing my office door.

I sighed, checking my phone just to make sure. There was no action on the door camera. No texts from the group chat. But there was a picture of Riley and her sisters. I checked for Grace on the location finder app. *Location not found.*

The pack was up at the cabin, as planned.

Why had I let Riley get my hopes up? I knew that I'd never see Grace again the moment I opened the door and saw him. That suit, which smelled of neutrons, brought everything back from when they'd come for my father and Dr. K.

Still, I pretended to be optimistic for Riley's sake. As much as I worried for Wes and Evan, they had each other. Riley didn't.

As for me, maybe I didn't deserve love after Elaris.

I went to the closet in my office where I kept extra clothes and quickly changed my shirt, using some wipes from my gym bag. I'd still smell like an angry alpha all day. Oh well. I *was* an angry alpha. I should be at the cabin, with the pack, with Grace. Who I'd hoped to finally get knot-deep in—or at least balls-deep if she wasn't ready.

Though I had a feeling she was. I could smell her desire, her arousal, see the want in her blue-grey eyes. The only reason why

I hadn't pinned her to the bed sooner was that she seemed to be enjoying the game.

Certainly, I was.

It was enjoyable to woo someone again. Especially someone who clearly had never been courted properly. Delighting her always made my day. I'd even bought some gifts to give her up at the cabin.

And now...

My head bowed in defeat as I buttoned my shirt and changed my tie. The main reason why I'd stayed here in the office was because not only was the house empty, but her peachy scent was *everywhere.* The couch. My office. The kitchen.

The air purifier wasn't enough. I'd need to convince Brennan to have the house professionally de-scented.

No. I couldn't think like that. She'd be back.

No, she wouldn't.

I'd even combed over every inch of the little I had of my father's research and all of mine, trying to see if there was anything helpful.

Any hope.

I'd even reached out to a few old contacts.

Nothing.

I'd obsessed over the door camera footage, trying to figure out what had happened, what I could glean from the situation. It was different from what I remembered, with my father. The two officers had identified themselves back then. They *arrested* my father and Dr. K. Then an entire team arrived.

This man never identified himself, he simply asked for Grace. He never arrested her, just repeatedly told her that they needed to go. That there was no time.

But clearly she hadn't expected him, not with her cries and pleas. Also, she would have told us.

My shoulders slumped as I checked my emails. What I needed to do was to keep my promise to Brennan and figure out a way to explain Grace's absence, so another investigation wasn't opened.

"Spencer?" Mrs. K knocked on the door.

"Come in."

She came in and set a cup of coffee and a container from the cafeteria on my desk. "There you go. Is everything okay? Is something wrong with Grace? I noticed that you pushed her start-date a week. Is she in the hospital again? You can go to her. Things will be fine if you leave for a bit. Family is important."

I wished I could go to Grace. Hold her. Kiss her.

"It doesn't matter. Thank you for bringing me breakfast." Usually, I'd go to the cafeteria myself. It was good to be seen, and to talk to my employees. But I'd go down for lunch. Get my mind off everything.

"I... I got what you asked for," she added. "I'll bring it to you."

She disappeared as I took a long drink of strong, black coffee. When she returned to my office she had a large, battered folder—and closed the door.

"Spencer, you know I love you like one of my children. I support you and your research. But what are you doing? You need to be careful, or you'll end up like them. I shouldn't even give this to you. Not that it's much and probably won't be helpful. Selfishly, I hope it's not helpful." She clutched the folder to her chest.

Mrs. K sunk into the seat on the other side of my desk, weathered hands still gripping the folder. "You should know the truth before you get too deep like they did. I tried to warn Demitra, but you know her—stubborn to the core. And, well, they were doing something good; illegal, but good."

My heart thudded at her unexpected words. "What do you know?"

She set the folder on the table, but kept her hands on top of it, as if trying to trap the information inside. "I'm pretty sure the super collider explosion and their deaths were on purpose. You see, they were doing things they shouldn't."

Mrs. K knew. I didn't think she had, since my mother knew little about the specifics of my father's research.

"What were they doing?" I wasn't sure I wanted her to know what I'd seen. Especially before discovering what knowledge she possessed.

"Things they weren't supposed to. Things they were warned not to continue doing. I understand why they did it. They were helping people, good people, and giving them the life they deserved. But after that man showed up the first time, they didn't stop. Or the second. Or the fourth. They trusted the network who said not to listen to them. They also took risks they shouldn't, and then..." A sob ripped from her throat.

I pushed the tissue box to her. "Oh, Mrs. K. They were involved in something? Moving people from one world to another? I know that they'd actually discovered parallel worlds. I didn't think they knew how to move through them. That is what you're saying?"

Network? They were working with other worlds? A shiver went up my spine. This was very bad indeed.

And so different from what I'd thought they'd been doing, what I'd helped with.

"They were approached by a group of scientists from another world. They asked them to be part of a network of worlds that offered sanctuary and new lives for omegas from places where being an omega was illegal or dangerous. It seemed noble, and they were able to tap into the Omega Protection Program that the Omega Center has. They gave them new lives and identities here where they could be happy and safe." She grabbed a tissue and dabbed her eyes.

"There are worlds where being an omega is *illegal?*" The very thought baffled me. Omegas were treasures.

"We were one of many worlds accepting omegas through the network, so that no one was overwhelmed. Mostly we got male omegas, since many worlds in the network didn't welcome them," she sniffed.

"I see." That was a lot to take in. I understood some designations being illegal, but *omegas?*

And not wanting male omegas? Evan was my packmate, my best friend. While they weren't as numerous as female omegas, I couldn't envision a world where male omegas were unwanted.

"It seems like a noble thing, to give shelter to omegas. Did they do the same, send our illegal designations to other places?" Illegal designations had become quite rare, but the fate of those few was unkind, and in my opinion, quite unnecessary. It's not as if they chose to be an illegal designation.

Mrs. K opened the folder. "That had been the idea, taking in omegas and sending our illegal designations to safety, but it didn't work as planned. Still, they made a difference in the lives of those omegas."

"I'm proud of them for that. They must have saved so many lives."

"They did. I only met a couple of the omegas, but they were so lovely." Her hands hesitated on the folder, then she pushed it forward. "Please, be proud, even though they hid so much from you. The mapping research they were doing was also important. They loved it; it wasn't just a cover for the other operation. On that end they were mostly just a receiving depot . They'd just get omegas and help them. They never went elsewhere or got much knowledge about other worlds or how their technology worked."

I took the folder from her. "Thank you, I appreciate you being honest with me."

She left and returned to her desk. That had been enlightening. My father had been smuggling omegas to safety. Huh.

I ate my breakfast and went on with my day. My mind kept wandering as I wondered who else I could call, what else I could do. But it wasn't as if the Temporal Police had an office here that I could march into. They had no permanent presence here at all that I had been able to find.

If I wasn't going to do my work here, I should be working on a cover story regarding Grace's disappearance, so no one thought that we'd harmed her. The easiest would be to say it didn't work out with Wes and she went home.

But Mrs. Beekman would want to talk to her. While I could possibly pull off texts, I didn't sound anything like Grace. The integration team from the Center, who was helping Grace assimilate into our pack, would want to know what went wrong and if they could do things differently. The Center would ask for her new address so that they could put her in touch with her local one so that she could continue to receive healthcare and educational opportunities.

No, it wouldn't be easy at all.

"Spencer, just go home. Or go to your club and work it out on small balls or something." Mrs. K came back in, concern etched on her weathered face.

"You're right. I have no meetings anyway." I closed my laptop. While I didn't want to go home, I wasn't doing anyone any good here.

She was right, I'd go to my club and work it out on the court. Then I'd return home, de-scent an area, and drink myself to sleep, hoping that I didn't dream of Grace.

Chapter Five

Grace

Once again, I was locked in some room, with weird food, not knowing what was happening. My phone was dead and tucked in my bra because the latest dress Agent Weigmier had brought for me didn't have pockets. Heathens.

At least it wasn't itchy like the last outfit.

Time seemed to have no meaning here in the interdimensional police station and I wasn't sure how long I'd been gone. Days at least. My very soul ached for Wes.

The black kitty jumped up on the table, as if coming out of nowhere. But then again, who knew what powers otherworldly kitties had?

"Hi." I scratched the kitty's ears. "Still hiding or did you escape again?"

His eyes gleamed as if to say *Don't you want to know?*

"Do they have you chasing interdimensional mice in the basement or something? I hope they're nice to you." The desire to go home to Wes and Evan raged inside me. Especially since I'd given my testimony at the other trial and we were just waiting on verdicts. Or something. No one would tell me anything.

Please please please let Professor Jaffey be guilty so I can go home. I couldn't handle being relocated. Short of stealing Agent Weigmier's interdimensional-traveling car, I didn't know how else to get home.

Not that I knew how the car worked.

The door opened. The cat jumped off the desk and hid. Captain Claussen strode in, alone. She was the one that hadn't wanted me taking the stand without knowing what I was going to say.

"Hi, Captain. Do I need to make more statements?" I asked.

She was just an unyielding stickler for rules and protocol–and did *not* like how Agent Weigmier had taken control of things.

"I need you to come with me." She huffed a little as if it was a massive inconvenience.

The captain had a disdain for my class of world. Class and type were two different things. *Class* referred to a world's level of knowledge regarding parallel worlds and travel along with their ranking in the Temporal Authority food chain.

My world was Class IV, meaning while we had some tech and were developing, we didn't know about interdimensional travel, and all comings and goings of the sort were strictly prohibited except for official business.

Type referred to the people that lived there. My world was Type-H, just an ordinary humanoid world without magic, paranormal beings, superheroes, or alphas.

To Captain Claussen, I was just some backward country bumpkin who had little use beyond putting away the bad guys.

"Okay." I stood and trotted after her as she was already at the door, without any concern for me and my short legs.

Certainly, I wasn't worth any special treatment.

I followed her through the warren of sterile halls, wondering where I was going now. Back to the judge? More testimony? The cafeteria? I'd like to choose my food. Maybe something would finally taste right.

She took me to a room that said *Processing*. An uncomfortable feeling fluttered in my belly.

"What's going on?" I frowned.

"The case is over. We're done with you." She opened the door, expression hard.

"Oh." My belly dropped further. "Where's Agent Weigmier?"

"Probably doing his actual job. I have no idea who he pissed off to be made to babysit you." Her face scrunched up with distaste as she pushed me inside.

A hard-featured woman with predatory eyes sat behind a desk. "Captain." She eyed me. "Return?"

Shivers crawled up my spine. "Where's Agent Weigmier."

"I told you, he's *busy*," the captain snapped. "Judge wants re-location. I don't know why. Gloria, if you want to throw her back home and lose her record no one would care. Why do we even bother with trials for lower-class worlds? Waste of time and resources, we should just turn and burn." Scorn filled her voice.

Without a backwards glance at me, or even a *thank you* to the woman at the desk, the captain left, the door slamming behind her.

"Well." The woman stood. "Hi, I'm Gloria. Let's get you set up."

Fear filled me, because I didn't want to be relocated any more than I wanted to be returned to my sad little apartment and lonely life. Not that I probably had an apartment anymore. My landlord had most likely thrown away my stuff and rented my studio to someone else.

"Can you get Agent Weigmier? Please?" I didn't want to tell her I had a place that I needed to go back to.

"It's going to be fine, Dr. Ellington. Type-H world? Pity, you're such a tasty little thing. Maybe we can send you someplace a little better. Hmmm…" Her eyes went a bit black around the edges as she led me through another door and down a hall. "Has anyone ever told you that you smell like peach pie with vanilla ice cream? Mmmm."

"I… I have been told that." No. Things weren't right. Agent Weigmier said that I could go back to Wes.

No, he said he'd try.

Still, something felt wrong.

She opened the door to something that looked like an exam room. "You sit here. We'll get some readings and find a nice place for you. Relax, I'm very good at my job."

Before I could protest the door shut. I tried the handle, but it was locked. "Let me out, please?" I cried, banging on the door with my good hand, as fear consumed me. "Please get Agent Weigmier. Let me out."

I banged until my hand hurt, yelled until my throat was raw. Sadly, the kitty never appeared. Spent, I sank to the ground, tears streaming down my face.

"I want to go home." I sobbed until everything went dark.

When my eyes opened, I was in something like a reclining pedicure chair–and not in the room where I'd been before. It looked a little like a fancy medical clinic. Monitors beeped. Gloria and some other woman, who wore a lab coat, were talking.

"You're not actually sending her to a Type-H world, are you?" the other woman inquired.

Gloria laughed. "You know we can't keep them, right? But she is so very tasty. I was considering sending her somewhere where she'd be more… appreciated."

"She's ill and needs care. If she is what I think she is, I'd recommend a dynamic world. Preferably one of the more civilized ones.

She might qualify for special placement under Precious Population Protection," the doctor replied.

No. No. No. Both heads turned as I whimpered.

"Shh, it's going to be okay," the woman in the lab coat soothed. "I know this is scary, but it's going to be okay. Gloria's going to find a very nice place for you."

I frowned at the IV, chest shuddering as I tried to sit up. "What are you doing to me? Making me forget again?"

"Easy. We're just stabilizing you." The unknown woman came over to me and checked the monitor.

"Oh. Did I have another seizure?" It had been a few days of a whole lot of emotional upheaval. Not to mention the longer I was separated from Wes, the greater the ache grew in my chest. I couldn't sense him here and it made me feel empty.

Lonely. Hopeless.

"Is everyone okay in here?" A very large man strode in. He wore a uniform like Gloria and had blonde hair. "It's none of my business, but..." His eyes fell on me. "Why hello, Precious."

Fear shot through me. Alpha. It was evident in his scent and bearing.

"Can I talk to Agent Weigmier? Please?" I begged.

"Everything's fine. Just a nervous relocation," Gloria said, going to the wall and pushing a button on a small terminal.

He got close enough for me to smell his woodsy scent. "Exquisite."

"We can't keep them." Amusement tinged Gloria's voice.

"I'm not a pet," I frowned. "Please, let me speak to Agent Weigmier."

"Oh, but you are. The best, sweetest pet. You're going to make someone's year. Doctor, you might want to do something to suppress her scent before every alpha in the building barges in to check on her," he warned.

You smell like alpha bait. No one had given me any de-scenter in a while.

"Is someone hurt? Can I be of assistance?" Another very large man came in, this one older, elegant, wearing a suit, and holding himself with authority.

The first man chuckled. "See."

"Oh. It's going to be all right, Little One. What do you need?" His eyes were kind, but almost animal-like. His musky scent held an undertone that I couldn't identify.

"I need to go home," I sobbed.

"You know what she needs," the first one laughed. "Soon, precious, you'll get everything you could ever need or want, very soon."

"Lupa bless, you're such a lovely little thing," the older one said.

"Top of your class at the academy, I'm sure," the first one added.

"Gloria, please take very special care of this one. Though I'd be happy to make some recommendations," the older one offered.

Gloria gave them a scathing look. "I need both of you to *leave.*"

The doctor was busy studying the monitors and fiddling with dials. She glanced over at Gloria as the men left. "I told you."

"Well, this complicates things. But not in a bad way. Yes, let's run those tests so we can get her an extra special place." Gloria winked at me.

No, thank you.

"Go do your thing, I'll make sure she's stable enough to move," the doctor said. "Let me know if your placement requires anything specific."

Gloria left, but the doctor continued to tap on things, and I started to feel sleepy.

"It's okay to be scared, but it's better to just relax before Alfie comes back with a teddy bear and a bag of candy." The doctor chuckled.

"I don't need to be placed. Please, I need to speak to Agent Weigmier," I begged, as my eyes closed. Though I wouldn't mind some candy.

"That's it, just go back to sleep," the doctor soothed.

Everything went black. Then something poked me.

"Mmmph," I sat up, startled, heart racing. "What?"

Agent Weigmier stood there. "We need to go. Unless you wish to be relocated."

"I'm so glad to see you. I just want to go back to Wes." There was a stuffed bear in my arms, and a little box of candy on the table next to me. Someone had covered me with a fluffy blanket.

He shoved a hat on my head. "You're detached. We need to get out of here before they return."

I climbed out of the chair, grabbing the bear and candy, but leaving the blanket, and followed him. He quickly led me out a back door, up some stairs, through halls, and down an elevator until we were back in the parking garage. A combination of panic and relief flowed through me. I'd been this close to being sent someplace else. But once again, I had no idea what was happening.

He pushed me into his car, eyes sweeping it as if looking for something. "Sorry for the delay; you're not my only case. I told the captain I'd handle it myself. I didn't think she'd take it into her own hands."

"Thank you." So many feelings overwhelmed me. I also felt weird.

He got in. "Drink the juice in the utility box. I'm just glad that I wasn't too late. If you'd been processed there would be nothing I could do. Hold on."

Agent Weigmier pressed the button and once again it felt like I was plunging down a very fast roller coaster.

I closed my eyes, holding the bear, steeling myself against the nausea.

"Did they go free?" My voice trembled as I bent forward, trying not to puke.

"Everyone from your world was found guilty. The judge liked you. She thought she was doing you a favor by giving you a chance at a new life, considering your previous one is in disarray. Between my other cases and needing time to reverse the *relocation* order to a *return to world of origin* order, and wipe as much of your footprint as I could, it cost precious time. You being ill saved you," he mentioned, the car slowing.

"I think I'm going to be sick." I squeezed my eyes shut, holding the juice.

"Drink the juice. While it's been nice getting to know you, you'll probably never see me again. I've done my best to wipe everything, so that you won't be found," he said.

"Can't they track your car records? Surely they know when and where the car jumps or whatever we're doing?" Taking a deep breath, I downed the juice, though it made me feel worse. *I will not vomit all over the car. I will not vomit all over the car.*

"Per protocol, you won't recall anything about the trial, the involved incidents, or the Temporal Authority. Please take care and be cautious. Avoid any fields of study that could put you in our path, and I do hope that you're not using your identity from the other world," he said as the car came to a stop. "Also, you didn't take the cat, did you?"

"No, I was just joking." Okay, if I'd had the opportunity I might have.

I opened my eyes as we stopped in front of Wes' house. Happy tears pricked my eyes. *Home.*

"I haven't been gone too long, have I?" How much had they worried?

He shook his head. "Just a few days."

"Thank you for everything. Why are you helping me?" It seemed like he was breaking protocol not just for my safety, but for my happiness.

For that I was grateful.

Agent Weigmier shrugged. "It's my job."

My eyebrows rose. There was more to it, I'm sure. Not that he'd tell me.

Something pricked the space between my neck and shoulder, and I rubbed it.

"Ow. Again with the stabby-stab. Was that really necessary?" I glared at him.

"Yes. I hope I got the dosage right this time. Goodbye, Dr. Ellington. I wish you and your husband a happy life." His voice went faint.

For the third time today, everything went black.

Chapter Six

Spencer

It was a lovely spring afternoon, making me wish Grace was here to play chess with me in the backyard. I sat outside with Mrs. K's folder and a bottle of merlot, mostly because it didn't smell like Grace out here.

There wasn't much, and it seemed that it was all regarding their dimensional mapping project. The idea that my father and Dr. K hadn't been taken simply for a discovery was comforting. That meant if Grace stumbled on something accidentally then perhaps she'd still return to us.

A sigh escaped my lips as I continued to go through the documents. How long had they smuggled omegas? Months? Years?

Mostly male omegas, Mrs. K had said. Huh. The male omega population had grown in the past couple of decades. There'd been some miracle births by male omegas as well. Perhaps they had come from worlds where male omegas were capable of having children. Fascinating.

It was probably better that I didn't know too much. The last thing I'd want is for any of those omegas brought here to be in danger.

If they were still even here.

Would the Temporal Police take them back to a world where their return could mean their death? They were sticklers for the rules, but were they that harsh?

It wouldn't surprise me if they were.

I swirled the wine in my glass and shook my head. Omegas being illegal. I couldn't imagine a world like that.

The few illegal designations on this world were supposed to prevent public violence, genocide, and other horrible acts.

At the same time, was the death of them *all*—even ones with no personal or familial history of violence, the answer?

The most well-known illegal designations were sigmas and omicrons—both offshoots of alphas. Sigmas often passed as alphas, but were actually ultra-dominant, arrogant, violent loners who liked to exist outside the hieratical structure. Something that many governments saw as a threat. Especially since they had hair-trigger tempers and were prone to extreme acts of violence to make their points. Many terrorists, anarchists, bombers, mass shooters, and dangerous sociopaths had been sigmas.

Same with omicrons, though instead of keeping to themselves, they were ultra-charismatic. They didn't exist *outside* the structure, they believed they *transcended* it. They gathered followers and tended to be fanatics or zealots, believing they were making the world a better place with their often violent extremism—versus sigmas who did it to punish or retaliate. Over the course of history many narcissist rulers, colonizing sovereigns, evangelical cult leaders, and perpetrators of genocide had been omicrons.

The illegal designations were also incredibly uncommon, even before they were illegal. Also, there were still very bad people in this world with perfectly legal designations.

My mate Elaris didn't think executing them was the answer. That was a project she hoped our pharmaceutical company could accomplish. After her death, no one wanted to take over the project because of how politically volatile it was, given people who spoke of it often ended up *dead*.

But I wasn't talented enough to continue it without her.

With a sigh, I continued to look through the old papers.

Once again, I glanced at my phone. No location for Grace. Just a photo of Riley and her sisters at a theme park and a lone text from Jett.

Jett

> **This might take a while. If you come, please bring food.**

Perhaps I'd go up to the cabin in a day or two to clear my head and cook for them, even though I'd promised Riley that I'd stay. After all, they were my pack, and even if I wasn't mated or married to any of them, I cared for them all.

When I was younger, I'd never thought much about having a pack. I didn't grow up in a pack, though many of my relatives had them. Elaris and I were content for it to just be us, unless fate brought us someone. After she passed, I was just trying to heal and survive. My alpha instincts to care and protect were satiated by taking care of my mother, like I had since my father had died, as well as Evan and his family.

Joining Evan and his pack had never been a thought, until it was. There was no magic. I didn't look at them and go, *Yes, this is my pack*. But it was comfortable and safe. The pestering about moving on after Elaris stopped. I was more on the outside of the pack, but content to be there.

Then Grace came. Intriguing me. Growing on me. She made me realize that being safe was complacency.

Grace. How scared she must be. I ached at the thought of her being alone and afraid.

My shoulders slumped as I shut the folder and finished off my wine. I couldn't concentrate.

It wasn't dinner time yet, but perhaps making something complicated would help calm me. I took the folder and the empty glass and bottle to the kitchen. As I contemplated what to cook, someone knocked on the door.

Odd. I wasn't expecting a delivery or guests.

It could be one of the sisters coming to check on the house. I couldn't remember if Lexi and Katie had been told that I stayed behind.

No. Not the sisters. They had access, they'd just walk in.

I opened the front door and there stood that man, the one who'd taken Grace, dressed in that same suit, once again smelling of neutrons.

He held an unconscious Grace in his arms. In broad daylight.

The world stopped.

"You brought her back." The words barely escaped my lips as I stared into the face of the man who'd destroyed our world four days ago.

"Apologies for any worry. I couldn't promise her return." He thrust her limp body into my arms.

"She's innocent." I'd never seen the dress she was wearing. Her face was tearstained, and she reeked of fear and chemicals.

Oh, my sweet darling. What happened to you?

"She was never on trial." His expression was impassive, unyielding.

Oh?

"Then why did you rip her from us? What did you do to her?" All my anguish, anger, and fear came out at the agent as I clutched her small body to my chest. Did they drug her? Was it the effects of being away from her mates?

"She should wake in a few hours this time. This is hers." He dropped an unfamiliar backpack at my feet. His eyes swept the area, then he turned to leave.

"Will you come for her again?" I needed to prepare my heart.

"By the stars, I hope not." The man walked to his strange car.

Using my foot, I scooted her backpack into the house and closed the door.

"Grace." The growl was primal, possessive, as I buried my face in her hair, then made a face. So many strange smells.

She was here. Home. Not dead. They'd brought her back to us.

My good doctor looked so fragile and helpless, her skin clammy, breathing a bit shallow. Part of me wanted to take her to the hospital. But what would I say?

No, I'd care for her here and if she didn't wake up by morning, or became distressed, I'd take it from there.

I carried her upstairs to her room, hoping that she'd forgive the intrusion into her most private space. Flipping on the lamp, I took her to her window seat, since it was perfect for helping her to feel safe.

Yes, that's what she needed right now.

Wrapping her in her favorite fuzzy blanket, which smelled of her and Evan, I hauled us into the sea of pillows and blankets. Bringing down the net curtain that separated the seat from the room, I threw another blanket over us.

"I'm right here, Darling. You're home, safe, and here in my arms," I murmured, peppering her face with the lightest of kisses. I felt a hardness between her breasts.

What?

"Pardon me." I put my hand down her dress, my hand curling around the rectangular object in her bra. "That is a strange place to keep your phone."

It was also dead. I texted the group chat.

Me

> Grace was just dropped off at the house. She's unconscious and in my arms.

Immediately, I got a text from Riley with a screenshot of me holding Grace in the doorway, probably from the door camera.

Riley

> Grace!!! I knew it. Did they take her phone? No location.

Me

> It's dead.

Riley

> She okay?

Me

> She's unconscious. I'm not sure what happened other than she's back.

I didn't see visible injuries, though the brace on her wrist and walking cast on her foot were different.

Riley

> Aren't you glad you stayed at the house?

Me

> I am.

What would have happened had I not answered?

Running my fingers through her hair, down her face and arms, I let Grace know that she was here with me.

I replayed the strange encounter with the agent over and over in my mind. If she hadn't been guilty or suspected of anything, then why did they take her?

The idea of the Temporal Police bringing her back was bizarre. But, then so was her appearance on the exact park bench that was special to her and Wes, when she couldn't even remember her name.

What did I know about the Temporal Police anyway?

I sat there, curled in her little window seat, talking to her softly, occasionally checking my phone to see if anyone responded.

Perhaps it was better that they didn't reply. Wes and Evan would want me to take her to the cabin right now. While she'd want them, she had much more immediate needs. I'd care for her, then see if she was up to the drive tomorrow.

Holding her so that her head was on my chest, I dozed off. Whimpering woke me, as she thrashed in her sleep.

"Grace, it's all right, you're home and safe," I whispered.

She continued to toss and turn. Panic rose inside me. I laid her so she was no longer on top of me, but in a nest of pillows and blankets. Gently, I covered her with my body, trying to position myself so she was pinned, but not squashed.

"That's it, Baby Girl," I purred, as her body relaxed from both my weight and scent. "Relax. You are safe and I'll take such good care of you." The tossing stopped. "Good girl. Just relax for me, oh yes, that's it. So good. So perfect."

I purred for her until darkness came, her body tucked under me feeling so right. My cock was pressed right up against her ass, and so very hard. She stirred under me.

"It's okay, Baby Girl, Daddy's got you," I whispered, moving a little so I could see her face, but still giving her the comfort of my weight.

Her eyes fluttered open, and her body tensed with panic.

"Grace, you're home. It's Spencer. You're safe and in your room." Purring again, I curled my body around hers, making sure we were covered with a mound of blankets so that she felt secure.

"Spence." She turned so her face could bury in my chest as sobs wracked her body.

"I'm right here," I soothed.

"I'm home. I came home." Fear and anguish rolled off her, making the room reek of burnt and sour peaches.

Every alpha instinct I had wanted to make it all better.

"I've got you." I held her as tight as I could without crushing her.

The sobs stopped and she lay there in my arms, trembling. I ran my hands over her, kissed her head, her face, her jaw, and did everything I could to soothe her without actually touching her in the way I truly wanted.

She cupped my face with one of her small, delicate hands. "Spencer."

"I'm right here, Darling." I think I liked that better than *Dearest*.

Her head tilted. "Did you call yourself *Daddy*? Is that what you want me to call you?"

There was no judgment in her voice as she bit her lower lip, eyes going half-lidded.

"We did agree to try out different names." I started rubbing her shoulders trying to relax the tension in them.

She nodded. "We did."

"You don't have to call me that. But I'll take care of you and protect you. I'll encourage you to achieve your dreams, push you to try new things, and show you the world. I'll keep your secrets, shelter you when you're vulnerable, talk you up, and remind you how wonderful you are. I'll always be there for you, good days and bad, to get support from, confide in, and give you whatever you need. As your alpha, I promise that to you, regardless of what you call me, or I call you, both in public and private." We might as well have this chat now. Because I was making love to her tonight.

"Oh. That sounds nice." She made a little happy noise as I kneaded a tight spot in her shoulders.

"I'm so glad to hear that. It might be fun, sometimes?" I added gently. "Or perhaps use it as a bit of code, when you need something particular?"

"Sorry, Daddy, I've been naughty." Her voice was husky as eyes danced, and she giggled. "Sorry, sorry. I'm not trying to mock the moment. It's a reference from my world."

"You, naughty? Never." My lips brushed her ear, heat building between us. "You're such a good girl."

It was nice to hear her laugh after seeing all that anguish on her face.

My legs curled around her. "I do love good girls. I'm not much for physical punishments, I'm more for rewards, like good girls get orgasms. Lots of orgasms."

Oh, how my alpha wanted to comfort her by knotting her over and over until I'd wrung every last orgasm out of her.

She moaned, arousal dusting her peach scent. "I like orgasms. How about being bent over the desk in your office? Sorry, too many boss romance novels."

A little growl emitted from my chest as I continued to rub her back. "Oh, my good doctor, I'm happy to oblige. You'd look so lovely lying across my desk as I take you, perhaps wearing nothing but garters. Mmmm. Exquisite."

She groaned again. "Oh, yes. Maybe giving you a blowjob while you're in a video meeting..."

Oh, yes. I was enjoying this immensely. We did need to talk about these things if we were to take our relationship to the next level. Which I so desperately wanted.

Especially now.

"I'd also love to see how long you could warm my cock in your mouth—with delicious rewards increasing the longer you were able to." A happy little growl rumbled through me, and I got another burst of her sweet arousal.

Her eyes went wide. "That growl just made me wet."

"You make me hard." I nibbled her ear, my teeth aching to bite her, claim her, even though we weren't ready for that yet.

"Warm your cock in my mouth? I just hold it there? That's a thing?" Her breath came out in little pants as my hands rubbed her lower back.

"Oh, absolutely. So is you sitting on my cock without moving, perhaps while we watch a movie. With a reward for accomplishing the task, of course." I pushed her hips into me as I continued massaging her.

She groaned. "Mmmm, I like the sound of that."

"What don't you like, Darling?" I asked, knowing she was probably soaking wet for me. The more I understood her limits the better I could meet her needs.

She was going to need a lot tonight.

"I...I think I might like to be Baby Girl sometimes? But I don't like bad names." She grimaced. "I also don't like being taunted, humiliated, or hurt."

Those weren't my interests.

"Noted. I just want to take care of you, spoil you, love you, and give you what you need." Again, I watched her face, felt for the movements in her body, so that I could interpret her reaction.

"I'm okay with that."

"Communicate with me—and I'll do the same for you. While I might push you, I don't want to cross your boundaries. Also, never ever be embarrassed about not wanting to do something—or wanting to try something new. I want to know your desires and fantasies as well as your limitations. If something interests you that isn't something I can give you, we'll find another way, understood?" I needed her trust.

She nodded. "Yes, Alpha."

Yes, Alpha. That went straight to my cock—which was curious as to why we weren't knot-deep in her, especially since her peach scent was taking on undertones of *fuck me, Alpha.*

"I need you to tell me what you need, but I know sometimes you can't. So, I would very much like your consent to be able to give it to you. It's a learning process, so I might have to try things out, but ultimately, all I want to do is please you and care for you." I nipped lightly on her neck.

Please her. Protect her. Make her happy.

Her body bucked. "Oh, yes, Alpha. Mmmm. Please, give me what I need."

The last part was a little whine, which shot right through me.

"Also, you can tell me to stop at any time. No matter what. *Stop.* That's it. You can also tell me to slow down. If you want to choose a safeword and sign, we can. We can do whatever makes you most comfortable." I gently cupped her face with my hand, so she was looking at me. "Understood?"

"Understood." She kissed my nose.

"Would you like a shower first? Perhaps have something to eat. Then I can take you to my bed and tend to you properly? Though I'm happy to take the edge off first." It was definitely dinner time.

"Because alpha cock and cuddles cure everything in this world? Not that I'm complaining." She nuzzled my chest, making a contented noise.

Oh, I loved those noises.

"There's science behind it. Do you know that, my good doctor?" I held her tight, trying to keep her from grinding against me before I threw her on her pink fluffy daybed and knotted her into oblivion under the canopy of fairy lights.

I would make love to her soon. But not yet.

"Alpha cum helps your body produce serotonin, dopamine, and oxytocin," I murmured, nuzzling her pulse. "That's why alphas have a tendency to shove their cock in their partners when their partners are unhappy or unsettled."

Which was my first instinct when she had her terrors in my arms, but I hadn't had her permission yet.

"Mmmm, magic dicks," she groaned. "Full of happiness."

"Indeed. Also, there are pressure points inside you that react to the weight of my cock. I'm so happy to sit you on me and hold you close whenever you need or want it," I nuzzled the other side of her neck. "It induces calm and relaxation. Cuddling, well, that has more to do with pheromones and skin to skin contact. But the science is all there. Now, tell me what you need? If I get to pick you're going in the shower." To rinse off all those strange smells. She also needed food and water.

Grace looked around. "It's night? Is anyone else home?"

"It's evening. You arrived this afternoon. You've only been asleep for a few hours. Riley is with her sisters. Everyone else is at the cabin for Evan's heat. I let them know that you're here." I checked my phone. Nothing. I sent another text.

Me

> Grace is awake. She's physically fine from what I can see but needs a lot of care. I'll keep you updated.

"You stayed and waited for me?" Tears pricked her eyes.

I held her to me, reassuring her that I was there, that she was safe. "Yes. Though I admit it was partially because Riley insisted."

Grace took my phone and sent a picture of herself to Riley. Immediately there was a picture of hands in the shape of a heart.

"We... we don't have to go to the cabin yet, right, after I shower?" She began to shake. "I want to see them, but can I stay here with you for a bit first?"

My heart swelled. "Whatever you need, Darling. I'm happy to care for you here—and I'd rather not make that drive in the dark. We can always talk about it in the morning."

I desperately wanted to know what had happened, what she remembered. But first, and foremost, she needed to feel safe and be cared for. The look in her eyes, the tension in her face, the curve of her shoulders, all said that this had been difficult. That she'd need to be lavished with tender loving care for some time.

"Now, what first?" I kissed her temple.

"As much as I want those orgasms, a bubble bath and some food should be first. Can I have food and orgasms in the bath? Please, Alpha?" She looked up at me with those big blue-grey eyes, batting her eyelashes, gaze playful.

"How can I say no to that? I'll start you a bath in my room, then make you some tea. What would you like to eat? Something quick like pasta? Or perhaps some chicken? I could order something? Whatever you'd like." As long as I could get some nourishment in her, she could have anything she desired.

"I think I'd like some pasta. Thank you." She smiled, though there was a haunted look in her eyes.

"My pleasure." I would happily feed her dinner in the tub and wash her just right.

I extracted myself from the window seat and went to my bathroom where I started the bath, setting it to shut off automatically when full, hoping I got the temperature correct. It wasn't a giant bathtub but would fit the two of us fine–if she wished for me to join her. I put on some soft music, lit candles, placed a bath pillow, and added some of the bubble bath I'd gotten for her, as well as set out a silky robe that I'd originally bought for this week. Grabbing some of my fluffiest towels, I put them on the towel bar and set it to warm.

Going downstairs to the kitchen, I started the tea and the pasta and defrosted some chicken. I'd make her something warm and comforting. When I brought the tea upstairs, I found the bathroom dark except for the flicker of the candles, and Grace neck-deep in the bubbly tub, eyes closed.

"Spence, this is amazing," she whispered. "Thank you."

"My pleasure. I brought you some tea." I set the cup of tea and a glass of water on the large flat edge of the tub. Maybe I should get her one of those bathtub trays. I placed a kiss on her cute freckled nose. "I must run back to the kitchen, but I'll return."

I finished making us food–orzo pasta with lemon, chicken, feta, spinach, and tomatoes. Putting two bowls and silverware on the tray, I added a glass of wine for myself and a beer for her, and more water.

"That smells amazing." Her eyes opened as I walked in. "You brought me a beer."

I sat down on the rug in front of the tub. "Did you finish your tea and water?"

She drained the mug, finished the water, and held out her hand. "Beer me, please."

I handed her the beer. "I probably shouldn't, due to whatever drugs they injected you with. But you're an adult, don't seem to have a concussion, and seem like you could use one."

Getting a forkful of pasta, I held it out to her. She opened her mouth like a baby bird and allowed me to feed her.

Grace closed her eyes as she swallowed. "This is amazing, you're such a good cook. I…" She frowned, opening her eyes. "Everything is so foggy and muddled, but in a different way from before."

"I'm just beyond relieved that you're home." I took a bite for myself.

"Um, I almost didn't get to come home. I don't remember why. Though I wasn't in trouble." Her chest shook.

"Do you remember why they took you? Or how you ended up here in the first place?" I fed her some more. If she wasn't in trouble why did they take her?

She rubbed her forehead. "Ow. I… I don't think I'm supposed to remember."

"Which makes sense. If you remember anything, or just want to talk, I'm here. But it's nothing that we need to discuss tonight, unless you wish. Have another bite." I offered her another forkful.

"Mmmm. So good." She made a happy noise, which went right to my cock.

"Here, have more." I needed her to eat.

Grace took the offered bite and looked around. "How did I get here?"

"The agent that retrieved you brought you back. This time with a backpack?" I took a sip of wine. "Your phone is charging. I'm just glad you're back. We… we thought we lost you."

The fact that she was alive, well, and back with us was *everything.*

Her head bowed. "I didn't mean to worry you."

"That's not what I meant. Relax and let me take care of you." I fed her the rest of her dinner and finished mine.

Food eaten, I positioned myself on the edge of the tub, where I washed her hair, giving her a nice, long, head massage, carefully working in shampoo, then conditioner, followed by a hair mask.

"This is amazing." She groaned.

"I'm glad you like it." Certainly, I enjoyed pampering her. I finished rinsing her hair. "Would you like me to wash the rest of you?"

"As long as it involves you getting naked. I believe orgasms were promised." She grinned at me, blue-grey eyes dancing.

"As you wish, Darling." I removed my clothes, carefully sliding in behind her and settling her on my lap, my hard-on pressed against her. Because that was all for her.

She curled into me. "Mmmm."

Taking the soap, I carefully soaped up the rest of her, scrubbing off the odd smells from wherever they brought her, washing away her fear, her tears.

The first time around was gentle, and more about getting her clean. The second, I lingered on her breasts, my fingers barely grazing her nipples as my mouth latched onto her throat.

Even though these weren't the best of circumstances, I'd take my time with her. If anything, it was even more reason to. Her sweet body called me. As one hand toyed with her breast, my other hand cupped her pussy, and she gasped.

"Would you like me to touch you there?" I breathed in her ear.

"Oh, yes, please, Alpha," she sighed, eyes closing, as I ran my fingers down her length, her hand running across my chest.

"Just lay back and let me care for you. Let go and feel." I began to massage her clit with my fingers.

With my other hand, I slipped two fingers inside her, her body against me. Under the warm, bubbly water, my hands explored her, making her gasp in delight. Each little noise made me harder and harder, as I wanted to impale her with my cock.

But this wasn't about me.

I continued to work her with my hands, bringing her to her peak. As she rode my fingers, my mouth got well acquainted with her neck and shoulders.

"Here..." I bit gently down on the place where her neck and shoulders met, where one of her scent glands was. "When it's time for me to bite you, I think I'd like to bite you right here," I whispered, as I made her climax again, three fingers now inside her.

"There?" she moaned, writhing on my lap.

"If you want it to be visible. It would look beautiful right there for everyone to see." My kisses worked lower.

My hand left her clit and brushed her inner thigh. "Perhaps there if you don't. I would lavish it with attention every time I went down on you."

"Spence." It came out as a gasp as she bucked in my arms. "You'd bond with me?"

Grace turned her head to face me, trailing my jaw with tiny kisses.

"Oh yes. Not today, but soon," I murmured. Though if she keened for my bite today I'd give it to her. The desire to mark her coursed through me with ferocity.

Never had I thought I'd want to mark someone again, to be bonded emotionally like that. Until her. Just a couple of months and I was hers, heart and soul.

"Do you like the places I've chosen?" I withdrew my fingers from her as her body melted back into me.

"Mmmm. Yes, please." Her hand settled around my cock, and it throbbed with her attention. "Alpha, I want your cock inside me."

Alpha. How sweet it sounded on her lips.

Without waiting, Grace turned and slid herself on my cock, so she faced me, the water sloshing slightly with her movements. She stopped just shy of my knot, a scintillating moan escaping her lips.

"You feel so good. So nice and thick." She sighed, resting her head on my chest.

"You feel amazing as well," I groaned. "Ride me, Darling, take what you need. If you want my knot, have it when you're ready—and if you'd rather wait, that's fine, too."

We had all night. I'd most definitely knot her before morning. Probably more than once.

I gripped her hips, urging her to go faster, as I ensnared her lips, kissing her deeply. My hands moved to cup her sweet ass, then ran up and down her back, loving her, supporting her as she worked herself and I toward the brink of pleasure.

"I want all of you," she hummed. She rocked into me, running her tongue over my nipples, the water sloshing over the sides of the tub as we moved.

"Take it. Though once you do that, I'm not sure how much longer I'll last." Right now, I was staving myself off for her.

Her lips once again claimed mine, as she moved herself up the length of my cock, then impaled herself on me.

Holding her tight with my arms, I thrust myself the rest of the way in. She stretched around my knot, seating me deep inside her, joining our bodies together.

"Spence," she cried. "I..." Grace came around my knot, and my own heat exploded inside her, filling her.

I pulled her to me, kissing the top of her head, as our bodies trembled together. It had been a long time since I'd knotted any-one. I felt so *full,* not just in the sense that I filled her, but in that my heart brimmed with love, my soul complete.

"That was so wonderful. You are perfect. Are you all right, Darling, do you want more?" I caressed her gently, peppering her with little kisses. We were knotted together but I could still please her. Softly, I rocked my pelvis against her clit to show her what I meant. She gasped, body shuddering.

"Please, Alpha, give me more," she begged, the bathroom filling with the sweet smell of her arousal.

"Oh, you beg so sweetly, my good doctor," I murmured. "I'll gladly give it to you. I'll give you everything."

Chapter Seven

Grace

Wrapped in a long, dark green silk robe, I sat on the foot of Spencer's bed as he brushed my hair. It was getting long—well, longer than I liked to keep it. Still, I sat and enjoyed it as he took his time, turning what I thought of as a necessary chore into a nearly orgasmic experience.

"You're an expert hairbrusher," I told him. And hair washer. And bather. And cook.

All of my memories about what had happened while I was gone bumped around in my head so fast I couldn't grab onto them, like I was trying to catch bubbles. But I did get a sense of things—like when I'd told Spencer I wasn't in trouble. That I knew.

But I still wasn't sure *why* the agent came. I *was* pretty sure that I'd previously met him. That where I'd been, I'd been before.

I also knew that I almost hadn't come back, which terrified me so much that I wasn't sure I wanted to recall anything.

"Just relax," Spencer said softly. "Just feel. You don't have to think of anything, do anything, just let me take care of you."

Yes, Alpha.

While I had no complaints with how Wes treated me, I was thoroughly enjoying Spencer's pampering. Sure, Evan and Wes treated me like a princess. But Spencer worshiped me like I was a goddess.

All the attention to details made everything even more perfect. Like all the lavender-scented things. How had he known that I preferred lavender? Wes and Evan usually got me peach or vanilla, which I did love. But it wasn't my absolute favorite.

Somehow Spencer had noticed. The hair mask was for fine hair. The robe was just the right shade of green. There was a *bath pillow.* He'd been prepared so when he had the chance he'd be ready.

The goddess treatment was exactly what I needed right now.

We weren't bonded. He couldn't feel me. Spencer was going off of alpha instinct or reading my body language or whatever.

No one had ever paid me this level of attention and care. He was so gentle, so kind, so patient. Getting fed a homemade dinner while in the bath? *Yes please.* I loved every moment.

I took a deep breath and exhaled. Because I wasn't ready to process what had happened. *Just feel.*

"That's it. So perfect," he murmured, one hand caressing my face, sending shivers straight through me.

Mmmm, yes Daddy. I could see how he saw himself as a nurturer and protector. He always took care of this family in so many ways. Ways I wasn't sure everyone even noticed, and there were probably a million little things I didn't.

It was hot as hell.

Spencer's bedroom was done in burgundies and greys, with dark wood furniture, carpet my feet sunk into, and stunning artwork on the walls. The room smelled of lavender, like he had a diffuser going someplace.

Everything seemed simple yet luxurious, like he'd rather have a few well-made items than a room full of ones that just worked. It was a perfect balance of aesthetic and function with no expense spared. Even the comforter under me was soft, probably of a higher thread count than I'd ever felt.

But then I knew Spencer was a man that liked his comforts and appreciated quality. Like whatever hairbrush he was using on me. So much better than anything I used.

Finally, he put the brush down and caressed my neck and shoulders, which sent heat right down my core, pooling between my thighs.

"Would you like to lay down on the bed and have a massage? Or we could watch a movie? Sleep? Would you like more food?" Each suggestion was punctuated with a little kiss on my throat that made me moan.

"A sexy massage with a happy ending? Please." While that bath was so very nice, I really wanted more. But I could be patient, as long as I got a knot in the end.

"Happy ending?" He grabbed a blanket off the chair and laid it across the bed.

"A massage ending in orgasms. In this case I mean orgasms with knots." It would be worth the wait.

"You want my knot, Darling?" He carefully removed the robe from me, eyes dancing with lust. "I'd love that. Could you lay face down on the bed for me, please? Oh, that is perfect."

All this praise made me wet. I was enjoying this care and attention so much that I was content to let everything take its course, knowing I'd get exactly what I'd needed. Just like in the bath.

I laid down on the soft blanket as he laid the robe on the chair and dimmed the lights, and pushed a button, lighting up a bunch of electric candles. Spencer only wore briefs. He was *very* fit. You could make pancakes on that stomach.

I would eat pancakes off that stomach. Yeah, I was thirsty.

"We should put the wrist brace back on, just to remind us of any limitations so that you don't get hurt," he said, putting the wrist brace on my arm. "This is different from what you had. The walking cast as well."

I frowned, struggling to remember. Hmmm. I could see a clinic in my mind. "I might have gotten sick. But I don't quite remember."

"Ah, yes. Some sort of interdimensional police station is probably a very good place to catch something that you're not resistant to," he nodded.

It made sense to me. I was a little surprised that I hadn't been sick with something here. Though when I arrived here, between the clinic and the hospital, I'd been vaccinated for all sorts of things since I'd had no records.

Spencer straddled my back. "Let me know if the pressure is too firm, not firm enough, or if you need attention in a different area."

"Oh, I will." Closing my eyes, I listened to the soft music, as warm lavender-scented oil glided across my skin. That must be what the blanket was for, so we didn't get oil all over everything.

His fingers kneaded into my shoulders. "Too warm? Too hard?"

"Perfect," I hummed. His cock dug into my back, and my pussy was on fire, but that smooth pressure was worth it.

"Good girl. Relax and just let all the tension float away," he purred as he massaged all my cares away.

Good girl? Oh, I'll be so good.

I drifted in and out of consciousness as his oiled hands glided across my body, tenderly working over every inch of me. The gentle pressure reminded me that I was home, I was safe, and people cared about me.

They'd missed me when I was gone. Had anyone even missed me back in my old world? There'd probably been no search, no posters. My own family probably didn't know I was gone.

Or cared.

Finally, he kissed my temple. "Are you doing all right? Turn over for me?"

I nodded and turned over, as he once again straddled me and began to massage my arms. His hard dick kept rubbing me through his briefs. As he worked me over, his hands kept brushing over my nipples, and the heat inside me that had lulled started to build again.

When his hands grazed my hips, my insides quivered, anticipating his next move. He moved so he was sitting between my legs and began rubbing my good foot, then working his way back up my thighs.

Tease.

"Are you still doing all right?" he inquired.

A groan escaped my lips. "This is amazing."

"I'm so glad that you're enjoying it."

He gently caressed me, lightly exploring and massaging me, but not actually entering me, as my breath came out in little pants.

"Would you like me to continue, or may I taste you now?" Spencer leaned forward, body almost covering mine, his breath warm on my cheek.

"That was wonderful but taste me, Alpha. Please?" I gazed up into his beautiful eyes.

Spencer smiled and let out a little growl of pleasure that made me wet. He moved me onto the bed, pulling back the covers and positioning me carefully among the pillows.

"I love you like this. So beautiful." He made a happy noise, and his eyes went half-lidded as his hands caressed my body with a featherlight touch.

Spencer positioned himself between my legs. My gaze fell down to that mouth, that delectable mouth full of sweet kisses and words.

"Yes, I'm most definitely going to taste you now." His tongue caressed me. "You taste a bit like peaches."

He devoured my pussy as if it were his favorite snack, licking and sucking every inch of it. I moaned and rocked my body, trying to grind down on his face as he teased my entrance with his lips, and circled my clit with his tongue.

"Come when you wish and as much as you need," he purred into me, his tongue flicking my clit. "I want you dripping down my face, to be aching, wet, and ready for my knot, so I can give you the very happiest of endings."

Yes, Daddy.

My thighs trembled as he sucked on my clit, hard, his fingers entering me. A gasp escaped my lips as my body spasmed with pleasure. His fingers continued to twist and pump, his mouth never stopping, sending me quickly to another peak.

"Spencer," I screamed as my back arched, as an orgasm shuddered through my body.

He purred into my pussy, curling his fingers to find all the sweet spots. "Oh, I think I could feast on you all night long. You taste divine."

I squirmed against him as I flooded with desire, loving the attention he was giving it, but ultimately wanting something else. He hit just the right spot and my body exploded. Again. I'd lost count of how many orgasms he'd given me tonight.

"Please, Alpha. I need you inside me, I need your knot," I begged, still not quite satiated.

"Do you, Darling?" He continued to lap at me languidly.

"I do, please, Alpha, please?" I pleaded, wiggling against him.

He sat up, my pussy juices dripping down his face. "You ask so sweetly."

Spencer stood and got off the bed, wiping his face as he removed his briefs.

All I could do was stare. While the lights were soft, I had a very, very good view of his very, very large, erect cock. It was longer than Wes' and as thick as Evan's. His knot, that fleshy bulb alphas had, was fully inflated, and ready for me.

"Beautiful," I murmured from my perch among the pillows, bending my knees and arching my back.

"Oh, you are," he breathed as he climbed back onto the bed. "Before breakfast tomorrow, I'm going to kiss every inch of you."

He took my breast into his mouth, teasing it with his tongue.

"Oh, yes, Alpha," I moaned, my hips jutting forward, again enjoying the attention but still wanting.

A smile played on his lips. "You're so sweet, so good."

Taking his cock in his hand, he leaned over me and guided himself inside me inch by inch, teasingly, maddeningly slow, his length stretching me.

A happy sound escaped my lips.

This. This was what I wanted.

"You look exquisite taking my cock. You *feel* exquisite taking me." His eyes met mine as he seated himself in me almost to his knot, then withdrew, then pushed himself back in, and withdrew, over and over.

The languid rhythm of his swollen knot slapping against my clit seeped through my body, filling every pore, every inch, with a slow burning desire. He continued murmuring praise in my ear, shifting my body into different positions, as he made me come again and again. Finally, a scream ripped from my throat and black spots danced in front of my eyes, as my orgasm seared my very soul.

"Are you ready for my knot, Darling?" he whispered. "I'm ready to come inside you."

"Yes, please," I keened, absolute jelly in his arms.

In one smooth gesture, he thrust his full length into me, joining us tightly. His body trembled as his heat flooded me. I orgasmed again, in a flash of warm lightening, making my entrance flutter around him.

"I love it when you come around my knot," he praised, kissing me deep, as he continued to pump his cum inside me. He pulled me close.

Spent and content, he rolled so I was on top of him, us still joined, and pulled a blanket over us.

"Are you all right?" he asked softly, stroking my back with his hands in a soothing gesture.

A happy hum thrummed through my chest. "That was amazing."

And exactly what I needed.

"It was. Rest now. You'll need your energy. After all, I did make you a promise," he murmured, holding me tight as he started to purr.

To kiss every inch of me. I couldn't wait. But until then, I'd let myself be lulled by his purr and his leathery scent. I was safe. I was warm. I was loved.

There were more knots waiting for me. Right after I had a little rest.

Chapter Eight

Jett

The dim nest at the cabin reeked of sweat, sex, and us. Evan moaned as Wes fucked him. Brennan dozen, but he'd wake as soon as Evan called for him.

"Grace, where's Grace?" Evan whined.

"I have you, Babe. I love you," Wes assured as he pounded into him.

This wasn't the first time that Evan had asked for Grace, but he'd picked up asking for her in the last couple of hours.

Hunger rumbled in my belly. Grabbing my phone, I took a bunch of bottles and wrappers and brought them down to the sitting room.

Evan had gone into heat almost immediately after we'd arrived here Saturday afternoon. It was Tuesday. Or was it Wednesday? Things should be tapering off. Instead, things were just as intense as that first round.

It was probably because of what had happened Friday night. Fuck. I still couldn't wrap my head around Grace being taken from us. Never could I have anticipated that. Or that she was from another world.

That had also broken Wes and Evan. Both had been inconsolable. Even now, I think the ferocity of this heat was because the two of them were trying to fill what they lost with each other.

I hoped that Riley was right, and Grace came back. Spencer telling us she was probably dead didn't help.

Was Spencer here? I hadn't anticipated things lasting longer so we'd gotten the normal amounts of things. Also, usually, Spencer would come by and fill up the fridge. Sometimes, when I came out of the nest during a lull he'd even make me something to eat.

Opening the last bottle of sports drink, I downed half of it along with a granola bar as I checked my phone, hoping that Spencer was here with groceries. Maybe he'd bring up a plate of sandwiches.

Oooh, Spencer had texted several times since I last checked my phone.

Spencer

> **Grace was just dropped off at the house. She's unconscious and in my arms.**

> **Grace is awake. She's physically fine from what I can see but needs a lot of care. I'll keep you updated.**

Oh? She was back? What?

Happiness flooded me. Not just because it would mean everything to Wes and Evan, but because for all her secrets, I genuinely liked her.

I texted him back.

Grace was back. But why had they taken her in the first place? I texted her as well.

Yeah, that would be just what Evan needed. Though it might make everything last even longer.

Getting some clean sheets from the basket I put them upstairs along with the last bottles of water and granola bars.

Now everyone was asleep. Good. Maybe I should go downstairs and see what we had in the fridge. Also, I wasn't going to tell anyone that she was back until she actually arrived. Just in case.

The kitchen was dark and quiet. According to my phone it was very early Wednesday morning. It reeked down here, too, but I didn't have the energy to air it out.

Opening the fridge, I found the things we'd brought to make food in case Spencer didn't come. Did I have enough time to make some bacon? No. I'd just make some eggs and hope I could shower and get in a little nap before Brennan hunted my ass down.

Heating a pan, I got out the eggs, whisked them together, then cooked them. Feeling Brennan stirring through the bond, I began eating them straight from the pan as soon as they finished cooking.

Given we'd been living on protein and granola bars, they tasted like the best, most wonderful eggs in the world.

"Jett." Brennan's voice cut through the darkness.

And there he was.

"Want some eggs, Honey?" I'm sure he could use some food.

He was still in the throes of Evan's heat. I could see it, in his eyes, in his face.

I held out a forkful of eggs and fed it to my alpha. My love.

"Mmmm. Perfect." He licked his lips. Lust filled his eyes as he grabbed the back of my head and kissed me.

"Here, have another." I fed him another bite, then took one myself.

Brennan and I stood there, in the kitchen, both of us naked, eating the eggs from the pan. As soon as the pan was empty, he took it from me and placed it in the sink. He picked me up and threw me over his shoulder.

"Do you want to take a shower?" I asked. This part always amused me, when the alpha took over.

"I want you," he growled, as we went up the stairs.

So, no shower. Oh, well. Maybe later.

Brennan dragged me straight back into the nest. "Found him."

"Jett." Evan pounced on me, kissing me deeply.

"I'm here, Baby, I'm right here," I soothed. "What do you need?"

His whine cut me deep and I kissed him back, trying to ease him, as the haze of heat, pheromones, and desire dragged me back under. Brennan grabbed my hair and kissed me as Evan reached for my cock.

Hopefully Grace would arrive soon, because I was pretty sure what he needed was her.

Chapter Nine

Grace

"Mmmm, now that was a wakeup call." I laid on Spencer's chest, lazily running my fingers through his dark hair, his knot deep inside me.

Sun peeked through the curtains of his room, and my stomach told me it was time for breakfast.

"That was very nice indeed. As lovely as spending the night with you in my arms. Why don't you doze a little more, then I'll make breakfast. Perhaps a frittata or some crepes?" he purred, pulling the comforter over us so we were nice and cozy.

Last night we watched a movie with his cock buried inside me. After, he took me to bed, made good on that promise to kiss every inch of me, then I'd fallen asleep curled in his arms... and he'd woken me up most deliciously.

Nothing like being tongued awake, then languidly knotted.

"Crepes? You're an amazing cook. Why don't you cook more?" My mouth watered at the thought of homemade crepes.

He smiled, a lock of hair falling into his eyes. "The guys generally don't appreciate all the time and effort that goes into my cooking. Also, most of the time Jett and Brennan beat me home. I do make crepes for Riley on the weekends sometimes. She appreciates my cooking."

Spencer stroked my hair while I dozed on his chest until his knot softened enough to release us. Giving me a kiss, he rolled me off him, fluffing a pillow under my head and making sure I was covered in blankets.

"Don't feel like you must get up right away. Would you like me to bring you some tea?" he offered.

"I'd love some coffee. I haven't had coffee in days." This bed was like a giant pillow, everything was so perfect, so soft. I made a happy noise.

He eyed me as he grabbed some briefs—not the boring white kind, but burgundy ones. "All right then. Oh, your phone is charging in your room. You hid it in your bra?"

"They didn't take my phone. Wow. Not sure. My brain feels mushy." Phone. Something about my phone. Did I make a video or recording to remind myself?

"Your backpack is downstairs," he added. "You didn't have it last time. Perhaps it's from before?"

My backpack? It awoke no memories. "It just might be."

Spencer left and I laid there a moment before getting up. I hobbled to my room, feeling very sore. If I was going to see Wes and Evan anytime soon, I needed those green bath fizzies.

Using the door from my room that went straight into Evan's bathroom, I started Evan's giant tub, glad it filled fast, and threw in two soothing green fizzies, along with a glug of bubble bath.

I went back into my room. It was a long, airy room. The daybed was festooned with lights. The window seat had been put back together neatly, the net curtains tied back. My phone was charging by my bed. Riley had messaged me.

Riley

I'm so glad you're back. Going to ride more roller coasters today.

Me

Have fun!

I texted Wes and Evan.

Me

I'm at the house. Love you. Miss you.

There was also a whole string of texts from Wes, starting not long after I left on Friday to Sunday.

Wes

I miss you.

I'm sorry I failed you.

I'll love you to the end of the universe.

Please come back to us.

Do you know where you are? I would invade an otherworldly police station for you.

I love you with my very soul.

We're going to the cabin for Evan's heat, when you come back head there. We'll save some for you. I love you.

My heart broke.

I scrolled through my phone looking for hints of where I'd been and what happened. No pictures. No texts to myself. No emails or unsent emails. No videos. No voice recordings.

Huh.

But then again, it wouldn't surprise me if the Temporal Police deleted them. I should just be grateful I was back.

And I was. Just knowing what happened would give me a piece of mind. There was also a text from Jett.

That was my biggest hesitation. Brennan would be pissed at me for keeping secrets, for sure.

I took off the robe, turned on the towel warmer, flipped on the jets, and slid into the bath, letting the water and fizzies soothe all my squishy parts, so that when I did see Wes and Evan I'd be ready.

Being with Spencer was amazing, but I needed to be the filling in a Wes and Evan sandwich.

Spencer came in with my coffee. "Please excuse the intrusion. I come bearing coffee. The bath's your happy place, isn't it?"

I accepted the coffee and took a sip. "Before coming here, I hadn't lived in a place with a bathtub in so long. The novelty of being able to take one whenever I want hasn't worn off yet."

"You enjoy your bath. I'm going to let the office know that I won't be in for the rest of the week. When you're ready, I'll make breakfast. I've already taken the liberty of pushing your start-date for work. We didn't know when you'd come back, and we were trying to buy time." Spencer leaned down and gave me a kiss.

"Oh, thank you." Ah, yes, my disappearance could cause problems. Thank goodness Mrs. Beekman thought I was on vacation.

I took another sip of coffee. It was nice and strong, but he used a smaller mug than I usually chose. It was *adorable,* with a little saucer. It was just *tiny.* I liked my coffee in a mug the size of a soup bowl.

"Think about when you'd like to head up to the cabin. Jett would like us to come today and to bring food. I know you want to see your mates. But there's no rush unless you desire it." He kissed me on the forehead and left.

Closing my eyes, I sipped my coffee and relaxed. It would be so easy just to stay here and let Spencer spoil me until they came home. Yet that desire for Wes and Evan clawed at my chest.

Still, I needed just a little more quiet and solitude. Spencer might be happy to let me process everything in peace. But everyone else would be peppering me with questions, pushing me to remember.

Part of me just wouldn't rest easy until I saw them in person. Yes, I'd ask Spencer if we could leave after lunch.

Spencer kept giving me looks as he drove. We had breakfast, watched another movie, made love again, ate some lunch, then left for the cabin, which involved several stops to get everything we needed.

Grocery shopping with Spencer had been fun. I could see us doing this years from now, me pushing the cart as he selected the right hunk of lamb, chose the freshest produce, and fed me tastes of things from the deli.

As we left town, we'd stopped at that very fancy coffee shop where he'd brought me treats that morning back when I'd been in the hospital. He'd gotten me one of those delicious tea lattes and a pastry for the road.

Perfect.

I took a long sip of my coffee slushie that I'd bought when we'd stopped to get gas. I'd also grabbed some hot chips. Road trip food for the win.

"You drink too much coffee." He eyed my drink.

The tea latte was nice, but I loved my coffee.

I gave him a look. "Have you been around PhD students? I've had so little today compared to what I used to drink. I pretty much ran on coffee and ramen."

Mostly because it's what I could afford—even after graduation.

"It's not good for you. You and Evan don't eat right. You might not understand, but Evan knows better. Actually no one eats right. Our pack has dreadful eating habits," he muttered. "Me included. I should fix that."

"Right, the nutrition unit I didn't watch. You can pry my coffee from my cold, dead hands." I ate some chips, which were purple and deliciously spicy.

He chuckled. "I understand and feel the same way. You just need to be careful not to drink too much."

Yeah, pretty sure his definition of *too much* was more than one tiny mug in the morning.

I gave him a stern look. "If you take my potatoes away from me, so help me."

"Never." He squeezed my knee. "Sweet potatoes are better, but never."

Good. Spencer liked them as much as I did.

"I like sweet potato fries, and sweet potato tots. I'm excited about trying your food," I added.

He gave me a fond look. "I can't wait to see what you think. Also, I'm going to get the boat out, since the weather should be nice. How does that sound?"

"It sounds perfect," I replied.

Finally, we arrived and pulled into the garage which held Jett's convertible.

When we walked into the airy kitchen of Evan's cabin, my nose wrinkled at the onslaught of overpowering aromas. "What is that smell?"

"Them. Usually it's not this pungent." Spencer immediately opened the kitchen windows, then started opening up all the doors to the outside.

A pan, a small bowl, and a fork sat in the sink. The fridge had basics—bacon, eggs, juice, some yogurt, and fruit. Nothing nearly as exciting as the lamb Spencer was going to rotisserie.

I put my stuff in my room upstairs. It was a tiny room, mostly bed, with everything built into the walls. The little bookshelves folded *into* the big picture window the bed nestled into. It was cozy and comfortable, but I didn't plan on spending much time here.

No one had texted me back. But I could feel them. They were here...

A wave of lust hit me so hard that I fell backward on the bed. Desire burned inside me. *Oh?*

He was still in heat. For some reason I thought that he'd be done by now. I wasn't sure if I was ready for all four of them. Though I wanted to see Evan and Wes so badly it hurt.

Spencer leaned in the doorway, looking casually handsome in a T-shirt and chinos. "You're going up? Will you take a tray of water and snacks and put it in the sitting room for me, please?"

"Yeah, I'll pop in and let them know I'm here." I got up off the bed. So many nerves bumped around inside me. But I had to see them.

"Darling?" Spencer cupped my face with his hand. "One of your mates is still in heat, and you've been gone for days. There is no *popping in.*" He pressed his forehead to mine. "You need them—and they need you. Go on. I'll be fine."

Spencer was right. Even if Evan wasn't in heat, he would drag me into his room—and relish the thought of Wes breaking down the door to get to us.

"Don't be nervous. You'll feel so much better after being reunited with them. I'll happily give you another back massage later—I also have a very nice bathtub here. I'll feed you while you bathe." Spencer held me to him, his leather scent curling around me, comforting me.

I held him for a moment. "I'd like that."

We went downstairs and got the tray. I stopped in Evan's room, which I loved with the big window and fireplace. I exchanged my dress for one of his shirts and took off the walking cast and wrist brace.

When I opened the door to Evan's turret, all four of their scents, as well as desire and sex nearly knocked me over. Wes and Evan's sheer lust and need washed over me–and the door to the actual nest wasn't even open yet.

Setting the tray on the table of the turret's little sitting room, I put a couple waters in the mini fridge which was empty except for a half-full bottle of sports drink. The garbage can overflowed with bottles and wrappers. A stack of folded sheets sat next to a basket of crumpled ones.

The door to the bathroom opened.

"Peaches. I was just about to go find you." Jett stood there, completely naked. "I'm so fucking happy to see you."

I'd seen Jett shirtless, but *hot damn.* Tattoos decorated his golden back. Brennan's silvery bite mark sat at the juncture of his neck and shoulder. The gold hoop in the tip of his dick gleamed at me.

He had a dick piercing. I'd never seen one in the flesh. My breath hitched in my chest.

"They almost didn't let me return. I... I didn't know they were coming, and I can't... I can't quite remember," I blurted, everything going a bit hazy.

Jett wrapped his arms around me so hard he lifted me off the ground. "It's okay. There's time for that. You brought food, thank goodness. We didn't get enough, but usually by now we're winding down, or done."

He set me down, opened a bottle of water and downed it.

"How pissed is Bren?" Tears pricked my eyes. I hid something major from him, and he wasn't going to be happy.

"Hey, don't worry about that right now. He won't be pissed. He'll be glad you're back. Though he'll probably want to talk about it later. Because this is Bren." Jett held me to his bare chest again, his amber scent comforting, though he also smelled of all of them.

"Only Evan's been asking for me? Is Wes pissed at me, too? I didn't mean to cause emotional damage." The tears kept coming.

"Shhh. It's okay, Babydoll. I didn't tell anyone that you were coming, and they've been too... occupied to check their phones. I'm guessing Evan's feeling you through the bond, which is why he's been asking for you a lot." His dark eyes met mine, his hair was down and in disarray.

Oh, that made sense. While I could feel both Evan and Wes through our bonds now, Evan's and mine were more nuanced.

"Could they not feel me when I was gone? I couldn't feel them," I added.

He shook his head. "They couldn't. Hey, this heat is turning out to be hardcore. You need to understand that if you walk into the nest, you are consenting to getting fucked long, hard, and everywhere. I can't promise it will just be Wes and Evan. I'm usually not this deeply affected by their pheromones. If Evan whines to help him make a Grace sandwich, I can't guarantee that I won't. He's told me the fantasy of you being between the two of us and I find it hot as fuck."

I gulped, the need to be with my mates growing, despite my apprehension. Jett's amber scent smelled so good that it made me want to lick him.

"I... I'm okay with being the filling. Though I've never had a pierced dick in me." I bit my lower lip.

Yeah, I'd try that.

"I'll be gentle. It's okay. I was afraid the first time I was with Evan in his heat, too, but it'll be fine." He went to the counter in the kitchenette behind the couch.

"When I'm done I'll just slip out, right?" I rubbed my thighs together as my need increased, but not my bravery.

"Only if they don't see you, and even then your ass might get dragged back. I usually take naps in my own bed. Bren has been hunting me down as soon as he's free to do so after he realizes I'm missing." He brought out a first aid kit.

"Oh." My chest shuddered.

Jett held out a tablet. "Here."

"What is it?" I eyed it.

"It keeps you from getting UTIs during a heat. Believe me, that isn't something you want to be dealing with after." Jett handed me a bottle of water.

"Oh. That makes sense." I took it and drank some of the water.

Now Jett had a big tin. Opening it, inside were tiny tins, holding different colored gummies.

"Are those drugs?" That was quite the assortment there.

"Legal recreationals." He held up one with little pink gummy strawberries. "You don't have to, but I got this one especially for you since you were so nervous. It's a mild relaxant and takes the edge off. It's what you take when you're going to a theme park when you don't like rollercoasters or a party when you don't like people."

"Oh, thank you for thinking of me." I took it and eyed the other things as he pulled out one with green lightning bolts.

"These are what I use when I've been on duty for three days straight during an emergency and have to function. Do I take this one or that one?" He held up one with orange hearts. "Betas sometimes take these to help them enjoy a heat better."

"Oh?" I reached out.

"Maybe next time, when we know how pheromones affect you." He put the hearts back and took two lightning bolts.

"The doctor at the clinic said to pay attention, since with gammas it could range from no reaction whatsoever, to being buzzed like a beta, to being driven into a heat spike. Which given my fucked up hormones, isn't likely." I sighed. "Yeah, TMI." I held up one filled with little colored bears. "And these?"

"Evan's favorite to unwind after a rough day." He grinned.

I heard the sound of a door and nerves shot through me. I took one of the strawberries.

He put a few bottles of water in his arms. "They told us that you're from another world. That's really trippy but given all the really common things you don't know—and random things you do—it makes sense."

"Yeah, I'm a stranger from a strange land. I was afraid. I'm sorry." The tears started again.

"Let's get you upstairs. I can't purr for you, but they can." Jett's voice went soft, as he put his free arm around me.

A low growl vibrated through the room, one that simultaneously overwhelmed me and made me gush. The scent of pine filled the room to the point of suffocation. My knees grew weak as fear washed over me.

Brennan.

"I'm sorry. I know I should have told you, but I didn't know how you'd take it. Telling people weird stuff hasn't gone well for me before. I didn't know they were coming to take me." Overwhelmed, I fell to his feet as pain shot through me.

He was also naked—his big cock *right there*. One with a whole bunch of barbell piercings.

For the love of baby Jesus, what was *that?*

"I wasn't trying to hurt anyone," I sobbed. "I don't even remember what happened. They took my memories *again.* Please don't be mad."

"Evan's shirt. You do that on purpose, don't you?" Brennan's voice grew rough and rumbling.

All I could do was cry as everything went fuzzy. "Please don't hate me. I'll even play Volkov the right way."

"Oh fuck," Jett whispered. "Do you really have a problem with bringing her upstairs, Honey? I guess I could bring her down to Spencer. I'm pretty sure she needs Wes, though."

Brennan scooped me off the floor. "Grace, I don't hate you. I'm not mad. Worried. Yes. Concerned. Yes. Do I have questions? Yes. Am I going to keep you from them? No."

There was an almost hypnotic quality to his voice. Even though I didn't mean to, I melted into his arms, as sobs continued to rack my body.

"Jett, grab all the waters you can. Evan's going to fucking lose it." Brennan started up the stairs, holding me to his bare chest. "Shit, you're warm. But then you've been away from them for days. I should have fucking seen this coming, but I didn't know you were back."

"I'm sorry." I whimpered as pain stabbed me again.

"It's not your fault," he assured.

"Spencer texted. I was a little afraid of telling them until she physically got here, given the state they're in." Jett followed with water bottles and snacks.

Brennan opened the door and the full force of their four scents and sex hit me. My body shattered as the pain intensified. My whimper turned into a whine, as the space between my thighs grew soaking wet.

The inside of the disheveled room was dim. It was small, round, and cozy, with a low ceiling, a stained-glass window, and filled with colors like saffron, cinnamon, and turmeric, making me feel like I was in a spice box. The ensconced lights on the warm brown walls gave everything a soft glow.

Evan panted as he laid face up in the nest of pillows and blankets, Wes fucking him. That beautiful sight made me gush so hard wetness trickled down my thighs.

"Wes..." It barely came out as my body shook. "Evan."

Here. They were here.

Need overwhelmed me as I bit my lower lip to keep from moaning as Evan took Wes' knot. Jett set the bottles and the snacks near the edge of the nest.

"Grace." Wes' voice broke as he stopped and looked at me.

"Alpha, don't stop," Evan moaned.

"Sorry, Babe," Wes soothed, continuing to move. "Peaches." He reached out to me with one hand, the other on Evan.

Brennan put me down and I stumbled into Wes, desperate and needy for everything he had to offer. Wes was naked and disheveled, dark blonde messy hair in his hazel eyes.

"You came back." Wes' mouth smothered mine, as I frantically met lips, kissing him deeply as if I could pull what I needed out of him.

"Wes, Boo-Bear," I moaned, as one of his hands grabbed me, the other stroking Evan. "I... I didn't think I'd get to come back."

"Boo-Bear?" Jett chuckled.

"You're here. It's going to be okay," Wes purred.

"Grace? Where's my Princess Peaches," Evan keened.

"I'm right here." I laid my head on Wes' chest as one of my hands searched for Evan's. Need and longing overwhelmed me. "Alpha, please."

"You're next, I promise, Peaches." Wes' hand cupped my pussy. "Fuck, you're soaked."

Wes slipped two fingers inside me and happiness shuddered through me, though I still felt empty.

I whimpered and squeezed Evan's hand. "Evan."

"Grace..." Evan moaned.

"Do you want Evan's cock, Peaches? Does your pussy ache for your mates' dicks? Because they ache for you. We're going to fill *all* your holes, don't worry," Wes murmured between kisses, his fingers starting a maddening rhythm.

"Please, Alpha," I whined. My soul ached for their cocks.

"Let's get you undressed. Look, Evan's dick is right there, just slip on it. I'm *right here*," Wes murmured as my shirt and panties came off with Jett's help.

"Slide right down and ride him as hard as you need; he's nice and slick for you," Jett said softly, getting me to straddle Evan.

Body trembling, I impaled myself on Evan's cock, which was dripping with slick and precum, my knees sinking into the soft nest as I exploded all over Evan's hard shaft. *Oh, that's it.*

"Oh fuck." Evan's eyes flew open as Brennan stuffed a wedge pillow under Evan's back.

"Hey, Love, look who came to see us," Brennan whispered, cupping Evan's face and giving him a deep kiss, while he stroked Evan's chest.

Jett lay next to us, his tongue caressing Evan's nipples.

"Evan." It came out like a sob. They were here with me.

"Grace. You're here. I missed you." Evan's chest shuddered as he kissed me again, forceful and needy.

"We're right here," Wes purred, stroking my back. "I'm going to finish with Evan and then we'll make a Grace sandwich."

Evan's lips attacked me, arms pulling me down on him. Our bodies melded as he held me to him. I rode him, moaning his name over and over. Longing and want coursed through my bond from both of them so forcefully that I wasn't sure where I ended and they began.

"We missed you so much," Wes whispered in my ear, leaning forward. "I'm going to touch you and get you ready. Then, when I'm done with Evan, we'll pump you full of cum."

"Oh yes, please, Alpha," I begged, my need for a knot growing.

"Omega, do Grace's breasts taste as delicious as they look?" Jett asked, his mouth latching onto one and sucking.

"Oh yes, they do," Evan sighed, attacking the other.

I moaned and my pussy fluttered around Evan's cock as I licked his chest.

"Grace," Evan groaned. "I'm going to come."

A moment later I felt his cum shoot into me, making me cry with delight.

"Me too," Wes stated.

I was sandwiched in between their two bodies as they came. My body shuddered, but I still wanted more, and a little whine escaped my lips.

"Shhh, just give me a little time and I'll put my knot inside you, promise," Wes said. I could feel his fingers brush my ass as he massaged his knot, trying to deflate it sooner.

"Maybe I should do a taste test," Jett teased as he started alternating his attentions between Evan's nipples and mine.

My hand reached out and grabbed Jett's cock, and I began to stroke it. Pre-cum beaded on the tip.

"That feels good, Peaches, keep going," Jett murmured, still kissing our chests, teasing our nipples with his tongue and unnerving me with nibbles.

Brennan had his cock in Evan's mouth and something in me twitched. Evan moaned, taking Brennan deep as he continued to move inside me. What did Brennan's cock taste like? Any reservations or inhibitions I may have had before I entered the nest had fled. Right now, all I wanted was that beautiful pierced alpha cock in my mouth. I moved forward and my lips brushed his balls. I started to suck them lightly like Evan taught me. *Delicious.*

My movements made Brennan look at me and my heart jumped, a whimper escaping my lips.

"Go ahead and taste me, Grace," Brennan encouraged quietly. "Jett, hold her head better."

"That's it, there's enough of Bren to share," Jett muttered, hands around my throat as Evan and I attacked Brennan's cock with our mouths.

"Keep going. You're still warm." Brennan's fingers brushed across my forehead.

Wes groaned as he continued to play with my ass. "Shit, that's sexy as fuck."

Pain shot through me, and my whine became a whimper.

"Trade. There you go. Take what you can. You're doing fine. Look at the two of you, giving my cock such attention," Brennan soothed, pulling his dick out of Evan's mouth and thrusting it into mine as he pushed Evan's head over to suck his balls.

Brennan's cock was large and I gagged a little. But it was also delicious–his pre-cum tasted like Christmas.

"I'm going to come in your mouth," Brennan finally said, as ropes of hot liquid squirted into the back of my throat, his hands tangled in my hair.

"So beautiful," Jett whispered, holding my face.

"That's it, Little Butterfly. Suck it down like a good girl so you feel better." Brennan held my head, lightly stroking me.

I swallowed as much as I could, because I desperately wanted to be a good girl for him. But there was still some left in my mouth when Brennan withdrew his cock. Immediately, Evan kissed me, taking the rest, and licking any remainers off my face.

"That's sexy as fuck," Jett breathed.

"You're both so good, not wasting any," Brennan praised.

The pain subsided, though I felt fuzzy. I rested my head on Evan's chest. Wes ran his hands up and down my back. Brennan and Jett were making out.

"Okay, there we go." Wes pulled out of Evan. "Give me a moment to clean up, Peaches, and I'm all yours."

I laid on Evan, feeling intrinsic, that need for cock building inside me again.

"Evan, can you go again? Pussy or ass? Grace, do you care?" Wes carefully cleaned up me and Evan.

"I want her again," Evan panted.

Pain shot through me again and I whined, needing cock *right now*. "Just fuck me."

"Okay, Peaches, just sit yourself right here. Evan, take her ass." Wes leaned up against the edge of the nest and helped me settle onto his hard dick.

A sigh escaped my lips and my body shuddered as he filled me. "Alpha."

Wes buried his face into the crook of my neck as his hand stroked the bond mark under my breast, making my body buck. "I missed you so much. Shit, you're warm."

"I missed you, too. Both of you." My lips fumbled for his.

Evan kissed my shoulders and neck as he guided his cock into my ass. "I missed you, three."

My body spasmed as my mates filled me, their love for me pulsing through the bond.

"I love both of you," I told them, my need for them frantic, as my hands roamed over their bodies, my lips searching for theirs.

Their rhythms synched, and Wes said sweet things to the both of us. Scents flared around me making me let go of everything but how I felt. Of the sensation of Wes' knot, the pleasure of Evan's hands on my breasts, the softness of their lips as I kissed them.

Everything else happening around me floated away until it was just us, reunited and bringing each other to a peak.

They both came inside me as my body trembled with an orgasm so fierce I seemed like it tore me in half. Wes held us and began to purr, coating us with warmth. As I rested my head on Wes' chest, him knotted to me, Evan at my back, once again everything felt right with the world.

Chapter Ten

Wes

I awoke to Evan and Grace kissing while on top of me. Such a lovely sight. I ran one hand through her tangled hair, my other hand stroking his bare light brown back, which no longer burned with fever. Evan's heat had, for the most part, finished.

But Grace was nowhere near satisfied and the two of them kept feeding off each other, sending each other into spikes.

She pounced on Evan, and he let her push him down into the messy nest. Brennan was dozing next to me, Jett in his arms. Jett watched Grace and Evan with interest as they fucked, the sweetness of their arousals filling the nest.

I crawled out, needing a bathroom break before they started whining for me. Grabbing some wrappers and empty bottles and cups, I went down to the sitting room. More water and sports drinks had been left along with a note from Spencer saying that there were sandwiches in the fridge.

Sandwiches. Fuck. My stomach rumbled as I hit the bathroom. I gazed longingly at the shower. I reeked. The room reeked. The sheets were going to need to be washed multiple times, and the room would take forever to air out. Maybe I could lure them into the shower...

In the sitting room, I downed a sports drink and hungrily devoured a sandwich, not even aware of what sort it was.

Grace was back and for that I was so fucking grateful. When Brennan had carried her into the nest it felt like the world had restarted after being on pause. I had no idea what had happened, but we could talk later. Also, she didn't need to talk right now. She needed us.

And our dicks.

While she hadn't gone into actual heat, she kept having something very close to one of Evan's heat spikes. There was no slick, but I'd never seen her this wet, this desperately needy. She had no actual omega perfume, but like the last time we'd been here, her scent had taken on irresistible undertones that definitely stated that she needed to be fucked long, hard, and often by her alpha. *Eau d'fuck me alpha.*

Sometimes in response to trauma or lengthy separation from their alphas, omegas needed to be reassured by being held and knotted, repeatedly. There'd been a little bit of this after both the shooter on her birthday and the incident with Caroline at the gala.

But this...

This was on a whole different level. Which, of course, made me want to satisfy her, because that was my job. That then set Evan off, hence the cycle. Also, I was pretty sure his heat had been fiercer for the same reasons. We'd had our mate ripped from us and sought solace with each other.

Now she was back.

I filled up Grace and Evan's cups, which had lids and bendy straws to make it easier to keep them hydrated, and grabbed some more water bottles, along with snacks.

When I went upstairs, groans and moans met my ears. Grace's eyes were closed, an expression of delight on her face, as Evan and Jett fucked her. Being the filling in a dick sandwich seemed to be her favorite position. She nestled against Evan's chest. Grace looked too deep into it to do more than hum with delight. Evan and Jett murmured sweet things to her and each other between kisses and strokes.

It also looked like Brennan had finally let go, no longer maintaining the control he so often had in the nest, as he took Evan from behind, his hands tangled in Jett's unbound hair.

So beautiful. So perfect.

It was nice to see Brennan surrender for once. He always felt like he had to be the heat cruise director. But Bren did have a need for control that went far beyond the usual alpha dominance.

He'd been tender to Grace, stroking her, and giving her little kisses here and there. Her and Evan sharing Brennan's cock had been so very hot. While I wasn't sure Grace and Brennan would ever be mates, it would be nice for them to have a deep enough relationship to trust each other.

I put down the drinks and snacks, and sat on the edge of the nest, stroking my cock, watching the four of them, knowing that it was only a matter of time before someone whined for me.

"Wes, I want your knot," Grace keened.

I was on my feet and at her side in an instant, Evan still fucking her. I gave her a kiss. Shit, she was warm again.

"As soon as Evan's done," I promised. Her little pout broke my heart.

"Do you think you can take them both in your pussy, Babydoll?" Jett nipped her earlobe. "That would feel so fucking good."

That was an idea. I looked around and found a bottle of lube.

"Oh, fuck, yes," Evan moaned. "Do you want Wes and I in your pussy at the same time, because I know I want to feel his knot rub against me when he's inside you." He kissed Grace.

"Yes." Grace sighed, pure bliss on her face as the two of them continued to fuck her.

"Go slow, use a lot of lube. Check in with them often," Brennan murmured to me, scooting to one side, as he kept thrusting into Evan.

There was the cruise director. But it wasn't bad advice, because Evan and I had yet to do this with her.

"Ready?" I lubed her up, putting a slick finger inside her alongside Evan's dick when she nodded. "How does that feel, Peaches?"

She made a happy noise, eyes closed, head on Evan's chest, since she faced him.

"Let me know if it's too much and I'll stop. Evan?" I asked.

"Mmmm," Evan smacked his lips as he moved inside her, the feeling of him against my hand making my dick weep.

Slowly, I worked a second finger in, stretching her out so she could take the both of us, as Jett continued to take her ass.

"Ready for me?" I asked both of them, lubing my cock.

They both nodded. Evan stilled, making her whine.

"Hold on, my sweet peach, I don't want to hurt anyone." I slowly worked the head of my cock in, checking on both of them as Evan groaned with pleasure, and Grace mewled for more. It was a tight fit, as I slid in inch-by-inch my dick rubbing against Evan's.

"I feel that, shit. I'm going to come soon," Jett breathed, stroking Grace's hair.

"Do you feel nice and filled now, with three dicks inside you?" Evan asked her.

"So good," Grace moaned, her pussy squeezing my cock as I finished working my way in.

"Evan, I'm going to come," Bren said, stroking Evan, his face blissed-out.

Seated, I started to move inside her tight wetness, Evan staying still.

"Jett," Grace called, spasming around my cock, as I felt Jett come in her ass, at about the same time Evan yelled Brennan's name.

I continued to move inside her, as Jett stroked her, and Brennan murmured to Evan.

"I need your knot," Grace begged.

"Are you ready for that, Babe?" It felt so fucking good to be inside her like this, with Evan.

"Please," Evan groaned.

I pushed in, locking myself and Evan inside Grace's pussy. The sight of the two of us deep inside her made desire shoot through me. "Fuck." as I shot my cum into her

Yeah, I wasn't expecting Evan and I to take her *at the same time* today. Shit, it felt so good.

"I'm going to cum, too," Evan said, squirting into her, as Grace ground against me, coming again.

Jett had slid out of her, and they kissed.

"Fuck, that feels good," Evan murmured, eyes closed, Bren's arms around him.

"More, I need more, please," Grace whined pitifully.

"Let me clean up. If you suck me in your pretty mouth, I should be able to give it another go. Do you want your ass filled again with two dicks in your pussy," Jett murmured, lowering her body to the nest as he got up.

She nodded.

Jett grabbed the wipes. "You like that, don't you? To be nice and full of dicks. To have everyone's cum inside you?"

"Please, I need more," she whimpered, almost as if in pain, eyes closed. The scent of her desire, her need, filled the room.

Brennan stroked her hair tenderly. "Such a greedy body you've got there, Little Butterfly. You just need all the dicks, don't you? Every hole pounded by cock, and dripping with cum."

Little Butterfly. Bren had called her that before. Hearing him talk dirty to her was hot.

Yeah, my needy little mate needed all the dicks, and it was fucking beautiful. Jett came back over, and Grace greedily started sucking his cock. A low, needy whine, one that cut straight through to my alpha core, came from deep within her throat.

Tears pricked her eyes. "Please," she begged, mouth full of dick.

Brennan bent over and whispered to Evan.

"Oh, yes, Alpha," Evan groaned, as his omega perfume filled the room with suffocating force.

Brennan's eyes met mine, and his head tilted toward Grace.

Wait, what? *Go for it,* I mouthed. I wasn't expecting that.

He grabbed the lube, lubing up his fingers and her ass, sliding one inside her, as she lay beneath Evan and me. "Is that what you need, my greedy little butterfly. Do you need two knots at once?"

"Yes, please." She sighed, eyes still closed, lips closing over Jett's cock again.

"That's it, just like that." Jett's hand wrapped around her throat like a necklace, taking control of her mouth.

Oh, fuck, that was hot.

"You beg so sweetly. But if you want this ass knotted, and stuffed full of my cum, then you need to be a good girl and keep sucking Jett's cock," Brennan instructed, two fingers now pumping inside her.

She was still pretty gone, moaning, as she sucked Jett's cock, and took mine and Evan's dicks, and Brennan's fingers.

"You're doing so well." I kissed her.

Brennan rubbed his cock and her ass with lube, as she keened, lips still around Jett's dick.

"Here we go, Little Butterfly," Brennan murmured.

Evan and I stilled, as he worked himself underneath her, moving her to assume the position Jett had been in when I'd entered the room.

"I'm going to go nice and slow. Not sure your pretty little ass has ever taken a cock pierced like mine. But you're going to take it perfectly for me," he told her.

She immediately came, her pussy spasming around my cock, making me shoot my load into her wanting pussy.

"That's it, come as much as you need," Brennan murmured, as he lowered her onto him, easing into her, as she ground against Evan and I, still not satisfied.

The sight of Brennan's multiple frenum piercings slowly disappearing into Grace's pale little ass made me hard again.

"Oh, fuck, that feels good," Evan groaned. "Peaches, you look so beautiful with all your holes filled."

That blissed-out expression had returned, as she made little kitten noises while sucking Jett's dick, still clinging to Evan, as she seated fully onto Brennan.

"You're doing perfectly," Jett added, hand still around her throat.

Brennan's balls slapped against her ass, the sounds of their pleasure filling the room, as we moved her up and down on our cocks.

It was so fucking beautiful.

"Keep going, Babydoll, I'm almost there," Jett gasped. "That's it, that's it." He held onto her throat as he came into her mouth. "So good."

She swallowed and Evan kissed her, Jett running his hands down her back, murmuring to her.

"Please, Alpha," Grace whispered to Brennan.

"I love hearing her call you that," Evan breathed, eyes closed.

It was so very hot.

"If you think you're ready." Brennan pulled her body up with his hands, withdrawing almost the entire way, then slammed her back down his length, knotting her tight little ass.

Grace shrieked in pleasure, coming, and Evan did the same. Their arousal through the bond was nearly overwhelming. I loved that we could make them feel like that.

I took over moving, trying to match Brennan, our pace unrelenting. Both of us had knotted her, Evan along for the ride. Grace orgasmed two more times. Finally, we collapsed into a pile of bodies.

"Everyone okay?" Brennan asked, running his hands through Grace's hair. "You did so well." He gave her a kiss on the temple. "You, too." He kissed Evan, long and deep. "And you. I love seeing your cock sucked. You're so good with them." Brennan captured Jett's mouth.

"Mmmm, that was nice." Grace's eyes closed, contentment rushing through our bond. Bren and I were still knotted to her. Evan had managed to somehow slip out.

"Drink a little water, you're still warm." Jett held her cup to Grace's lips.

Evan threw a blanket over us and curled into Brennan. "Being inside Grace *with* Wes was intense, but I'm good. Mmmm. I am good."

"It was nice feeling you while I was inside her," I told him, reaching out to grab his hand as satisfaction came through our bond.

He squeezed mine. "Let's do that again."

"Jett? Are you doing okay?" Bren took a gulp of water.

"I'm fine. Hungry, but fine." Jett drank some water, then ran his hands through Bren's hair.

"There's sandwiches in the fridge," I told them, stroking Grace's warm back.

Delight broke out across Jett's face. "Shit, I need a sandwich."

"And I need the bathroom. I think I'll get a sandwich, too." Evan gave Grace, Bren, and I each a kiss, and he and Jett went downstairs.

Leaving me and Brennan alone with her. Her eyes were closed, breathing slow, as she napped sandwiched between us. Good. Maybe after a little nap I could carry her to the shower and feed her something.

Brennan's fingers lightly stroked her face. "I hope she's here to stay. It would break Evan's heart to lose her again."

"It would break my soul to lose her again." I pressed my lips to her temple. "But she's here, with us, where she belongs."

"Okay."

I don't know what I expected Brennan to say. *Okay* wasn't it.

"I still want to know what happened," Brennan added.

"Me, too." But the most important thing was that she was back and in my arms. Right where she belonged.

Hopefully, this time, she'll stay there for good.

Chapter Eleven

Jett

"That's it, you take me so well, Babydoll," I told Grace as I fucked her in the ass, again, as she took Evan in the pussy. Even though the air purifier ran on high and we'd changed the sheets, the smell of sex, heat, pheromones, and us permeated the nest. That was probably why every time we thought everything was over, one of them pounced on us.

Wes was passed out on a pile of pillows, but Brennan watched us as he drank some water. We were all fucking exhausted. I wasn't sure how much more of this I could take. While this heat had affected me more than any other, I still wasn't like them.

"I'm going to cum, Peaches," Evan said to her as he kissed me.

"Cum inside her, Omega," I directed. "You fuck her so good. Peaches, come for us as we cum in you." Thrusting harder, I let go, flooding her sweet little ass with my cum.

One thing about this heat was that I'd gotten to spend a lot of time sharing Grace with Evan.

And I fucking liked it.

Of course, seeing Brennan fuck her had been extremely hot. I loved how careful he'd been with her. Sweet Bren was such a turn on.

Even now, he watched us carefully, ever the vigilant alpha, waiting to see if anyone needed him.

Grace came in our arms.

"Mmmm. I'm better now." Grace sighed and flopped on Evan.

"Good." I kissed her head as I pulled out of her. She didn't cry for a knot. That was positive.

Grabbing the wipes, I cleaned her, Evan, and myself up.

"Are you okay, Dear?" Brennan pulled me to him and gave me his water.

I took a long drink. "We need to get everyone out of here and try to break the cycle. Get them showered and in other beds. Feed them. Maybe we can all go out on the boat while the house airs out?"

If they spiked again, well, there were plenty of places in the cabin that we could fuck them.

"Good idea." Brennan kissed my temple. "Go find Spencer. Maybe we can get the cleaning crew here while we're out on the boat. I'll get Evan to his room, Wes can take Grace."

I looked over and saw Wes fucking Evan.

"I want a sandwich." Grace looked up at me.

Brennan stroked her hair. "You're hungry? Food and a shower will probably make you feel better."

"Okay. Come on." I took her hand, grabbed my phone, and led her downstairs. The sitting room was a mess, full of dirty sheets and wrappers.

Opening the door of the fridge, I found one last sandwich. I gave it to her along with some water.

"Eat," I told her. I started texting Spencer about the boat, the cleaning crew, and trying to get this wrapped up. It was really early in the morning, but he was probably awake.

Grace ate her sandwich. "No more?"

"No, but if you want to take a shower, I'll get Spencer to make you something?" I cupped her face with my hand.

Her eyes welled up. "I..."

"It's okay. You're with us and safe." I held her to me as she started to cry. Who the fuck knew what happened to her? But she'd cried a few times in the nest.

I held her until she was done sobbing.

"I want a bath." Her teary eyes looked up at me.

"That sounds amazing. Though you might want a shower first."

Grace nodded but didn't move.

"Come on." I picked her up and took her over to the bathroom shower and turned on the water. Gently, I put her inside. "You rinse off. Do you want me to make you a bath? Or have Spencer make you one? I bet he'll give you a nice bath."

She nodded. "Please?"

I kissed her. "I'll find Spencer."

Grabbing a robe, I gathered up the trash and took it out. I went back up and got the laundry. She was sitting on the floor of the shower, crying. My heart broke for her. I wasn't sure if she needed Wes or a little alone time.

"Grace, what do you need?" I said softly. "Wes? Spencer?"

"Ice cream," she sobbed. "And coffee."

Well, then. Grabbing one of the baskets of sheets, I went down to the laundry room and started the washing. Some of these might need to be washed twice.

In the kitchen, I found Spencer, spices all over the counter. I guess he got my texts.

"You look exhausted," Spencer said, as he made the marinade for the meat.

"I need a nap." I went straight to the coffee machine. While I wanted to sleep, Grace asked for coffee. So, I'd make her coffee. I wasn't sure we even had ice cream.

"It's still early yet, so yes, naps for everyone then we'll have lunch." Spencer added more garlic. "You do know it's Friday? It was a lot? I figured Grace being reunited with Wes and Evan might cause a bit of a frenzy."

"That it did. After lunch let's go on the boat? Fresh air would be good for everyone. Did you get the boat out?" I got down the coffee.

Spencer nodded as he brushed the marinade on the meat. "Indeed. I even had it checked over and I took it out last night to watch the sunset."

"That sounds nice." I pushed the button and leaned against the counter.

"It was. Also, the cleaners will come after lunch while we're on the boat." He shot me a look.

Usually, we didn't have the cleaners come until after we left, and we'd done a lot of work to clean up after ourselves first. I'd make sure we tipped them extra well. This place needed some major airing out, too.

I briefly explained how intense everything was and how this was an attempt to finish things. "Oh, someone would like coffee, a bath, ice cream, and probably some food."

"Grace." He covered the meat with plastic wrap and put it in the fridge. Spencer took a container out. "I made some soup knowing she'd want to be fed in the bath. I have her favorite ice cream, but I'd like her to have some food first."

He made her soup? How adorable.

"I'm glad she's back." I opened the fridge and grabbed some yogurt. While I was wrung out, I should eat something.

"Me, too." Spencer started putting spices away.

At some point I wanted to know what happened. But now wasn't the time.

A little body in a bathrobe flung herself at Spencer.

"Darling." Spencer held her tight and kissed the top of her wet head. "Would you like me to draw you a bath and feed you some soup?"

She nodded, sniffling.

I poured her some coffee, making it how she liked, and handed it to her.

"Thank you." Still nestled in Spencer's arms, she drank her coffee, making happy noises.

I finished my yogurt and threw the container away, putting the spoon in the sink. Grace was quiet, snuggled with Spencer.

"Why don't I go get your bath ready?" Spencer kissed her and left.

"I'm going to take a shower and have a nap," I told her. Hopefully, Brennan didn't hunt my ass down and was instead getting Evan showered.

I looked in the cupboard and took down a bottle of pain reliever because I ached. Taking two, I grabbed a bottle of water out of the fridge and swallowed them down.

"Need some?" I offered Grace the bottle.

Grace took two with her coffee. "Thank you."

"Anytime, Babydoll. Welcome home." I kissed her on the cheek and went upstairs to the nest to bring down more laundry. Evan, Wes, and Brennan were in the shower. Good.

I brought more sheets down to the laundry room then went up to the room that Brennan and I shared.

It was a simple room with a big wooden bed and matching furniture. Everything was done in dark blue and grey. I closed the blinds and turned on the lamp. Did I want the fireplace? Maybe.

Shower, sauna, bath, maybe another shower, nap? Or maybe just shower, sauna, shower, nap...

There was a knock on the open door. Grace stood there holding a little box.

"Hi, Peaches. You can come in."

Grace ran in and snuggled into me. Someone needed all the cuddles? Fine with me.

"Hi." She looked up at me.

"I thought you were getting fed soup in the bath?" I stroked her damp hair.

"Yes, but..." Her look grew bashful. Squirming out of my arms she held out the little box. "I... I'm so sore. If I am, then you must be, too. Need anything?"

"I am sore. What do you have in there?" I eyed the box which looked like a little paper treasure chest.

She put it down on the bed and opened it, taking out little tubes, packets, tea, fuzzy socks, and little green balls.

Grace handed me a tube and a green ball. "Here."

"Thanks?"

Her look went bashful again. "The bath fizzy makes your squishy parts feel better. Evan gets them from the Center. They gave me this whole kit."

I glanced over at a paper on the bed that said *post-heat kit.*

"So, I put this in my bath, and it makes me feel better?" Okay, I'd try that.

"Yes. I like them. I haven't tried the cream, but it's supposed to do the same, after your bath. You can have other things if you think they'd be better." Grace showed me everything in the box.

I looked at the cream and the other lotions and potions. Wow. I had no idea they made all this stuff.

In the end, I took the green ball and the tube she'd picked out originally.

"Thank you so much, Grace. I appreciate you sharing." I gave her a kiss.

Giving me a shy smile, she left.

I looked at the green ball in my hand. Might as well give it a try. I'd never tried a bath fizzy. While the bath filled, I rinsed off, because I was gross.

Unwrapping the green ball, I threw it in the water. With a fizz, the green spread through the water. Okay, that would be why it was called a *bath fizzy.*

I turned off the tap, lowered myself in and...

Oh fuck. Comfort surrounded me as I fully immersed myself in the green water. I lounged in the warm scented water, which definitely made me feel a whole lot better.

Evan had known about these this whole time and never told me about them? That was practically treason.

Wes walked in and saw me. "Um, hi."

"Hi, Wes. Just taking a bath. I think Grace is with Spencer," I told him from the tub. His room shared a bathroom with ours.

"Yeah. He's feeding her soup. He'll wake us for lunch." Wes went and took a piss. "Are you okay? That was a lot."

"Yeah. Bren's with Evan?" I asked.

Wes nodded as he washed his hands. "Yeah, they're asleep in Evan's room. I'm going to take a nap in my bed."

"Sounds good to me." I finished my bath and rinsed off again. Fatigue pressed down on me. I'd use the sauna later.

Reaching out through the bond, it seemed like Brennan and Evan were still sleeping. Good. Selfishly I'd like a nap alone, followed by a really big lunch, and maybe some of that ice cream.

Chapter Twelve

Evan

I leaned into Wes as we fished off the edge of the boat. It wasn't a yacht, but it wasn't the little two-person wooden fishing boat my grandpa had. It was perfect for lazy afternoons, sunsets, and a little fishing.

We hadn't caught anything, but we weren't trying very hard, either. Some fresh air while the house got some major airing out and cleaning was just what we needed. I was still a little edgy, but a lot of that came through the bond from Grace.

Brennan was on one of the benches, laying on his back, on his phone, looking really sexy even though he just had on jeans and a sweater. Jett laid on top of him, reading a book, occasionally reaching for his beer.

Spencer lounged in the corner, also on his phone. Grace, in one of her little dresses, napped on his lap. She wasn't wearing her walking cast or wrist brace but I'm not sure she had been this whole time she'd been back. Her face buried in his chest, his arms and a blanket around her. Occasionally he gave her a fond pat, or a kiss on the head. It was so sweet to see him like this with her.

I was also pretty sure his dick was buried deep inside her as she slept.

We were wrung out from this heat, physically and emotionally. Even in the aftermath of Caroline and me being in the hospital, I hadn't been so needy, my heat so forceful. But then, Grace was literally taken from me while I watched, helpless.

It was traumatizing. Terrifying.

At another point in my cycle, it would probably cause me to spiral. In this case, it pushed me over the edge, making me seek comfort in my alphas with ferocity.

Then add back in my sweet Grace, needy, aching, and scared.

Dicks for days. I was so glad I'd brought an entire box of those green bath fizzies Grace liked.

My phone buzzed.

Carly

> **I can fill in for you Monday and Tuesday if you take my weekend evenings.**

Perfect. I was on call afternoons and evenings this week, anyway. I could handle the weekend, too.

"Hey." I nudged Wes with my hip. "I was thinking of staying a few extra days, trading shifts, and driving back Wednesday morning. I don't think Grace is ready to re-enter the world yet."

We were supposed to head back tomorrow morning.

Wes looked over at Grace, concern in his eyes. Grace hadn't said much. She needed constant physical contact. While we burned to find out what happened, it was apparent she needed time. She was so fragile. There was no laughter in her blue-grey eyes, only shadows and longing.

"Do you want me to stay with you?" Wes' offer was soft, tentative.

I appreciated him wanting to offer me alone time with her, even though he probably wanted some himself.

"If the boss will let you off, I would. Considering, while she loves my cock, I'm not sure she should go without alpha dick for long," I whispered back. Certainly, I couldn't be without my mate so soon after my heat.

Wes chuckled as he got out his phone and sent a text. "You two only keep me for my knot."

I pretended to think for a moment. "Well, that and your purr."

"Okay, I have a meeting Wednesday late afternoon, but the boss says other than that, it's all good," Wes whispered back, glancing at his phone. "The boss would also like to stay with us."

"I don't have a problem with it. We'll have to see if Lexi or Katie would get Riley at the airport and take her to school." Because Riley got back tomorrow.

"Sounds good." Wes nodded.

I glanced over at Brennan, who was now holding Jett as they talked softly. "Can I ask them if they want to stay, too?"

"Yeah. If they stay we should see if Lexi could be bribed to bring Riley here. Let Riley ditch a couple days of school. Grace probably wants to see her," Wes said.

Leaving my fishing pole in Wes' care, I slipped in next to Jett, putting my arms around him. Poor Jett. This heat had been rough on him.

"Hey, doing okay, Baby?" Jett asked, giving me a little kiss. His turtleneck made him feel extra snuggly.

"No fish, Love?" Brennan looked up from his phone.

"Nope, but I'm enjoying being outside." The weather was pleasant with a light breeze. Still too cold for swimming, though. I rested my head on Jett's shoulder.

"Wes, Spence, and I were thinking of staying a bit longer and going back Wednesday. If you can get off, I'd love for you to stay, too," I said.

Relief flooded Jett's face. "I'd love to. Oh, I don't care if I have to call in sick. I really need some sleep."

"Why are you reading instead of sleeping, then, Dear?" Brennan asked gently.

Jett's look went sly. "Honey, are you offering to let me nap on your cock? Peaches has the right idea."

"For you, anything." Brennan gave Jett a kiss and caressed his face. He looked at me. "I should be able to reschedule my meetings, at least for Monday and Tuesday. I might have to go back Tuesday evening, but we have two cars, so that shouldn't be a problem."

Jett nodded. "That works for me."

"What about Riley?" Brennan asked. "It will cost us, but we could ask one of the sisters to bring her here. Let her miss school for a couple of days. Believe me, she won't be the only one coming back late from spring break."

"That's what Wes suggested, and I like it. I'll ask Riley if she's interested." I sent her a text.

Me

> **Want to ditch school for a couple of days and join us at the cabin?**

Riley

> **Fuck yeah. I need a vacation from my vacation.**

From the photos, it did seem to be busy.

Me

> **You won't miss skate smash tryouts will you?**

> **No, they're not until the end of the month. I have another practice clinic that someone set up but it's not until next weekend.**

> **Great. I'll bribe a sister to deliver you. Have a safe trip. Love you. Send Sonja and Sasha my love.**

"They're staying. Will you text Lexi about playing shuttle?" I asked Wes, making myself comfortable with Bren and Jett.

Grace began to whimper and thrash a little in her sleep.

"Shhh, I'm right here," Spencer murmured, arms now tight around her, his legs bouncing slightly as he purred for her. "Settle, Darling, I'm right here and you're safe."

The whimpers quieted though the bouncing and purrs continued.

"Well then," Jett said softly.

Spencer was a little old school when it came to caring for an omega. His mom had enrolled him in a fancy training course and sent him to an exclusive alpha summer camp in Greece so that he'd grow up to not be an alphahole.

I had a feeling his approach would suit Grace just fine.

"Not complaining. Jealous." Jett nuzzled Brennan.

Same. Given my size, it was a little harder for me to tuck myself into an alpha lap for a long period of time like she could.

"I think I could use a nap when we get back. I have a little headache anyway." Brennan's eyes locked with Jett's.

"Hey, are you okay with that, Wes?" I rejoined Wes, taking back my fishing pole. I nodded to Grace. While I thought Grace and Spencer were adorable together, I wanted to check in with Wes. They hadn't been physical before this.

"He thought she was dead." Wes' voice went rough.

"Yeah, he did." Which had devastated him, I was sure. He'd lost one mate, then almost lost Grace, too.

"What's for dinner? Spence, do you have something planned? Should we go out? Get takeout? Order food and grill?" Jett asked as we made our way across the lake back to the house.

Yeah, that feast had been delicious, but I was hungry again.

"I have something planned. It will take time to prepare though," he stroked Grace's hair.

Okay, I'd take care of Grace so that Spencer could cook and Bren and Jett could 'nap.'

Grace's eyes opened with a start. "Where's my phone?"

"It's in your room," Spence replied, rubbing her back.

She relaxed. "Okay."

"Peaches, we were considering staying here for a few more days, does that sound good to you?" Wes asked.

Grace nodded. "What about Ri?"

"Lexi's going to bring her here tomorrow afternoon," Wes said. "We should probably place a grocery order."

Grace nodded and her eyes closed as she settled back into Spencer.

"I can do that. Any requests?" I asked.

"Ice cream," Grace told me.

Spencer stoked her hair. "We still have some."

"Marshmallows for roasting," Jett suggested.

Giving my fishing pole back to Wes, I spent the rest of the ride back making an order. Finally we headed back. Wes and I hadn't caught a single fish. When we docked, Spence carried Grace inside. Brennan and Jett went straight upstairs.

Spence came down the stairs and went into the kitchen. "I'm going to get dinner started. Grace is in her room."

"I'm going to go make sure everything's set so that I can stay a few more days," Wes said.

"I'll cuddle Grace. Join us when you're done?" I gave Wes a kiss.

"I'd like that." He grinned, showing off a dimple.

Grace lay in her little room, buried in pillows. But she wasn't sleeping, she was on her phone. Tears pricked her eyes. Pain shot through our bond.

"Is everything okay? Do you want privacy or a cuddle?" I asked from her doorway.

She held out her arms and I kicked off my shoes and joined her in her bed, getting snuggly. Still holding her phone, she started to cry.

"Hey, what's wrong?" I squeezed her to me.

"I left myself written notes on my phone," she sobbed. "I haven't read them all yet—and there aren't notes for everything. But already the memories are becoming clearer—especially the final ones before he did the stabby-stab to make me forget again. I really did almost get sent away for good."

I covered us with a blanket, so we were inside it, like a fort. My purrs filled the room, and I held her tight.

Again. Shit. *Stabby-stab.* I caught that needle to the neck as he took her.

"You're here where you belong," I soothed. "You don't have to talk about it right now. But we all really would like to know what happened. It might be better to do it before Riley comes tomorrow, too."

She nodded. "Will you hold me while I read them?"

"Of course." I held her as she scrolled through everything on her phone, occasionally sobbing.

While I was so curious as to what her notes said, I respected her privacy and just held her, flooding the bond with my love for her, my happiness that she was back in my arms. She'd tell me when it was time.

"Hey, can I come in? What do you need, Grace?" Wes asked, concern shooting through his voice and the bond.

"Boo-Bear! Hold me," Grace demanded, putting her phone on the ledge of the window.

Wes joined us in bed, holding her, purring while she sobbed. He looked at me.

"She's remembering and it's hard," I said softly, rubbing her back.

We sat there holding her until she was almost asleep.

Spencer stood in the doorway. "The main course is in the oven. Grace..."

Her hands went out. "Hold me, too."

I rolled Grace on top of me, making room for Spencer and patting the space beside me.

With a shrug, he joined us, the bed a little small for the four of us.

"Perfect." A contented look crossed her face.

"I'm glad." Spencer smoothed her hair.

Alpha purrs filled the room, cocooning us in warmth and love as we all just laid there for who knew how long.

Finally, Jett stood in the doorway. "So, that's where everyone is."

Grace waved and blew him a kiss.

Sharing her with Jett had been mind-blowing—and I was looking forward to seeing if I could extend that outside the nest. He even called her *Babydoll.* Not that seeing Brennan come in her mouth and take her ass wasn't sexy.

She motioned at him with her hand.

"Peaches, your puppy pile is a little crowded." Jett grinned at us, lounging against the wall in only some shorts.

Brennan stood at his shoulder. "Oh."

Grace's hands went out. "Gimme."

"She wants you two to join the pile," I translated, glad she wanted them to be with us–because I certainly did.

"Twist my arm." Jett dove in, partially laying on top of her. She giggled.

Brennan stayed in the doorway, a frown tugging at the corners of his mouth. "I don't think there's room for me."

I got just a touch of something through the bond from him. Not jealousy or hurt, but longing.

"There's always room for you." Grace gave him a firm look. "Now come over here or I'll do the dishes the wrong way for a week."

"I don't respond well to threats," he tried to growl, clearly suppressing a laugh. Jett chuckled.

"It's a promise, not a threat. Now please, Head Alpha, please stop being a drama llama and cuddle us?" She batted her eyelashes.

Drama *llama?* I snorted at the imagery.

Wes scooted over so there was a smidge of space between me and him, I moved her until she was partially on Spencer.

"Please, Alpha? We need cuddles," I added, batting my eyelashes, too.

"You two are ridiculous. This is how it's going to be now?" Brennan joined the pile.

"It's always been this way, it's just more obvious with two," Spencer replied.

The alphas thought that they were in charge, but Grace and I ran the show.

Grace made a happy noise. "Thank you."

"Of course." Brennan got comfortable, partially smooshing me in the best way. *This.*

Jett's amber. Spencer's leather. Bren's pine. Wes' fresh laundry. My lemonade. Grace's peaches. Everything wove together in a big tapestry of scent as the purr of three alphas, and the hum of three very contented people filled the room.

And my bond lit up with happiness. Not just Grace and Wes, but Brennan and Jett, too.

This was what I needed, everyone, all together, in a giant pile full of love. My family.

All we needed was Riley, and we'd be complete.

Chapter Thirteen

Grace

We sat on the floor around the living room table eating some sort of delicious eggplant, meat, and potato concoction that Spencer made. I lounged on Wes' lap. Evan was between Brennan's legs. Jett sat between me and Evan, Spencer was on my other side.

Most of my memories of what happened in the nest were *very* foggy other than there was a lot of sex. A whole lot. Between *everyone.*

Like I recalled being between Jett and Evan. More than once.

Music played in the background as we ate. I'd put my wrist splint and walking cast back on, but really, they felt so much better.

While I had my own food, it was much more entertaining to try to steal bites off Wes' fork as he attempted to eat.

"Peaches!" Wes chuckled, as I snuck another bite.

"Evan, what are you doing?" Brennan asked as Evan tried the same.

Evan grinned and tried again. "Peaches has good ideas."

"I'll feed you, my good doctor." Spencer took my bowl and started feeding me bites.

"I want someone to feed me." Jett laughed.

"I'll feed you." I tried to feed Jett while Spencer fed me, which resulted in food all over mine and Jett's faces, and the floor.

"Here, Hot Stuff, let me clean that up." Evan started licking Jett's face.

Wes kissed the food off mine.

Brennan rubbed his forehead while trying not to laugh.

"This is so good," I told Spencer as we finished.

"I'm so glad. It's not quite as good as my mother's, but we'll visit her." He patted my knee.

He wanted me to meet his mom? Awww. "I can't wait."

Jett and Spencer cleared our dishes and brought out dessert—some sort of light, citrusy cake.

"Peaches. Babydoll." Jett squeezed my bare leg lightly. "Could you please tell us what you remember? At least, can we know why they took you? I know you've been through a lot, but we have, too. It was scary as fuck to see you taken like that. And well, I have questions about you being Wes' soulmate from another universe."

I gulped. I didn't want to. Though many memories were clear now, there were things I wrote down but didn't actually remember. Still, they had a point, but...

"Grace." Brennan's voice was a low rumble. "We can't have secrets in this family. I understand why you kept it—and why the others helped. But secrets hurt people, and you need to understand, and follow our rules just like everyone else in the house."

My chest constricted. Wes wrapped his arms around me.

"He has a point, Peaches. We were terrified for you. You're not in trouble with them, right? The secret world police or whatever they are?" Evan squeezed my hand.

I shook my head. "No. I wasn't on trial. I did nothing wrong. They came and got me because I was a key witness."

"Oh. Well, that makes sense. You weren't arrested–and he was in a hurry. It would have been nice if Agent Asshole actually *told* us that." Jett's look went thoughtful.

"Yeah. There's a lot regarding me actually waking up on the bench in the park that I don't remember. But I do know that someone tried to kill me, which was why Agent Weigmier stashed me here with my memories erased for my own safety until I could testify. I'm not supposed to remember things now. It's Temporal Authority protocol for worlds where parallel travel is illegal," I said. "Also, technically it's Temporal Authority Enforcers not Temporal Police who bust you when you break their laws."

Evan exhaled sharply. "Someone tried to kill you?"

"So that I couldn't testify. The defense was killing witnesses, and I was almost a statistic. Those injuries I had on the bench were from that." My professor's betrayal made me wince. Evan gave me a kiss on my temple.

"While I'm so glad that you came to me, how did they even figure that out?" Wes asked, pulling me to him.

"I think Agent Weigmier got it from my head. He thought you telling me in my dreams to wait for you on the bench was some actual reunification plan. I think he's psychic. There are all sorts of worlds out there. Some worlds are part of the Temporal Coalition, which means they know about parallel worlds. The Temporal Authority oversees everything, so it doesn't go to shit. The enforcers, you know, enforce. I have no idea what agents do. Investigate maybe? This world and the one I came from, are not members of the Coalition but are subject to their rules," I replied.

"There are other worlds? Are they all just a little different from each other? Yours is *really* close to ours, right?" Jett asked. "Are we talking about the multiverse?"

"We do *not* exist in the multiverse." Spencer shook his head.

"No, we do not. Think of it like a specific section of a bookstore. There are only so many unique ideas out there. Some books are really different from each other, others *very* similar, but ultimately every book is their own story," I explained. "In my understanding, the multiverse would be like fanfiction for a particular fandom–same characters with many, many variations."

Fanfiction existed in this world. I checked. I just didn't know any of the fandoms here.

"Got it." Jett nodded.

"Anyway, let me start at the beginning." I settled into Wes' lap. Really, I wasn't ready for this. But they were right. They deserved to know.

No secrets.

"When I thought people were after me for my research, I was wrong. That memory was of the night I saw too much..." In the safety of Wes' arms, I told them everything I could. About the weapons smuggling. My professor setting me up. Me turning witness.

Her trying to kill me.

I buried my face in Wes' shoulder. "That's the hardest part. Professor Jaffey was like a second mother to me. She encouraged me, fed me, and knew a shit-ton about my past. For her to set me up like that, to isolate me, and manipulate me into being the perfect scapegoat is devastating."

Wes squeezed me, purring. "Of course it is."

"Weapons smuggling. Was it a ring?" Spencer asked.

"Just two worlds. Which meant two trials–one for each." I continued, telling them about everything that I could recall.

"Most of the time I had no idea what was going on. Agent Weigmier was clear that while he wanted to get me back here, to all of you, he couldn't make promises. In the end, I almost didn't. Normal protocol for witnesses is to wipe their memories and plop them back into their world with little concern for the after-effects on their lives. The captain didn't even think worlds like mine deserved trials." For a moment I shook in Wes' arms.

Spencer patted my hair and Evan squeezed my hand.

"Anyhow, I guess the judge took pity on me and authorized relocation. There's literally nothing left for me in my world. Fortunately, Agent Weigmier got to me before I was sent someplace else." Yeah, so glad I was not the pet of some otherworldly pack.

Jett nodded. "That makes sense. They have some sort of program in place to protect and relocate witnesses. But I'm happy they returned you to us."

He was? Awww. "Me, too."

"Are they going to come back for you?" Brennan frowned.

My heart twisted. "I hope not."

"When he dropped you off, the agent said that he didn't think he would need to," Spencer assured.

Relief filled me. "Agent Weigmier seems decent. It also seemed like he was bending rules for me. Which is weird, because I got the idea that the Temporal Authority *loves* their rules. When I asked him he said that it was his job."

"Well, I'm happy he hid you with us. I'm still confused about leaving you in the park with all your injuries," Wes said.

"From what I remember, we were out of time. Also, he was trying not to leave a trail in order to protect me." I frowned. "He didn't ask me anything about you or my association with this world. I don't think it was jankiness. With all their rules, everything was deliberate. I think even me keeping my phone was intentional."

"Making notes for yourself was brilliant," Jett praised.

"Do you recall why you went to the infirmary and got new casts?" Spencer asked.

"All I remember was crying, then waking up there. They were relocating me so it might have been a seizure? Also, I apparently smell like alpha bait." I shrugged, leaning into Wes.

"You do smell like alpha bait." Wes nuzzled me.

Evan gave me a look. "There are other worlds with alphas?"

I nodded. "There are other worlds with lots of things. I sort of wish that I would have brought home the cat I made friends with."

That wouldn't be breaking a rule, would it?

"You're from another world?" Brennan frowned. "One with no alphas."

"No alphas–or designations of any kind. No packs. No knots. No delicious smells. No bonds. You're also a little more advanced in science and social programs. I'm sorry, Brennan. I always tried to tell you the truth. Really, I do have a PhD. And I used to compete in piano. I first met Wes in a dream when I was ten. Also, I'm so glad that I didn't go back to a world where no one probably even noticed that I was even gone." A sob escaped my lips, and I buried my face into Wes again.

"I'm happy you're back." Brennan's voice went soft.

That made my heart grow two sizes. "Really? Even though I play Volkov too fast?"

"Do you even have Volkov?"

"No. But I'd love to play some of my pieces for you sometime when I have full use of my hands again. I still have my competition pieces memorized," I sniffed.

"I...I'd like that."

Jett and Wes asked me a ton of questions about legalities and science. Spencer was quiet. I squeezed his hand.

"What happens to people convicted?" Spencer finally asked.

"I... I asked about your dad. I don't remember the conversation, but I wrote it down," I said quietly. "I can show you later?"

"No secrets. Seriously," Brennan grumbled.

"I told them about my father," Spencer said.

"From what Agent Weigmier told me, your dad is still alive, just in prison. But Dr. K died a few years ago. They wouldn't let me see your dad or write him a letter. But they said he might be released for old age, and I said I'd take him. I don't know if that was overstepping but–"

Spencer dragged me into his lap and pressed me to him. "Thank you."

I nuzzled his neck. I'd tell him the part about the smuggling ring later.

"You volunteered to do *what*?" Brennan scowled.

"If my father, by some miracle, gets returned to us, I'll figure it out. Most likely he'll want to return to Greece and my mother," Spencer said. "Hopefully he'll remember something. How common is it to not remember anything, like when you first arrived?"

"I'm small. The dosage was off." I shrugged. "But I'd expect your father to have a very long memory gap. Oh. I wonder if that's why some people go missing and then turn up years later with no memories of the time that passed?"

Jett rubbed his chin. "Quite possibly."

"I'm sorry. I didn't know why I was here. Certainly, I didn't know Agent Weigmier was coming for me. I didn't mean to upset you. My phone didn't work there so I couldn't text you. He wouldn't let me get a message to you." Tears streamed down my face.

"We know, Grace, we know," Spencer said softly. "It was just frightening."

"Especially since Spencer didn't think you were coming back," Jett added. "Ri was adamant that you would."

"Anything else?" Brennan asked.

"There are some things that I need to remember that didn't get written down. Probably because I never let anyone see my phone.

But I do remember an agreement to not research parallel worlds and travel. So–" I shrugged.

"Sorry, Peaches." Wes squeezed my shoulder.

"The whole point was to find you. Now I have you." I leaned in and kissed him.

"I'll make sure you don't take on illegal projects. I want to keep you here." Spencer kissed the top of my head.

I looked at Brennan. His opinion as head alpha was important.

"Can I stay? Please?" My heart squeezed a little. What if he said *no?*

"You can stay. But I'm still confused about the dream traveling." His brows furrowed.

Relief flooded me. I could stay!

"Thank you. And I don't understand the dream traveling, I never have." I mean, that whole thing about putting the wedding cake under your pillow to dream of your future husband was just an old wives' tale. Right? None of my friends had dreamt of anyone.

"We'll go with the fact that you're scent matches and that's why you dreamt of each other. Your love is so strong that it spans the universe. It's romantic," Evan stated.

"Also, I'm not twenty-nine, I'm twenty-eight. Evan fucked with my birthdate. We should change that back at some point." I grinned at him. Might as well lay down the secrets.

"Why?" Brennan made a face.

Evan grinned back. "Wes is a perv."

Wes play-smacked Evan. "She was an older seventeen when I bonded with her. Also, it was extenuating. I wouldn't have bit her then if I hadn't been worried about her life."

A pang of regret zinged through the bond, and I crawled back onto his lap.

"It's okay that you didn't find me. I still love you to the end of the universe." I gave Wes a kiss.

"Why don't we clean up and go roast some marshmallows around the fire pit," Jett said, getting up off the floor. "If you're up for it, I do have some questions, especially about your interdimensional mate bond."

It was late. Jett put out the fire in the fire pit down by the dock. Brennan and I folded up and carried the chairs back to the cabin. Spencer had already headed up because he couldn't remember if he'd put all the food away. Evan, Jett, and Wes were cleaning up around the fire pit. Brennan and I walked in the dark, the sound of the lake lapping on the shore filled the cool night air.

"Bren?" My heart beat hard in my chest. "I... I'm sorry. I didn't mean to break pack rules. I don't even know what they are and–"

"Relax before Wes and Evan crash our conversation. I understand. It's my fault, too. We don't have that trust between us that you do with the others. I'll keep your secrets; we all will. We just don't keep them from each other. That is very important," Brennan explained.

I tried to gulp the lump out of my throat. "I get that. I'll try not to keep secrets."

"Good."

For a moment we walked in silence, and I shivered a little.

"Also..." I didn't even know how to broach what happened in the nest. Things between Jett and I seemed fine. But I felt like maybe Brenn and I should talk about it?

"Grace?" He stopped, facing me, body close but not touching. "You confuse the shit out of me."

"I'm not that different from other girls." I snorted.

"No. You're not. You're just not like the kind of woman I'm used to being in my life. Take this–you broke a pack rule. You should get punished. But I can't punish you like I'd punish anyone else in the pack."

"Punish? I'm not sixteen." I looked up at him, way up, eyebrows rising. "You ground Spencer, right?"

The idea of punishing Spencer, or anyone, except possibly grounding Riley, seemed funny. But I also understood that breaking rules had consequences. Especially ones about trust.

He laughed. "Yeah, no. We have an understanding. And well, he might just make donations to my family's foundation to support all the scholarships Evan gives away."

"Who punishes you?" I blinked.

"Spencer and Wes."

"Oh. They ground you?" My head cocked as I smirked.

He laughed. "Only Riley actually gets grounded."

"Well, you can make me eat plain vanilla ice cream for a week instead of cookie dough? I don't like punishments." I shrugged.

"I'm sure you don't." Brennan snorted. "But you *have* to follow the same rules as everyone else. Understood?"

"Okay." I closed my eyes. A little sound rumbled through my chest, greater than a hum.

"Oh." His head leaned down to touch mine, our bodies very close. "That's it, you've almost got it. You should work on that with Evan. blowjobs, too," Brennan teased.

I play-punched him in the chest. He grinned and grabbed my wrists.

Panic filled me and I froze. Immediately, he let go and pulled me into his arms. His chest rumbled in a very soft purr, and I relaxed.

"Sorry," he whispered in my ear. "I wasn't trying to trigger you. They tied your wrists in that bad place, didn't they?"

"It's okay. Sometimes I don't know what's going to affect me." I closed my eyes and leaned into him, letting his pine scent comfort me.

"You've been through a lot. All this is probably dredging things up. We'll find someone safe for you to talk to, okay," he assured.

I nodded, knowing I really needed that if I was to move forward.

"Is everything okay?" Evan joined us.

"We're okay," I said quietly, letting go of Brennan.

Evan put his arms around us as we continued walking. "Okay."

"I was teasing her that she needs purring and blowjob lessons," Brennan said, as we reached the edge of the back downstairs yard.

We could either go inside to the bottom floor, or up the stairs to the gazebo or the porch.

"You can purr?" Evan kissed my temple. "Aww, you tried to comfort Bren. So cute."

"Is that what I did? We need to practice blowjobs on actual alpha dicks." Even though I'd play smacked Brennan for his tease, I wasn't going to deny the need for more blowjob lessons. Usually, I practiced on Evan.

Evan nodded. "We can do that."

"We're okay, Grace?" Brennan asked.

"Yeah." I could purr? Well, I could growl.

"Everything okay?" Wes asked as he and Jett joined us.

"We're okay," I confirmed.

The five of us went upstairs, and I entered the kitchen to do the dishes. Spence was there, washing large pans.

"Hey, I can do that." I put my arms around his waist. It was my turn to clean up.

He gave me a fond look. "I'll finish the special pans, and you do the rest?"

"Spence?" I needed to tell him the rest of what I learned about his dad.

"Yes, Darling?"

"Your dad didn't go to jail just for discovering things. He was part of some sort of really big people-smuggling ring. But the good kind. Agent Weigmier wouldn't give me details. He said that even though they were helping people, you couldn't just send people from one world to another without consequence, and that they were still cleaning up the mess, years later–though he didn't elaborate. I hope they didn't send people back when it would endanger their lives." I rested my head on his back.

Putting down the pan he turned and enveloped me with his arms. "Thank you. And I know a little of this. I was trying to figure out if there was anything I could do to get you back and stumbled upon the information that my father and Dr. K were part of a group of people smuggling omegas. My father and Dr. K would take omegas from worlds where they were illegal and set them up here with new identities. A lovely and worthy cause. But considering they'd done it for years, I could see how people might get upset. I do hope that no one sent those omegas back. It means the world to me that you asked about my father."

"I hope they let him come home. I'd love to meet him." Saving omegas? That sounded extraordinary.

Spencer tipped his head to mine. "I'd love for nothing more."

Chapter Fourteen

Brennan

Unable to sleep, I left the bed in the room Jett and I shared in the cabin. Everything was dark as I went out into the hall. A little tug on my mate bond with Evan told me that he was not only awake but... busy. I shut that down as I went to the kitchen to get a drink.

I was still really confused about Grace. About her return. About what happened in the nest. About her too-crazy-to-be-true story about being from another world and taken by the interdimensional police to testify in an inter-world weapons smuggling ring trial.

Taking a bottle of bourbon from the cupboard, I poured myself a glass. I took a sip, letting the liquid burn my throat as I leaned against the counter, the only light coming in through the big windows.

What I'd told her earlier, about being glad she was back was true. I was happy she'd returned to us.

But the thing that ate at me was that it wasn't *just* because she meant everything to Evan and Wes. At some point I started to care about her. Which was why I'd pulled her to me when I'd triggered her and tried to comfort her.

"Can't sleep?" Jett put his arms around my waist, he was only wearing boxers.

"Are we really believing that whole story about Grace being a witness in interdimensional protection?" I took another sip. It was a wild tale.

"Are you asking Officer Jett or Packmate Jett?" He left my side and opened the fridge. "Snack?"

"Both and yes." I swirled the liquid in my glass, watching that ass as he bent over and rummaged through the fridge. The main tattoo on his back was of a dragon, surrounded by some smaller ones.

"Officer Jett feels like it's perfectly plausible. If key witnesses were being *killed,* and someone *tried to kill Grace so that she couldn't testify,* I could understand her being stashed somewhere until the trial. Shit, I've been that officer, helping to hide someone then get them to the stand without other people finding out." Jett closed the fridge and set some chicken wings and butter on the counter. "Don't know what they're for, but they're not labeled, so they're my snack now."

I mulled over what Jett said as he got down spices, flour, oil, and hot sauce.

"Did you get anything from her body language indicating that she might be lying? Both tonight and ever?" I leaned against the counter.

"No. I mean, there were holes in her story, there still are. While I knew that she was hiding something, I never got the idea that she was outright lying. Packmate Jett also believes her. Tonight, it was pretty obvious that she was trying hard to tell us some painful shit. I felt flickers of her pain through our bond with Evan. Her professor tried to pin a crime on her and then attempted to kill her—and now *she remembers it*. She was literally dropped into another world with no memory in order to protect her. I think no one's paying attention to all that. Not to mention, they almost sent her to another world away from Wes. That probably scared the shit out of her." Jett mixed the flour with spices.

I rubbed my chin, considering this. "You're right, the story is so big, so wild, that I really didn't consider all of that."

While Spencer and Wes did drop this on us days ago, I'd been so busy with Evan and his heat that I hadn't had time to process it. It was a lot to take in. Other worlds existed.

And Wes fell in love with someone from one.

Jett put some oil in a pan. "It is. Grace is from a fucking different world. Again, I don't think anyone's realized how much that's probably affecting her. I mean, what would it be like to grow up *without* designations? That could be the unease we get from her sometimes. Just not knowing the cultural norms and body language could do it. I see it when we get recruits that grew up in mostly beta or equalist areas."

Equalists didn't believe in designations. They thought we'd be better off doing away with the classification system that had been used for thousands upon thousands of years. Of course, there *were* physiological differences. But they ignored that.

There were also large swaths outside the cities that were mostly beta, especially in the middle of the country and parts of the south that had been settled by betas to farm.

"Cultural cues. She's lacking in expected cultural cues." Now *that* I could grasp, working in international markets.

"Exactly. Not only did she not grow up expecting to be a certain designation, she didn't even grow up internalizing them. Evan didn't anticipate being omega, but he knew from health class, the media, and just life, about the societal views and expectations of them." Jett dipped the wings in the flour mixture as the oil heated in the pan.

"I'm a little worried about her," I sighed. She'd been through so much and Wes wasn't handling his shit.

Jett gave me a look as he continued to coat the wings with spiced flour.

"When did I start caring about her?" I drowned the last of my bourbon and poured more, remembering pulling her into my arms to comfort her—and her trying to *purr* for me. Like with alphas, omegas didn't purr for just anyone.

Her first purr was for *me*.

"If this isn't rhetorical, I think that it was sometime between her disarming a gunman to save your mate and her getting pushed down the stairs by your ex." Jett carefully put the wings in the hot oil, and it made a sizzling sound.

I thought about this for a moment. "That sounds about right."

While I'd made an active choice to not be a dick after I saw how I was hurting her, it was her smacking the shooter with a chair that made me realize she genuinely cared about Evan.

"You're head alpha. You *should* care about the people who are mated to your packmates. She's *bonded* to two of them and Spencer wants to be the third. You know, I feel her sometimes." Jett got down a large plate.

"Me, too." Just twinges through Evan's bond. Like little dust motes dancing through a ray of sunshine, occasionally reminding me that she was here. I sighed. "But... I... I'm not ready."

It came out raw. They were all asking so much of me. To let someone else be part of our home, our family.

To open my heart again.

"Not ready to not be a dick? Because no one is asking you to mate with her." He gave me a measured look as he lined the plate with a paper towel.

"I'm glad, because I don't intend to. But I think I truly care about her. I'm *happy* she's back and safe and not just because it tore Evan and Wes up inside." I frowned and took another sip.

"That's a perfectly normal way to feel about someone who lives in your house, is bonded to your mate, and will eventually join your pack. There's nothing wrong with caring about her." He smirked.

It was still a lot. Caring for someone meant opening yourself up for hurt. Loving someone meant that you could have your heart broken.

"She has to follow the rules," I grumbled. Though in some ways, some of this felt like my fault. Grace kept secrets because she didn't trust me.

"I think she understands that now. I believed her when she said that she wasn't ready to tell you. It's a huge thing to tell someone, even without that little tidbit she slipped in around the fire about being fucking institutionalized as a teenager for saying the wrong things." Jett made two different sauces out of butter, hot sauce, and spices.

"I accidentally triggered her tonight. I was trying to be playful and grabbed her wrists when she was play-hitting me. They fucking tied her wrists when they beat her." I winced. It tore me up inside that someone would do that to her.

"Fuck." For a moment Jett went quiet, the only sound in the kitchen was that of sizzling chicken. "Does anyone even know what actually happened to her when they made her forget that Wes was real?"

Just the thought made my blood boil. It was an awful thing to do. That was probably why she was a gamma, not an omega.

"Wes, I'm assuming. But I still don't quite understand how it all fits together. Like why did her mom hate alphas if she lived in a world without them? Why make her forget him for the same reason? If Grace is from a world without designations, how could she be a gamma?" I was so confused.

How could omegas even survive in a world without alphas? A heat without an alpha was a painful experience. A lifetime of unsatisfied heats could be devastating.

Jett shrugged as he used tongs to turn the wings. "If it's that important to you, ask her sometime."

"I just want to understand. Jett, I'm not used to people like her." I'd meant it when I'd told her that she confused me. It could be that she was lacking in those cues I expected.

It also went beyond that.

Jett snorted as he drained the wings on the paper towel covered plate. "Well, yeah, the only woman living with us is a teenager who likes to fund her overseas bank account through hacking, and the ones you have regular contact with are either alpha females or people like Lexi who you mess with at your own risk."

"So, we just accept this story?" I rubbed my forehead, trying to make sense of all this.

"What other choice do we have? I don't quite understand the scent-match-from-another-world part. What if they never were brought together? That would be horrible. Wes would have been fine, he has Evan and us. But her... I still remember seeing her in the Center that first time. How scared she was." Jett frowned as he brushed sauce over the wings on one of the plates.

"How willing she was to come home with a stranger?" I rolled my eyes.

"That stranger was *Evan*. It was probably her bond with Wes that affected him." He took a different bowl of sauce and brushed it over the wings on the other plate.

True. Honestly, I think most people would go home with Evan if he asked them.

"Considering Grace and Wes *mated*, I'm surprised she even lasted as long as she did," Jett added.

That made me pause. I'd never truly considered that. Being apart from your mate for so long could be deadly for an omega. It was probably due to the strangeness of their bond. I was still unsure of how you could actually bond a mate in your dreams.

Jett took the plates and nodded toward the table. Grabbing the bourbon, I took a seat at the wooden table.

"That plate is mild. You won't like this one." Grinning, Jett pulled one of the plates to him.

I chuckled. His tolerance for spice was much greater than mine.

"Are you okay with Grace staying? If she stays, things are going to change." I bit into a wing, which despite being *mild* was still a bit spicy for me, but not unbearably so.

"What is the real question, because we know Grace leaving isn't an option?" Jett gave me a look as he took my glass and drained it.

True.

"This heat was a lot. Are you okay? I'm worried about how hard it was on you," I admitted. It had been fierce, and there were a few times where I'd lost control. Usually, I didn't allow myself to let go.

Jett's hand covered mine. "It was a lot. I'm exhausted mentally, physically, and emotionally. But I'll be okay, and I appreciate your worry. I'm guessing a lot of the ferocity of this heat was driven by Evan and Wes watching Grace get taken away. It probably won't usually be that intense, even with her joining us."

I toyed with my wing. "True. But Evan and Grace feeding off each other like that–that will probably be normal. She fucking spiked, which I didn't know she could do."

"She didn't know she could do that." Jett shrugged. "Her doc was no help. Basically, she was like *See what happens and report back.* Grace probably doesn't even know what a spike is."

Shit. "She might not. Is that why Evan is always making her watch videos?"

"Yeah. The little she knows about alphas was courtesy of teenage dream Wes." Jett snorted, rolling his eyes.

"Oh fuck." I laughed. While my sister and I went to private alpha summer camps, Wes just had what the school provided us, and his alpha family members.

"Her in the nest during his heats changes things. I didn't really consider how much," I admitted.

Or that her reactions would be that female-omega-like.

"I'm still okay with it. It was different, but it wasn't a bad different. I could get used to it." Jett devoured another wing.

"What *did* you think of lady ass? I forgot to ask earlier," I joked, since he'd talked with me ahead of time about possibly acting out Evan's fantasy of the two of them taking Grace together.

"While vagina is still not my favorite, I have to admit, lady ass felt pretty nice, especially feeling Evan *through* her. Mmmm." Jett licked his lips.

I took another sip of bourbon. "It was a pretty sight, her between the two of you."

"And when Wes *joined Evan inside her,* fuck me. She is so fucking responsive. Fucking wasted on Wes. At least Spencer will appreciate it." He laughed and devoured another wing.

"True. Though Wes being her scent match really does tell me a lot about her." Which circled back into me not knowing how to care for her.

"So does Spencer being so into her." Jett's eyebrows waggled.

I rolled my eyes. "What Spencer likes and what I like are *very* different."

"Yeah, but seeing you fuck her gave me dirty ideas." He grinned and swiped one of my wings.

"Are you okay with that? That I fucked her? I know you mentioned being fine with it, but I wanted to check in." I worried that in the thick of things I overstepped. I'd reacted on instinct.

"Of course I'm okay with it. That look on her face undid me." He grinned. "Now I have this fantasy of her being tied up and on her knees in the playroom as you fuck her mouth until she shatters."

Fuck, I could see it. Totally at our mercy–and Evan wouldn't be allowed anywhere near her. She'd be ours and ours alone. With Jett's hand around her throat...

"That's probably only in your dreams," I told him. "*Wes* is her scent match. And she's not very good at sucking cock."

"But she has enthusiasm and follows directions. It could be what she needs. After all," his voice grew soft as he squeezed my hand, "it was for you."

Though those were different circumstances. I'd been injured in an accident, she'd been intentionally harmed. Tying her up was probably never going to happen–and that was *fine*.

"If you want to give it a go, I'm not going to stop you. But I'm not sure I want that kind of relationship with her," I admitted.

Though I might want to watch. They did look nice together.

"No?" He smirked.

"What would we do with *two* of them?" I rolled my eyes. I was actually glad Spencer was interested in Grace. Not just because it meant that he was finally ready emotionally for someone else, but because Wes was floundering trying to balance both Evan and Grace's needs.

"Because it would be so bad to have one that actually listens?" Jett joked.

"Good girls aren't my thing." I shrugged as I finished the last wing.

Jett smirked. "Good girls can still be a good time. But I get it if you're not into Grace like that. Most of my fascination is because of Evan's fantasies."

"I can imagine." I rubbed my temples.

"Are *you* okay with what happened?" Jett scooted close to me and put an arm around me. "After all, as beautiful as it was, I wasn't expecting that."

"Me either," I admitted. "But she was in pain, and Wes-the-dumbass didn't even notice. But I was with Caroline through years of her heats. Wes was just involved in a couple. I don't think he realizes that female omegas are different during their heats than male omegas. Female omegas need to be knotted. Male omegas are just driven to fuck and be fucked." Because alpha females had locks, special pussy muscles, that clamped down on a dick.

"Not that Grace was in heat or is an actual omega but..." I hit the table in frustration, because the problem was I *didn't* regret it one bit. "Fuck."

I should regret it. Never could I open myself up to a woman again after what Caroline did to me.

Jett climbed onto my lap and put his arms around me. "It's okay, Honey. She was in *pain?* Though I did smell her need–and I heard that whine."

"Yeah." I could still almost taste it in the back of my throat. "With females it's so much worse. She was really unsettled, which was probably a lot of it. I... I just couldn't sit back and let her hurt."

That whine. The look on her face.

His hand cupped my face. "Well, of course not. No one would want anyone in the nest to need or hurt or be unsatisfied."

Which was why we had the rules we did. It was actually mostly for Jett. The last thing I'd ever want is for him to feel that he wasn't enough because he didn't have a knot. Especially because we could do it without sacrificing what Evan required of us.

"Her body was so greedy, so wanting, and I just couldn't let..." My voice broke.

He wrapped his arms around me. "You were just doing what you do—caring for us. It's okay to care for her, too."

"I don't want to make it weird." I knew she wanted to talk about it tonight, but I wasn't ready for that conversation.

"Then don't. Still, I'm keeping the image of your piercings sinking into that ass one-by-one as you lowered her down your cock in my spank bank." Jett grinned and stole a kiss.

Same. Being in her ass with Evan and Wes in her pussy *had* felt amazing. And she'd taken it so well. *Such a good girl.*

Which was why she should stay far away from me outside of the nest.

"We should have Evan assign Wes a video." Jett snorted.

"We should. But you're okay? What do *you* need?" My fingers trailed his neck, lingering on his bite mark.

"Those couple extra days here will help. I was able to get off work without a problem. Okay, I owe Cam, but I feel like I always owe her and Lexi. I could use a few more *naps* like today." His eyebrows waggled and a wave of lust hit me.

"Mmmm, that was delightful." My lips trailed down his neck. I really did want to focus on him and make sure he had as much time alone with me as he needed. Grace would help occupy Evan.

"I worry about you overdoing it," I added. His body was different.

Though Grace's body took everything like an omega.

"Naw, I'll just swipe more fizzies from Grace. Fuck, why did no one ever tell me they made all sorts of lotions and potions for sore bits?" Jett frowned.

I blinked. "What are you talking about?"

"*Evan* has been giving Grace these fancy little bath fizzies they make for omegas that soothe your sore parts. He's known this whole time and never been like *Jett, that was intense, wanna try?* But Grace comes to me with a whole fucking treasure chest of shit from the Center and a bashful look on her face, and was like *If I'm sore, you are too. Need anything?* That fizzy was amazing. I should totally punish Evan for never offering, especially since he gets boxes of them free from his work," he said in a tone that was only partially serious.

"It probably never dawned on Evan that you'd even use a bath fizzy. And well, it's probably one of those omega mysteries and Grace doesn't know better. It was kind of her to think of you."

"Yeah, it was, though it was probably because I shared my drugs." His grin widened.

"You did not." I made an exasperated noise. "What did you give her?"

Jett rolled his eyes. "Just the same shit I give you before your mom's parties. Only I bought omega-sized doses because I wasn't sure if cutting yours in half would still be too much for her."

"Oh. It was nice of you to get her special ones." Those were nothing. Even Wes used those once in a while.

"She was scared, even though Evan explained things to her. Of course, now I understand why. Grace had no references. She's probably never even seen any heat porn." He put his head on my shoulder.

"I should punish her for breaking a house rule, but how do I even do that?" I sighed, rubbing my forehead.

Jett's eyebrows waggled. "I have ideas."

"I mean ones I actually could do without harming her," I toyed with his hair. "The only one I can think of would probably be too intense."

His eyes lit up. "Are you going to tell me?"

"It involves you holding her while I make her come," I replied. "Hard and forcefully. One after another, not stopping even when she begs me to. No, I'd keep going until her body simply can't take anymore and shatters in your arms–and then you get a turn, while I pin her down, and you'd be just as unrelenting."

His scent got sweet with arousal. "Oh, I could see her face. Mmmm. She'd probably understand after."

"Yeah, but I'm not going to do that." It would be very intimate. I'd also probably enjoy it way too much.

"Honestly, I think it's fine that you just warned her this time. Good snack?" He gave me a kiss on the cheek.

"It was very tasty. Thank you so much for making it for me." I wrapped my arms around him and brought him to me.

Evan might be my omega, my heart, but Jett was my soul, the glue that kept me together.

"We should probably clean up the kitchen and go back to bed." I kissed the top of his head.

Jett nuzzled my neck. "Yes, but maybe not go back to sleep?"

I made a little growl of delight as his words went straight to my cock. "Only if you're up for it."

Jett pressed his lips to mine, giving me a long kiss that tasted of too-spicy chicken. "I'm up for anything with you."

My everything. I kissed him back. "You and I always."

Chapter Fifteen

Evan

The smell of delicious rotisserie lamb drifted in off the back porch. That was part of Lexi's delivery fee. My phone buzzed.

Lexi

> **Got the package, delivery en route.**

I texted my sister Sonja as I plopped down on a chair on the patio, to enjoy the afternoon breeze and the lake view.

Me

> **Lexi has Riley and is taking her to the cabin.**

Sonja

> **Thanks for letting me know.**

> **When do I get to meet Grace? When's the wedding? I've heard so much about her from Riley that I feel like we're besties.**

Sonja and Grace besties? Actually, they'd probably get along well or at least have a lot of respect for each other. I replied.

Me

> **Don't worry, I won't use your date. Do you have one yet?**

She was younger than me, lived outside Portland with her fiancée, and worked at an exclusive academy for gifted students. It was her dream job, and she was so happy.

Sonja

> **We were thinking of eloping. Thoughts?**

Me

> **I volunteer one of Brennan's resorts. We'll cover the costs. Promise we won't crash.**

> **Unless you want us to.**

I sent her a link to his properties. Spencer and I had already talked about offering to pay for it.

Sonja

> **I always forget that your packmate owns luxury hotels. Actually, this might be nice. We'll look it over and get back to you. Thank you.**

Me

> **We'll probably get married next May. Get together soon? I'd like you to meet her.**

Grace and Sonja's fiancée might get along, too.

My sister knew a bit about Grace. We texted frequently and talked occasionally, mostly regarding Riley, but other things slipped in there.

Riley had sent a bunch of pictures. There were texts from my other sister Sasha, berating my life choices. There was a reason why Riley did things with my sisters without me.

Sasha

> **You're letting Riley ditch school? Seriously? What kind of guardian are you?**

We didn't get along. I'd made mistakes, like letting her, Sonja, and my grandparents bear the brunt of caring for Riley for far too long. I'd tried my best to own up, apologize, and make amends.

But when it came down to it, it was me awakening as an omega that Sasha had the biggest problem with. With a sigh, I replied.

Me

> **It's two days.**

Sonja didn't have an issue as long as Riley did her homework. Riley had already made arrangements to get assignments and notes.

Sasha

> **I can't believe that you went on a vacation without Riley.**

Me

> **It wasn't a vacation.**

I sighed again. Sasha knew what it was for. But she didn't like me to talk about anything omega-related—my job and mates included.

Why are you telling her that she's a theta?

Um, because she is a theta? This time, I didn't respond, I just sent the test results—and the follow up testing. Then I texted Sonja about it.

None of this is your fault. You know Sasha.

Sasha had been one of those little kids who'd dreamed of awakening as an omega and being 'special.' She was devastated when her middle school prick-test marked her as beta, though we fully expected it, given we had beta parents and our family's mostly beta. When I awakened as a surprise omega in my twenties, she got her hopes up, and every year she hadn't blossomed made her more and more bitter.

While thetas weren't coveted like omegas, they were exceedingly rare. Rarer than deltas, but not as rare as iotas or kappas. I wasn't actually sure where that gene even came from; especially since thetas were closer to alphas than betas. They were hyper-independent misanthropes who liked collecting wealth. Yep, that was my baby sister.

So, I could see Sasha being angry that *two* siblings became something other than a beta. She'd also been a little jealous of all the extra attention Riley got growing up because our parents were gone.

My phone buzzed again.

Who the fuck is this woman you're letting around Riley?

Me

Grace is Wes' other mate. She's a mathematician and works for Spencer.

My sisters all knew Spencer very well. Why was I even doing this? I loved Sasha. I just didn't know how to fix things between us.

Me

If you'd like to meet her we'd be happy to visit or fly you here or meet someplace at my expense. It looks like you three had an amazing time. I appreciate you spending your spring break with them. It means the world to Riley.

I love you very much and I hope you have a safe trip back and that your studies are going well.

Sasha was at her dream university studying to become an anesthesia nurse, after having completed numerous smaller courses while living at home and helping with Riley.

Shoving my phone in my pocket, I went inside to find Grace. She was in her room, curled into a ball, smothered in blankets, watching the boats on the lake through the window. She smiled when she saw me and opened her arms. Warmth shot through the bond.

"You want me to join you?" I asked.

"Yes, sir." Grace gave me a smile that always made me hard.

I joined her in her nest, holding her to me. "Riley will be here in a bit. Do you want to watch a movie? Take a nap?"

Grace pressed her face into me.

"Or we could go find an alpha and have blowjob lessons," I teased.

She laughed and I kissed her freckled nose. It was nice to see her laugh.

"Are you doing okay? A lot of things are happening all at once. The stuff with the temporal dudes, my heat, you and Spencer really becoming a thing..." I loved seeing her with him.

"I keep thinking about dicks," she said softly.

I grinned as my phone beeped. But I ignored it. "I think about dicks all the time. Dicks in me, dicks in you. Fuck, I keep seeing you full of knots. It was so hot."

She blushed. "Should we talk about this kind of stuff? Kiss and tell and all that."

"Between me and you, yeah, I think we should. I know so much of this is new, and I want to make sure you're okay–and I have a burning desire to know what it feels like to nap on a giant cock." While I wouldn't have the patience or be able to just relax and go to sleep without being satisfied first, it still would be fun to try.

"It's amazing and I don't know why I want it all the time." She hid her face in me again.

"Hormones. It's normal to want your alphas. Especially right now."

"Okay."

"Spence may not have bonded with you yet, but he's yours. You know that, right?" It was obvious in the way he doted on her. This morning he'd surprised her with an electronic book reader, with an unlimited book subscription, given she'd been reading a lot.

"Spence has a giant dick." She giggled into my shirt. "Not that I have an issue with yours and Wes'."

"Spence is being good to you?" I needed to make sure that she was okay. I wasn't afraid to talk to him if she needed me to.

She nodded. "Spencer makes me food and feeds me while I'm in the bathtub. He hides little surprises for me."

Her ears sparkled with tiny peach blossom earrings, not unlike the necklace he'd given her for her birthday. Just tinier, like little every day earrings.

"You can save the food for his bathtub. Drinks and chocolate only in mine." The idea of dinner in the bathtub was weird to me. But if it made her happy…

Still, she could clog his drain with dropped food.

"Also, he's really good at back massages." She made a happy noise.

"A lot of alphas are good at stuff like that–especially alphas like Spence and Bren. Ooh, Bren gives a foot massage like you wouldn't believe. Hey, make sure you talk to Spence and communicate. Especially since I'm pretty sure you've never been with anyone like him before." I ran my fingers through her hair.

She looked up at me. Surprised.

"I've literally known that man my entire life. You think I don't know what he's into? He's perfect for you." I was dying to ask more. Like did she call him *Daddy?*

"He thinks we don't eat right, the whole pack, but especially me and you." She made a face. "Apparently, I drink too much coffee."

I ran my fingers through her soft hair. "He's right. The whole pack has crap eating habits, but you and I, we're the ones that really should take care. Different designations have different nutritional needs. Believe it or not, it makes a difference. Have you watched that module?"

Probably not. It would help her hormones. All those years of her eating garbage because she couldn't afford decent food had probably seriously affected her. Not to mention, her world might not even have some of the nutrients she needed. That could be why she was so small, even for an omega.

"So, you teach omegas to eat properly but eat crap?" Her eyebrows rose.

My head rolled to one side then the other. "I guess that because I do zero cooking I feel bad asking for certain things? Each designation has little differences. But we could make small changes—not necessarily getting rid of coffee, but other things."

"I guess." She rolled into me. "How do I separate feelings and biology? Do you have videos for that?" Her voice was muffled by my shirt.

"I do. You can talk to me about anything. Bren's a good dude and he's trying to deal with his issues." That was probably what she and Brennan were talking about last night.

She and Brennan were only starting to develop any sort of friendship. For them to have such intense intimacy in a very vulnerable moment might be confusing. Though I was glad I remembered most of it, because it was beautiful. He was tender and caring with her—and that gave me hope.

"I think that you and Jett should start something privately, just the two of you." I stroked her hair again.

"Would you be okay with me being with Jett?" She looked up at me. "I liked being between you two. He was also really kind to me when I was scared."

I hadn't known that, but it didn't surprise me.

"I fucking fantasize about it," I grinned. "Please, take my dudes, as long as you don't try to replace me, which I know you won't. Sometimes, I might want to watch or participate." I snuggled her back into me. "Though, I'll share you with Jett anytime."

"The swing fantasy when all three of you have me at once." She giggled a little.

"That and so much more." I grinned, thinking of all the fun the three of us could have with her.

"Yeah?" Her eyebrows waggled.

"Jett's a rigger. One day I want to see you suspended from the ceiling and railed until you are nothing but a pile of goo." The very thought made me hard. She'd take us so well and make so many cute noises.

She blinked. "What?"

"Jett likes to tie people up–consensually and safely, of course," I assured her. Guess she'd never heard of that.

Grace frowned. "Tie them up and do what?"

"Whatever's agreed upon. For me it's usually fucking, but not always," I explained.

Her frown deepened, and anxiety shot through her.

"It's always with permission, and while he's tied me to the bed-post, he prefers these really beautiful, elaborate designs. Here, can I show you some special pictures, so you understand?" I got my phone and pulled up a professional black and white photograph of me suspended from the ceiling, tied in knots so elaborate that I'd become a work of art.

I handed it to her. "This is my favorite. Everything he does is with consent and care. It's talked about and he's constantly check-ing in to make sure nothing is painful or triggering."

"Oh. That... that's not what I was expecting. It's really pretty." She bit her lower lip. "And he doesn't just tie you up and do whatever he wants even if he knows you don't like it?"

So much to unpack there.

"No, he never does anything that isn't agreed upon by both parties–and you don't have to be suspended or fucked. Sometimes, if I'm really stressed he'll just tie me and hold me, and we'll watch a movie. Also, he doesn't have to tie your hands. You don't even have to take your clothes off." I showed her more pictures of me.

"Oh."

"This is just my fantasy, Grace," I assured, holding her tight and peppering her face with kisses. "Nothing like this would ever happen without your consent. There's a lot of love and healing in what he does, and if at some point, you want to try, talk to him about it."

She nodded slowly. "Those pictures are beautiful."

"Sometimes it's nice to surrender control. To just relax and let them take care of me. But we have that trust and can stop at any time for whatever reason. And not just me, if it gets too intense for anyone, they can stop it."

"So, you sometimes... with both of them?" She buried her face in my side. "Bren likes to do that too?"

"Bren's not the artist Jett is. He's also more about absolute control. But again, it's about consent, safety, and meeting each other's needs," I explained. "Bren knows my limits and what I like and dislike, and what I need—and I know what he likes and doesn't, what he's willing to do and not, and what *his* needs are. Most of all, I trust him. We trust each other."

It was very different from what Wes and I did. Though Wes and I were rougher when it was just us compared to how we were with her.

"As long as you're okay with it," she said slowly.

"I am. We haven't gotten to any of those modules. But we can watch them together," I added.

"Okay?" She peeked up at me. "I... I'm not adverse to seeing what's out there, it's just..."

"I know." I kissed her.

She'd had little relationship experience outside of teenage dream sex with Wes. Grace had also had a very sheltered upbringing with sex being taboo. Not to mention the harm caused to her because of who she loved.

For a moment she was quiet. Her brow furrowed when she finally spoke. "Last night Bren mentioned punishments for breaking pack rules. That is a thing?"

"It's more like consequences, but yeah, it's pretty common in packs. It's something you have difficulty with, isn't it? Because of how you grew up?" I continued to stroke her hair.

She nodded. "Being punished for no good reason. I just wasn't ready to tell him where I was from."

"I know. We're not super punishy, as I'm sure you figured out. Usually, it's extra chores or the guys just beat the shit out of each other. They call it sparring, but it's different from the usual sparring. Jett is *very* strong and fast, but Bren can get you down to the ground so quick."

"Oh." She went quiet again.

"Anything else bothering you?" I ran my fingers up and down her arm.

"I'm okay." For a moment she just lay there in my arms.

I held her tight, and I purred for her. "Do you want to try purring?"

A look of concentration crossed her face as a little rumble came from her chest.

"That's good, let's try again." I gave her another kiss, and we practiced purring a little more. It was nice to be able to talk with Grace like this. Omegas did talk to each other about this sort of stuff, especially in omega-only spaces. But most omegas I knew were through work and I had to be professional.

"Can we watch a movie? With popcorn–and those candies Ri likes to put in it," she asked.

"If we have them, sure." Yeah, snuggling Grace wasn't a hardship.

We went downstairs where Brennan, Jett, and Spencer were cooking. Wes was still napping. Snacks in hand, we settled down in the movie alcove with a pile of blankets, where we watched another one of my favorites as I tried to get her 'caught up' on the movies most people her age would know. Right now, we were watching a space movie.

I'd dozed off when someone jumped on me. Someone smelling of anise. "Hey, Ri."

"Fuck of the morning to you." Riley grinned. She tackled Grace. "I knew you'd be back."

"Thanks for believing in me. I don't know what would have happened if no one had been home when I returned," Grace said, holding Riley tight.

"Well, this is cute." Lexi stood there, grinning. "Where's my brother?"

"Sleeping. We keep him tired. He's less argumentative that way," I laughed.

Lexi snorted.

"Oh my fuck." Riley rolled her eyes.

"Your hair is pretty," I told her. Her hair now hung in long braids with green in them. Sonja must have taken her to get them done.

"Thanks." She grinned.

"Ri." Wes dived-bombed the couch, making a pile of us. "Oh, hi Lexi." He smiled at his sister. "Thanks for doing this."

"I believe I was promised food." Lexi looked at the back porch where Spencer was taking the lamb off the rotisserie.

"Soon." Jett appeared. "Hey, Lexi." He turned to us. "Someone needs to set the table. Someone else needs to pour beverages. Ri." They fist-bumped.

Grace shut off the movie and stood. "We'll watch the rest later."

The eight of us had dinner outside on the raised gazebo, then roasted marshmallows around the fire pit by the water. Lexi headed back and we all went inside to watch another movie. This was the first in the Defender League, a superhero blockbuster franchise that most everyone knew—and I couldn't wait to see Grace's reaction.

Armed with more snacks, courtesy of Lexi picking up a grocery order for us, all seven of us piled onto the couch in the movie nook, a tangle of limbs and blankets, as we dimmed the lights, and settled in.

Like yesterday, all our scents tangled in a soothing concoction. Only this time, Riley was here.

Everyone was all here. It was perfect.

Chapter Sixteen

Jett

"Are you sure you're going to be okay?" Brennan asked as I laced up my hiking boots.

I rolled my eyes. Brennan had been in full-on overprotective alpha mode since Evan's heat ended. While charming, it was also wearing on me.

"This is a hike that Evan and Wes can go on, it's *fine*." It was sort of funny that the two members of our pack that were ex-military were the worst hikers. Even Riley was better.

"Just checking. Do you need to take tomorrow off and come back with them instead of returning with me tonight?" Brennan sat next to me on the bed, dressed for our hike in cargo pants and an athletic shirt that showed off his muscles.

"Fuck no. I'm looking forward to a drive back all alone with you." I gave him a kiss. "Dinner alone with you." I gave him another. "Having the house to ourselves all night long."

The last kiss was lingering, a promise. While he'd gone out of his way to make time for me here, it would be nice to have complete privacy.

"Mmmm. I like the sound of that. Maybe we can stop for dinner at that little Italian place? The one with the patio?" he offered. "Share a bottle of chianti and some tiramisu."

"That sounds great." I finished tying my shoes and we went downstairs where Riley, Evan, and Wes waited in the living room.

Everyone was dressed pretty much the same as us, only Riley's boots were black, and she wore makeup and big earrings.

Grace was curled in the alcove with Spencer as they watched a documentary on something sciency. They waved at us as we left, Evan and Wes giving her kisses.

We piled in the car and drove to the trailhead. Riley was very talkative, but Wes was quiet. As we started our hike Wes lagged and kept checking his phone, frowning. I hung back with him, as Brennan and Evan chased Riley up the trail.

"She's with Spence, she'll be fine," I assured him, trying to set him at ease. He really hadn't been away from her since she'd come back.

Wes' frown deepened. "I know. That's the problem."

Oh. What?

"Did they mate, and I not realize it?" That's all I could think of. Wes and Spencer were like brothers.

"No, but they're fucking now." His fresh laundry scent became bitter.

"Now? They weren't fucking before?" My head tilted.

Wes shook his head. "They were having fun playing games. But, I guess while we were up here, everything changed."

"Oh, I would have thought after he gave her the motorcycle–" I stopped as pain filled Wes' face. "Hey, if you're not okay with it, talk to them."

"And be the asshole? I've already said that I was fine with it. And I was. When he got her the motorcycle, him planning a special trip for her, even when they were on the boat. But then, suddenly, I'm not and I don't know why." He raked his hair with his hand. "I should be fine with it. But..."

"Wes, Grace isn't going to love you less, or not want to spend time with you, just because she has Spencer, too," I assured, kicking a rock out of the middle of the trail. "If you're feeling neglected, talk to her."

His head hung. "Everyone can take care of her better than me apparently. Bren gave me a fucking lecture. Sure, he's been with female omegas before, but Grace is *mine*. I know her better than anyone else."

Wow. He was still blaming himself for shit he couldn't control.

"You *do*. After all, she's your scent match. No one can care for her like you can. But that doesn't mean there won't be a learning curve–for you, for her, for all of us."

He pouted, picking up a rock and throwing it at a tree. "So even you can take care of her better than me."

The urge to literally slap some sense into him overwhelmed me.

"No, I can't," I said honestly. "That was painfully obvious as she cried in my arms when she first arrived during Evan's heat. I could hold her. I could try to ease her fears. But I couldn't purr for her. I couldn't give her what she needed, because what she needed was *you*. Not Spence, not Evan, *you*."

Okay, maybe Evan a little.

"Oh." His expression softened.

"Are you mad because of what happened between her and me?" I took a sip of water. It was starting to warm up now.

"Fuck no. It was beautiful. Bren, too. I just could do without him being a sanctimonious asshat." Wes rolled his eyes.

"We can all do without him being a sanctimonious asshat. But he's also struggling with the fact that he's actually starting to give a shit about her," I offered.

Only Brennan would be worried about caring about someone who lived in his house and was mated to his omega and one of his packmates.

"I'd like for her and Bren to be friends. He can take her to the piano shit you and Evan hate," he said. "I'd really like once her injuries heal for you to teach her some self-defense."

"Absolutely. And Spence will take her to all sorts of science shit that we'd find boring, but she'll love. Just like there's so much that only the two of you can do together." I'd happily hand off all classical music concerts and science dinners to Grace.

Wes' shoulders slumped as his hands went deep into the pockets of his shorts. "Spence was there, and I wasn't. She came back, scared and confused, and *I wasn't at the house.* I was up here with Evan. But Spencer was there, to comfort her, to care for her in the immediate aftermath. I'm her alpha, I should have been there to take care of her."

And there it was.

"Wes, Evan was in heat. It was more important for you to be with him than waiting for Grace, given we didn't know when and if she was coming back. I hope she understands that. Do you need me to talk to her? Is she upset about it?" I asked.

He shook his head.

I thought for a moment. "Did you want her to be upset about it?"

He blew hair out of his eyes. "I'm a shit alpha. A shit, jealous alpha."

"You're still working through whatever happened between you two all those years ago. Those feelings are valid. Grace loves you.

She dreamt of you across the universe. How fucking special is that?" I goaded. It really was something out of a movie.

A smile twitched on his lips. "True. But dude, Spencer. Fuck." His head bowed again. "I didn't feel like this when you and Bren were courting Evan. Which just makes me feel even shittier."

I snorted. "Yes, you did. Do you need me to refresh your memory?"

Wes and Evan hadn't been mated very long before we'd decided to be a pack.

"That was about the money. I felt bad that I couldn't financially give him all the things you two could. It went away when you took over courting," he admitted.

"Um, no, it didn't." I rolled my eyes. Brennan had gone overboard, being flashy with his money, overwhelming not just Wes, but *Evan*. Because that's what Brennan thought omegas liked.

So, I'd taken over. But it hadn't fixed everything. Time and communication *had*.

"But if that's what's bugging you, then talk to Spence and set financial boundaries. Also, you know Grace really just wants ice cream." It pained me to see him this insecure. But at the same time, he also needed to accept it.

"What if he gets a flavor named after her or some crazy rich people shit like that?" A smile glimmered in his eyes.

I could see that completely. "It would be fucking great."

"Yeah, it sort of would." He stopped and took a drink of water.

I could no longer see everyone else, but they'd stop for us at the waypoint. "It's okay to set boundaries. Bren set boundaries with Evan regarding Grace."

"He did? What sort, if you can tell me?" Wes said as we started walking again, the path getting a little steeper.

"The main one is that Evan can't come to bed smelling like her. Boundaries are normal. You can even set them with Evan since he likes to hog her." I originally set boundaries with Brennan regarding Evan.

As attracted as I was to Evan, I still had some initial fear because he was an omega and Brennan and I were newly married. But, we'd talked it out, taken time for each other, and eventually found our rhythm. They would too.

If they *talked* to each other.

Wes nodded. "That's a good idea. I... I guess I'm not really mad that she's with Spencer. I'm just jealous that he was there and I wasn't."

"Then be there for her *now.* Now comes the really tough shit. This is her world now, and you need to help her through all the adjusting," I stated.

"True." He sighed. "I'm just so relieved she's back. For a moment there I thought that I'd never see her again."

"We all did. Hey, why don't you take her out tonight? Just you and her. Spend some time together. Reconnect." I wasn't sure if they'd actually talked since she'd come back.

Wes huffed. "Like Spence will let me drive his car."

"Take the boat, dumbass. Make a reservation at one of the places on the other side of the lake. Be all romantic and shit. Talk. Do more than just cuddle and fuck," I offered.

"Oh. That sounds nice." He went quiet. "I really haven't had her to myself to just talk."

"Then do that. Carve out some standing time for just the two of you. Maybe Thursdays, since that's Evan's night with Riley? Even if you don't go on a date, you can still watch a movie or sit in the hot tub or something?" I suggested. "Bren and I schedule regular time for each other."

He rubbed his chin. "That's a good idea. I still have shit to deal with, don't I?"

"Yeah, and so does she. But you're mates, so you'll work through that shit together. Be there for each other." I made a face. "When did I become a marriage counselor? Evan's the fucking social worker."

"Evan's biased. You're not." Wes smiled. "Thank you."

I clapped him on the back. "Anytime. Now, we should walk faster and catch up."

Chapter Seventeen

Wes

"Grace, are you almost ready?" I called, knocking on the closed door of her room at the cabin.

"Five minutes," Riley called with a giggle.

"Sure, I'll wait downstairs." Straightening my tie, I walked past Spencer, who was standing in the doorway to his room, and went downstairs to the living room.

Spencer followed. "Wes, are you avoiding me?"

Yes. I plopped down on the couch and gave him a look. "Maybe?"

"I overstepped, didn't I? Apologies." Stricken, he sunk into a chair.

"No, not really. I'm just being a jealous asshole," I admitted quietly, not meeting his eyes.

"I see. Would you like me to step back? I should have waited longer for you two to settle in. I got carried away, I'm sorry." His head bowed.

Spencer would, too. Which made me feel like an even bigger asshole.

"Thank you for being there when she was brought back, and for taking care of her." It was difficult to say, but the truth.

What *would* have happened if no one had been there? She'd been *unconscious.*

"Of course. I'm sorry for not bringing her to you immediately. When she was lying there unconscious, it just brought back a lot and my alpha instincts to care for her just took over." Spencer's look went glum, and his scent went a little salty.

Now I was an even bigger asshole. Spencer had trauma too. His *dad* got taken away by the same dudes and never came back. He seriously thought that Grace was *dead.*

Not to mention, once upon a time, he had a mate. Who died. And he hadn't been there. Losing your bonded mate was apparently a painful and traumatic experience because you felt it happen... then you didn't feel them at all.

Shit, I felt awful.

"It's fine," I said. Also, the truth. He hadn't kept her long and she probably needed a good night's sleep before joining the chaos that had been Evan's heat.

"I'm glad she had you there," I added.

"What can I do? I don't want to cause any issues between you, especially right now, when she really needs you. Would you like to accompany her to the PIIP symposium instead of me? I can transfer the invitation to you. I was just trying to make her happy," he confessed, an earnest look on his face, pain in his eyes.

"Shit, why would I want to subject myself to that when you're willing? But thank you." I knew he hadn't planned that to one-up me. He'd organized the trip to the exclusive science conference because she wanted to see some particle thingy. I'd go if she wanted me to, but I had no issue with Spencer attending with her instead. He'd enjoy it. I'd find that shit boring as fuck.

Also, I knew with Spencer she'd be taken care of. Fuck, he could be her travel buddy for all the science shit I knew she'd be doing. It was only a matter of time before she was the one speaking at conferences.

"There are a few weeks before the conference, you could take her on some sort of special solo getaway. Is that the issue? While you went to the cabin for her birthday, you haven't whisked her away on a special trip yet?" he asked.

I paused. "Oh, I could do that, couldn't I?"

A romantic weekend would be nice. Maybe I could take her to the little seaside town my grandparents always took Lexi and I to when we were kids. Yeah, my grandma would let me borrow their beach house for the weekend, right?

Jett did say it would be good for us to spend some solo time together.

"This is all a me problem, not a you problem, Spence. I'm feeling guilty for not being there, for not protecting her, for not being alpha enough for her." My head bowed.

"Wes, you're a good alpha to her. You make her so happy. My interest in Grace doesn't mean that she isn't getting what she needs from you." His brows furrowed.

Oh.

"I... I didn't realize I needed to hear that. When that asshat took her, I felt so helpless..." My shoulders slumped.

"I did as well. I honestly thought I'd never see her again." Pain leaked into his voice. "I will do whatever you need of me. The last thing I want is to come between you. It's been so long since I've gotten to spoil someone in that way, and it's very easy for me to get carried away. It's okay to tell me to back off—or piss off," he admitted.

"Just don't get an ice cream flavor named after her?" I joked.

His look became amused. "I was actually thinking of an ice cream store."

I froze, then realized he was joking.

"A car shaped like an ice cream cone?" I countered.

"Perhaps." Spencer smiled. "Are we all right? My offer to back off stands."

"We're good, thank you."

He patted me on the shoulder. "I'm glad. She needs you so much." Spencer's gaze shifted to the stairs. "Have fun tonight."

My gaze followed and I sucked in a breath. Grace wore one of her usual cotton dresses, but in a cute floral print, and she'd dressed it up. She had her splint and walking cast back on. Riley had done her hair and makeup.

I stood and met her at the stairs. "You look amazing."

"So do you." Grace's smile melted my heart as she grabbed me by the tie and gave me a searing kiss. There was a jacket in her hands.

Yeah, this woman loved me.

Taking her arm, we waved, and I took her outside and we got onto the boat. Nerves wafted off her and through the bond as we set off across the lake toward the restaurant.

Shit. I had to remember that our bond worked better now. Much better. Grace also probably didn't know how to filter it.

"Come here." I held out a hand to her.

She took it and I pulled her onto my lap as I steered one-handed.

"I've got you. Promise." I kissed the top of her head.

"Did I do something wrong?" Her voice broke. "That's why we're going to dinner alone to *talk*." Her blue-grey eyes went misty.

Fuck.

"You did nothing wrong. I wanted to spend some Evan-free time with you. Check in, see how you're doing, because this has been a lot for all of us," I said honestly.

"Okay." She rested her head on my shoulder. "You're not mad at me for being with Spencer?"

"No. Be with anyone in the pack. It's fine. I'm just being, what do you call it, a *sad panda,* because I wasn't there when you came home and I feel like I failed you." It was a raw and honest admission.

Grace tipped her head up and kissed my nose. "You could never fail me, Boo-Bear."

My heart bloomed as she pelted me with love through the bond.

"I'd probably be mad if you'd abandoned Evan to wait for me, especially now that I really understand what it's like." She snuggled into me.

Yeah, I needed to hear both those statements.

"I'm so sorry that I worried you," she added. "All I could think about was getting back to you. And... and they almost sent me somewhere else." She started to cry. "My professor tried to kill me."

Fuck, fuck, fuck. She now remembered *why* she'd come here. And it wasn't pretty.

"You're safe now. You're here with me, Evan, Spencer, and everyone. We're all so happy that you're back with us." I planted a kiss on her head.

"Okay." She sniffed. "I... I should have gone hiking with you. I didn't–"

"Stop, please?" My voice broke, so did my heart. "You still have a broken foot and shouldn't be hiking on it. Please, watch weird science documentaries and play chess with Spencer."

Which was all they did, well that and he made her chicken soup.

"Okay." She sniffed again, her makeup now a little smeared. "I'm sorry. I feel so weird inside, and everything's all jumbled and…"

I wiped away the makeup smear with my thumb, then held her as tight as I could with one arm, as we made our way across the lake. "I love you, Grace. I love you so much, and I'm glad you're home, and *I'm here.* And I'm so sorry if I made you anxious. I just wanted to spend some time with only you. Evan's been a little greedy."

A smile played on her lips. "He really has been. Has anyone thought to tell him *no?*"

I chuckled. "Not really."

He was our omega. We tried to never tell him *no.*

"You don't have to let him, at least when it comes to me." Her look went coy, then she bit her lower lip. "I mean I love Evan, but I like time with just you, too."

"I'm so glad. Maybe we can make a regular date night? We could go out or stay in, but you know, just us?" I steered us toward the restaurant as that edge of the lake came into view.

She beamed. "I'd like that. When I start at your work can we drive and eat lunch together?"

"That sounds perfect. What about if I take you away for a little getaway, just me and you?"

"Oh, I'd love that," she breathed.

All felt right again.

I shifted so I could use both hands to bring us into the restaurant's dock.

"Oh, this is so pretty. It has its own dock? Fancy." Grace grinned. "We're by town. After we eat, will you go for a walk and hold my hand? Maybe we can get ice cream? That shop had such fun flavors."

How could I have doubted her? This was my Grace, who for all the fancy trips and jewelry, really just wanted ice cream.

"That sounds perfect." I cut the engine and tied up the boat. "Here." I helped her out and took her arm. "Let's go have a nice dinner."

Turning to face her, I took both her hands and gazed right into those blue-grey eyes. "I know things are hard and strange. I'm not super good with details, and sometimes I forget how weird things must be for you. But I love you so much and I'm so glad you're here with me. Talk to me, and I'll talk to you, and we will figure everything out together."

Grace leaned up and gave me a kiss. "That sounds good to me. I love you, too."

I took her arm which felt so good, so right, as we went into the restaurant.

Chapter Eighteen

Grace

"Whose backpack is this and can I have it? It's super nice." Riley barged into the third floor sunken living room and held up a black leather backpack.

Wes, Evan, and I were piled on the couch watching the latest episode of Evan's favorite show. That was how we were spending a wild Friday night together–though we'd had family game night earlier, which had been fun. Evan was on call.

"I've seen it around, but I have no idea," Evan said.

I sighed and paused the TV. "I should probably deal with it, shouldn't I?"

"It's yours?" Wes blinked.

"When Agent Weigmier dropped me off, he left that as well. I... I don't remember what's even in it. Probably whatever was in it that day I went to work and never came back." I'd been ignoring it since we'd come back from the cabin.

"Oh." Riley held it out to me.

I took it from her, the leather soft under my fingers. "It *is* nice. It was a graduation present when I got my PhD."

Riley squished in on the couch with us. Her eyebrows rose. "You got a *backpack* for getting a *PhD*? That kinda sucks."

"It was from my roommate's parents. They were really nice to me, especially when they found out that I didn't have anyone there. Dad, well, the man who raised me, offered to attend, but it's far. He helped me get into my new apartment instead." Which had been a godsend. I toyed with the straps. That backpack was one of the only presents I'd gotten.

"Are we going to open it?" Riley prodded, bouncing on the balls of her bare feet. Her toes were painted lime green.

"We don't have to." Wes pulled me close.

Our dinner together helped a lot. I now had a better idea of how Wes felt after I stopped appearing in our dreams all those years ago. Of how it had affected him, his relationship with Evan, and the buried emotions both me appearing and being dragged away caused.

He'd started to understand not just how strange and new everything often was here, but how wrecked I was by these memories I hadn't had when I arrived.

And I was glad he was okay with me being with the others in the pack.

Evan tugged on the strap. "I'm so curious to see things from Grace's world."

"Things aren't *that* different." Opening the top pocket, I removed a pair of scratched hot pink aviator sunglasses and my car keys. "I wonder what happened to my car, my place?"

"I thought you had a motorcycle." Riley sat on the arm of the giant couch.

"It got stolen my last semester and I'd gotten a car." A cheap car. I'd used my apartment money for it because I had to get to work, and taking the bus there got complicated.

Riley toyed with the colorful beads on the keychain. "You made this?"

"No, just some kids I used to babysit." My heart twinged. Professor Jaffey's kids.

At one point, after we'd all been hauled in together, Professor Jaffey tried to talk me into taking the fall, using the fact that I adored her kids as emotional blackmail. After all, she had kids, a family, and a career. I had a plant. Why shouldn't I take one for the team and go to jail so that she could go home.

After all, who'd miss me?

I'd almost relented, too. Because she had a point.

The front pocket of the backpack held gum, a romance novel, and lip-gloss.

I pulled out the strange little teddy bear that had appeared in my arms at the clinic. It felt weird to have it. "Oh. Shit. I don't know why I even took this. Some old guy gave it to me at the Temporal Authority hospital while I was scared. I think I'd had a seizure or something when they told me they were sending me someplace else. I can throw it away."

Wes wrinkled his nose. "It smells odd."

"If you're going to throw it out, can I have it? I want an interdimensional stuffie. I'll wash it first?" Riley held out her hand.

"Sure. I also have interdimensional candy. Not sure if we should eat it?" I handed her the stuffie and pulled out the little blue box.

Riley opened the box, which was filled with colorful star-shaped candies. She reached for one.

"Don't eat them. We don't know what they are." Evan smacked her hand.

She smacked him back. Rolling her eyes, she popped it in her mouth. "Delicious. They're chewy."

Wes took the box and sniffed it. "Smells like fruity candy."

"My interdimensional candy." Riley grabbed the box, though she looked at me.

"Go for it." Next, I pulled my floral fabric purse out of the main compartment. My money, bank card, driver's license, everything was all there–and completely useless here.

"Her Fake Billionaire Boss's Secret Baby?" Riley laughed, reading the back of my romance novel.

"I like boss romance novels. We had a book swap cart at work." My water bottle was still there but it was empty. My earbuds held no charge. No phone though. Not that I expected it, because it had been broken by my boss.

I unzipped a compartment and frowned. "What the actual fuck?"

"If there are actual fucks are there theoretical fucks?" Riley opened a piece of gum, put it in her mouth, and made a face. "Grape? Are we five?"

"There are theoretical fucks. We did a whole project on it in one of my classes," I laughed. "And yes, I have childish taste in gum. But this... they gave me my *laptop*. I didn't even have this that day at work. This is my personal laptop. Oh, they raided my apartment, looking for evidence. I wonder if it'll run here." I withdrew my battered, old, sticker-covered laptop and power supply. I frowned, running my fingers over the colorful stickers.

"Give it and the power supply here." Wes held out his hands.

I handed it to him. There was nothing else from my apartment. Not that I had many mementos. Still, there were a couple of things I would've liked to have.

Wes examined the power supply. "I think I have a cord that would work, and the voltage seems compatible, do you want me to try to charge it?"

"Please? I'm curious as to what they left on it. Like, there's movies and music and stuff. I'm making you watch movies I like." I grinned at the thought of sharing things with them.

"Fuck yeah." Riley smelled my hand cream and examined my lipstick.

Evan put my pink sunglasses on and struck a pose. "Me?"

"Absolutely." I laughed. He looked good in them.

We put the show back on and watched the rest of it. Afterwards, Wes brought the laptop over. It booted up and I started looking for my files.

"Sweet baby Jesus, my dissertation is here. Wow. Actually, I think everything from my PhD program's here."

Well, almost. I frowned as I looked for something else. No. It wasn't there.

But did that really surprise me?

"Why are you frowning?" Wes put his arms around me and kissed my temple.

"All my parallel world research is gone." It wasn't like I had access to my backups, though they'd probably deleted those as well.

"I guess that's to be expected, and I don't really need it now." I wasn't going to do anything with it, of course, but still, for so much work to have been deleted...

Especially since I'd been so close.

"It looks like most of my movies, music, and books *are* here. We'll have to watch them at some point." There were a few on here that Riley would love.

I opened my music. A playlist caught my eye. I put on a song and held out my hand to Wes. "Dance with me?"

"Do you feel up to it? You're not wearing the splint or walking cast." He frowned.

"I'm feeling better. I'll put them back on when I need them." But really, I felt well enough to leave them off. They just got in the way anyway.

Wes cocked his head, listening to the opening of a song I knew he'd never heard. I wrapped my arms around him, and leaned my head on his chest, letting the music entwine around our limbs.

"While I love this song. It always made me a little sad," I said as we swayed to the music in the living room. "Now I know why. This song is *us*. This is the sort of song we would have danced to at our wedding."

My eyes misted as I looked up at him, as the pieces fit together. They'd done more than make me forget he was real, they caused me to lose a part of myself.

Now I had him back and felt whole in a way I never realized I wasn't.

Wes leaned down and kissed me. "We still can dance to this at our wedding."

He twirled me and we danced around the living room; not like we danced at fancy parties, but how we'd danced in his room as awkward teenagers. My eyes closed and everything faded away. It was just us, alone with the music, like we'd been all those years ago. As the song ended, he twirled me out and back again, then dipped me.

A self-conscious look crossed his face as he brought me to his chest. "I don't know how to dance to a song like this."

My lips met his. "That was perfect."

Evan got up and wrapped his arms around us. "I love it."

"That was sappy, but I can see that being a dance at a wedding. I can't wait to hear your good songs. Can we watch one of your movies *now*?" Riley looked hopeful.

"Is your homework done? Given you've got all sorts of stuff going on all weekend?" Evan gave her a look.

She made a face. "I was actually up here so I could get Wes' help on my homework."

"My help? Okay." Wes looked at me. "I can't wait to dance with you at our wedding."

Riley took his hand and dragged him downstairs.

Evan's phone rang. He looked at it and grimaced.

"It's work." He answered. "This is Evan. What do we have?"

While he talked, he paced around the living room. I took a look at what other songs I had. There were a bunch on here from old cheer routines with lyrics about ass shaking and stuff. Riley might like those.

Evan finally ended the call, turned to me, and gave me a kiss. "I've got to go to work. Love you."

Homework done, Riley started playing a video game, getting on her headset with her friends Marcos, Kilroy, and Hiro.

I stood and closed my laptop, then went to find Spencer. Wes had gone with Evan to the Center considering how late it was.

Spencer was in his office, hunched over his desk, frowning at something. Those slutty little glasses that he wore sometimes perched on his nose. He had on a polo and khakis, feet bare.

I stood behind his desk chair and started kneading his shoulders. "Everything okay, Spence?"

"Why hello, my good doctor." He smiled and gave me a kiss. "I found a cypher in Dr. K's research and am attempting to solve it.

I wish Elaris was here, she was so much better at things like this."
Spencer froze.

"Her name was Elaris? That's so pretty." Oh, that was the love
he'd lost. I kept rubbing his shoulders, though I wasn't anywhere
near as good as he was at this.

Pain crossed his face. "I didn't mean it that way, I'm so glad I
have you, Darling."

"I didn't take it that way at all." I knew nothing about her.

The room grew quiet for a moment.

"I'm glad I have you. Elaris was good at puzzles? She was really
smart wasn't she? Will you tell me about her?" Given we should
have this conversation before we bond.

His eyes closed and he leaned into my hands. "We met at Rock
Tech–Rockland Institute of Technology. I was studying science
business, she was in the chemistry program. Oh, she was *brilliant*.
I knew from the moment I met her that if given a chance she could
change the world."

"Oh, yes, you two had a company together." Wow. No pressure
there. Oddly enough, I felt no jealousy, even though I wanted to
be told that I was brilliant and would change the world.

Oh, wait, he did tell me that sometimes.

"We did." His voice was soft. "We were still at university when
we started it, and it took off quickly. But she knew what she was
doing; she just needed someone to believe in her and the funding
to put her ideas in action."

My fingers worked out the knots in his neck. "You... you were
mates, right? She was an omega?"

"We bonded right out of university. She was a beta, with the
fierceness and confidence of an alpha." He flinched.

"She died in an accident?" I bit my lower lip. Apparently it
hurt when a mate bond broke in death. Sometimes omegas didn't
survive losing all their mates. The Center told me about it. Losing

your bonded soulmate hurt so much that they called these omegas *soulbroke.*

"A car accident. So they say. Sometimes I wonder." He raked a hand through his hair. "Some of her ideas were... controversial."

"What did you make? Do?" Did he just casually admit that he thought she may have been *murdered?*

"Her first pharmaceutical was a take on alpha suppressants, refining them to have less side effects so that alphas would actually take them," he told me.

I blinked, my hands working where his neck met his skull. "I didn't know alphas took suppressants."

"It's not common. Mostly it's young alphas who have trouble controlling their urges, inmates, and those ordered by the courts, mostly. They dull alpha senses and emotions and can suppress alpha rut. In addition to the side effects, there's stigma around them—people think you're 'less' of an alpha if you take them. That's why more development wasn't poured into them and why many who should take them don't. Which can cause... incidents, especially in places like high schools and universities." His voice grew quiet.

"Oh. That was controversial?" I could see that. Just because the alphas I lived with had control didn't mean they all did.

"Only to the alphas who didn't want to take them." He shrugged. "Our main contracts were with prisons. Her most controversial idea was that she wanted to develop ways to keep the illegal designations from being executed. She died before it could be developed. Most of her research was in her head, and no one wanted to seriously take it on." He sighed and tugged me onto his lap.

"Wow, that... that seems very noble. They *kill* illegal designations? Why? Isn't that government-condoned genocide? That is terrible. It's not like you can control what designation you are." I didn't know much about illegal designations.

"You are very right, and I agree with you. They're considered a danger to society but I'm not sure that they all are. Certainly, I don't think our current methods are the answer. But that's a conversation for another day." His look went pained.

For a long moment the room went quiet again.

"Thank you for telling me about her," I finally said.

"I've been thinking about her a lot lately. Like how she would have loved you–and immediately had you helping her with formulas and calculations. Elaris had a thing for smart blondes."

"I would have loved to help her amazing endeavors." What else could I say? "What are you trying to decode?"

"Some of Dr. K's research. I'm very curious about the smuggling ring," he replied.

I nodded. "Me, too. The idea of omegas being illegal is weird."

We'd looked through what he'd given me of his father's research to see if there were any secrets in the margins but had found nothing.

"It is. Omegas are a gift. As are you. The fact that I was once mated to her doesn't diminish what I feel for you, I promise you that. You don't need to compete with a ghost." His lips brushed mine as he pulled me closer.

"I believe you." I cupped his face with my hand as I straddled his lap. "After all, I love Wes, Evan, and you." It took a moment for me to realize what I'd said. But it was true.

He beamed. "You love me? I love you, too, Grace."

Spencer's mouth seized mine and we made out in the desk chair. Finally, he broke off the kiss. "Is there a reason why you came to me, my good doctor, not that you need one."

My breath hitched as his fingers slid under my bra and brushed my nipple. "Just that my laptop was in my backpack and it has some of my research and my dissertation. Not that it really does me any good here."

"I'd love to look over it with you at some point." Kisses trailed down my jaw as his hard cock jut into me. His other hand slid up my thigh, under the hem of my T-shirt dress, and toyed with me through the fabric of my panties.

My lips seized his as two fingers slipped under my panties and slid inside me. The other hand unhooked my bra, setting the girls free. He grabbed it and threw it someplace, along with my dress. Spencer caught my nipple in his mouth, and I gasped.

"Are you all right, Darling? Let me know if I'm too rough. All you have to do is tell me to stop and I will," he whispered, his fingers picking up the pace.

"More, please." My eyes closed as pleasure rolled through me.

"Anything for you." He stopped and I whined as he lifted me off his lap, pulling off my panties. "Bend over the desk, Baby Girl."

Excitement shot through me as I stood there, naked. He wanted to take me on his desk? My pussy gushed. "Oh, yes, Daddy."

It just slipped out.

His entire face lit up as he cleared a space. "Such a good girl. Now, turn around."

I had barely leaned over the desk when he spread my legs and drew his tongue up the length of me.

"Mmmm, you taste so good." Spencer teased my pussy with his tongue, licking and sucking until I was panting and squirming.

"Hold still." The pat on my ass was light.

I tried not to move as waves of pleasure washed over me, building inside me.

"Come when you need to," he directed as I lay on the wooden desk. Spencer continued to tease me with his mouth and fingers.

But I didn't just want an orgasm.

"I want you inside me, please, Alpha," I begged. Not that his tongue wasn't heavenly. Still, the space between my legs ached for more.

"Come for me first." He picked up the pace, adding two fingers while he nibbled at my clit.

As if waiting for that command, my body bucked, the orgasm shooting through my body like lightning. "Spence," I gasped.

"So good. You look so beautiful spread over my desk," he praised, his hand running over my ass.

I heard a zipper and cloth falling to the floor.

"Do you still want me to take you from behind while you're bent over my desk, Baby Girl? Are you going to be a good girl and come all over my cock as I fuck you?" he growled, hands running up and down my body, sending shocks of heat through me.

"Please, fuck me hard, Alpha," I begged, holding onto the edge of the desk.

"Mmmm, that's what I want to hear. You're so perfect." Kisses trailed down my spine as his hands grabbed hold of my hips. "Look at you. Your pussy is so wet and ready for me."

His long, hard, length thrust into me, his hips slapping against me. One of his hands stroked my clit as he unrelentingly fucked me. The air grew thick with his desire and pheromones. All I could do was hold on, moan, and surrender.

"So good," he murmured, as he continued to fuck me hard, hand on my hips, helping him angle into me.

"Right there," I gasped, seeing stars as another orgasm shot through me.

"I'm going to knot you now," he told me. His knot pushed inside me as he filled me with his cum.

For a moment he just lay lightly on top of me.

"Are you all right, Darling?" he murmured in my ear. "That was a little... fiercer than I intended."

Wrapping his arms around me, he pulled me into his chair with him, our hearts thumping with exertion. My head rested on his shoulder. He began to purr, filling me with warmth.

"That was amazing." I hadn't visited him with the intention of being fucked on his desk, but now that I had, I didn't regret it one bit.

"I'm so glad." He kissed my temple.

"I can take care of you, too, you know." I picked up my head and grinned.

His lips seized mine. "That you do."

"Oh, I wasn't wearing garters," I said.

A little growl escaped his lips as he kissed my neck in that place that always sent shivers through me. "Next time."

"Promises, promises," I laughed.

He growled again, this one making me wet. "Oh, I always keep my promises, Darling."

I kissed him again. "And I can't wait for you to show me."

Chapter Nineteen

Brennan

My muscles ached, but it was a good ache. I hadn't made it to a wrestling workout in a while. I hadn't been keeping up on my workouts at home, either. While I'd played rugby most of my youth to please my father, I'd gotten into wrestling because I enjoyed it.

Really, lately only Jett *wasn't* slacking in the workout department. I should fix that. Part of Evan's freedom hinged on him being able to defend himself. Wes now had more to protect. Grace and Riley should know the basics. Though Jett had taken Riley to the gym this morning for an early morning workout before she went to another skate smash clinic to get ready for the upcoming tryouts.

Parking my motorcycle in the garage, I checked my phone.

"Terrance, it's Saturday, play with your kids," I muttered, looking at all his texts. Once again, he had concerns about the estate property I'd bought to make Evan happy. I'd been ignoring them with everything else going on. But I should deal with Terrance's concerns at some point.

Perhaps not right now. Jett would be at his gym for a while–and Evan and Spencer's cars were gone, and they all had plans.

Which meant I got the house to myself for a bit...

As I opened the door to the kitchen, I was hit with a wall of chocolate, banana bread, and anxiety.

...or not.

"Oh, hi, you're home," Grace stammered, nearly dropping a tray of those chocolate cookies with the powdered sugar on them that Jett liked.

She wore a fluffy pink apron and had flour on her face.

"Sorry. Sorry." Grace put them on the kitchen table, which was *covered* in baked goods.

"Grace, what are you doing?" I asked as she hustled around the kitchen, turning things onto racks, opening drawers, and putting more things in the oven.

And I didn't mean the obvious task.

"Sorry." She dropped the spatula on the floor. "I... I didn't know you'd be home. Sorry. Do you need to make yourself food? You can have some cookies or banana bread, though those aren't lunch. Should I make you coffee?"

Grace practically spun in circles, her anxiety ratcheting up with every word, filling the kitchen with the acrid tang of nerves.

I took a step towards her. She didn't answer the question, but I wasn't sure this was the time to push her. Grace was wound so tight the tension was palpable.

"It's fine. I'm not hungry. Though banana bread sounds good," I soothed, trying to put her at ease.

"Good, okay." She bent down to get the spatula and hit her head on the open drawer. "Ow." Grace sunk to the kitchen floor, spatula still in hand, her lower lip quivering.

What. The. Fuck.

"Hey. I thought you were going to the movies?" I sat down on the floor next to her. Where was Wes?

"They went to the movies, since Evan's on call tonight again." She leaned toward me, like she was going in for a cuddle, then moved back.

"They left you alone?" My eyebrows rose. Grace was *not* ready to be left on her own. If she wasn't going to be working with Wes *and* Spencer I'd suggest that she postpone starting her job.

Her eyes rolled. "I'm not a puppy, Bren. They went on a *date*. Spencer asked if I wanted to come with him to his club, but sitting in the golf cart reading romance novels and drinking beer didn't sound fun today."

"Okay." Ugh, they all left her alone?

A sigh escaped her lips. "I should be studying, but," she made an exasperated noise. "I... what am I doing? They're gonna know. Everyone's gonna know."

Scrunching up her body, she rested her head on her knees, as her voice broke, and her peach scent grew burnt with fear.

I had no idea what she was talking about.

"Come here. If you need Wes to come home, tell him." I wrapped my arms around her, enveloping her tiny, shivering body with my own.

"I'm fine. Just nervous about starting work." She sighed and settled into my arms.

Grace really believed she was fine. This was why we had fucking problems.

"It's okay to be nervous. It's okay to not be fine," I whispered.

"Okay." She closed her eyes.

"It's also okay to not go to work right away. Spencer owns the company. If you need more time, then let him know," I added. "There's no rush."

"I know. But my family had a business, so I've been working since I was useful. It feels weird to *not* work." Her voice was quiet.

"Now that, I understand." I nodded.

A tiny smile played on her lips. "Pretty sure putting on a tiny tux and going to a dinner and doing inventory are two different things."

"Inventory sounds more fun. Those tiny tuxes are itchy. What sort? I started helping with the budgets of various company and foundation projects when I was in high school," I told her.

"We had a hardware store. Not like the fancy one Evan dragged me to for doorknobs, but the kind where you can buy nails, chickens, and hot sauce all at the same time. My favorite was counting the baby chicks on chicken delivery day to make sure that we got the right amount." Her eyes sparkled with the happy memory.

Hot sauce? Chickens? At a *hardware store?* Not that I knew where you could buy chickens around here.

"Also, in high school I helped on the neighbors farm. In undergrad and while getting my PhD, I always had a couple of jobs. So yeah, it's been weird not going to work. I'm looking forward to starting. I get to use my degree and do really interesting things, but I'm afraid that I'm going to mess up. So many little things are different." She slumped against me.

"You will mess up. It comes with starting a new job. Or an old one. Terrance thinks I've fucked up badly by buying that estate." I kept my arms tight around her, so that she felt safe.

She peeked up at me. "It will be beautiful. But what if..." Her chest heaved.

Telling her that she was overthinking wasn't going to help.

"While your fears are valid, no one in this house will let anything happen to you," I assured, stroking her hair because I didn't know what else to do.

"Okay." She went quiet and just sat there with me on the hard kitchen floor until the timer dinged.

Grace made a face, then used me to get herself up off the ground. She'd been leaving off her walking cast and brace, which worried me. All that baking probably wasn't good for her wrist.

She got the cookies out of the oven, then started moving the others around–the ones on pans went on racks, the ones on racks went in containers, as she became a ball of nervous energy pinging about the kitchen.

"Any more in the oven?" I peered around the kitchen trying to discern what else needed to be done.

She shook her head. "No, but eventually I need to wrap everything individually."

"What are these for?" There were *a lot* of baked goods.

"We can eat what we want, but they're really for the bake sale for Riley's school." Grace never stopped moving, loading the dishwasher, rinsing things, and putting stuff away.

This wasn't healthy. With the amount of energy she had, a movie wasn't going to work. I didn't want to push her recovery by working out or playing the piano. But...

"Let's get out of here and go for a ride," I finally offered, blocking her with my body to keep her from moving but not grabbing her. Yes, I think that would be okay.

She paused, head tilting. "Like on your motorcycle?"

"If you feel up to it, yes. Put on some jeans, and we'll go for a little ride while everything cools. Given they're for *Ri's* bake sale, *she* can help wrap them later," I told her. Grace shouldn't be doing this all herself. Riley needed to take responsibility, too. Also, with the amount of money that school costs, no one should be needing to hold a bake sale.

Though it was probably a fundraiser for art club or something.

"That sounds nice. Thank you." Grace gave me a shy smile then went upstairs.

I grabbed my phone and texted Wes.

Me

> Wes, your girl is a bundle of nerves. I'm stealing her.

Then I sent a text to Jett.

Me

> Wes left Grace alone. I'm going to take her for a ride before every surface is covered with baked goods.

I sent a picture of the pile of baked goods. My phone buzzed.

Jett

> I get to eat some of those? Have fun. Where are you going?

Me

> I'm considering taking her to see the estate.

I helped myself to some banana bread. Not what I'd been planning on doing today. But it needed to be done, and I couldn't let her wind herself up like this; she'd get sick. It might be nice for her to see the place Evan wanted to marry her in. Right now, there was enough time for her to object.

My bite of banana bread was overly sweet. I grimaced. Who the fuck put chocolate in banana bread?

Wes didn't answer my text, but he was at the movies.

I was finishing cleaning up for her. She came back down in jeans and one of Evan's flannels, which could be a dress on her, and her jacket over her arm.

A heavy sigh escaped my lips as I eyed the shirt. Her head ducked and she wrapped her arms around herself. While I understood why she stole Evan's clothes, part of me still thought it was to annoy me, not because it brought her comfort. We put on our shoes.

"Come on." I walked out of the kitchen and into the garage.

She shrugged on her jacket and grabbed her helmet from the garage, as I grabbed mine and my bike.

Her gaze lingered on her own tiny green motorcycle with a sidecar. "I can't wait to ride it."

"It's really nice. You should probably take the written test first, before practicing. Also, get cleared to ride from the doctor." I still couldn't believe Spencer did that. Not buying her a motorcycle, it would be good for her to have one that suited her. It was that he got her *that* particular one. Top of the line, limited edition, and *custom.*

Show off.

Not to mention he'd gotten himself a matching one. It stood by Evan's. I didn't even know that he could ride.

"I suppose." She sighed. "I'll ask at my next appointment."

We went out to the driveway, and I closed the garage behind us. She was fiddling with her helmet.

"Here, I can turn it on for you." I grabbed it and enabled the com-system and handed it back to her.

"On?" She blinked and put it on.

I put mine on. "Can you hear me?"

"I didn't know it did that." Her voice was soft over the coms.

I guess she and Jett hadn't talked during their ride.

"In case you want to talk–or just tell me something. Would you like a short ride or a long one?" I helped her on.

"It doesn't matter. It would be nice just to get out. This is a big seat."

"Evan sometimes rides with me." I got on in front of her. "I should look at some stuff at the estate before Terrance gets pissed at me. It's a nice long drive and then you can see where Evan wants to marry you. Or we could just ride around town a bit, then go bug Jett."

Either one would be fine. Jett had mentioned wanting to take her to the outdoor market.

"You'd take me to see the estate?" She put her arms around me, holding on tight.

"I could use your opinions on stuff anyway." Why the fuck did that feel nice? She was tiny and boney, and not someone I could fall in love with.

Care about. Take care of. But never love.

We set off for the estate.

"Is it okay that Evan marries me? He didn't marry you and Jett, right?" her voice finally said over the coms.

"Please, marry him. Legally, a mate bond between two omegas doesn't count like it does between an alpha and an omega. It would be good protection for you, since you fall under omega law," I explained as we merged onto the freeway.

Omegas could bond with each other, creating a connection, just like an alpha did. Their bites just didn't leave a permanent mark. Apparently, she was close enough to an omega that she could bond Evan and Wes back.

"Jett and Evan have a civil partnership, and Jett and I are married for the same reasons. I did bond Jett, but alpha-beta bonds also don't have legal standing, and he can't bond me back. Evan and I have a registered mate bond, which for an alpha-omega pair legally means the same thing as being married," I added.

She and Wes were registered, but I wasn't sure if she understood what everything meant.

"Oh. Okay. So that's why no one's married Evan? I... I'm just trying to understand. Where I'm from, your options are marriage or living in sin." She laughed.

Yeah, I didn't want to touch that.

"Jett and I had been through a lot together, so it felt appropriate to have a ridiculous wedding, and I'd recently acquired that resort," I said, keeping an eye out for cars, since it was busy this morning.

"Which is where you met Evan," she added.

"Yes. And part of why we didn't have an actual wedding with Evan. Don't get me wrong, we had a giant mating party with all the things a wedding does, except for the legal officiant. We brought out his sisters, grandparents, and family. A great time was had by all," I explained. "I have a great picture of little Riley in a ruffled dress. The three of us do wear rings. When we went to have a party for Evan with Jett's family out on the West Coast, he dressed us up and hauled our asses off for some ceremony in a temple, that was just us, some old temple guys, and the ancient omega matriarch of his family. I'll show you pictures because those two looked so hot in his traditional clothes."

It was very beautiful.

"That sounds nice. Wes and Evan just never got around to it, because it's not legally necessary for them, right?" she added.

"Exactly. They mated and registered their bond, which is all you really need to do. Wes' dad threw them a party. Jett and I attended, and Spencer brought in Evan's family. Between you and me, I think Evan wasn't ready for a wedding, because it meant facing the death of his parents. Weddings are a huge part of beta culture, and he grew up in a beta family in a mostly beta neighborhood," I added. "To me, him wanting to marry you means that he's ready to face things–like having a wedding without his parents there to see it."

"Oh. That makes sense. It's also really sweet when you put it that way. I figured he just wanted to see me in a pretty dress and have a party," she said softly.

He didn't need a wedding for that.

"Weddings are important where you're from?" I asked, trying to ignore how comfortable it felt to have her behind me.

"Very. It's considered one of the most important days in a woman's life. I'll have to read up and see what traditions are different, but everything Evan's mentioned sounds good to me," she replied.

Things would be different. Important in a *woman's* life? Not the man's?

"Just to warn you, after you and Spencer actually bond, a party *will* be expected. It's a society thing," I said.

"Oh. I guess someone like him would be expected to have a big party." Her voice went guarded.

"It doesn't have to be big, it could be a very exclusive, lavish party. Think about what you want, because you might as well have fun at your own party," I told her.

Suburbs gave forth to grass and trees, though soon enough this would probably be built up too, between Redstone's new research complex, the Space Authority, and the expansion of the nearby military base.

"Oooh, yeah. I think I'd like that—no, it's not small, it's *exclusive*." She laughed again. "Tell me about your wedding? I'm having trouble visualizing a *week-long* wedding."

"It was fun. Ridiculous, but fun." And exactly what Jett and I needed to celebrate us, our journey, and the strength it took for me to choose living. Also to celebrate him, his patience, and persistence in helping me through that process.

As we continued our ride, I told her about the activities, location, and meeting Evan.

Finally, we got off the highway and made our way down the winding, tree-lined road to the estate.

"This is beautiful. Even wild, I can see how this area could make for a great venue, think of the pictures," she breathed. "Oh, there's something for your website–availability for people to book parts of it for photos."

"That's a good idea. Even if people don't have a party when they mate, they often get photos and send them out." The giant iron gate stood open, and it was evident that renovations were in progress.

I parked at the house and helped her off.

"Oh. Oh." Grace took off her helmet and turned around, taking it all in. "When you said *old estate* and that it needed renovations I was thinking something like a gothic haunted mansion, something mysterious and spooky. But this…"

She eyed the elegant stone home, with the large front staircase and sprawling front with a fountain.

Grace curtseyed. "I'm so sorry, but the duchess is not in residence right now," she stated, adopting an accent. "If you'd like to leave your card, I will let her know that you called. This is straight out of England. At least my England."

"It *is*. When the family was kicked out of Britain, back in the day, they had it relocated stone by stone out of spite," I replied. "The upkeep on this is enormous and it's been neglected for some time–not just the grounds but the infrastructure. The plumbing, electrical, and roofing all need upgrades."

"Of course it's expensive to keep. Ten thousand a year isn't nearly as much as it used to be." She giggled.

Then I got it. "Oh, yes, very *Tea-Time British*. I suppose you like dramas from that era."

She seemed like the type.

"Terrance thinks we should just fix what we need to bring it to code," I told her. "But I think that it would be better to gut it to the bones. Then of course, do we match the interior to the exterior or go modern?"

"Restore it, if not to how it looked then, to at least the time period," she breathed. "There's your hook right there. You could go the school visit route, showing them what life was like then. Or perhaps cater to recreationalists or LARPers–live action role play. Think of the costumed balls you could have here."

Grace hummed and started swaying, eyes closed. Her eyes snapped open. "Or be wild and make it a themed resort. Like an expensive one, where you're immersed in the era. I have that movie on my laptop–from my world." She laughed. "Might be a little too out there."

I thought for a moment. "Terrance might not be on-board with an immersive resort, and school visits sound like a lot of work, but I love the theme angle."

A man in a construction hat came over to me. "Mr. Morris, we weren't expecting you."

"Hi Reg. Is it still safe to enter? I wanted to take a look around, also see how things were going with the gardens."

"Yes, of course. Always a pleasure to work for the family," he said, then left.

I turned to Grace. "The company Reg works for does a lot of work for my parents but is also well known for being on time and budget. I've known him most of my life. I tried to get Wes' dad on the project, but he was already on something else."

"Oh, that's nice." She smiled then offered me her arm. "A tour m'lord."

Why did that sound so nice from those little lips?

"Absolutely, m'lady." I escorted her up the stairs then used my access to get inside. I'd been here enough times to feel comfortable showing her around. Taking hard hats off the stand, we each put one on. Just for safety.

"This was once so beautiful. Even though it would cost more, I think a complete restoration would be perfect if you can swing it. Wait," she stopped in the foyer. "Why were they kicked out of England?"

"For being extremists. You see..." I grinned, knowing she'd like this detail. "They thought that omegas should have *rights*. Like the right to be educated, the right to have a voice in choosing their alphas, and, *gasp,* the right to have a job—or at least money or property of their own."

Her hand went to her face in mock horror. "Oh, the horror."

"I know." I laughed. "England has always been behind in the omega and beta rights department. Even now they're not quite as progressive as here."

She paused. "Can only an alpha be king or queen?"

"It depends on the country. Though traditionally, for many years, the answer was *yes.* There was once a great war that was fought over succession because the king only had an omega child and no alpha children. She had the knowledge to be queen, just not the designation," I told her as we entered the great room.

Grace bowed and twirled around the great room like she was at a ball. "What happened?"

"I think people underestimated what alphas would do for an omega, especially then. She rallied an army, won the hearts of the people, got herself a pack of alphas who made up for what she was lacking, and became the most beloved queen their nation had ever seen. Katie and Lexi would *love* to watch the movie made about her with you." I wasn't about to offer because I'd seen it more times than I cared to remember.

"Are only alphas political leaders?" She peered out the window.

"Many political leaders are alphas, but most places no longer have laws prohibiting other designations from running for positions other than the ones specific to them." I came up behind her. "Nice view, right?"

"Yes. Oooh, look at the chandelier and the ceiling. This would be a lovely room for a party," she breathed.

"Absolutely." I led her out of the room.

Her look went pensive. "Wait. When the president's omega goes into heat does he just dip for a week? Like who runs the country? Does he or she have a pack? Do we have a president?"

Oh, fuck. Not having designations would change a lot of things. For example, why did people even come to this country if it wasn't for designation freedom?

We wandered into a library, which still had some books and furniture.

"Yes. We have co-presidents for that exact reason. The current ones both have packs, and their omegas coordinate so that they aren't going into heat at the same time. Your co-president is *very* important because you have to trust them enough to run everything when you're away. Same with your vice president, because they'd take over if something happens to both. It works pretty well, though, because it allows them to not just have heats but take vacations and ensure their pack and families aren't neglected for the sake of the country," I explained. "Traditionally, one of the presidents is usually a beta, for parity, but it's not a law. Given this nation was founded on designation freedom, betas have always been able to run for office. After the omega rights act passed, omegas can run as well, but we've yet to have an omega president."

I looked around. The family had only taken what they wished and left the rest. Someone had been going through everything left, determining if it should be thrown out, sold, or potentially kept.

"Well, at least if you have co-presidents they can't use the excuse of not having an omega president because he or she would be irrational around their heat." She rolled her eyes.

Mmmm, people did say that. Most of it stemmed from a fear of other countries using their alpha barks to sway an omega president. Beta politicians usually worked long and hard to overcome that and had alpha staff members whose jobs were to keep that from happening. Omegas had a harder time of it.

"There are omegas in the other branches of government, not to mention, we have omega judges in all courts, including the Assembly, which is the highest court in the country," I added. It was a dangerous, but necessary job.

"Omega judges. As there should be. Ooh, a ladder." Grace climbed up on the wheeled ladder in front of the tall bookshelves. She flung herself out, making the ladder careen across the shelves as she started *singing*.

"Grace." I rushed over and caught her just as she nearly crashed into the wall. She was laughing. Laughing!

"Don't do that," I growled. "Wes will beat my ass if anything happens to you."

She rolled her eyes as she opened a door and walked into the adjoining study. "Excuse me, but the boys and I are going to retire for a cigar."

I surveyed the dark paneled room, which smelled faintly of cigars. It most likely was exactly that–the alpha study. "Pretty much."

"How did you and Jett meet, will you tell me?" she asked.

I paused. Should I? Though if anyone would understand it would be her.

"Oh, is it embarrassing? Jett said it wasn't his story to tell. Sorry, not trying to pry." Her head bowed.

"It was a very dark time in my life when I met him. After I graduated from university, as you know, Caroline and I broke up, and she went to travel the world. I went to business school—much to my mother's chagrin, since it wasn't for accounting. My undergrad *was* and she wanted me to handle accounts for her company. She said that she didn't see me actually managing properties, just handling numbers." My voice went bitter.

No, I wasn't good enough to follow in her footsteps. My brothers, but not me.

"Oh." The corners of her lips tugged in a frown as she ran her fingers across the panels.

I put a hand on her shoulder as we left the room and entered the hallway. "She thought my idea for a luxury hotel business was a waste. I'd acquired my first hotel in undergrad and was working on turning it around."

"You acquired a hotel in college." Grace nodded. "How?"

"In a card game. I figured out my niche. I acquired partners, invested, and found a corner of the market. Each of my properties are very special. Unique. Private. By the time I graduated from business school, I had three hotels and was considering a fourth. While my mother still thought I'd work for her company, perhaps fold my hotels into it, she *was* proud of me. So was my father—and Katie, who was still in law school," I explained as we walked through the formal dining room. "My older brothers were pretty indifferent."

But they always had been. There was a decade between them and us. We were not only an *oops,* but surprise twins. Mother had always wanted a girl, though.

"I'm glad your parents were proud," she said softly, looking wistful, like she'd never been told that.

"Me, too. Those moments are fleeting with my mother. Anyhow, I graduated with honors. We had a lovely party. Caroline even called me from her travels. Katie and I decided to meet some friends for a night out. I'd gotten a new car as a gift, and Katie desperately wanted to drive it, so I let her…" I winced, hearing the glass shatter.

Grace put a hand on my arm. "Oh. The car accident."

"It wasn't Katie's fault. It was a drunk driver. I was thrown through the window and onto the expressway. Katie was trapped in the car but ultimately was relatively unscathed. Again, not her fault. The model of the car was new, and the safety system on the passenger side failed." I looked away as we went into the kitchen, which would need a lot of work to make it into a commercial kitchen.

My fingers ran across the countertop. "Jett was part of the responding team. While Katie was cut out of the car, I was brought to the hospital. I remember him holding my hand and telling me that it would be okay. I recall him being there when I woke up. Unable to move."

"Oh?" Grace's arms wrapped around me and for a moment I just let her hug me.

"They told me that I'd probably never walk again. I went from having one of the best days of my life to that worst. That cute beta police officer that smuggled me treats didn't even help," I replied as we went into the pantry and wine cellar. It had been crushing to wake up to that news.

"I… I'm so sorry that happened to you." She squeezed my hand.

I squeezed hers back. "Jett was very persistent. After I was released, I eventually agreed to go on a date with him. We had sparks. Oh, did we ever have sparks. He also was trying to get me to go to therapy, take my meds, do my PT–even sue the car maker, which my mother didn't want because *we don't sue.*"

Those sparks. When I was still in the hospital, we may have done a few things that could have gotten him fired.

Grace rolled her eyes. "If it was their fault they should pay. So, things with Jett were good?"

"So good. Who would have thought that a beta police officer who boxed and liked spicy food would have been a match for me?" Taking her arm, I led her upstairs.

Much better than I deserved. He gave me a reason to *try*. Especially since my parents pretty much neglected me after the accident, and initially I was angry with Katie.

One at a time we peeked into the bedrooms, most unfurnished, dusty, and neglected.

With a sigh, I went back to the conversation at hand. "My recovery was long and hard. Sometimes it felt impossible. Eventually, I got so frustrated with everything that I ignored my business–which would've failed if not for Terrance. I refused physical therapy. One day I ghosted Jett, because I felt that I had nothing to offer him. He was so amazing, I was nothing. I just... wallowed. My mother suddenly took interest and tried to convince me to move back home–and sign everything over to her so that she could *take care of me since I refused to take care of myself*," I confessed. "This would be mostly the assets I'd come into eventually."

"You ghosted Jett? Poor Jett." She frowned.

I put my arm around her as we continued the tour. "It was wrong of me. Everything was dark and I couldn't find the light. I felt like I didn't deserve him."

Oh, how I regretted doing that. Everything had felt so bleak and hopeless, why drag him down with me?

Grace buried her face in my chest. "I'm so sorry. What happened?"

"I confided in Katie. For all our differences we were really good friends. I thought maybe, somehow, she could help me." I winced. "This... this is the part where I understand you being afraid to talk to people. Now, Katie had no malicious intent, she wanted to help me. So, even though I told her not to tell our parents, she did."

She sucked in a sharp breath. "They put you somewhere."

"Yes, and my mother tried to get me legally under her care. This wasn't what Katie had in mind. She'd been thinking more of a fancy physical rehabilitation facility where I could learn to walk again and get some counseling. Not a psychiatric unit where they'd try to declare me unfit." I winced. This was the root of my current issues with Katie–even though it wasn't her fault. She'd trusted our dad, who apparently regretted bringing our mother into it.

"Oh no." Concern crossed her face.

"Katie and my father tried to check me out. My mother then had me moved to someplace else. She had me locked down, so that no one could see me but her–not even Katie and my dad. While he thought I needed help, he didn't think I was unfit." It was part of why I did what my mother told me. She had a lot of power and I'd seen what she could do when you angered her.

"I can't believe they did that to you." Grace started crying.

"I promise, no one harmed me. But in the second place she sent me to, they didn't help me the way I needed," I assured, trying to comfort her.

"The drugs were the worst. That's what they tried first, to make me less rebellious and bad at math." Her voice was muffled by my shirt.

"I'm sorry they did that to you." Yeah, we were going back to that.

We went up the stairs to the next floor, which was mostly storage.

"In the meantime, Jett, being a persistent asshole, got worried about me, and showed up at my place. When he found out that I wasn't there, he tracked down Katie and she told him what had happened," I said.

"Please tell me he busted you out." Her look went hopeful.

"He did." My chest shook a little.

I didn't deserve it. I'd ghosted him. And there he was, rescuing me.

"It involved getting a favor from a friend of Jett's that's an ambulance driver, Katie dating a judge's son, and Terrance doing some browbeating. But yes, they got me out of there–and, much to my chagrin–into the place Katie wanted me to go to. There, the three shitheads assholed me into learning to walk again to spite my mother who was pissed at us. I also got my shit together there, both personally and regarding my business."

I'd needed that ass-kicking and was grateful to have people in my life that cared enough about me to do that–even when I was being a knothead.

"I'm so glad," she told me while we went down the backstairs.

"Me, too. Jett was by my side the whole time–not just while at the rehab facility, but after. Also, a lawyer at the firm Katie was interning at took my case and I sued the fuck out of the car company. That money helped to buy the resort Jett and I got married at."

My mother never did quite forgive me for that–and certainly she never completely trusted me again. Which was why she was always forcing me to play the good son to 'prove' my loyalty to her and the family.

"You're better now?" she asked.

"I still get headaches, but I recovered more than they ever thought I would," I assured her.

We were now in the main ballroom, which opened out into the gardens.

"Thank you for opening up to me." She hugged me again. "Sorry, not sorry, you feel nice to hug."

"Jett and Evan would agree." I patted her back. "It's a hard story to tell. It was a long journey. There were times I hated Jett, especially when trying to get my life back together. He hated me sometimes, too. But in the end his persistence saved me. He believed in me, pushed me." Loved me. Gave me a way to heal–and a way to regain the control I'd lost.

"I'm glad you shared it with me."

"I had a feeling that you'd understand," I told her. Wes had resonated with it as well. Even though Wes had been in the military at the time, he'd really been there for me, too.

There were a lot of people that hadn't.

We entered another room. "This would probably be the room where you'd have the party after your wedding–or be the backup in case of rain. He's looking for the ceremony to be outside in the gardens. Evan's set on a May wedding. Though June would be better because the flowers would have more time."

Something about his parents being married in May.

"This is beautiful. Look at the moldings." She looked up at the elegant ceiling. "This could be something so special, Bren."

"It really could," I agreed. "Would you like to see the gardens? Or have we done enough walking?" Though she'd been doing well. Maybe she was fine.

She smiled and took my hand. "Let's go. I can't wait to see them."

Chapter Twenty

Grace

My phone rang as we toured the gardens, which were mostly in disarray but starting to bloom, creating a chaotic, but enchanting display.

"Hi, Wes, how was the movie?" I walked in the opposite direction of Brennan, going into another garden.

"It was great. You're with Bren?" he asked.

The anxiousness from the bond made my belly twist as I sat on the edge of a non-working fountain. "Is that okay? I was stressed about my new job, so we went for a ride on his motorcycle."

I'd texted Wes to let him know what was going on.

"Grace, Peaches, it's totally fine. I'd like you two to be at least friends."

"At least?" My brows rose. Though I was enjoying this kinder and protective side of Brennan.

There was a jostling of the phone. "Having fun? What are you and Bren doing? Each other?" Evan asked cheerfully.

"Evan! He took me for a ride on his motorcycle. That's okay, right?" Memories of him taking me flitted through my mind, making my insides tingle.

"If he asked you to go somewhere with him, go for it. I mean, none of us would be mad if you abducted him and made him take you somewhere, as long as you eventually brought him back," Evan laughed. "Motorcycle ride. I hope you enjoyed that. I know I do. Does he play with your ankles when he's at a stoplight? I always like that."

"It was nice. We're at the estate. I guess he needs to make some decisions." This was a lovely place with so much potential. It meant a lot that Evan wanted to marry me here–and that Brennan *bought* it so that he could do so.

"Grace, we want you to be friends with Bren. Besides, aren't you going on a date to a concert with him at some point?" Evan teased.

Anxiety shot through me, as I recalled the piano concert he'd invited me to back before I'd been taken by the Authority. "It's a date?"

Sure, he was cute, and I was so curious about what that pierced cock felt like when I was not high on orgasms and pheromones. But I was still getting to know him, trust him–especially the not-asshole him.

"Hey, it's okay. I'm teasing you." Evan's voice went soft. "We're a little horny, so ignore us. We love you, have fun."

"Okay. I love you, too." For a moment I just sat there. It was an unassuming little garden with a bunch of little benches. This, too, could have so much potential. I could almost see the wallflower sister hiding here with her book, and hear the laughter of a young couple off in the distance...

"This is a night blooming garden, so I'm told. Is everything okay?" Brennan sat down with me on the fountain's edge.

"Oh. That sounds lovely. I just wanted to make sure no one was mad that I ran off with you. I'm still trying to figure all this out."

"Given no one had anything planned, I don't see why they would. Now, if you spoiled Jett's plans then he might get cranky with you." He smiled. "Jett wants Spencer to grill ribs for dinner. Does that sound good?"

"That sounds amazing." Would he let me make the sauce? My sauce literally won an award at the fair. I texted Spencer and asked him.

"So much of our life must be so new and strange to you. We sometimes forget that you're not used to this." He looked up at the cloudy sky.

My lower lip quivered. "I get so confused. Like you can barely stand me sometimes, but back at the cabin you..." My body flooded with heat with the little I did remember. "Then Evan was cracking jokes and..."

Brennan started rubbing my shoulders. "Easy or Evan's going to call and scold me. You're right. When you first came here, I was so blinded by what Caroline did to us that I could only see you as a threat. But I see beyond that now. You make my packmates happy. And well, I like playing the piano with you."

I relaxed into his hands. It felt different from when Spencer did it.

"As for the cabin, I'm sorry for not talking with you beforehand, and I hope it wasn't unwanted. Wes is still trying to figure out how to manage both your and Evan's needs. My actions were beyond duty or instinct. When we're in the nest, we care for each other's wants and needs regardless of who we're with on the outside, because we have trust. We're a family and the last thing I'd want to do is leave someone hurt and wanting."

"Oh, I... I like it when you're sweet with me. And I don't necessarily even mean kissing. Like this–getting me out of the house before I become a wreck. Though what I remember was good." I ducked my head. It felt weird saying these things out loud.

Trust. Care. Before I came here I didn't experience a whole lot of that. Now, I craved it.

"I take care of everyone in this family—even those I don't have a bond with. We'll get it all figured out. Getting used to the hormones can be a bitch." He chuckled.

That was an understatement, because just him sitting this close and touching me so tenderly was getting my lady parts a little jumpy.

Down girl. We're not getting with Brennan.

Like I'd admitted to Evan back at the cabin, it was hard to wade through hormones and feelings and all that. Part of me wondered if Brennan and I would ever be intimate outside of Evan's heats. Even if it was just carrying out some of Evan's fantasies.

They could be good. *Very good.*

Though I also understand that his ex had caused him a lot of emotional damage and I appreciated how far he'd come since I arrived. We were also still getting to know each other, trust each other. Who knew what might happen...

I'd be okay if it did.

Yeah, I'd just be patient with him and figure out how he needed to be loved, since he was so busy taking care of everyone else.

"Thank you for telling me all that," I added, refocusing on the present.

"I need you to know that I understand where you're coming from. Okay, not parallel worlds, but things like your fear of saying something to the wrong person being perfectly valid," he assured.

"I also appreciate you and Jett taking me being from another world all in stride." What would have happened if they hadn't believed me?

"While I understand how you came *here,* I'm still confused about why your mom was such a bitch about Wes if you don't even have alphas in your world? How did she even know?" His face scrunched in confusion.

"That's a complex question," I replied as he continued to rub my shoulders.

It was probably time to explain a few things.

"Should we see the rest of the gardens while we talk? Not that I don't like this. Did Wes miss the massage lesson in alpha school? Not that I have any issue with Wes," I groaned as he hit a good spot.

Brennan stood. "Spencer and I went to private alpha training camps. Wes didn't. Should I get him massage lessons for Christmas?"

I adored Christmas. Would they let me cover the lawn with inflatable Christmas dragons? I'd always wanted to do that. Also, wear matching Christmas pajamas.

"I think you should." Taking his hand, I stood. "Alpha training camp. It sounds miserable."

"It's pretty fun. Well, the one Katie and I went to. You learn how to care for your omega and how to run a pack or household. We covered everything from accounting and investing, to cooking and cleaning," he said. "And, things like sailing and massage."

We continued touring the spacious grounds and I felt like I was in a regency novel, wandering through a dilapidated manor.

"I was *too into* math in high school. My mom was really into appearances. She wanted me to be acceptably social, to participate in the right activities, and get good grades–but not have a schedule full of advanced classes. When I wanted to join the mathletes, that was it–she'd had enough–even though I promised not to drop cheer or miss any piano competitions. One thing I never figured out was why she was so obsessed with me playing the piano when she didn't, but she also said she never wanted to play it as a kid."

I shrugged. "I did get a little obsessed with math and my theories. Which worried her."

Brennan looked puzzled. "There are so many worse things teenagers can do."

"I know, right? Like get drunk and pass out in a field." My eyes rolled. There wasn't a whole lot to do in our little town.

He nodded. "Exactly."

"Still, nothing I could do was right. She didn't like my attitude and behavior. Also, she thought that I rebelled against her rules and mouthed off. In hindsight, I really didn't do anything bad. I got top grades, did extracurriculars, volunteered, played the piano at church, and worked two jobs. Though I did keep a messy room and was overly fond of blankets and stuffies." It was never enough for her.

I was never enough.

"Still not a bad thing." He shook his head.

"I made a mistake, confiding in my guidance counselor in high school about what I wanted to study in college–and where I wanted to go. I thought that he could help me with my college applications and find scholarships. He thought my interests were unsuitable for a woman and told my mom that I was delusional because I believed other worlds existed. Really, he just didn't understand quantum physics." By then my relationship with my mom had already been strained. Confiding in him was what started the really awful things.

"You should be able to talk to your teachers. Girls can do quantum physics." He frowned.

"They can. But getting a three-day hold because your guidance counselor was worried about your mental state because of what you wanted to study in college and hoped to accomplish was horrifying. It also made me more secretive. I got meds and therapy, and weird treatments. When the real professionals wouldn't give my mom the answers she wanted, she switched me to unlicensed church people, who just pandered to her and not my needs. My mom and I were always at odds, and I couldn't wait to escape to college." With my eyes set on an elite university on the other side of the country.

"So that's when the drugs started," he said quietly.

"Yeah. I didn't like the way they impacted my academic performance and had to figure out how to make her think I took them. Anyway, the future was in sight, and one day I confided in my best friend that I had a boyfriend. I didn't mention that he was from another world, just that there was someone and it was secret. She… she told." I flinched. She'd been my ride or die. I kept so many secrets for her—and I never knew why she told on me.

"Oh." Horror crossed his face.

"Remember, in my world there are no omegas or alphas. My mom didn't deny me stuffies to curb omega tendencies. Just like she wasn't angry about Wes because he was an *alpha* the way you mean it here. She freaked out because he was a guy and I was *sneaking around,* as she put it, instead of dating the *nice church boys* she wanted me to. She took everything in my room as punishment, even the bed and door. Leaving me my rug, one blanket and a pillow—and a couple of basic outfits." I winced because it had been humiliating, and she hadn't listened.

She'd also let my brothers take whatever of mine they wanted.

"While taking everything, she found my notes. There weren't just formulas, but theories, my dreams—and a whole lot about Wes. This all freaked her out, because I believed this *alpha* I saw in my dreams was real and one day I'd use math to be with him. Anyhow, the next day I found myself at some religious *wilderness camp* since apparently everything else wasn't *helping my delusions.*" I plopped down on a bench, we were back in the rose garden where we started.

That had been a horrible day. I still didn't know why my mom was so angry. Maybe my bio-dad had been a self-styled 'alpha male.' Our church had been full of them. They weren't kind and protective like my alphas. They'd been mean and used their size and the fact they were dudes to get their way.

Concern flickered through his eyes. "Camp. That's where…"

"It was terrifying and dehumanizing in a way my other experiences never were. Even the church-run summer camp for 'troubled kids' I'd gone to wasn't like that. This was not the sort of *wilderness camp* where you lived in a tent and hiked for three months. It was a religious behavior modification camp that used extreme measures." My heart sped, recalling the sheer misery of that place–and the pain.

I hunched over, my breath hitching, at the memories of that place. Brennan sat next to me, putting an arm around my shoulders. My phone buzzed.

Wes

Are you okay?

Me

Bren and I are getting deep, but I'm okay.

I'd come to terms with it. I just didn't like to dwell on that place and what she and the church did to me.

"And I was scared–so scared." My chest shuddered as I leaned into him, filling my lungs with his pine scent.

"It sounds awful. I am so sorry they did that." He rubbed my back.

"It was nothing short of torture. They even messed with our sleep cycles, which made talking to Wes, the one positive thing I had, difficult. I got through everything else because I could still visit him in my dreams. I could be wrapped in blankets and hold

Mr. Hippo, snuggle him, and get a pep talk. But between the sleep deprivation and the new drugs it got harder and harder to reach him." Tears streamed down my face. Slowly they stripped me of *everything.*

Brennan started to purr. "I've got you—and you don't have to talk about it."

I rubbed my wrists. "I tried to hang on, especially for Wes' sake. I knew he wasn't going to find me, but I thought maybe the mating connection would enable me to hang on. But I'm weak."

A sob escaped my lips. I wasn't strong enough.

I wasn't enough.

"Then they moved from just hurting me to shock therapy. I was so tired. My soul hurt so bad. After I'd had a heart attack, I'd gotten to talk to my parents on the phone. My dad begged me to just go along with it because he was afraid I'd die. In the end, I thought Wes was just a dream—a sinful dream that was best to not remember, and that advanced math wasn't for girls like me." My head bowed with the weight of those memories.

"You're not weak, Grace. If that didn't happen in another world, I'd kill someone for you. I can't believe that it's fucking legal." Brennan held me tight, and I rested my head on his chest.

"Oh, they're not. But because they run as *religious camps* they skirt by because in my world, my country values religion over the lives of children." My voice went bitter, and I kept rubbing my wrists. "So, there it is."

Brennan entwined his hand with mine. "As Evan would say, there's so much to unpack there. I can't believe someone would do that to their kid. You had a fucking heart attack?"

"Yeah. I went through a shit-ton of actual legitimate therapy to be able to talk about it. I still don't like to," I whispered. Kids died at that camp. Like my roommate.

"Understandable." His finger very lightly ran over my wrist.

"There were marks on my wrists, too. One of my therapists found someone who removed them for free. I'd looked into getting my back done, but even with help it would be a long and expensive process." I closed my eyes again and leaned on his shoulder.

"If at any point you want to get the scars on your back removed, I'll cover whatever the insurance doesn't. The Center might even be able to help you," he told me.

I thought about that for a moment. It hit differently coming from him, considering his own scars. "Thank you. I'd want to make sure it's for the right reasons."

"As you should. I'd once thought about it, but ended up not, because I wasn't doing it for me," he replied.

I started to sob again, and Brennan continued to hold me and purr. My phone rang, but I didn't want to let go of him.

"Wes, it's Bren," Brennan said, answering it for me. "I didn't make her cry, promise. I told her about my accident, and she told me about wilderness camp."

For a moment there was quiet.

"Yeah. No, we don't have booze. Or chocolate. Maybe we'll get ice cream on the way home. We'll probably head back soon. Okay." He pressed the phone to my ear. "Please tell Wes that I didn't yell at you."

"I'm okay, promise. Like I said, we got deep," I assured Wes as I got love from him and Evan through the bond.

"Okay. I love you," Wes replied.

"Love you, too." I ended the call and sighed.

"Thank you for sharing that with me. It... it explains a lot. I'm glad that you found your way back to Wes," he said quietly.

"Me, too. You mentioned ice cream? I could use that right now." I felt wrung out emotionally.

He stood. "Yeah. I think we're finished here. Let's get some ice cream."

Chapter Twenty-One

Grace

Giddiness filled me as I shifted my weight on the stool in my little office lab. Today was my first official day at Compass BioTek. My attention kept focusing on Blaise's adorable baby as they video-chatted with me.

"I'm so excited. I've had an interest in simulating particle acceleration since undergrad," Blaise said on the screen of the computer as they bounced their infant. "I'll send everything I have over to you. It's not much, but I'll include all the general project checklists so that you can start filling in the gaps and laying the groundwork."

"Absolutely. Thanks for making time for me while you're on leave."

"No problem. When Deb told me that Spencer had finally started hiring for the project, it made my day." They gave their baby a kiss, short brown hair falling over their brown eyes.

Blaise was something called a quantum coder, and on parental leave. We'd be working together along with the team we'd assemble. There was also a quantum physicist that was on sabbatical, and a project manager currently working on other things.

"I'll also take a look at who's presenting at, and attending, the PIIP symposium, in case there's someone worth talking to. We're going to need an expert on super colliders and that would be the place to find one," they said. "We might even find a quantum mechanic."

I nodded. "Perfect."

"Deb said that you're helping with the interns and fellows–keep an eye out, because you never know if what we really need is some nineteen-year-old with a penchant for arson." They grinned. "Oh wait, that's how I got hired back in the day."

I laughed. "You're right, though. One of the high school applicants submitted a proposal that used hacking to solve Garamoci's Theory of Everything."

It wasn't even Riley.

Garamoci's Theory of Everything was one of this world's unsolvable equations.

"Overachiever," they coughed, chuckling. The baby fussed. "I've got to go, but we will talk again. Let's get this simulation started."

The screen on the laptop went blank. While I still felt like I was massively in over my head, I liked Blaise.

There was a knock on the door and Deb popped her head in. "How'd it go? Blaise is great, right?"

I nodded. "I'm really excited."

And grateful I'd gotten a bunch of project management experience at my other job, even though then I'd resented roles like that instead of the positions I'd really wanted.

"Ready for lunch?" Deb entered. She was older than me, with a little grey in her short dark hair. She was a smartly dressed, no-nonsense alpha and head of all of Special Projects. Since this project didn't have a team leader yet, I'd directly report to her. While this project was still in the early development phase, I'd have other projects and duties as well.

My stomach grumbled, it had been a while since we had welcome pastries. "Sounds great."

I stood. Today I wore one of my new outfits. I'd also brought the messenger bag with the equations on it that I'd gotten for my birthday from Evan.

"I thought we'd have lunch for all of Special Projects so that you can meet everyone. We even invited the locals who work remotely and this afternoon there will be an online mixer," she said, looking very serious in slacks and a blazer, her jewelry just right.

It was nice that so many people worked remotely, at least part of the time. Not just in Special Projects, but in a lot of departments. It meant me working remotely a day or two a week wouldn't be weird.

"Considering your past work with qubits, you'll probably get along with a lot of them, especially Margie's team, which is the ultra-secure communication project, and Narif's which is the nano-quantum-computing project. Some of them will be going to the PIIP symposium with us," she added as we walked down the hall.

"Narif is presenting, isn't he?" The PIIP symposium was something that I was very excited for. I'd already been in touch with Dr. Harlowe and was trying to set up a tour of PIIP and a demonstration of the particle cutter for our whole group.

"Yes. His work is amazing. We're so lucky to have him." She beamed as she opened the door to a room that had some tables with balloons on them set up along with a display of food.

A banner said *Welcome Dr. Ellington.*

My hand went to my heart. "This is for me?"

"Yes." She grinned. "Any excuse to order catering. While the cafeteria food is great—and free—sometimes it's fun to bring in something else." Deb led me around the room as people came in and got food.

A middle-aged woman with chin-length dark-blonde hair, who reeked of *nosey Karen,* came over to me.

"So, this is the mysterious Dr. Ellington? I thought Blaise was running the simulator program." She gazed at me with pursed lips.

"Blaise and Grace will be working together, Margie," Deb assured. "The team is still being assembled. Grace is laying the groundwork and working on some other projects while Blaise is on leave."

"I see." Her mauve nails tapped on her soda can as she looked me over. "You're helping with the interns, right? Please make sure we get a good one this year. University, not high school. Why are we adding high school interns?"

For Riley, from what I could determine. So far not very many high school students had applied, and most weren't suited to our division.

"I'll try my best. I'm meeting with the intern coordinator tomorrow," I answered, though we'd already met before today. It didn't sound like I'd be doing the actual assignments, more like coordinating the needs of the department, acting as a liaison, planning some activities, as well as running a small project of my own.

I could do that. It would be fun.

Someone called Deb. "I'll be right back."

She left, leaving me with Margie.

"You're Grace." Another woman joined us. "I'm Tish, I work with Margie. Welcome."

"I'm Jordie," a guy added. "Also with Margie. First day, exciting. What brings you here? I heard you were working on a quantum-computing project previously?"

I nodded, nerves in my belly, as I clutched my can of soda. "Yes, I was. But those were very different applications."

Military applications.

"Why did you leave?" Margie pressed, making a nosey face.

Time for my backstory. I waggled the finger with the beautiful antique sapphire and diamond ring that Wes had given me on my birthday. "I finished my PhD program and moved here to be with my mate."

Which was true. We'd tried to root everything in the truth.

"Oh. A new mate. How exciting," Tish giggled. "Did you do anything special? Travel someplace exciting?" She was younger than Margie but older than me, her dark braids swinging as she moved.

"Tish is always looking for new places to travel to," Jordie replied. He looked like he was probably around my age. He was slight and very well dressed.

"The pack is going to the Mediterranean this summer," I said. "But my mates and I are going on a special trip next year. I'd love to hear recommendations."

I didn't miss Margie's eyebrows when I said *mates,* as she looked at my neck. There weren't any bites on hers, but I did see one on Tish's wrist, and one on Jordie's neck. All three smelled like betas. Not that I was really good at smelling designations yet.

"A new pack, a new city, and a new job. So exciting! I have tons of recommendations. We'll have to sit together at lunch and talk." Tish's hands moved while she talked, and her nails were a pretty gold color.

Tish seemed nice. Wes had mentioned her as someone he thought I'd get along with.

Margie studied me, eyes narrowing. "I'd love to read some of your work. I couldn't find any."

Inwardly, I groaned. *And here we go.* "I didn't have a lot of opportunities previously, but I do have some things that I'm working on."

Which was true. Spencer and I were going through all my work, including my dissertation, to see if anything could be redone and published with this world's sources. Especially since I *was* going to need an actual dissertation to have on file at the university I'd supposedly gotten my PhD from. Thank goodness for Spencer and his incredible network of people who owed him favors–and Evan and the Omega Protection people who helped make identities real.

"No?" Margie smirked.

Tish frowned. "You *can* report them if you think you were denied opportunities because of your designation. We all know it still happens. I don't know if you're part of the Daedalus Society but reach out to them. They can help you."

The Daedalus Society was a professional society for omegas in the sciences. I'd gotten quite the education on how omegas fared in science PhD programs, and a lot of it paralleled my professor's stories from their experiences as being young women in science. This was why some omegas did what was basically independent-study PhDs. Rami, Katie's omega, had done such a program and now worked for the Space Authority.

And in this world, supposedly so had I, since it would help explain why other people in the program I'd 'graduated' from didn't know me.

"Thank you. I joined Daedalus. It was more because I didn't have family support and couldn't participate in anything that didn't fill a requirement, was for a class, or paid," I explained truthfully.

That was why I'd begged Professor Jaffey to include my under-funded ass on one of the Rydor Corp teams. It *paid.* Though I had later learned that Professor Jaffey intentionally kept opportunities from me, because I couldn't serve her purposes if I got on someone else's radar.

She'd played a long game with me. And almost won.

Jordie raised his cup. "Here here. I was a bartender all through my PhD program. I feel like that taught me just as many skills."

I nodded. "I worked in bakeries. *Lots* of life skills."

"You worked in a bakery? I didn't know that." Wes came over to us.

"It was perfect because it was bright and early before classes. That's where Jett's favorite cookie recipe came from." My heart fluttered a little. We'd driven in together and while I missed my special morning time with Evan, it had been nice.

"Wes, whatever you think we did, we didn't do it." Margie's voice went tart.

Wes put his arm around my waist. "I'm here for her. How's your day going?"

Looking up at him, I beamed. "Wes is my mate. My day's going great. Yours?"

"Better now that I'm with you." He grinned.

Tish and Jordie chuckled.

"Congrats, Wes." Tish raised her can of soda.

"Oh. I see." Margie looked over at the door, her expression went bland. "Oh my. Look who's gracing us with his presence. How exactly did Spencer find you, because he found *you* right? You, or Wes, didn't put in for this position because it doesn't exist."

Ummm...

Spencer was immediately greeted by people.

"The kitchen, I believe," Wes interjected, giving Margie a hard look. He turned to me. "That's where you first met, right?"

I thought for a moment and laughed. "You're right. He did find me in the kitchen. In my pajamas."

Well, Wes' clothes.

"The kitchen." Tish laughed. "That's a good one. I always forget that you two are packmates."

Whatever answer Margie was expecting, that wasn't it.

"Getting the job the hard way. That's the way to go." Jordie grinned. "My mate works in accounting. Spencer found me in the cafeteria doing my homework. I wouldn't have known they had post doc programs otherwise."

"I tried the easy way once and it didn't work out so well." My breath hitched a little.

Wes squeezed me. "You're here now."

Spencer joined us. "Hello everyone. Margie, Jordie, Tish, Wes." He smiled. "Grace. How is everyone doing?"

Something about the way he said my name sent shivers of delight up my spine.

We all chatted for a few moments, finally Spencer excused himself, but not before his hand grazed mine, sending sparks through me.

Wes pulled me to him. "Let's go get some of that delicious food. I don't know about you, but I'm hungry."

Wes squeezed my hand as his truck pulled into the driveway of the house. "I love this. I get to drive to and from work with you and we get to eat lunch together. Well, if Tish doesn't monopolize you. I work with one of her packmates."

"I like her. Margie doesn't like me." I sighed. Though most people seemed nice.

"Margie doesn't like anyone. Especially me when I tell her that they can't do things to the firewall." He rolled his eyes and got out of the truck, coming over to the other side to help me out.

We went into the kitchen where Riley was cooking under the direction of Jett and the assistance of Brennan.

Riley grinned, waving around some tongs, my apron with peaches on it over her outfit. "I'm making dinner, fuckers."

It smelled delightful. "I can't wait. Should I set the table?"

"Please," Brennan said. "Wes, pour drinks. We're just waiting on Evan and Spencer."

I put my stuff upstairs and changed, then went back down to the dining room to do my assigned task. As I was setting out plates, arms circled my waist, and the smell of lemonade went straight to my pussy.

"Mmmm, I missed you this morning." Evan nibbled on my ear, heat searing me.

"Me, too." I leaned into him, rubbing my ass against him. "But we'll still get a couple of mornings most weeks." Which made me so happy. I loved that time with him, too.

"Hello." Spencer leaned in the doorway, in his suit, holding a bottle of champagne.

"Hi." I went a little giddy inside.

"Oooh, you got the good stuff." Evan let go of me and went to the hutch and got out champagne flutes.

"But of course." Spencer gave me the softest of kisses on the lips. "Hi, Darling. Your first day went well?"

"It did." I rested my head on his chest, putting my arms around him.

"Dinner time, fuckers," Riley yelled from the kitchen.

A moment later Riley brought out a platter of something fried, gleaming with sauce, sesame seeds, and green onions. "Looks good, right?"

"It does." Brennan set a bowl of fried rice and a bowl of sautéed vegetables on the table.

"But these, these will be best because I made them. My aunt's secret recipe." Jett placed a plate of eggrolls on the table, along with some sauce.

"Oooh." I practically drooled at the delicious smells.

Spencer poured the champagne and we all sat down.

"A toast to Grace's first day of work." Spencer held up his glass.

We toasted and dug into the delicious dinner.

"So good, Riley. You planned the menu?" I asked.

"Fuck yeah. I apparently need to cook more. Jett and Spence know how to make the good dinners. Don't worry, we'll work on dessert," she told me.

Cook more? That sounded like her sister Sasha talking. Sasha had a whole bunch of opinions on how Riley was being raised here. But Riley should learn to cook. Along with all the other tasks you needed to know when living on your own.

"I'll teach you whatever you want to know. I can do more than bake," I said. Did they have smokers here so I could make some real barbecue?

"Grace apparently worked at a *bakery*." Wes took another eggroll.

"I did. I baked cupcakes and cookies mostly. Sometimes I helped with the pastries and cakes. It was fun. Also, it made me popular in classes, since I often brought stuff that had been made the day before and didn't sell."

"Your baked goods were a hit at the art club bake sale," Riley added.

"I'm so glad." I'd worked hard to make everything.

"So, who got in trouble?" Wes teased.

Riley told us all about who got in trouble at school today.

"Work went well?" Jett asked me.

"Yep. No trouble there. I like it." I dipped my eggroll in sauce. "Jett, these are so good. Riley, make sure you get your application in for the internship program, and encourage your friends. Maybe I can reach out to your science and math teachers? There aren't very many high school applications, and it closes soon."

"Hiro and I are going to work on ours," Riley said.

"Friday night is the Finchley Academy talent show. I've got a bunch of clients in it, including Rose. Does anyone want to come with me? They always put on a good show." Evan took a bite of rice.

"Me. Rose's routine is fire." Riley stole Evan's eggroll.

"Speaking of Finchley..." Brennan rubbed his forehead, grimacing. "My mother has informed me that there will be no funding for scholarships for next year."

"What?" Evan looked like he was about to cry. Those scholarships were used to get young omegas out of bad situations by sending them to omega boarding schools.

"That bitch. Let me at her." Riley made a face.

"This is unacceptable. You know why she's doing this. To punish us," Jett stated, taking a sip of champagne.

"I know." Brennan sighed.

"I've already found a lawyer that specializes in small family foundations. To start, we won't need a staff, other than an assistant. The board is right here." Spencer took another bite.

Jett nodded. "Let's do it. You've been talking about starting our own foundation for years."

"You're right, it's time. Spence, we'll talk later and figure out how much we'll need to get started. I need to determine if I'm going to have to demand my share or not," Brennan told us.

"Do it anyway. Force property sales if you have to. Katie's gotten her share, so should you. You got degrees, found mates, started a pack. There's no good reason why the Queen Mum should still be holding out on you." Jett said. "Seriously, the scholarships? That's a low blow on her part. They're kids who need help."

"Was it because of me?" My shoulders rounded. The guys had left in the middle of Brennan's mom's big foundation gala because an encounter with Brennan's ex left me injured.

"No. It's because Caroline's a bitch—and so is my mother." Brennan made a face. "Okay, we'll do this. Which means that we need to actually decide on a family last name."

While some people did keep their own last names, especially professionally, it apparently wasn't uncommon for packs to choose one that everyone then took or had a pack name. I liked the idea of choosing a last name together.

"I have more thoughts," Riley stated.

"More swear word last names?" Jett laughed.

They were all very creative.

"No. If we truly want to piss off the Queen Mum, let's take Grace's last name. It's pretty," Riley suggested.

My last name. I tapped my lips with my finger. What was there about my last name?

"I like that," Jett said.

"That's an idea, just take someone's last name here in the pack instead of creating our own." Brennan nodded. "Grace, you're frowning hard. What's wrong?"

I do hope that you're not using your identity from the other world.

"I have to change my last name," I blurted, sucking in a breath. "I remember now. I... I forgot. Sorry..."

Spencer patted my shoulder. "It's all right, Grace. They told you to change your name?"

I nodded. "Because of the whole *people trying to kill me* thing. Also, the *not sure if I'm actually supposed to be on this world* thing."

"That makes sense," Jett added.

"If you don't want to create one, we could use mine," Spencer offered. "I don't mind. We could pick a pack name, as well. Whatever you wish."

"Really?" Jett asked. "Oooh, the Queen Mum would be *pissed*. The Thanukos Pack. It has a nice sound to it."

"That's a thought. If we do this, I'd like to stay head alpha. I'm happy handling the family finances and investments. But I'm no longer interested in going to events simply for appearance. Since Spence and Grace like them, they can do most of it, and the rest of us will just go to what we want. How does that sound?" Brennan offered.

"Sold," Jett said.

"Me, too," Wes agreed.

"I don't mind." Spencer looked at me. "Grace?"

"I'll go to all the things with you. The science dinner was fun." I got a little giddy.

"I can't believe your mom would cut the scholarships. She's literally saving omega lives." Evan looked defeated.

"I know, Love," Brennan soothed. "We'll work quickly to make sure they're covered for the next school year. Just try not to hand out new ones without talking to me. At some point we should have actual guidelines, maybe a formal application process."

Evan nodded. "Yeah, we probably should. As long as my current school babies are covered, I'll do whatever you need."

"It's one thing to demand that we attend events or hire a housekeeper, it's another to play with people's livelihoods. These kids are innocent," Jett said. "We'll back you."

"We will," Wes said.

"Oh, look, Marcos took our pack crest and turned it into a really great tattoo design. Let's do this." Riley got out her phone.

"Can Riley get a tattoo?" I asked. The design was really cool.

"A pack tattoo with a guardian present, once she's sixteen," Evan said. Her birthday was in November.

Brennan had a pensive look on his face. "Okay. I know what we need to do. It's just hard."

"I know, Honey. We're here." Jett squeezed his arm.

"Okay, first thing first. All in favor of starting a family foundation to cover the scholarships?" Brennan asked.

We all raised our hands.

"Okay, Spence and I will get started. We should also find a new housekeeper, unless you want to go back to the chore rotation." Brennan said.

"Let's just do the chore rotation," Jett offered.

"We should warn the sister pack. So, they're aware when your mom makes them take sides," Wes said. "I'll do that."

Brennan nodded. "Also, we're *not there yet,* but if we're doing this, then I'll also get the paperwork started to add Grace to the pack. Because it's a process. Grace, do you want a house like Evan?"

What? I just stared at him as so many feelings bombarded me. Did Brennan just ask me to eventually be part of the pack? While I knew it would happen at some point, after everything we'd been through I hadn't expected him to be the one to say it. Especially so soon.

"Yes. On her own island. And a horse," Riley said.

Words didn't form. What the what what?

"Just breathe, Darling, this is a wonderful thing." Spencer said as Wes squeezed my hand.

"That would be great, Bren," Wes said for me.

"Oh, you ride?" Spencer asked me.

"Cowboy style," Riley answered.

That was true. But I still had no words. This was a big deal. I obviously wasn't going to say *no*, but for Brennan to mention it like this?

Huge.

Wes hauled me into his lap and held me to him. "Breathe."

I took a breath. "I'm okay. Surprised. But okay." My chest shuddered. "Thanks, Bren."

"It's just practical," Brennan brushed off. "I mean you're here to stay, and you live here in the house, and if we're altering the charter anyway we might as well..."

I got off Wes' lap and gave Brennan a hug. His arms wrapped around me, as did his pine scent.

"Don't we need to vote?" Jett joked. "Also, we never voted on how Evan and Grace are getting married. I still vote for pushing them out of an airplane."

"Absolutely *not*." Evan gave Jett a playful push. "Grace, them deciding how we get married is not a thing."

"When it's *time*, all for adding Grace to the pack?" Brennan asked, my arms still around him.

Everyone's hands raised. My heart thundered as Evan gave me a kiss. I was going to join the pack. At some point. Wow. So many feelings.

"While we're voting, ass tattoos or arms?" Riley added. "Design is good?"

Arm won. The design *was* good. Though Wes wanted to adjust it a little.

"Okay. All we need is a last name and we'll do this." Brennan looked at Spencer.

"I'm serious. But I understand if you'd rather make one up," Spencer said. "It's also a decision that doesn't need to be made today."

"I like it. It works. I'm tired of being a Morris," Brennan told us.

There was power behind Spencer's last name. Morris had power too. But Spencer's last name was more widely known. His family back in Greece was powerful and very rich.

Also, I'm guessing it really would piss off the Queen Mum.

"Let's vote," Spencer said.

It was unanimous.

"Final vote. Are we going to war with the Queen Mum if it becomes necessary? Wes and Ri, um, I might need your help to handle fallout," Brennan looked at them, probably silently asking them to do computer hacker things.

All of us raised our hands.

"It's settled then." Brennan's look went grim. "If it comes to it, the Thanukos pack is declaring war on the Queen Mum. Because it's one thing to mess with us, it's another thing to punish kids."

Chapter Twenty-Two

Brennan

I sat in my office, going over spreadsheets on my laptop, doing the math. Again. A sigh escaped my lips. Why wouldn't the numbers magically bend to my will?

Of course, I knew very well that wasn't how accounting worked.

Terrance knocked on my open door. "Bren?"

"Come in." I sighed again.

"That good?" Terrance took a seat in the chair across from my desk. "While I trust you, and know you're a visionary, are we really going to take the financial risk of historically renovating that old estate?"

"We specialize in unique properties. What would be more special than being transported to the era of Tea-Time Britain? I'm not saying the guests would have to dress the part–or even the staff, but think of the possibilities?" I suggested, seeing the entire thing in my head.

Grace had made me watch a movie on her laptop about the immersive resort, and while I wasn't completely sold on the idea, I'd gotten some good ideas.

His fingers tapped on his chin. "True. But the cost."

"Considering it's a historical property, and we have to meet certain criteria anyway, it's not that much higher. Reg and his crew will only be able to do so much, we might have to bring in specialists," I told him, checking the numbers again.

"All I hear is the sound of money leaving." His look wasn't completely serious. "Are you sure we can't negotiate with the historical office?"

I sucked in a breath. "I pissed off my mother. Now the historical office is on my ass, and they've changed the rules. I'm guessing there's a correlation."

When we'd voted at family dinner a couple of days ago, I hadn't counted on her making war on the business front.

"Is this over whatever happened at the gala?" He frowned. "After you left with Grace she was grumpy for the rest of the presentation."

"That and I fired the housekeeper she made me hire." I sighed.

You'd think I'd done something horrible by the way my mother reacted to that.

"Though honestly, this is on us," I added. "We were checking with our county's office. Turns out, it's registered in both this and the next county because when it was built the lines were different."

"Shit." Terrance rubbed his bald head.

"It won't be that bad. I'll send it to you along with the proposals we're getting from restoration specialists."

"Are you okay?" Terrance got up, shut my door, and sat back down. He knew exactly what my mother was capable of, having been there for me—and the company—after my car accident.

"I think I'm about to start a war with my mother. Short version—she's stopping the funding for all the scholarships the foundation gives omegas." I glanced back at the numbers on my laptop.

He whistled. "That's low."

"It is. My pack is starting a foundation of our own to cover the gaps. I actually have to go over to Compass BioTek so Spencer and I can meet with the lawyer." Which is why I'd been crunching numbers.

"Honestly, that sounds like a good call—but maybe have better galas?" he joked, having been to plenty of my mother's.

"We now own an event venue." I grinned.

He chuckled. "That we do."

"Things could get bad. She has a lot of contacts in this town." I winced at the potential fallout. Those who went up against her seldom won.

"We're not in our twenties anymore. If she starts messing with our business, we'll fight back," he assured. "Also, very little of our business is here—and while people know who she is here, most of the places we operate don't know or care about her."

"True." Sometimes I forgot that.

I thought for a moment. "We need to go over *everything* and make sure it's tight so there are no more oversights like this one with the historical office. We also need to lock down communications and be very careful. Wes will help us."

Riley had already built a backdoor into the Morris company server. It wasn't paranoia when your mom had spies everywhere.

"Got it." He nodded. "What about Grace?"

"Grace sadly isn't a scientist that makes explosions. She just maths." I grinned. Terrance had set so many things on fire in chemistry when we were in high school.

"You're okay with Grace now?" Terrance asked.

"I have to be. Two of my packmates are bonded to her, one is courting her. Also, she's sort of growing on me. Don't get me wrong, she does so many things that bug me, but she checks out, and she's not the mountain I want to jump from," I admitted quietly.

"I see."

"Anyhow, let's be careful. You know how quickly things can spin out of control with my mother." This phone call I was about to make could shove it into motion.

"I've got your back, Bren. Always have. What she's doing to you isn't healthy or fair. It's been a long time coming and there are people who will support you in this."

"Thank you. You're a good friend, Terrance," I said.

Terrance grinned. "Who? Me? I just want to keep this company in business. My children have expensive hobbies."

He stood and left. I closed the door and called the Morris family lawyer.

"Brennan, what can I do for you?" Ian Murphy drawled. He was an old man who'd literally watched me grow up.

"I'd like to claim full access to the trusts and all my assets," I said.

"Now Brennan, you know I can't do that without permission from your mother."

I clicked out of the spreadsheet on my laptop and over to the trust documents Katie had sent me. "She's not the executor of either. I meet all the criteria–and I'm happy to furnish any documents you need proving my age, pack, and marital status."

"Well, Brennan, there are issues," he mumbled.

"I've sent letters of wellness to you multiple times. Katie has full access to hers. I meet the same criteria." This wasn't the first time I'd tried to get full access–and not just the small allowance my grandmother's trust gave me.

"I'll talk to your mother," he blustered. "Also, the assets for your trust are not... liquid."

To make it harder for me to claim, my mother had 'invested' most of it–including buying the building that was now the foundation headquarters.

"Never mind, I'll just have my lawyer call you." I winced as I ended the call.

That *was* a declaration of war. But Jett was right. There was no legal reason for them to keep my money from me. I'd read the documents and had our new pack lawyer look over them as well.

I called our pack lawyer and left her a message. Letting my assistant know that I was stepping out, I got my motorcycle and went over to Compass BioTek, a pass waiting for me at the front desk. I went up to Spencer's office.

"Brennan, dear." Mrs. Katsopolis smiled at me from her desk.

"Mrs. K." I grinned back. "Is the boss ready for me?"

"Absolutely."

I entered his office, which was understated and sophisticated. There were tiny wisps of Grace as I took a seat in the offered chair.

"Are you okay?" Spencer asked over his laptop.

"I'm having the pack lawyer start the process of getting my trusts." I gulped, because I was kicking the hornet's nest here.

"If it's too much–"

I shook my head. "It's my money and I'm tired of my mother trying to control it."

And me. Though me acquiescing had been less about getting access to my money and more about the fear of her upending my life like she'd done years ago.

Not to mention the financial plan I'd drawn up to get the foundation started required contributions from both Spencer and I, as well as the pack. While Spencer could fund this foundation himself, given this was going to be *our* foundation, he shouldn't have to.

"I know at the start we're just trying to cover the outstanding scholarships for the omegas currently enrolled. But when we get situated, there's something I'd like to do," Spencer said quietly.

"Of course. I'm sure Riley has lots of ideas." I grinned. She'd already mentioned getting her school a new computer lab and better art stuff.

He laughed. "Oh, I'm sure." His look turned wistful. "I'd like to endow some scholarships for betas in the sciences. One at the university Elaris and I attended, and one at Hadley Hall, or some equally prestigious academic institution, such as the one Sonja is dean of. Elaris never got the opportunity to attend a high school like that. I'd like to give others the chance. I've been thinking about it for a while."

Elaris. He so seldom mentioned her. All I knew was that she was smarter than Spencer and had radical ideas.

"That's a great idea, go for it. Maybe do all three." I wasn't about to argue with scholarships. No one in the pack would. It also seemed like a nice tribute to her. I'd never met her but to be both the love of Spencer's life and to have accomplished everything she had at such a young age, she must have been something.

Mrs. K appeared in the doorway. "He's here."

The foundation lawyer came in and the three of us went over everything we needed to do to lay the groundwork for the Thanukos Family Foundation.

"Well, we have our homework," Spencer stated when the lawyer left.

I looked at the list of action items. "Indeed."

There'd be lots to talk about at family dinners as we got the logistics ironed out.

"I'll speak to the headmistress at Finchley to get things going in regards to making sure those students keep their funding. Don't worry, everything will be fine," Spencer assured. "We won't let your mother win."

My phone rang. My mother. I silenced it. "No, we won't. Spence, you're okay with all this? The names and everything?"

That was a very strange dinner conversation. I'd never expected him to offer his name. He'd always been content to be in the background. Not that I'd minded. Though I absolutely didn't mind him taking over as the face of the pack. I liked being in charge, but I didn't like being social. Neither did Wes. Something required for a pack of our stature.

Not to mention a drawback to us claiming his last name was that it would catapult our social status. Everyone was going to invite us to everything. Everywhere. *No thanks.*

Spencer nodded. "Of course. As long as you're okay with it."

"I am. I'll get that process started, too."

"Can I choose her house?" Spencer's look went pensive.

That took me a moment. "Grace. You want to choose the house she gets when she joins the pack? Is that what she wants?"

It didn't need to be a house, it could be any sort of asset. Paintings. Stocks. Jewelry. Money. Horses. It just had to be hers alone.

"It is. Please? If I'm not overstepping. Wes is fine with it." He looked so earnest.

"Go for it." I didn't have time to do it, and Spencer would choose something she'd adore. "But we're not there yet."

"I know." He nodded. "I can get her whatever I'd like?"

"Go for it." Then I told him about the historical office and what was happening with the estate. "This could get messy."

"While I generally respect Siobhan, if she crosses lines with my company, I'll show no mercy," he stated.

"I appreciate that." While I believed him, because like me, he was a businessman, I also really wanted to see what him showing no mercy looked like. I seldom saw him as anything but congenial.

"At some point we should talk about how far we want to take this," he added.

"That's a good point." While this was a war I wanted to win, I didn't want to stoop to her level.

Then again, I'd do anything for my pack—and I wasn't quite sure my appearance-oriented mother truly understood that.

Chapter Twenty-Three

Evan

Friday night, Grace, Riley, and I filed into the packed auditorium at the Finchley Academy for Exemplary Omegas. I winced at all the alpha smells permeating the state-of-the art building, even though the air filters were running.

"It's so nice that all these families are here for a talent show." Grace looked around, holding my hand.

"Yeah, that's not why people are here." Riley checked her phone and led us down and to the right.

"Well, there are families here. Mostly for the local students," I said. Finchley was one of the best omega schools in the country. People sent their omegas to get an excellent education. Many of their graduates transferred to top universities or took jobs at prestigious companies. Or made *very* good matches. Often all three.

Every year *omegas of note* were chosen from graduating omegas worldwide. It wasn't uncommon for Finchley to be represented.

As we made our way to our seats, a lot of people ignored me, but looked Grace up and down with interest. Shit. We should have brought alphas with us. I got out my phone and texted the group chat. I'd forgotten who else Finchley events drew.

"They're *shopping*. Well, that's what Rose calls it." Riley waved at someone, and we sat. "Finchley goes from high school all the way through undergrad. Packs come to school events to see who might be available."

That they did. Especially younger alphas that might not be quite ready for an omega and perfectly willing to wait for the right one.

Grace frowned. "Even college is a little young, isn't it? I mean I had a bunch of friends get married in the last year or right after graduation, but it still feels early."

"Even though a lot of work has been done to make it a choice, not a necessity, plenty of omegas do still choose to mate in their early to mid-twenties. A lot of it is biology. That pull to want an alpha or two of your own." I put an arm around Grace as a group of alphas in suits that looked like trouble stared unabashedly at her.

There was also the fact that a heat without an alpha could be very painful–and too many of those could have long-term health effects. While the Omega Center did help you find heat partners, provided comfortable places to have a heat, and even offered safe ways to go through it partnerless, it was an intimate experience, and you craved a permanent partner to share it with.

I'd already been dating Wes when I'd awakened as an omega, so I never had to worry. But with my clients, there was often a big biological push. Heat suppressants were something many chose, especially when trying to get through university or establish a career. However, heavy-duty blockers and heat suppressants could only be taken for so long without causing health problems.

"Still..." Her frown deepened.

"That's why the Center exists. To make sure matches are above-board and in everyone's best interest. The Center even looks over agreements for matches they didn't make. Like mine," I offered. "And yours."

They also had a calculator to help determine the value of a mating gift. Both to make sure the omega wasn't shorted and ensure the alphas didn't want an omega so badly that they went into debt.

"Me?" Her head cocked.

"You don't think Mrs. Beekman won't be all over the pack agreement to make sure you're being treated fairly?" I grinned.

Grace's advocate had come for another home visit accompanied by our dear friend Luc the integration counselor, who'd met with the whole pack.

"True." She nodded.

Riley rolled her eyes. "Alphas. They just seem like so much work."

"Which is why all your friends seem to be young alphas in the making?" I teased.

"Fuck you, you doofus." She scratched her nose with her middle finger. There were little spiderwebs painted on her black nails.

I looked at my phone, then waved at my coworker, Carly, who sat nearby with her alphas and toddler. She had a few clients in the show tonight, too. We tried our best to attend things for our clients, especially the ones that didn't have much—or any—family.

The lights dimmed and the show started. I peered at the program to see who was in what number. This wasn't like my high school talent shows with students singing karaoke and doing marginally appropriate dance numbers. There were sets, costumes, and lighting. Everyone's talent was at a high level. Some school groups also performed tonight—like the cheer team and dance squad that Rose was part of, the choirs, and music ensembles.

It was also quite *long*.

"Those kids," Grace breathed, as the cheer squad performed. "That is so much better than we ever were, and we competed."

"We're in fancy-land, Grace," Riley whispered. "Tons of rich kids. Most of them have been in dance classes or music lessons since birth."

Children didn't take the basic blood test, the prick-test, that showed which of the three main designations they were until middle school. However, families often had a general idea of what their children might be, and some tendencies did sometimes manifest early.

Like baby Grace building nests in the laundry.

The team certainly was good. The show finished and everyone poured into the adjoining gym for a reception.

Grace darted off to find the omega science teacher who'd once been one of my clients so she could talk to her about recruiting students for the Compass BioTek internship program.

I made my rounds, finding all my clients and complementing their performances. Finally, I went over to Rose.

For a moment she looked anxious, and her voice lowered. "I thought I saw some bad alphas, like the ones my uncle always owes money to."

"Thank you for telling me." That didn't sound good.

Had the uncle wanted part of the money to pay his debts? Perhaps they were who the doctor had gotten the drugs from that had made Rose an omega? There was so much we didn't know about Rose's circumstances even with her mom and uncle being in jail.

Wes joined me. "There you are."

"Where's Grace?" I leaned into him.

"With Spence, who's chatting up the headmistress," he said. "Thanks for letting us know we were needed."

Rose looked at Wes and her mouth formed a little 'o." The first time I met her, she looked at a picture of my mates and told me that Wes was her favorite.

"This is Wes. Wes, this is Rose." We went back into the gym. There were less people now, as families took their students out for an ice cream or a late dinner, but there were also alphas talking to omegas–and students speaking to each other. I spied Riley in a group–some of her schoolmates probably had siblings here.

"Thanks for coming." Rose gave me a hug then went off to join her friends.

"Let's find Grace," I said to Wes.

Headmistress Nikita found me first. "Evan. Did you like it?"

"Amazing as always," I said. "So many people."

"I know. But it's nearing the end of the year, which always brings interest. Speaking of interest," she looked around and lowered her voice. "Can we talk?" She was tall for an omega, and on the younger side for a headmistress.

"I'll round up the others," Wes told me, giving me a squeeze and leaving.

"Some men were asking about Rose. Something about her uncle talking to them about a possible match. It didn't feel right because I know Rose is a ward of the Center." The headmistress frowned. "Also, beyond the age gap, they were... how do I put it? Not the type of pack I'd encourage a Finchley student to choose? Not that alphas in, um, the *family business*, don't deserve to be matched with omegas, but these particular ones... you understand my concern here?" Her eyes pleaded with me.

Gangsters. Gangsters were asking about Rose. These were probably the bad men Rose was talking about.

"No. Rose's uncle isn't allowed to do such things. She's still a ward of the Center. And sixteen." I frowned. "Are those men still here?"

"No, they asked when the next mixer was, and left. They didn't ask for an introduction and I didn't see them speak to her. It was a little odd," Headmistress Nikita said.

"We don't have any record of who they are, do we?"

She shook her head. "Other than getting a clip from security footage and running facial recognition?"

"We can do that. Sorry, with everything going on, this makes me worry," I said.

"Me, too. Because it affects everyone's safety," she stated, expression serious.

"I know." I recalled what she'd said previously about not being able to keep Rose if she put everyone in danger.

"Also, I got notification from the Morris Foundation that they are discontinuing funding for the scholars here. However, it seems that Spencer Thanukos is starting a foundation and offered to cover it. Do you know anything about that?" she asked. "I definitely want these young people to continue their education, and we can't internally fund all of them. It just seems odd that he'd do that. I'm pretty sure his omega isn't a former Finchley student."

"Spencer's my packmate. When we were blindsided by the Morris Foundation's decision, he decided it was time to step up. And Grace, I wish she would have gotten the opportunity to go to a place like Finchley." What would it have been like for her, had she grown up omega?

The headmistress gave me a look of surprise. "You're in a two-omega pack? I didn't know that."

"Technically, Grace is a gamma. I love her," I confessed.

"You do?" Grace wrapped her arms around me. "Sorry if I'm crashing something important. Riley's getting restless."

"Hi." I gave Grace a squeeze. "This is Headmistress Nikita. Headmistress, this is my mate Grace."

"Hi." Grace waved.

"It's very nice to meet you. I'll send you what we discussed." She nodded and left.

"Everything okay?" Grace asked.

"I hope so." I took her hand. "Should we get Riley and have some ice cream?"

Grace nodded. "Absolutely."

Chapter Twenty-Four

Grace

"How's your memory?" Dr. Davidson asked me as I sat in a cheerful exam room at the Omega Center clinic, for yet another check-up.

Everything at the Omega Center was cheerful and relaxing, to help put omegas at ease. Something I appreciated.

"Um, I'm remembering more and more." Anxiety shot through me. In some ways it was better when I didn't remember my professor's betrayal, or the fear I'd felt when witnesses started dying, or how lonely I'd been back in my world...

She beamed and made a note on her tablet. "Wonderful. Anything new? You started your new job recently?"

"Yes. I like it." My legs swung. Everyone in Special Projects was pretty nice, and I was adjusting and learning. I liked the fact that I could work two days a week from home. The work days were also a little shorter here, with longer breaks and lunches. They actually wanted you to take them, too. Same with vacations and sick days.

I could get used to that.

"That's great." The doctor nodded and made another note. "Don't be afraid to sign up for a stress-management workshop. They're very good. A lot of people think omegas can't handle stressful jobs. They can, they just manage stress differently. Also, with your head injury you might find it helpful. Don't forget to take breaks when you need them. I know you're mated, but if you want scent blockers I can prescribe some. Sometimes work is more comfortable that way."

"I think I'm good?" I didn't truly smell like *omega*, I just smelled interesting–and mated.

"That is fine. Let me know if you change your mind." She looked at me and frowned. "You're not wearing your walking cast or wrist splint."

"I feel fine. Can I just not wear them anymore? They're annoying." I shrugged.

She peered at the screen, clicking through a few things, probably looking at the x-rays they'd taken today. "Wow, yes, you can leave them off if you don't think you need them. You're healing just fine. Though you'll want to wear sneakers for a while, and go easy on your wrist. Your alphas are taking such good care of you."

"Um, yeah." I wasn't sure what the correlation was.

Dr. Davidson chuckled. Um, what wasn't I getting here?

"Can I ride my motorcycle? I need to practice so I can take the test." I was itching to ride it. Brennan was like *No, you can't until the doctor says.* Ugh. I was fine when I rode behind him. Why couldn't I ride mine? Also, I wanted to get my driver's licence.

"Give it a couple weeks for the motorcycle. But you could try driving a car if you'd like." She made some notes then clicked through more screens.

"O-kay." I'd need to get some cute but comfy shoes for the symposium.

"Your hormone levels are looking good. Whatever it is you're doing, keep doing it." She grinned at me. "Or should I say *who*."

My cheeks burned. The doctors at the Omega Center always made a whole lot of sex jokes and I wasn't used to it yet.

She looked back at the screen. "No, really, your omega's heat finished a couple of weeks ago and your hormone levels are still great. Also, did you finally meet with a nutritionist? I know it seems silly, but good nutrition is really important for your hormones, especially as you age."

"Evan's been making me take supplements and drink this special tea. I haven't met with a nutritionist, but Mrs. Beekman gave me a cheat sheet for my phone to help me make better choices in the work cafeteria." Which was fine. I didn't have a problem choosing a yogurt with more protein, shrimp instead of chicken, berries instead of melons, or having a salad made with spinach.

Spencer had been serious about us improving our eating habits. It was a good thing Special Projects had a coffee pot in the break room, because one little mug of coffee in the morning was *not* enough for me. Though he did keep bringing me fancy tea lattes, which was sweet. Especially since he usually got me a pastry, too.

"Very good." She nodded.

"What does Evan's heat have to do with *my* hormone levels?" I didn't understand the correlation.

She grinned. "Having an omega in the house is one of the best things for a gamma. They're like walking hormone diffusers—especially during their heat."

I frowned. "I thought gammas don't always react to things the way other designations do."

"True. But the way you react and the way they affect your body are two different things," she explained. "This is good. I was getting worried about your hormone levels. Gammas can have so many problems if they don't take care of themselves—and it's important to your overall well-being, even if you don't want kids."

My belly twisted. "Right, kids."

"If you're not ready—or never ready—for kids, it's okay. Just communicate with your mates. Mrs. Beekman can even facilitate if you need her to," Dr. Davidson assured.

"My cycles are so screwed up, and well, that means I probably will have trouble, right?" I chewed on my lower lip, still unsure about kids. I'd had a terrible mother, so I worried that I wouldn't be a good one.

Though Spencer, Evan, and Wes would make such great dads. I had a feeling Jett and Bren would as well.

The doctor looked at her computer. "You mentioned last time that your cycles were irregular and painful and that you haven't had one since moving in with your mates. I suggested making a gynecological appointment to run tests to see where your cycles fall on the scale, since betas and omegas have very different cycles and gammas can be anywhere in-between. It looks like you haven't made one. Have you ever had a gynecological exam? You have practically no medical records before a few months ago."

"I didn't know I was a gamma until a few months ago. And well, between college and getting my PhD, going to the doctor wasn't a priority." Which was the truth.

"Oh? I thought that was just the memory loss. You were never tested and given an omega designation in school? Or were you just waiting to awaken?" She frowned at me, probably wondering, like so many others, if I'd grown up in some fringe group.

"I was never tested, ever, and no one ever said I was an omega when I was little." Except for Wes, but I thought it was just some cute phrase or something.

"Ever?" She frowned. "So, you thought you were beta until a few months ago? That explains so much." She started typing.

"I'll make a note. Does Mrs. Beekman have you doing any sort of education program? Gammas still need to know the basics."

"Between her and Evan, I have more videos to watch than I have time for," I laughed.

"Good. I wish we had baselines for you. But we'll figure it out. Let's talk about those cycles. You mentioned bad cramps and irregularity?"

"Yeah, usually it's months between them. The actual period isn't bad or long, but the cramps that come before it are *curling into a ball and crying* bad. Sometimes I have a fever, vomiting, and headaches—there are even times that I can't get out of bed." Which was always hard to explain to male bosses and professors.

Her eyebrows rose. "And you never thought to see a doctor?"

"I'd see doctors on campus, who would just change my birth control and tell me being a woman was painful." I played with my ring.

She sighed. "I hope you reported those doctors. Also, campus doctors should still be adding their findings to your universal medical record. I'm making you an appointment. The thing with gammas is that each one of you is *so* different. It might take a couple cycles to figure out what should be normal for you."

"Okay. If I do want kids, do you think there'd even be a chance?" I chewed on my lower lip. If I actually couldn't, Evan should know sooner rather than later, given having kids meant the most to him.

"We can run some tests. However, you're mated to a male omega, which is one of the best fertility treatments out there. I'd recommend, when you're ready, starting with Evan. Once you remove your birth control implant, get a round of hormone injections so you can sync up your cycle with his, eat well, let him have dibs on your pussy during a heat or two, and take it from there," she told me. "He can get you pregnant anytime, but he'll go into overdrive during his heat."

"Dibs on my pussy? Is that a technical term?" I laughed. Evan would love that.

"Yes." She grinned back. "Now, let's talk about your mate's heat. How did it affect you? Was it as scary as you thought?"

My cheeks warmed again. "It was pretty nice. What I can remember. Is that normal?"

"It can be. Like I said, every gamma is a little different. It didn't affect your cycles?" she asked.

I shook my head. "It can, right? This means I can't have kids?"

Because I had half thought that it would happen. I'd had a little spotting, but I'd also had a whole lot of dick.

"It means that you haven't synced. It's only been a few months," she replied.

"The guys think I spiked—or something close. But that was during the part I can't remember." I shrugged.

"Oh." She made more notes. "Did they mention why they think that?"

"Fever. I whined a lot. Wanted all the sex. Was really wet. Smelled like I needed to be fucked." My head ducked a little in embarrassment.

"Grace, this is all perfectly natural, no need to be embarrassed." Her look softened. "You said that you didn't know you were a gamma until a few months ago. You're a textbook gamma, which usually means there was a rough period in your life that forced your body to stop developing. Do you remember when that might have been? Maybe a time where you didn't have enough to eat or feared for your life?"

How did I even answer that? Also, I was still so confused about all this genetic-wise/

"Shit went down when I was seventeen. That might have been it." It was the truth. If anything was bad enough to stop a genetic process, it was wilderness camp. Though given I was from a different world, I still had no idea how this all worked.

The doc made some more notes. "The reason why I was asking was because the earlier it happens, the closer a body is to being a beta–the later, the more omega-like you can be. It just aids us in helping us figure out what is or should be normal for you." She eyed my shirt, which was the Rockland Raiders shirt Riley had made me for my birthday. "You like skate smash?"

"Evan's sister and I are going to a game tonight." I was excited.

"Then let's get finished up so that you can go have a good time."

Rubbing my arm from another shot, I found Evan in the center rec room, having a talk with a sad-looking Rose as they made bracelets. Riley had me help her make a lot of beaded bracelets in preparation for tonight. Apparently, bracelet trading was a big part of professional skate smash.

She waved and I joined them. "Am I interrupting?"

"Iris is bugging me again." Rose sighed as she strung another bead.

"Again?" I gave her a little hug. Her older sister was still giving her crap about staying in Rockland and attending Finchley instead of going home and getting a job–even though her mom and step-dad continued to tell her to stay.

"Yeah." She sighed.

Evan's look told me there was a whole lot more to it.

"I'll just take a car and get Riley and go to the game," I suggested.

"It's fine, Grace," Evan brushed off. "Rose, I want you to stay on campus as much as you can, okay? If you leave, make sure it's in a group—and call me if you need me."

"Okay." Rose rolled her eyes in that teenage way that meant us adults were overreacting. "Grace, have fun."

Evan and I left and got into his 4x4.

"Is everything okay?" I asked him.

He frowned, probably trying to determine what he could tell me. "Disconcerting alphas are interested in Rose. I'm not sure if it's just a pack being a little inappropriate, or if there's something more here."

"Oh. More? Like having to do with her uncle and whatever money problems he's having?" I frowned.

"Yeah. I need to call Detective Esposito." He sighed. "How'd the doctor's appointment go?"

"They said I can keep off the brace and walking cast. Of course, she also says that I should wait a few weeks before riding my motorcycle. But apparently they're healing well because my alphas take good care of me? I don't know what that means." I rolled my eyes as we plodded through traffic to get to Riley's school.

"Well, that's good news. It's also fast, isn't it?" Evan grinned. "So... alpha cum has many properties."

"Yes, they're full of happy juice. Spencer explained it." I nodded.

"Yes. However, accelerated alpha healing properties can be passed on through alpha cum." His grin widened.

"Wow, they really do have magic dicks," I laughed.

Evan nodded. "They do. Though, you said you ended up in the infirmary at the Temporal Authority. Maybe they healed you, too."

"Huh. I never thought about that." I frowned. They had given me different casts. "Um, the Center doctor and I also had a super interesting talk about having kids."

"Did you now?" His lemonade scent flared with lust.

"Yes, sir. Apparently I should try with you first, because you're a walking fertility treatment. When I'm ready, you get dibs on my pussy during your heat." I grinned, running my hand up his leg.

"Watch it, Peaches, or I'll be teaching you to give head in the car." His voice went rough.

I looked at the roof of the car and grinned.

"You've been holding out on me." He grinned. "No wonder Wes is so relaxed when you come home from work. He gets traffic blowjobs?"

"Only sometimes," I laughed. Then there was the whole cock warming thing with Spencer.

"So, I get a kid first? If you decide on them?" He grinned. "We'll have to try so much. Such a hardship."

"I'm not ready, but I thought you'd find that funny," I responded.

"I know. Your career is just starting, but that doesn't mean I can't fantasize." He squeezed my hand. "Just the fact you were talking about it is fucking hot. I wish I could take you home and *practice*."

Heat flared in my core and his nose twitched.

"I'm looking forward to seeing a professional skate smash game. Though Riley is going to be annoyed that you guys have seats two rows behind us." The overprotective dudes in the house didn't think Riley and I should go by ourselves.

"It's just me, Bren, and Jett–and we'll buy you food. Fuck, you smell extra good today."

"Is that a problem? Now that I have a job and stuff, should I take scent blockers? The doctor offered them to me." I chewed on my lower lip.

Apparently there were different sorts. The one she recommended to me just dulled your scent, there were also ones that blocked your perfume and pheromones, and ones that made you appear beta.

"Only if you want to. You can use my scent-nulling body wash and shampoo though, and see if that makes you feel more comfortable. I also have some spray. If someone is being weird, tell Wes or Spencer. I wasn't trying to make you self-conscious. It was a compliment." He gave my knee another squeeze.

"I know. I'm still trying to figure all this out. No one's being weird. It just struck me as strange since I'm not an omega."

"That's what makes people look twice. Because you don't smell like a beta–and it's all mine." He tried to lick my temple.

"Eww, keep your eyes on the road." I laughed.

We finally pulled into Riley's school, where she waited in a matching shirt. She also wore a black kilt, fishnets, and combat boots.

"Fuck of the morning, bitches." Riley climbed into the back of the car.

"Your brother tried to lick me," I tattled.

"Unsanitary." She made a face. "This is why I live at school."

Evan drove us to the arena and parked in the underground lot.

"See you later, be safe," he told us, giving me a kiss, then leaning against his car and checking his phone.

Riley led me toward the entrance. "Where are they sitting?"

"Two rows behind. He promised us food, though."

"Good. I'm going to make them buy me *all* the snacks," she replied.

We went inside the giant arena, which was full of fans wearing Raiders gear. There were also a lot of banners for Rockland's hockey team, which shared the arena.

Riley and I had come early so we could go to a bracelet-trading meet-up which was fun. Some of the bracelets were so pretty.

"Let's find our seats." Riley dragged me into the arena, and we found our seats. We were near the center of the rink, one section up from the ice. It was high energy, with electronic dance music playing.

Skate smash had sort of a rave theme going on—with dance breaks. It was a big-deal professional sport here. The pro teams were mostly alpha females, but there were a few betas and dudes.

"How are tryouts going?" I asked her. Her school skate smash tryouts for next year's team were this week and next.

"Good. Really good. I think I have a chance," she told me. "I'm going for swing, though. Not crusher."

"I'm so glad it's going well. I can't wait to go to your games next year." Swing was essentially the pivot in roller derby—they could switch between the other two positions. Crusher was the blocker, only this was pretty much full-contact and on ice skates.

"Maybe next year we'll win more. The season ended so early this year. Oh, Hiro and I submitted our intern applications today—complete with teacher recommendations." She beamed, looking pleased.

"I'm so glad. I'm proud of the both of you for getting them done." They'd started them over the weekend.

"Oh, I can't wait to work with you. Even Hiro's mom thinks it's a good idea, and nothing impresses her." Riley rolled her eyes.

True. My phone buzzed. A text from Kilroy's mom.

"Do I want to join Kilroy's mom's book club?" I asked. Generally, book clubs were an excuse to drink wine and gossip. It might be fun to meet more omegas.

"I'll check." She frowned and texted someone.

I felt someone behind us. Pine filled my nostrils, and I leaned backwards, and looked up into Brennan's blue eyes.

"Hey fucker, where's my food?" Riley asked. "I want a lime whirl, fried potato balls, and pizza nuggets."

"Beer me—and nacho me." I grinned. Two foods that I was glad this world had.

"Evan's in the food line, Jett's in the drink line. Text your requests." Brennan raked his hand through my hair, nails lightly grazing my scalp in a way that felt nice. Ever since our motorcycle ride he'd been more affectionate with me. Not like Evan and Wes, but it was nice.

I texted them both for us.

Bren still stood there. "We're right here if you need us."

"Sweet baby cheeses, back off, you overprotective fuck. We will be *fine*." Riley rolled her eyes.

"Love you too, Ri." Bren laughed, then left to find his actual seat.

Riley looked at her phone. "Kil says *yes*, because, and I quote, *They have good snacks*."

"Great." I texted Kilroy's mom that I'd love to. She texted me the book title and I looked it up. It was a super smutty boss romance. Oooh.

Both teams came out on the ice to warm up. The Rockland Raiders were in black and silver, the Capitol Crushers in blue and red. They wore jerseys with their nicknames on the back—which were a lot like roller derby names but without the pop culture references. Many wore fishnets, tights, or long socks with their shorts. Some of the helmets were a different color, which designated the *bullet,* the person who scored, which was pretty much a jammer. It was the position I'd played back when getting my PhD, because I was small, fast, and really didn't understand the rules.

Evan and Jett brought us our food, and I dug into my nachos. Yeah, this was the best part of a sporting event. However, it was cold. I texted Evan asking if he had a sweatshirt.

The teams had left, and the mascots were throwing things at the crowd. Riley stuffed a dinosaur-shaped pizza nugget in her mouth.

"Thanks for sharing this with me. Best birthday present ever." I grinned. "And I can't wait to see you play."

Riley leaned her head on my shoulder. "Thanks for giving a shit about me."

"How could I not?" I grinned, putting an arm around her. Just the idea she thought I might not, tugged on my heart.

While I loved Wes, Evan, and Spencer, getting a Riley was the best thing about coming here. Who knew I needed a teenager in my life?

"Hey, will you back me with my sisters?" She stole one of my chips.

"Of course. On what?" I tried to think of what issue her sisters might have now.

"I..." She sat up. "I want to change my last name when the pack does, and Sasha's going to shit a cactus. I... I barely remember my parents. I'm not tied to my last name like they are. But she'll be mad–and make some comment about me just using it for the opportunities. I mean, I will use those, but it's not the only reason. You're my pack, my family. Why wouldn't I? Sonja's going to take a different name when she marries her wife. I think they're merging their names and making something cute."

Oh, my heart. I put my arm around her. "I've got your back. Always."

"Thanks *Dr. Thanukos.* That is so *dope.*" She grinned.

It hit me. "I have consented to eventually being Dr. Thanukos."

Riley nodded. "Yep."

"Grace." Evan stood at the end of the row holding a sweatshirt. I held out my hands and he threw it at me. I caught it and pulled it on, then blew him a kiss. He blew one back and went to sit back down with the guys.

"You two. Fuck me with a pineapple." Riley rolled her eyes.

"Thanks for sharing your brother." I sent a picture to Brennan of me in Evan's hoodie. I still wasn't sure why it bugged him so much, since I'd been told over and over that stealing your mate's clothes was a perfectly normal thing.

"You and Evan have fun this weekend," I added. They were going to do something special while Wes and I went away.

"Why are we being sappy fucks?" She took a chip. The lights started to blink. "Oh good, the intros are going to start. This is gonna be so much fun."

"I'm excited." From what I'd seen online it was just as violent as ice hockey—only with dance breaks—as in the teams dance-battled and did synchronized routines to dance music, complete with lights and lasers.

The arena grew dark, except for blacklights, and some low light on the rink, as fog filled the ice. Music blasted, as lights and lasers flashed and the Capitol Crushers skated out, one after the other, doing spins, flips, and other fancy tricks as they made their way around the rink. Everyone out, they assembled in the middle of the rink and began to dance, in unison, on ice skates. After they finished, someone announced the night's lineup, their pictures flashing up on giant screens as they skated one by one to the bench.

"That's a good intro. But the Raiders' is better. Just you watch," she nodded.

The Raiders did their intro routine and took their seats. The ref came out and the starting six for each team assumed their place on the ice. The music started and lights flashed as the first two minute round, called a succession, started.

The main objective was for the 'bullet' of each team to try to make as many laps around the ice as possible without being impeded by the other team's 'crushers' whose job was to stop them. This was pretty much by any means possible, since this was full-contact, with fist fights, commentary, and penalty boxes.

I looked over at Riley, who was *beaming*, as she yelled and cheered for various players, and predicting moves. I'd found my family. And for that, I was grateful.

Chapter Twenty-Five

Wes

Grace dozed next to me in the passenger seat of the rental car as I followed the directions on my phone. I'd been here many times, but I wasn't usually the one driving. It had also been a while. Nostalgia shot through me as I remembered all the good times Lexi and I had here with our grandparents and cousins.

As I drove through a quaint little seaside town, I made note of what stores were still here, and what new ones looked fun. I pulled into a crowded lot at the pier, since it was a Friday afternoon, and parked the rental car.

"Wake up, Peaches." I shook Grace.

She sat up and looked out the window. Before us was a pier and boardwalk. The sky swing and bubble wheel were in full force.

"Where are we?" she breathed. "I mean, I know we're on the Northeastern Seaboard, but..."

"Welcome to Seaside." I grinned, waiting a moment to see if she figured it out.

Grace sucked in a breath as she put on her sunglasses and grabbed her purse. "Boo-bear, really? Where your grandparents have a beach house?"

"Yep." I grinned. "Grandma even said we can stay there." Anxiousness shot through me. "I wanted to show you the places I told you about when we were kids. I hope this is good."

It wasn't some fancy resort, just a beach town where I spent two weeks a year for a large part of my life. A place I shared things about with her during our seven years of dream visits.

The grin on her face erased my nervousness.

"Are you kidding? I was always so jealous that you got to go to the ocean *every year*." She bounced out of the car. "This is the best. Thank you."

I joined her as we walked toward the noisy pier that was a core memory from my youth. "I thought we could spend the afternoon here. Maybe I could win you a toy. We could ride the sky swing, have funnel cake, and do all the things I used to tell you about. I have a place that I want to take you for dinner, too."

Her fingers entwined with mine. "I can't wait."

The sounds of the boardwalk brought me home. But we didn't stop for snacks or games, yet. Instead, I walked her all the way down the pier to the railings, the smell of popcorn giving way to salt and fish.

"This is the ocean I used to tell you about. The water is *cold*. But we can go swimming later if you want." I held her in my arms, the blue-grey of the ocean stretching out beyond us. To one side was a stretch of beach dotted with beach goers.

She'd always longed to go to the beach, so I'd tell her about it. While I was able to bring her some places in our dreams, the beach wasn't one of them.

"It's so clean," she whispered, looking over the railing.

"Well, yeah." I blinked. Was the ocean dirty in her world? How sad.

She pulled me down for a kiss. "It's perfect."

"Tomorrow I thought we could go whale watching."

Her face lit up. "Really? I've always wanted to do that."

"Absolutely." For a moment I held her in my arms, feeling the sheer happiness radiating through our bond.

This. I needed more of *this*. Simple silly things, like hugging her while watching the waves.

We took a picture and sent it to Evan.

"What first? Food? I think I should eat something," she finally asked, gazing up at me with those eyes as blue-grey as the water.

"That sounds like a great idea" I took her hand, and we went back toward the food court, my own belly gurgling with delight at the idea of eating something deep fried. Spencer had us eating healthy.

I looked around, taking it all in. "It's been a while since I've come here. After my grandpa passed we stopped. I miss those summer trips. I would even come for part of the trip if I could back when I was in the military."

"Really?" She eyed the games of chance and skill as people called out to us.

"Yeah. I don't know if you remember, but it's my mom's family we did this with–not my dad's. Something special Lexi and I got to do with our cousins and grandparents each year, all by ourselves. After our mom left us, I was afraid we wouldn't get to go anymore. But my grandparents made it clear that not only did they not approve of her abandoning us, that we were still their grandkids. Which meant the world to me after so much upheaval." I led Grace to the line for funnel cake, popcorn, and pretzels.

She leaned into me, her arms wrapping tightly around me, her head on my chest. "I'm so glad they did that. There's something about grandparents being like that. My mom had no family that I knew of. But dad–I mean the man that raised me, did–"

"Grace, you can call him your *dad* if you feel like he deserves the title. Just like you can feel free to call your mom *birth giver* or *egg donor* or whatever," I assured her.

"Okay. He really did love me–and care for me. When he divorced my mom, he and Grandma still remembered me on my birthday and holidays and stuff," she said softly. "It took some of the sting out of it."

"It does. My parent's divorce cut me deep too," I said softly.

We got funnel cake with powdered sugar, strawberries, and whipped cream, to share, and sat down on a bench with a view of the ocean.

Grace took a bite and made a face of delight. "So good. We have this in my world, too."

I took a tiny piece of fried doughy goodness and threw it to the waiting flock of seagulls.

"Your mom... did she leave because she found her soulmate?" Grace asked softly. "I've been wondering about that. How it might affect your family if you suddenly found them–and how I could have wrecked things for you and your pack if I hadn't fit the way I could."

I planted a kiss on the top of her head. "None of that. Because you *didn't* fuck everything up. You fit."

She *absolutely* could have destroyed us. Which was part of why Brennan had been so wary–and why Evan wanted the integration team involved. I was beyond relieved that it had all worked out.

"It does happen, though, right?" She frowned, shoving another bite of funnel cake in her mouth.

"Sometimes. Usually, if it involves an omega, the Center likes to step in and make sure there's a compromise and the least amount of fallout. That's part of why the integration team exists. But there's nothing like that for betas," I explained.

She studied me. "Did the Center help with Caroline? She almost joined your pack, right?"

"It should have been a red flag that she *didn't* want the Center involved. They did help us deal with the aftermath–especially Evan." I sighed, because the effects on him had been horrible. "But Caroline was an entirely different situation than you."

"Because I'm not a heartless bitch?" She snorted.

"Yep." I gave her a kiss.

And, well, we were bonded scent matches, so Grace had legal rights that Caroline didn't. Grace *loved* Evan and he loved her right back. Also, she wasn't looking to displace anyone and wanted nothing more than love and ice cream.

"My parents were married, but they never bonded. My beta mom didn't want to. It wasn't that unusual where we lived. One day, she proclaimed that she'd fallen out of love with my dad and needed to be happy–and it wasn't with us. She picked up and *left*, then sent the divorce papers." My head bowed. "While she made it clear it wasn't us that caused her to leave, to a kid..."

"Yeah, I understand." She scooted closer to me. "I remember you telling me about her calling you sometimes. Did you ever see her again?"

"No." My voice went bitter. "My grandparents begged her to try to have a relationship with us, but she wasn't interested. I know she eventually settled elsewhere, remarried, and had a new family. I know nothing about them. She didn't even show up when Evan and I had our mating party–and my grandparents made sure she got the invitation."

Grace leaned her head on my shoulder. "I'm so sorry."

"It's fine. I don't need people like that in my life." I sighed and took another bite of funnel cake, tossing another piece to the greedy birds edging closer, as I stared out at the waves.

We finished our snack, and I took her to the row of games.

"What do you want me to win for you?" I asked, as people called to us, trying to get us to play their game.

"One of those." She pointed to a squishy pink rabbit in a row of toys.

"If that's what you want, then I'll try my best. Let's see what our game options are."

We continued to look at the games until I found one with the same pink rabbit that I thought I could win. I paid the guy and threw the darts, eventually popping enough balloons.

Beaming, she gave me a kiss as she held her new toy tight. An omega eyed Grace's toy, and tugged on her alpha's shirt, pointing to it.

"Sky swing?" I suggested as we walked past the bubble wheel, where the enclosed cars went around in a big circle. At the top you had a great view of the ocean.

"It's the one with the swings attached vertically to a pole, right?" she asked.

"It is." Did she still like spinny rides?

Her grin widened. "What are we waiting for?"

We rode a few rides and browsed the shops. The boardwalk grew crowded as people got off work and school. Grace shivered as a chill started to come in off the water

"Getting hungry?" I brought her to me, using my body to keep her warm.

She nodded. I took her back to the car, getting one of my hoodies out of my suitcase for her. Grace put it on, and I drove toward the fishing docks. We stopped at a little red shack and found a space in the dirt lot which was crowded with cars. I led her past the families, teenagers, and packs until I found an empty stone table with a view of the water.

"Sit here, I'll be right back with dinner. This is one of my favorite places to eat." I stole a kiss and went inside.

The little restaurant wasn't much—and was half fast-food window, half-fish shop. I waited in the long line, ordered two of the dinner specials with drinks, then carried it back out on a wooden tray.

Grace looked up from her phone and grinned. "What's for dinner?"

I put a paper boat in front of her. "For all the fine dining in the world, I have yet to find anything better than grilled lobster with butter in a paper boat eaten at a stone table by the water."

"Ohhh." She licked her pink lips as she took in the lobster with butter, potatoes, and corn.

"Yep." I dug in, regaling her with stories of fishing off the docks with my grandfather, adventuring in town with my cousins, and the other things we'd done here in summer.

"That sounds like so much fun," she sighed, polishing off her potatoes. "Because my dad owned a business, we didn't really go on vacations. A long weekend at the lake. Driving a day or two to see something special or visit my aunt who lived in the next state. While my high school cheer squad competed, we didn't go anywhere that far. I didn't fly on an airplane until college. When I was getting my PhD, I was too poor to do much and never got the opportunities to travel that some of my cohort did."

I put my hand over hers. "You've got a whole world to see. I mean, first Seaside, next the PIIP conference."

She giggled. "I know. Wild right?"

We'd take her anywhere and everywhere.

The sun set as the lights came on from the fishing boats on the water.

Gathering up our trash, we deposited it in the garbage, freeing up the table for a group of teenagers.

Taking her hand, I brought her to the water's edge so we could watch the sunset.

"Can we go for a walk on the beach while you hold my hand?" she asked softly, as the waves lapped.

"Is your foot up to that?" I asked. She'd stopped wearing her walking cast and wrist splint, but I still worried about it being too much.

"Yes. Your dick worked its healing magic on me, and I feel just fine." She grinned.

"I am here to serve." I gave a mock-bow.

She took off her shoes and held them in one hand, the other entwined with mine. A look of delight crossed her face as she squished her toes in the sand.

"Are you doing okay with work and everything?" It seemed like it. Though she would ask me questions at lunch and on the way home.

"It's only been two weeks. Our lunch times help—and the cheat sheet Spencer made for me. The science is brilliant, and my mind isn't sluggish anymore. Truly, I'm excited. Also, everyone's sort of weird so I hope any quirks I have will just blend in." She beamed.

Relief sluiced over me. Also, Grace was right. Special Projects was full of neurodivergent genuineness, of course she'd fit right in. There, quirks were expected.

"What about you? Are you doing okay? You swam a whole lot of laps after your therapy session." She squeezed my hand.

The sun was setting, and we weren't the only couple out here, though many of them were sitting on the rocks.

"It's hard sometimes. But dealing with everything that hap-pened when I was nineteen is a long time in coming," I replied. Though part of the difficulty was leaving out the bits about not being able to find her because she was in a parallel world. More because I didn't want to be judged. I tried so fucking hard...

"Hey." Stopping, she pulled me to her. "I'm here and we're going to have a wonderful life together."

"Yeah. We are." I kissed the top of her head. "It's actually really helpful–both our sessions together and my individual ones. We really need to find someone for you."

"Bren says that, too. But short of Spencer managing to find a list of all the omegas his dad hid here and figuring out who became a therapist or counselor, I don't know how we'll accomplish that." She shrugged. "I highly doubt that's what his dad's encrypted research is."

I stopped short. "That is a brilliant idea. If there's no list maybe somehow Evan can use his connections with the Omega Protection people to work backwards since they helped his dad."

Getting out my phone I texted both Spencer and Evan the thought.

"I mean, if we did manage to find someone it would be sort of nice." She bit her lower lip.

"It'll be something Evan and I can work on while you're at the science fair with Spencer." It was getting dark so I turned around so we could head back toward the car.

She laughed. "I love that you're referring to one of the top scientific symposiums in the world as a *science fair*."

I grinned. "It sort of is. Now, let's go back to the car so we can start that wonderful life you were talking about."

Chapter Twenty-Six

Grace

It was dark as we drove down a road, but the cute Cape Cod-Es-que houses were lit up. Wes had brought me to Seaside! My heart was near bursting that he remembered how much I loved his stories about his visits.

"Thank you for bringing me." I could smell and hear the ocean.

"I'm loving this. Tomorrow we can go to town and get fudge and look at candles and buy silly things." He grinned. "Oh, this brings back memories. We'd come here other times when I was younger, too, not just in the summer. But the summer visits were my favorite. My grandparents had their hands full with us. It was nice, because I'd been really close to some of them, especially the ones I'd been in a pack with before the divorce."

"So, packs can be a bunch of families together, not just one family like us?" The sky was full of twinkling stars, and the moon rose in the sky.

"Yeah. In some places it's very common. Especially in areas where there's not as many alphas and families band together for protection. That pack, my uncle's pack, was more for the sharing of child care and being able to afford high housing prices by pooling together and getting a condo complex. It's how a lot of working-class people survive. All-beta packs were legalized during the big depression for that very reason," he answered.

"That makes sense. At first I wasn't sure if you all were rich or if it was because you had five employed adults living together." I laughed.

"As you can see, it's a little of both. Life can be better with several working adults even if you're not rich. Multi-generational packs are a thing, too. Take Jett's family. Their pack is full of families, they don't all live together but they live close together, and sometimes have multiple generations in one house, and are all a pack overseen not by a head alpha, but an omega matriarch," he explained.

Oooh. "I love that."

"I'm sure you'll get to meet them." Wes pulled into the driveway of a cute little cottage. "Here we are."

He parked and helped me out. We got our things and went inside. It looked exactly how I pictured a grandmother's seaside cottage to look–including a beach glass mosaic in the bathroom and framed seashells.

We put our bags in the cute and cozy bedroom that had a *very* big bed.

"This was one of the rooms grown-ups got to stay in. We stayed in bunk beds upstairs," he told me.

"We're on the beach?" I looked out the sliding glass doors. There was a deck and possibly waves.

"Yes. We can go for a morning walk then have breakfast on the deck. Grandma had the kitchen stocked for us. Come on." He took my hand. "There's a fire pit and I got marshmallows."

"I'm so happy you're having fun. Miss you. Love you," Evan told us as we video chatted with him.

"I miss you, too," I replied. Wes and I sat on the back porch of the beach cottage, the fire pit going.

"We should start meeting with wedding coordinators," Evan added. "I'd love you to help pick one. They're all ones I've worked with through the Omega Center with my clients."

"Wedding planner? Aren't we fancy?" Though it seemed like a good idea.

"We are. It helps take some of the stress off. They'll also have vetted and trusted vendors, but I know a lot of those, too. And obviously, Wes, you can have as much input as you want. Anyhow, I'll send you their websites. Love you, good night." Evan ended the call.

Wes snuggled into me as we sat on the lounge chair. We'd roasted our marshmallows, our beers almost done.

My phone beeped with links, and I clicked a few of them. "Wow."

Wes leaned over my shoulder. "Hey, don't let Evan force you into a wedding you don't want. This is all our wedding, and everyone gets a say, okay."

"Okay. You do want to marry us, right? I mean it's okay if you don't but... I mean, I want to marry Evan. I love all the beautiful ideas. We also talked about our wedding, but it doesn't seem like it's as big of a thing here and..." I frowned. Everything wedding-talk oriented had been Evan driven, which wasn't a bad thing. But if weddings weren't a thing with people already bonded I didn't want to push him.

Wes kissed me, sending reassurance through the bond. "Peaches, I *want* to marry you. And if you want your own wedding with me, separate from you and Evan, we can do that. We can have a flower arch and a photo booth and everything either way. I want us to have a wedding as magical as we used to talk about. It is a thing here, okay."

"Okay." I snuggled back into him. "I don't mind it being the three of us. I just wanted to make sure you wanted to be there and weren't just going along with it."

"I'm here for it. I'll go with you to try cake, choose the flowers, whatever you want. But you can leave me behind, too. Just as long as I get input on the band and candy bar and can pick the whiskey for the fountain." He peppered kisses along my jaw in reassurance.

"That sounds good to me. We absolutely need a photo booth." I grinned.

"I want to marry you, Grace Cassidy Ellington. He might want to wait a year, but the two of us can get married whenever you want, wherever you want." Wes kissed me again.

"Good." That made me feel better. Though I wasn't sure I needed to marry him sooner.

"I love this. You sat out here every night, didn't you?" I gazed out at the ocean, a couple of boats winking at us.

"Usually." He nodded. "Often we'd play flashlight tag while my grandparents sat on the porch. Or I might do some night fishing with my grandpa."

"I can't wait to go whale watching. And swimming." My shoulders shimmied.

"When you're with Spence, the ocean will be warmer. You're probably staying somewhere beachside and fancy. Maybe he'll rent you a cabana." He laughed.

I stroked his hair. "You're okay with it?"

He nodded. "As much as I want you all to myself, please spend more time with Spencer. He's a good travel buddy and you can bring him with you when you start speaking at shit. I mean I will go anywhere you want me to, but I don't even like going to conferences for my own sector. But you... the things you'll do..."

"Thank you for believing in me. I'd love to speak at colleges and encourage people to go after their dreams." I kissed his temple.

"I love that." He kissed me back, his hand running up my back making heat build inside me.

We finished our beers, and he cleaned up, while I lazily laid on the lounger enjoying the beachy air and the fire.

"Oh, um, Grandma found one of my sketchbooks." Wes sat down with me. "Look at you."

"Awww." I drew my finger down the picture of me. It looked like a precursor to the one that won an award.

I flipped through it as he finished cleaning up. He came back out and turned off the fire pit.

"Bedtime." Wes scooped me up in a princess carry, sketchbook and all.

"Mmmm, don't need to ask me twice." I buried my face in his shirt.

As nice as this was, I wouldn't mind making use of that big bed. Though we should probably shower first.

Like he knew what I was thinking, he brought me straight into the bathroom, putting the sketchbook on the dresser. While the bathroom lacked a tub, it had a nice, big shower with several shower heads. A shelf held very beautiful bottles of soap, shampoo, and conditioner.

Wes turned on the water. Slowly, he undressed me.

"In you go." Picking me up, he placed me under the warm spray.

The water was perfect, but instead of raising my face to it, I watched Wes undress. Mmmm, those abs. The infinity heart tattoo on his chest. The military tattoo on the shoulder I always liked to bite.

His tight ass.

That cock. By its state, it was happy to see me.

"Gimmie." I made grabby hands.

"Yeah." He grinned, revealing his dimples, as he climbed in and pulled me to him.

"Yeah." I looked up at him.

"All of me or just my cock?" Wes laughed.

I pulled him down to me and kissed him long and deep. "I love every inch of you, Boo-Bear."

Wes pushed me up against the shower wall, adjusting one of the shower heads so I wouldn't get cold. His body pressed into mine. "You mean that?"

"You know I do." I sighed as he slipped his hard cock into me, his clean laundry scent permeating the shower.

"I know. Because I can feel it right here." He put my hand on his heart, the other hand toying with my clit as he thrust in and out of me. "I feel you so much more now. I love you so much."

Love and devotion flooded me as my body exploded. I sent all my adoration back to the man I loved until the end of the universe.

Chapter Twenty-Seven

Jett

...nine...ten...eleven...twelve... I finished my set of pullups as the scent of sour lemonade filled the gym we had in the basement.

Hopping down from the pullup bar I turned to Evan who leaned in the doorway.

"Hey, what's wrong? Bad day at work?" I wiped my sweaty face off with a towel.

"Yeah." Evan wrapped his arms around my sweaty body, resting his head on top of mine.

"Rose?" I knew her case was really bothering him. But it was a sad case. Not to mention the whole thing with her uncle trying to *shoot* Evan.

He nodded. "Yeah. Can we go in my room and talk about it? Maybe watch a movie and have some gummy bears?"

Anxiety shot through the bond.

"That sounds great. Should I get my bag?" There were a couple of ties I did on Evan to help his anxiety. The compression could ease the parasympathetic nervous system and was sort of like covering him with a weighted blanket.

"Please?" He nodded.

"Okay, we'll do that first. Then we'll watch the movie and get out the gummy bears?" I didn't like him mixing recreationals and ropes. While I was happy he trusted me that much, safety and consent were really important to me.

"Sure." Evan kissed me and left the room.

I cleaned off the equipment I'd used, and went upstairs to our suite. Like most of the suites, there were three rooms. Our living room also doubled as Brennan's office, because we'd turned the third room into something else.

Entering the code on the keypad, I opened the playroom. We had a bed, a complete rigging setup capable of safely suspending someone, as well as a number of other things, including a swing. All three of our scents hung heavily in here.

I got my bag out of the cupboard, which had everything I needed to do exactly what he was asking. Double checking to make sure I had scissors and the correct ropes, I closed the cupboard.

My eyes fell on the swing in the corner. Every time I looked at it, I thought of Evan's fantasy of me, him, and Brennan having Grace in it.

Maybe one day.

Ever since Evan's heat, my attraction to her had been growing. But with Spencer courting her, I hadn't made any moves. The last thing I wanted was to overwhelm her. At least Wes wasn't being insecure anymore. The two of them had come back from their seaside getaway relaxed and happy.

I also grabbed the gummy bear tin out of my box of recreationals, then texted Brennan who was working late on the estate project.

Me

> **Evan's having a bad day. We're going to watch action movies.**

Brennan

> **Work?**

Me

> **Yeah, the Rose thing.**

Evan got really attached to his clients. It was part of what made him so good at his job. But I also hated to see him hurting.

Brennan

> **You take such good care of him. Let me know if you want me to bring anything home or if you need me.**

> **Love you.**

Me

> **He'll probably get the munchies so maybe bring home the usual?**

Love you, too.

The house was quiet. Spencer had something tonight. I wasn't sure where Grace and Wes were.

"Can I come in?" I knocked on the ajar door to Evan's suite, which opened into his sitting room.

"Please?" Evan sat on the couch, which wasn't as giant as the one in the living room, but still comfortable for someone of his size. Everything was done in the oranges, browns, and dark reds he preferred. His desk sat in the corner.

Evan's suite only had this room and his bedroom, the third room had been gutted to enlarge his bathroom and closet, and add his nest.

A bunch of snacks littered the coffee table. He had the remote in his hand, the TV on.

"*Whale-cane* or *Drug Raccoon? Drug Raccoon* is subtitled. *Whale-cane* just sounds funny. If you want something dubbed maybe *The Last Stand of Small Penis Man?*" Evan asked.

"*Drug Raccoon?* My co-workers were talking about it the other day." I sat down on the couch next to him. "Do you want to tell me what's going on at work?"

Evan liked to talk about things as I tied him. Brennan preferred silence.

"Yeah, I would." Evan turned on the couch so I could tie him better. He now wore a form-fitting shirt that looked delicious on him.

Since he liked corset ties, I got out two different colors, brown and burnt orange.

"The usual?" I asked, making sure the scissors were within reach.

Evan nodded. "Yeah. So, those guys, the ones who were at the talent show asking about Rose? They're bothering her by sending gifts and trying to talk to her in public. But there really is nothing *illegal* about sending someone unwanted gifts, especially since they're just ordinary things. Though it's creepy because they clearly know things about her and it's reflected in the gifts."

As he talked I took the brown and burnt orange ropes and looped them together with a square knot. I wrapped it around the lowest part of his sternum, using the brown as the base and orange as the lace.

"Very true, but you should alert the police anyway," I told him, threading the orange rope through the brown, then wrapping the brown around him.

"We have. But Detective Esposito can only do so much. We have no proof, and no good reason for her to investigate them. Sure, they're bad news, but they have no outstanding warrants; they're allowed to visit Rockland." Evan sighed.

"You're doing all you can." I wrapped it around him again. "How's that feel? Too tight? Not tight enough?"

Evan thought for a moment. "Perfect."

"Good, let me know. I can always tighten it later," I reminded, continuing to wrap the ropes around him, building a corset.

"She's scared and those men are sketchy as fuck. But we can't actually prove a relationship between her uncle and them even though Rose mentioned her uncle owing them money. Even though she's *sixteen,* there's no actual law that they can't try to woo her. They just can't bond her before eighteen without a judge." He rubbed his forehead.

"Yeah the whole situation is fucking suspicious. Do you think the uncle is trying to sell Rose to them to pay off a debt or make money? Or even already sold her? Perhaps they're running an omega trafficking ring?" While this wasn't my area of specialty, I'd been called in enough times on stuff like this to foresee a number of scenarios.

"We can't prove anything. It could go so many ways."

I checked the ropes to make sure they were straight and symmetrical. "Still comfortable?"

"Yes." Evan nodded. "The gifts make me think that they want her for them, not for trafficking, and they're not known for that anyway. She's scared. They know exactly where the lines are and don't cross them."

"I feel really bad for Rose. She didn't ask for this. I wish there was something we could do to help. Now, does it still feel okay?" I asked, reaching out through the bond to double check, as I finished up the corset portion of the tie.

"Perfect." His eyes closed. "Mmmm. It's also freaking out the headmistress. I'm afraid that she'll kick Rose out because this could be a safety issue for the school."

"I can see that, and I understand where she's coming from." Adding another brown rope, I took my design up his chest.

"Yeah. I wish there was more I could do, too." He started to relax.

"You do the best you can, Baby. You're great at your job, and I love the compassion you have for your clients. I'll see if there's anything I can do on my end." Maybe someone would have some helpful information for me.

Continuing to work, I brought the ropes over his shoulders and across his back, forming a harness, leaving his arms free.

"That would be great. Hey, can you make it a little snugger?" he asked.

"Of course." I tightened my work a little, continuing to watch him for any signs of discomfort or distress.

Evan sighed happily and went quiet. I focused on my work, continuing to check in with him. I finished and pulled him into my arms, covering us with a blanket.

"Better?" Kissing his temple, I stroked his hair.

"Much better, Hot Stuff." He got cozy in my arms. "Tell me about your day? Anyone get in trouble? I love how that's a thing."

I told him about my day, and he let me know about other things going on at work.

"They want me to go through Crisis Response Team training. It would be amazing, but I'm not sure I want to leave being an advocate for that." Sitting up, he grabbed a bag of chips, then laid back down in my arms again, opening it and taking one.

"They do? That's fantastic. Would you have to leave your job, though? Couldn't you just be on a roster for big crises or be on-call or something?" I took a chip. They were the in-the-field crisis-response workers for the Omega Center. They were often referred to as the *Blanket Brigade* because of their big duffels full of blankets and other comfort items that they always had with them.

"I'd do that in a moment. I like my job, but I'm happy to help in an emergency. They're looking for people for their shelter roster, I think. If it was with your station, I'd take it in a moment." He ate another chip.

"I'd love that." I gave him a kiss.

"Yeah, if I could just be on the on-call list for disasters and big emergencies, I'll do it. I might do it anyway. Just because you take the training doesn't mean you'll pass," he told me.

"True. You'd be good at it." It required a lot of complex problem solving. But they were crisis workers and didn't maintain the long-term relationships advocates usually had with their clients. However, I could see why they'd want Evan in that position. He was magic in an emergency.

The Center's Crisis Response Team came into often traumatic and volatile situations. They were trained in a lot of different things including crisis management, conflict resolution, and field medicine. Sometimes, especially in hostage situations, they were our line inside. They also worked with shelters, hospitals, fire stations, schools, universities, jails, nursing homes, government agencies, the Department of Dependent Services, and so many other places. Also, they aided in emergencies, disasters, and humanitarian situations.

"Will they send you away for training?" That could be difficult, but if it was what he wanted, we'd work it out.

He shook his head. "It's here. I'd have to lighten my caseload, but I could keep some of my clients and I'd get paid for training. I could also do it in modules. Though if I do that, I might have to go to other places to fill in what I miss. It's a big commitment."

"It is. But it's amazing that they want you to do it. You'd be great at it." Yeah, maybe I should see if I could get him attached to my station. We'd take good care of him and he'd be working a lot with Lexi and the Special Victims Unit.

"Thanks. It would be really good training to have. I'm just not sure I want to leave working with clients," he told me.

There was a knock on the door.

"Come in," Evan called.

Grace came in. Her eyes focused on us. "Oh. Sorry. I didn't mean to interrupt."

"It's fine, Peaches. We're going to watch a movie–*Drug Raccoons*. Do you want to watch it with us? How did your event go?" Evan held out his arms.

Oh, yes, she had a Daedalus society thing tonight.

"The nice people weren't there, but the speaker was good. Rami and Katie dropped me off. Spencer and Wes are still working." Her eyes stayed on the ropes.

I got a little fear and apprehension in her peachy scent.

Evan looked down. "It's pretty, right? He'll untie me before we start the movie."

Oh. Brennan said someone tied her wrists when they hurt her.

"Here, touch." I took her small hand in mine, nails sparkly, and ran it along the ropes. "See, they're soft so they don't hurt him, and thick so they don't cut him."

"This makes me feel better. It's like being smooshed by an alpha without the smooshies," Evan explained.

"They are soft." She bit her lower lip but allowed me to guide her hand along it.

"They're not too tight. I take a lot of care to make sure he's comfortable. Everything is done with consent here. Promise," I reassured.

"It is pretty. I didn't know it could be like that–like art or over your clothes." Her voice was soft.

"Yeah, they can make people feel safe. They can be beautiful and healing, and not just used to hurt," I explained, just like I had to both Evan and Brennan. It had been a lot easier to convince Evan. For Brennan it was a step in helping him reclaim himself.

"He can do something on you if you want to try, maybe your arm or leg," Evan offered.

Grace shook her head. "I'm fine."

"Okay," I soothed. "It's okay if you're not ready. It's also fine if you're never ready." I had some incredible ideas for her if she ever wanted to try.

"Really?" She took a chip from the bag.

"Really. Here, let me undo Evan." I pulled Evan to me and explained to Grace exactly what I was doing, showing her every tie, every knot, just like I had with Brennan, and assuring her that I check in every step of the way.

There were a lot of ways that she and Brennan were alike, though I wasn't sure either of them realized it.

"And he can ask you to stop?" The anxiousness still lurked in her eyes.

"Always. Just like if I'm uncomfortable with something, I can stop. It's about comfort, safety, and trust. So much trust, Baby-doll." I put the rope back in my bag.

"Oh." She rubbed her wrists absently.

I nodded to the scissors. "In case we need a quick exit. Ropes are replaceable."

"Okay." Tears pricked her eyes.

I put the scissors in, zipped up the bag, and moved it out of her sight. I held her to me. "You can ask all the questions in this house, always, okay?"

"Okay." She started to cry.

I held her tighter. "We're right here."

Evan joined our hug, stroking her hair. "We love you, Peaches. You know, maybe we should watch *The Last Stand of Small Penis Man?* I think we need something silly."

"Okay. Jett, how did you learn it?" She stole another chip.

"I learned a lot of the same things my alpha brothers and cousins learned. Unlike some families, mine thinks knowledge is power. They figured it would make me more useful and valuable as a beta. I showed a talent for this, so when I moved here, my family arranged for me to continue studying it." Growing up, they made me feel special for being a beta, like there were things only I could do.

If only more families were that supportive of their beta kids.

"The pictures Evan showed me were pretty." She nodded.

He'd shown her those? They were extraordinary. We had one up on the wall in the playroom.

"I like creating art. Yes, I absolutely tie Evan up and rail him sometimes. But it doesn't have to be like that—and everything is with consent and is agreed upon," I assured.

"Using safewords is always okay," Evan added.

"If you want to watch sometime, we can do that," I offered.

"Now for the good stuff." Evan got the gummy bears out. "Want one?"

Grace nodded. I was about to have her try half when she put the whole thing in her mouth.

"While I didn't do anything in undergrad, we did occasionally take edibles and watch weird movies while I was getting my PhD.

I'm guessing these are about the same." She snuggled between us on the couch.

Evan took a blue gummy bear and turned the movie on. I put the lid on the tin. I shouldn't be getting high, since I had no idea how Grace would react, and no one else was home. Maybe when Brennan got home I'd have one.

The movie started. It was a very silly, over-the-top, badly-dubbed action movie, and didn't seem to have much plot. But Grace and Evan laughed hysterically like it was the funniest, most well-written movie ever.

Grace was also very snuggly, pretty much laid out over our laps. I stroked her hair, enjoying spending more time with her.

She and Evan started feeding each other cookies. The movie was nearly done. Yeah, it would be much better if I was high. Another time. I grabbed a cookie.

My phone buzzed.

Brennan

Leaving now with the requested food.

Me

Sounds good.

Wes also texted.

Wes

Is Grace with you? She's not answering me, but her location is at home.

Evan's not answering either.

I took a picture of her and Evan eating cookies.

Me

Wes

The movie finished.

"The snacks are gone. Who ate our snacks?" Grace sniffed as she held up the empty chip bag and the empty box of cookies. "Jett, who ate the snacks?"

"You did, silly." I tickled her.

"Who me?" She laughed and swatted at me.

There was a knock on the door.

"Hey, I have food," Brennan called.

"Come in," Evan replied. "I'm hungry."

"Oh good. Someone ate all our snacks," Grace announced.

Brennan slipped in and looked at Grace, then at me.

"I'll share." Whoops, I didn't tell him to get any for her. But also, that's not what the look was for.

He put the food on the table.

"You're the best, Bren." Grace leaned forward and wrapped her arms around him.

"Bren really is." Evan joined the hug.

"I try." Brennan just stood there, blinking.

"Here, it's spicy, you'll like it." I opened the spicy shrimp dish Brennan always got for me and handed it to her.

"Thanks, Jett. You're also the best. The bester? The bestest?" Grace leaned in and kissed me.

Before I could react, she'd grabbed some chopsticks and shoved food in her mouth.

"So good," she muttered, mouth full.

"I can't believe she can eat that." Brennan sat down on the arm of the sofa. "Grace joined you for movie night?"

"Yeah, I didn't take anything. They're fine." Grabbing another pair of chopsticks, I reached over Grace and grabbed a bite of shrimp.

Grace giggled as Evan fed her some of his food.

"Do you need anything for your trip, Grace?" Brennan asked. She was leaving in a few days with Spencer for the science convention.

"Sexy underpants." Grace nodded.

Brennan made a choking noise.

"Oooh, right, because you're going to get some *quality time* with Spencer." Evan's eyebrows waggled as he fed her another bite.

"Probably some matching sets?" I ate more shrimp.

"Yeah. He's totally that kind of guy." Evan nodded. "We'll go Saturday. Riley needs to go to the mall anyway."

"Okay. Bren, are you a thong guy?" Grace asked in earnest.

I stifled a laugh as I continued eating. High Grace was fun.

"No, I don't like to wear thongs." Brennan was trying not to laugh.

Her eyes rolled. "That's not what I meant."

"He likes thongs, and you'd look great in one." I kissed the top of her head, because it felt right to do so.

She grinned. "Well, maybe you'll be lucky enough one day to see me in one."

Mmmm. If only I should be so fortunate.

Chapter Twenty-Eight

Brennan

I sat in my office, working. Things had been busy, and not the good kind.

Terrance came in, looking frazzled, tie askew. "We have a problem."

My stomach dropped. "Now what?"

"Reg and his team quit the estate project. He claimed that he was overbooked, and the job was better suited to restoration specialists." Terrance sat down in the chair opposite the desk.

That was bullshit. "Well, we'll call other places. What about Wes' dad?"

"We are, but..." Anxiousness crossed his face.

"Oh. It's because of my mother, isn't it." My chest tightened. I knew something was coming–and this was uncalled for.

"That's my guess. Though Wes' dad's company did land a big contract. Look, I'm having people shore up all our local supply contracts, and everyone we deal with that she might be able to influence, but..." He rubbed his forehead, wedding ring gleaming. "This is going to cost us. Especially since the landscapers quit last week, too, for the same reason. But for right now we've found someone else."

"Shit. I'll make some calls. No, I will not let her destroy this business." I hit my desk with my fist. This wasn't a coincidence.

"Maybe it's time to get Wes to help?" Terrance said quietly.

"I think so." Actually, Wes had been a huge help, identifying my company's security gaps, and making sure everything was encrypted. But there were other things he could do besides assist us with defense.

Since Spencer and Grace left for their conference today and would be gone all week, it might be good to have something to work on in case he needed to be kept busy.

Riley had a terrifying plan, but I wasn't ready to do that. Yet.

"Bren?" Katie's voice came from my partially open office door, as she knocked softly.

"Come in." My heart sped. Hopefully, she wasn't acting as a messenger for my mother. I worked in a different building than my family, so the only reason she'd be here was to see me.

Terrance stood. "I'll keep you posted."

"Thanks."

Katie closed the door behind him. Her red hair was up in a neat bun, her dark suit crisp and impeccable.

"I know you fired the housekeeper, and you said that your pack was starting a foundation to cover the scholarships for the omega schools, but what *is* going on between you and Mom?" Her look turned serious as she paced my office.

"I'm not sure, since I haven't actually heard from her in a while." The last time was that phone call I didn't answer when I was in Spencer's office with the foundation lawyer. I didn't call back.

"Oh fuck." She stopped pacing and faced me, face stricken.

"I... I may have had my pack's lawyer talk to Ian Murphy about getting my trust," I admitted quietly. I hadn't heard back from him, either. However, the PI I'd hired, and our pack lawyer had been busy. So had Wes.

Her blue eyes blinked. "What are you talking about? You got it after you formed your pack and mated with Evan, right?"

"Full access like you? No. Just a small bump in monthly distributions—and that's just Grandma's. I have zero access to the others. I've been trying on and off for years. But this is the first time I've really pushed."

Katie plopped down in the chair Terrance had vacated. "She has zero legal right to keep that from you now that you meet all the qualifications."

"I know. I'm done with her games, Katie." Frustration leaked out of my voice.

"Why didn't you tell me? I thought you'd gotten it. I..." Hurt crossed her face.

"Because I'm an asshole. I also don't want to drag you into things. Which is why I warned you that things might get ugly—and I think they just have." I raked my hand through my hair, well aware that I still held an unfair grudge against my twin.

How dare my mother meddle in my company? Having to change contractors would cost the estate project time and money—which she knew. Not being able to find one could ruin it. Not the company, but the project—and Evan's dream of marrying Grace there next May.

"What if I want to get dragged into it?" she challenged me.

"You have a good relationship with Mother. Keeping it will make you and your pack set for life." There was no place in my mother's empire for me—she'd made that clear, and I'd come to peace with that.

I didn't want her money. I just wanted what was legally mine.

"We're already set." She frowned. "What else is going on? Bren, talk to me. I know she's unfair to you, how can I help?"

"Like I said, I don't want to drag you into this. You know what she can do." My voice went rough.

"I know. Still. Please? I didn't agree when she and Troy cut scholarships for the omegas. I know she did it out of spite, not just because Caroline's family withdrew their support. Rami's refusing to go to any functions out of solidarity," she said.

It was only a matter of time before I was kicked off the foundation board. That stung, since my being allowed the freedom to fund projects like the scholarships for omegas was one thing that made me feel like a part of the family.

But now I could make a difference without them.

"I'm tired of her bullshit. We're no longer attending anything. Also, we're taking a pack last name. And getting tattoos." I met her gaze.

"Nice. Again, not something she can legally stop." Katie nodded.

"But she can and will get pissed," I replied.

Most of Katie's pack took *Morris*. A few, like Lexi, used their other names professionally. They weren't called the Morris pack, though, they were named after Lana's bar. Katie and Lexi had met Lana at university as she struggled to save her grandfather's bar while studying business. With their help, she'd turned it around and now it was thriving. That bar was also where Katie met Rami on trivia night.

Katie sighed. "True. What last name are you using? Please tell me it's Grace's."

I frowned. Did I tell her?

"I promise that I won't tell. You *can* trust me. What do I have to do to prove it to you?" she pleaded.

All sorts of ideas ran through my head. But I wasn't about to ask her to sabotage our mother. Our family.

"Spencer's."

She laughed. "That is amazing. She'll be pissed. But at that same time, she really can't be, because who wouldn't?"

"Why are you here?" I asked.

Anxiousness crossed her face. "Do you remember the lawyer from the firm I interned at, the one that took your case against the car company?"

"Of course." I ran into him from time to time. He was a good lawyer and sometimes I sent him business.

"He and a couple of others are forming their own firm and asked me to be part of it. I'm tired of working for the family. I like doing transactional documents, but I never wanted to be a corporate lawyer. It's why I interned with the types of firms I did in law school. With this new firm, I'd get a chance to actually help people." Her look went earnest.

"You're leaving the Morris Company?" That surprised me.

She nodded. "It's time. I actually admire the fact that you've been brave enough to be on your own from the very beginning."

"After the accident, Mother never *allowed* me to work for the family. Not that I wanted to." Which my brothers resented me for. Why wouldn't I want to work for the family?

"Dad *allowed* you to not work for the family," Katie countered. "Dad's in your corner as much as he can be. He's proud that you have such a thriving international business, and a great pack. I know you think Mom makes you come to things for punishment, which, well, she sort of does, but Dad likes having you at things so he can show you off. He's proud of you."

I frowned. "He has a funny way of showing it."

With his teasing and jokes. Calling me *Sport.*

"He always has, and he's not going to change. But that is him showing it. So..." Her spruce scent grew sour with anxiety. "Will you back me? Because if she's at war with you and grouchy at not being able to close that building for her new project, *and* I leave?" She whistled. "It's shit timing, but I can't miss *another* opportunity simply because my leaving doesn't work for her schedule."

It hit me. "She's been stringing you along."

This whole time I thought Katie *liked* working for the family.

"She has. While I have no issue helping with the foundation legal stuff, my job with the business was supposed to be temporary. Also, I found out recently that she's been sabotaging me so I can't leave." Katie rolled her eyes. "I can still be a part of this family and do my own thing."

That wasn't how it worked. But she didn't want to hear that right now.

"I'm proud of you for wanting to strike out on your own," I told her, meaning it. While I didn't like it when Katie was forced to be our lawyer, she was a good lawyer.

My twin beamed. "You are? So, we'll back each other? Twin power?"

Katie held out her pinky.

I linked my pinky with hers. "Twin power."

"Good." She looked relieved. "Now to give my notice. I was all set to do it this morning, only to find her riled up about you and this whole thing with the State Street project." Katie's eyes sparkled. "I told her not to lowball them or use fear, because that's not going to work on this seller."

There was something about the way she said it, the curve of her lips.

"Are you giving me a tip?" I asked.

"Who me?" She feigned innocence. "It would be such a pity if someone met the price and bought such a key property before she worked things out. It could ruin the entire State Street project."

Huh.

"Also, what Ian is doing to you *could* be against the legal association code and could cause him to lose his license," she stated.

"I'd need proof beside him just saying *I have to talk to your mother.*" I'd looked into it. Though the PI was working on that.

"Hmmm." Her look went coy. "Hey, secret? Though it won't be a secret for long."

"Always."

"I'm pregnant. Mom's going to be pissed. She always says it will impact my career, but I'm in my thirties. The longer I wait... and I want more than one." She chewed on her lower lip.

I wrapped my arms around my twin. "Congratulations."

Nope, I didn't smell it yet.

She grinned. "Lexi and Lana are trying too. We're going to have a pack full of babies and we're going to bring them over to your place all the time."

The idea of small children making a mess made me freeze.

My sister laughed. "So, when are you going to catch up?"

I shrugged. Children were never that important to me. Though I wasn't averse to having them.

"It's Evan and Grace's call. I think Grace wanted to get a little more established in her career," I explained.

"Makes sense." Katie hugged me again. "This has been fun, but I have a notice letter to draft." She left.

Yes, and I had a building to buy. I picked up my phone. "Hey, I'm going to need some information on the Morris Company's State Street project."

Our foundation needed a building, too.

Chapter Twenty-Nine

Grace

"Dr. Harlowe, this is amazing. Astoundingly amazing," I breathed as I watched the demonstration of her particle cutter at PIIP, the Particle Institute for Interdisciplinary Physics. Spencer stood at my shoulder. A few others from Compass BioTek Special Projects were with us.

"It really is. Oh, the things we could potentially do," Dr. Harlowe replied. "So, who'd like to finish the tour?"

Dr. Harlowe, the dark-haired beta that I'd met at the science dinner, continued our special tour of PIIP. The symposium started tomorrow at a nearby hotel. As we toured the research facility, I couldn't help but feel I was being watched. Specifically, by one young woman who could be a grad student. But then a lot of people were interested in the Compass BioTek team, since the company wasn't synonymous with particle physics.

It was interesting to see all the things that they were doing here. I paid close attention to what I saw and who I met, making notes on my phone, since I was on the lookout for potential team members, including our super collider expert.

"Does anyone want to see our super collider?" Dr. Harlowe asked. "We have the most powerful one on this continent, well, for now. We also have one of the new micro particle accelerators."

"Oh, we have one of those," Margie dismissed, with a wave of her hand.

Which we did.

"I'd like to see it," I replied, curious to see in person how it was different from what I'd used back in my world.

I looked over at Spencer, who gave me the slightest of nods. He probably wouldn't want to see it. While he was okay with the micro particle accelerator we had in Special Projects, the large colliders brought back too many memories.

And I understood that completely.

We split off, my group going to see the collider and accelerator.

"You said *for now*," I asked. "Others are being built?"

Dr. Harlowe nodded, as we walked down the hall. "BaySci is building a large-scale laser-plasma circular collider, and the Research Circle Collaborative is attempting to build a CeCe."

"Oooh. That's pretty amazing. I'd love to see both of them." I wasn't quite sure what either of them were specifically–or where these places were.

She nodded. "Both are really exciting concepts, though the idea is to make them *smaller* and safer, not bigger and more dangerous."

"Someone's overcompensating?" I laughed, still curious as to what they used that made them so much more dangerous here.

Dr. Harlowe burst into giggles. "You said it, I didn't."

We rejoined everyone for some refreshments in one of their meeting rooms. The young woman who'd been watching me was there, as were a bunch of other young people.

"They're curious," Dr. Harlowe told us. "It's not every day that Compass BioTek comes to PIIP. Before Dr. Terik's research, we didn't even know that you were working in any of these fields."

Narif, Dr. Terik, was swarmed with eager young people, as was Spencer.

"Again, thank you for arranging a private tour and demonstration for us," I said. "I'm so excited to be here."

She smiled. "I look forward to one day coming to tour your facility and see what you are all up to."

"Anytime." I meant it. I wanted to keep a friendship with her and PIIP, especially if we hoped to actually make our simulator.

The young woman who'd been watching me came over, holding a paper cup and a bashful expression. She was younger than me, very graceful, and only a little taller, with golden skin and really long, dark hair.

She held the cup out. "I brought you some tea. There's more if you want it."

"Oh, thank you." I took the cup, and she smiled and darted off. It tasted like the stuff Evan kept feeding me. I didn't like it much, but I drank it.

"Inara's one of our research fellows. She's presenting Wednesday as part of the student forum," Dr. Harlowe said softly. "While her research doesn't dovetail with yours, she'd probably appreciate your support if you have the time."

Got it. She was an omega. That's why she'd been watching me and brought me tea.

"I'll definitely try to attend." I'd planned to attend the student forum anyway, to invite students to apply to the intern program.

When I went to get snacks, I looked for her, but she wasn't there.

Finally, we finished, and our group assembled outside of PIIP to wait for the called cars. PIIP was in the idyllic Southern coastal town that was home to cute shops, beautiful beaches, and a number of research facilities and universities.

The May air was warm and sticky, and we were all dressed accordingly in more summery business clothes. Except for Spencer, who still wore a dark suit.

And looked delicious in it.

"We'll see you later," Spencer said, as he and I got in a different car. Everyone else was staying at the hotel the symposium was at. We were all having dinner together later.

As we rode, I held Spencer's hand, looking out the window. The two of us had come straight to PIIP from the airport. Most of our team had arrived yesterday.

The water came into view as we drove to the resort the two of us were staying at.

"Ocean," I'd breathed. I'd gotten a glimpse as we flew.

"We will take you to see as many oceans and beaches as you wish." He squeezed my hand.

The car stopped in front of a *very* fancy hotel. The kind you'd see in movies with lush landscaping, uniformed bellhops, and brass carts. Spencer took my arm and led me into the lobby. Our things had already been brought here from the plane, which was mind blowing in itself. Money did seem to have its privileges.

One wall of the lobby was all windows. There was a cafe to one side, and doors opening out to a patio, beyond that was a bar area, a pool...

...and the ocean.

Letting go of Spencer, I went right out those doors into the gleaming sand. Ocean waves lapped on the sandy beach, as families built sand castles and children frolicked in the waves.

Spencer's arms wrapped around me. "The water's warmer down here than where you went with Wes. Tonight, we're having dinner on a boat."

"We are?" I perked. "That sounds fun."

Spencer nodded as we swayed gently in the very slight ocean breeze. "I thought it would be nice for everyone from the company to go on a sunset dinner cruise, especially since some people brought their families."

"Perfect." I snapped a picture of me and sent it to the group chat.

It was just me and Spencer on this trip and while I'd miss everyone else fiercely, I was looking forward to both the symposium and having some time with just him. And trying out the sexy panties I'd gotten. I also had some new swimsuits.

The group chat went off again.

Riley

I made the team!!!! I'm a swing.

She added a picture of the skate smash team roster for next year.

Me

Congratulations! I'm so excited for you.

"Would you like to go to the hotel room?" Spencer asked. "Or should we walk along the beach?"

I was already taking off my shoes. "Will you hold my hand and walk on the beach?"

He held out his hand. "My good doctor, it would be my pleasure."

In the morning, I woke up to the alarm, nestled in Spencer's arms. The hotel room we were in was *extraordinary*. It was a villa set aside from the hotel in a small grouping of other villas. We had a porch, hot tub, and more rooms than two people needed.

"Good morning, Darling. Excited for today?" Spencer kissed my temple.

"I am." I sat up and stretched. It was the first day of the three-day symposium, though I was most interested in today and tomorrow. "What do you have planned for today? Are you still coming with me for breakfast and the opening session?"

While there were a few speakers Spencer wanted to see, mostly he was having a lot of business meetings and a couple speaking engagements.

He took his phone off the nightstand and glanced at it. "For part of it. I'm going to try to make one of the breakout sessions on micro-computing. Tonight, we've got the party we're hosting."

"I have the Daedalus Society reception this evening, but after that I'll be up. If that works?" I gave him a kiss.

"Perfect." His look went fond. "After, I'd love to take you to a late dinner at a special place."

"I'd love that." Last night had been extraordinary, first a sunset dinner cruise, then a moonlit walk on the beach.

Spencer made us some coffee, and I got dressed in one of my new outfits that I'd gotten while shopping over the weekend with Evan and Riley. I looked all nice and professional, complete with some new jewelry that had mysteriously found its way into my suitcase. Also, I'd gotten some flats that were pretty, but comfy.

"You look amazing. I ordered us some fruit and pastries. Breakfast will probably not be very exciting." He handed me a very small mug of coffee and gave me another kiss. As usual, he wore one of his very nice suits.

"Thank you." I took a sip.

We finished up and took a car over to the hotel the symposium was at and headed to the ballroom the opening session was in.

I checked my phone. "Deb has a table for us."

We joined Deb, Margie, Tish, and Jordie, along with Narif and his team. The opening session was fascinating, going into depth as to what PIIP actually did, highlighting some of their programs and advances worldwide, as well as introducing some of the other organizations in attendance.

"The military is here?" I eyed a couple of tables of uniforms.

"There's a military base near here," Spencer explained. "Another branch of the Space Authority, as well. We're also a quick train ride to Research Circle, which has a lot of research universities, pharmaceutical and chemical companies, and think-tanks. We're also not far from the Capitol, via the ultra-bullet, and there are some amazing universities there as well. I'm heading to Research Circle on Thursday–you're welcome to come if there's nothing you want to see here that day."

That was a thought, since most of the sessions that day weren't my field. I loved how they had such a complex network of ultra-fast trains here. Even the planes and cars were faster than back home.

Spencer left for his meeting as the session was ending and everyone at the table started talking about what they were going to do next. Margie began assigning workshops for the duration of the symposium so we could take notes and share.

"Tomorrow I'm attending the student symposium, I also hope to catch Dr. Harlowe's talk," I said. As well as Narif's.

"Student symposium? It would be better for you to attend something else so you can share notes with the group." Margie frowned at me.

Deb rolled her eyes. "I'm pretty sure she's going to the student symposium to recruit interns."

That I was.

Afterward Deb caught up to me. "Margie isn't your boss. I am."

"I don't want her to be mad at me," I said softly. Co-workers being mad at you made work life harder.

Deb shook her head. "You know what you're here to do. Go do it. I've got your back."

"Thank you." I went off to catch a session.

Later, I entered the ballroom where lunch and the afternoon session was being held. I was looking for Deb and the rest of my co-workers when I heard my name being called.

"Come sit with us." Dr. Harlowe waved me over to a table with a bunch of people I didn't know.

Why not? It wasn't like I had to sit with my co-workers. I saw Narif with a bunch of other people. Also, I really didn't want Margie to try to make my schedule. I was here more for networking anyway.

"Thanks." I joined everyone. "I'm Dr. Grace Ellington."

Dr. Harlowe led some quick introductions, which included Dr. Alfonso from the Research Circle Collaborative and Dr. Mariano from BaySci.

From what I understood the *techies* were sort of like if MIT had siblings. Most were creatively named, like the Bayside Institute for Science and Rockland Technical Institute, nicknamed BaySci and Rock Tech, respectively.

Though there were plenty of good universities that weren't among the techies and an extensive network of state universities and community colleges.

"Grace is interested in seeing your project, Dr. Alfonso," Dr. Harlowe said. "Maybe, if she's free Thursday, she can come along when you give Dr. Mariano and her students a tour of the construction?"

"Oooh, I'd love that, if you have room," I replied. From what I could tell, a CeCe was essentially a cold copper collider–and this one was almost finished. I might be able to meet some interesting people, too.

Dr. Alfonso, who was older, and balding, nodded. "We could probably work that out. They were also interested in seeing the visualizer, which one of our member institutions has developed, and will be used in conjunction with Sissy. That's what we call her, since she's the bigger sister to the one overseas."

"That sounds amazing. I have time on Thursday." That made me excited and hopefully would prove fruitful—or at least interesting.

Dr. Mariano gave me a smile, which lit up her entire face. "What *is* Compass BioTek doing? You seem to have a very large amount of interesting research going on for a biotech company."

"Not building our own super collider or particle accelerator," I assured, as a server brought around salads for everyone.

Dr. Alfonso shrugged, pouring dressing on his salad then passing it around. "Given Nick Thanukos' field of study, it really doesn't surprise me that Thanukos-the-younger has an interest."

"True." I nodded. Of course. Some of the older people might know of Spencer's dad and his work.

"Are you continuing Dr. Thanukos' research?" He gave me a sly look, taking a roll, and passing the basket on.

I shook my head as I added dressing to my salad. "Dimension mapping isn't my field."

Not anymore. And honestly, I didn't feel that sad about it.

"Right," Dr. Harlowe said softly, taking a bread roll then handing me the basket. "His dad was a particle physicist."

"Speaking of fathers, your father's a chemistry professor, isn't he? I can't remember which university, but I've seen him around," Dr. Mariano continued. "Nice guy."

I passed the bread basket on. "No. But you're the second person today that's asked me that. Now I'm curious."

Especially since I'd also been asked that at the science dinner—and at a Daedalus Society function.

We chatted as we ate lunch then the program started. After, I caught a couple of sessions, then headed over to the other side of the hotel where the Daedalus Society reception was.

I texted Spencer.

Me

Off to the reception, see you at the party. Hope your meetings are going well.

The lobby and bar area were filled with people talking and drinking. A lot of them weren't even wearing symposium badges. But this was probably a good place to network.

An omega sat at a table with a Daedalus Society sign, checking people off a list. There was delta security present. Deltas were about as big and strong as alphas and often used as security. A few alphas sat nearby chatting and having drinks.

"Students aren't free? Usually, students are free. Are we at least half price?" the young woman in front of me asked.

"I'm sorry. This place is really expensive so we can't do that for this one," the woman at the table said.

"Oh. Should we just go? If we leave now maybe we won't have to pay for parking?" Her shoulders drooped and she turned to the guy with her.

My heart went out to them. I remembered those days. How many networking events had I missed because I didn't have money for gas or parking or a drink at the bar?

"I'll pay for them. Also, I'll pay for any students that don't have tickets. Here." I fished one of my brand new business cards out of my pocket and wrote my cell number on it.

"Really? That's very kind of you," the woman behind the table said, as I scanned my phone, paying for their tickets. I'd already paid for mine ahead of time.

"Thanks, but why would you do that?" the guy asked me.

"A couple months ago I was eating instant noodles for dinner every night, and now I have a job that pays me ridiculously," I replied, checking myself in.

We went inside and I headed for the bar.

"Thanks," the woman called, as the guy said, "I'm going to text Ina."

The reception was a little uncomfortable. The couple of people I recognized from my chapter were not very welcoming and a few others dismissed me because of who I worked for. Maybe I should just head over to the Compass BioTek party.

"Thanks again," the guy I'd paid for said. He was at a table full of what were probably students. "This is the person who paid for our tickets. I'm Russ."

"Um, you can sit with us, if you want. We're just students though," the young woman who'd been with him added.

"Thanks." I took an empty chair. "I'm Grace, I work for Compass BioTek, and I'm feeling massively out of place here." I laughed and took a pull of my beer.

Someone leaned in. "I didn't expect it to be stuffy. Our stuff is fun, but I'm also in a university chapter."

The students were chatty. Most of them went to university in the area, were presenting tomorrow, or were here with professors.

Russ looked at me. "You have a PhD, right? Do you have a pack? Did people give you shit about getting a PhD when you'll *Just get packed up like a good little omega?*"

Several people grimaced.

"I hate that fucking question," someone muttered.

"Um, I'm actually a gamma. I didn't really get any of that during my PhD. But I mostly did directed study." It felt weird to lie like that, though that's what my fake record said. "But I did get a little of that during undergrad."

Not from classmates but from church people, especially since I went to a state university and not a small Christian college. *Why go to college if you're just going to stay home with the kids?* I didn't even find a husband while in college, either.

More heads nodded.

"You're a gamma? I'll have to tell my friend Enid. She's a gamma, too, and would love meeting another. She's not a scientist, though," Russ told me.

"Please. Maybe we can all have pizza tomorrow night or something," I said. "I've never met another gamma."

"Your pack supports your work?" someone else asked, eying my ring from Wes.

"Absolutely. The whole reason why I'm here is because one of my alphas knew that I wanted to see the particle cutter at PIIP, so he arranged for us to come." I smiled shyly.

Someone put her hand to her heart. "That's so sweet."

"Any food? I'm starving." A young woman rushed in and pulled up the chair. "Thank you so much for letting me know it was free. I can't believe someone paid for all our tickets. Someone has a rich alpha." She grinned.

Everyone else laughed.

"What?" She looked around and I realized it was Inara, the one yesterday that had given me the tea.

"Yeah, I guess that, too." I chuckled. "I'm Grace. You're Inara right? You're a fellow at PIIP? Dr. Harlowe says that you're presenting tomorrow."

"Oh, it's you. You toured PIIP yesterday." She smiled. "Dr. Harlowe told you about me?"

"She did." I jerked my head over to the snack table. "Get some food before it's gone."

The students told me all about the work and studies. Just being around people like this made me miss my cohort. Where were they all now?

Inara kept staring at me, it was a little weird.

I caught her eye. "Do I have food in my teeth?"

"Um, sorry," she blustered. "It's weird, but do you, um, have a–"

Oh. "Sorry, no but my dad's not a chemistry professor."

She shook her head. "Actually, I was going to ask if your brother's in engineering school at Natty. You look just like him. But his dad *is* a chemistry professor."

"No, I don't." I shook my head, belly twinging. Someone else who looked like me? But then there were only so many variations in the universe.

"Creed's my best friend from undergrad. He's the one who encouraged me to apply to PIIP." Smiling shyly, she pulled up a picture on her phone.

I took a look at the smiling blond young man, with blue eyes. Who looked *absurdly* like me, only his eyes were bluer.

Shit. Had I actually found this dimension's Grace? Who was called something else? And a *dude*. Creed. Also, a virtue name.

Engineering? I'd always found Wes' engineering talk interesting and it did use a lot of math. Creed was younger than me, but my mom had also had me when she was in her early twenties.

Mind. Blown.

"That's why I was staring at you when you toured PIIP," she said, passing the phone around to the others who echoed her sentiments. "I was going to ask you, but Dr. Harlowe intimidates me. Then you were with Spencer Thanukos, and well..."

"He's actually really nice," I assured.

"Creed's taking the train down tomorrow to see my presentation and to hang out in the bar and see if he can make any contacts. He's graduating in a couple of weeks and looking for a job." She ducked her head. "Okay, he's hoping to get some sort of fellowship at Compass BioTek, but he hadn't heard yet and figured a little networking wouldn't go amiss after I told him there was a whole battalion of you here."

"Is he close by? I can get him into the Compass BioTek party tonight." I sort of wanted to meet this dimension's me. Hopefully it wouldn't cause an incursion or some other anomaly. If that's even what he was. Genetics *were* weird. It was probably just a coincidence.

As long as I didn't meet this dimension's version of my mother. If there even was such a thing. Yeah. That probably wouldn't go well. Especially if she was kind.

Inara shook her head. "He's not leaving until morning. But I'll introduce you to him tomorrow."

"Can *we* go to the party? Is the food better?" Russ laughed.

"Yeah, we can all blow this and go get better food," I replied.

"Seriously?" one of the others asked.

"Let's go." I stood.

I settled my tab for the student tickets at the check-in desk, then we went over to the ballroom where the party was. Someone from marketing frowned as we approached.

"They're with me, that's not a problem, right?" I flashed my badge.

"Not at all, Dr. Ellington, go right in," she ushered us in. Music played, the liquor was flowing, and food was *everywhere*.

"Have fun," I told them. "Good luck tomorrow." I went to find Spencer.

"Grace." Dr. Mariano waved me over where she and Dr. Harlowe were drinking glowing drinks.

"Hey." I looked around but didn't see Spencer.

"If you don't mind traveling with students, you're welcome to take the train with us on Thursday," Dr. Mariano said. "A couple of other people are going, too. You can also make your own arrangements."

"I'd love to join you. Thanks." We talked for a bit then I went off to find Spencer.

"My good doctor." Spencer beamed when I joined him.

We made the rounds as he introduced me to people.

Finally, he looked at his phone. "Shall we leave and get some food?"

My belly rumbled as he took my arm and led me toward the door. "Sounds fantastic."

Chapter Thirty

Grace

"Your presentation was amazing," I told a teenager, after the high school portion of the student presentations. "I'm Grace, from Compass BioTek. Applications for our high school summer intern program close soon. While we're far, and I know summer's almost here, I hope that you'll consider applying. We have a partnership with Rockland Technical Institute for housing." I gave her my card and a brochure.

"Compass BioTek?" She gave me a curious look. "Thank you."

I found a few more students and encouraged them to apply, as well as gave out brochures to some teachers. Then I sat and listened to the college and graduate student presentations, some of whom I'd met last night at the Daedalus Society reception. I took a few notes as I wondered if any of them would be our nineteen-year-old with a penchant for arson. Though by now most students had plans for summer.

Inara's presentation went well. Though all the presentations were short and there wasn't a lot of time for questions.

Afterwards, I went over to her. "You did great."

"You came." Her face lit up.

"Of course I did."

A guy joined us and swept her off her feet. "Inara. That was fantastic. Aren't you glad you applied? I knew you could do it."

"Creed!" She laughed as he spun her around. "Put me down."

My heart thumped. I didn't see his face. He was slim, but very tall. Brennan tall. Though he was a bit of a beanpole. A scent like peaches, but sweeter, with a dash of cinnamon tickled my nose. As did the scent of alpha.

He was an *alpha*.

"Creed, I want you to meet Dr. Ellington. She works for Compass BioTek," Inara said as he put her down. "This is my friend Creed Thorne. He's the engineering student at Natty I was telling you about yesterday."

"Hi. It's nice to meet you, Dr. Ellington. I'm Creed Thorne. I'm about to graduate from Engineering school at National University of Science and Technology in electromechanical engineering. What do you do at Compass BioTek?" Creed turned and froze.

As did I. While he looked like me in the picture, in person it was like looking in a mirror and seeing me without makeup through a social media filter that was meant to make you look like a guy but really only added some chin fuzz.

"Wow, the resemblance in person is even stronger," Inara breathed as we just stood there, staring at each other.

"Can everyone please clear the room so we can get set up for the next session?" someone announced. "Lunch is grab and go in the main ballroom."

"We should go out to the lobby. You can find us a seat, and I'll share my lunch with you." Inara took Creed's arm.

Creed continued to stare at me, as he allowed Inara to drag him out of the room. She pushed him into a chair in the lobby.

"Save the couch for us, we'll be back with food." Inara grabbed my hand, and we headed into the ballroom.

"Wow, we look a lot alike," I said softly, as we got in the food line.

"Creed's a good guy. He'd be an asset. Smart. Loyal. Hardworking. Great big brother," she stated.

We grabbed our food, and I grabbed an extra box lunch. "Just getting one for my colleague," I brushed off, striding out like I knew what I was doing.

Inara giggled. "They just let you take an extra, that's brilliant."

We went back to Creed who was frowning at his phone.

"Here you go." I handed him the extra.

"Thank you. You look a lot like my little sister," he said softly. "Perhaps we're cousins."

"Maybe?" Not in this dimension. "You have sisters? I always wanted sisters."

"She does look like a blonde, short-haired version of Mercy," Inara said.

He pulled up a picture of a tiny girl with blonde pigtails. "I was thinking more like a grown-up version of Hope."

A pang shot through my heart, because the little girl looked an awful lot like little me. My dad always braided my hair like that. Though her hair looked curly and her nose was different.

"Awww. You have a lot of siblings?" I asked as we ate.

"Tons," Inara answered for him. "All brilliant. Just like all his parents. He's from a pack full of scientists–not just everyone's favorite chemistry professor."

Creed paused. "You know my father?"

I shook my head. "No. People just keep asking if he's my dad."

He thought for a moment and nodded. "I could see that. You're in Daedelus Society, right? He's very well known there."

"Yes." Oh dear. If Creed was this universe's me, was this professor guy some version of my biological father?

My heart raced and I felt my phone buzz. I checked it.

Evan

Are you okay? I felt that all the way over here.

Me

I think I just met this universe's me. It's weird.

"Dr. Ellington, are you all right?" Creed's voice grew soft.

"Just one of my mates texting me," I replied. "Everything's fine."

Creed told me about his work and studies as he polished off his food. It sounded impressive.

"How do you like Compass BioTek? I'm really hoping to work there through their fellowship program," he said.

"I just started, but so far I like working there a lot."

A woman came over to me, the teacher of one of the students I'd invited to apply. "Excuse me," she said, "can any high school student apply for the internship program, or only the ones you invite?"

"Anyone can." I handed her my card and a brochure. "Please, encourage your students to apply. It's going to be a really good program. If they're busy this summer, please, keep us in mind for next year."

"Thank you." She left.

Creed took one of my brochures and looked at it.

"You know her entire class will be applying now and putting your name down," Inara said.

"It's part of why I'm here." I shrugged. "They're doing some really great things. This high school internship program is just one of them—it's brand new."

"If my parents weren't so anti-Compass BioTek I'd get Mercy and Dare to apply. They're in high school. Mercy is really good at math. She could do well if she applied herself, but she'd rather play skate smash. She's in some ultra-competitive travel league and wants to go pro." He shrugged, like sports weren't important.

"Yeah, an internship like this could be what she needs to like school," Inara agreed.

"Your parents don't like Compass BioTek? Will they be okay if you get the job?" I asked. "And I mean this as someone who was kicked out of the family for getting a PhD in math instead of teaching kindergarten."

"I'm sorry to hear that. I hope that my parents can see the opportunities it offers, even if they don't like the company," Creed told me.

"Why don't they?" I inquired, curious. "It seems like safe and affordable health procedures would be a likable thing."

I'd done some research before taking the job and couldn't find anything objectionable.

"It's more because Spencer Thanukos is a businessman, not a scientist, and at the end of the day, they think he's about profit, not humanity, which they are against."

"Oh, I see. My mom hated that I was good at math." So, this dimension's almost-me was from a pack of science hippies? I did see parallels.

"She's good now though, right? I mean a PhD, a good job that you like, and a stable pack? That would be everything I could ever want for my child." Inara looked anxious.

"No. She died before I graduated. I don't talk to my brothers."

"I'm sorry." Inara squeezed my knee.

"It's okay, now, thanks. This is dumb, but can I see a picture of your family, Creed? Curious if all your siblings look like you." I took a sip of soda.

"Most of them do," Inara said.

Creed pulled up a picture on his phone. There was a stack of kids, most of them looking similar to Creed, though not as similar as Creed and I looked. But I was studying the parents. Three guys. One was a smaller guy who bore a very close resemblance to Creed but looked most like the teenage girl. Three women...

I exhaled as I confirmed that none of them looked anything like my mother.

Yeah, this is not this dimension's you. This is not your parallel family. This is not a multiverse. You know that, so just calm down.

"Dr. Ellington, are you all right? Do you want me to walk you to your room? Perhaps find one of your packmates?" Creed offered.

My phone buzzed again.

Evan

I need pictures.

"I'm fine. Thank you. Stayed out too late last night," I brushed off. Which was true.

Dr. Mariano stopped and waved. "Grace, are we still on for tomorrow? We're leaving here bright and early, does that work for you? I'll text you the details."

"Perfect. I'll get my own ride back though," I replied. Spencer would be in the area, too. I'd just call a car and meet up with him after I was done.

"See you tomorrow." With another wave she left.

"Going on a field trip tomorrow," I added to Creed and Inara.

Creed cocked his head as she left. "Grace. Your name's Grace?"

Inara giggled. "Fits right in with your family's naming scheme. Dr. Ellington, do your brothers have virtue names, too?"

"Nope." My brothers had biblical names. Religion did exist here, but it wasn't as big of a thing. Even holidays like Christmas were more secular than religious.

"Ugh, I have to go soon and help with the afternoon sessions. But first I need a picture of you two." Inara checked her phone.

"As long as you send it to me," I said.

Inara took a picture of Creed and me. After she sent it to me, I texted it to Evan... and Riley.

Riley

> **Who in the fuckity fuck is that?**

Me

> **Interdimensional me, I guess?**

"Sending it to your mates?" Creed grinned. "I might have sent it to my sister Verity."

Evan

> **Oh shit. Dude you?**

Me

> **Alpha dude me.**

"I've got to go. Hey, my friends want to know if we're really having pizza tonight?" Inara said.

"Sure. Pick a place, invite your friends, and anyone you think should be there. We'll call it a Compass BioTek student mixer, and I'll pick up the tab." Why not feed the students? Free pizza had meant a world of difference some weeks.

Inara went off, but Creed and I just sat there, talking. Conversing with him was easy, and thanks to Wes, I could follow a lot of what he was doing.

"You never told me what exactly you do for Compass BioTek. What's your PhD in?" he asked.

"Theoretical mathematics. My specialty is string theory, and I work a lot with qubits. I'm doing a project with simulations and quantum computers," I said.

"With medical applications? You're doing something with nano-quantum-computers for medicine?" he asked.

I nodded. "They are, not me, though."

"You mentioned your mom, but what of your dad? I don't mean to pry but..." He spread his hands. "I'm guessing you're just a few years older than me?"

"Yeah, not why I wanted to say *hi*." I shook my head.

Creed nodded. "So, who is he?"

Shit. Of course he'd wonder that.

My heart pounded. "I don't know and don't care. That's not..."

"It's okay." His voice went soft again. "Hazards of having a sister like Verity. Though her specialty is plant genetics not people. She works with omega lilies mostly."

"That sounds fun. She's probably trying to figure out the probability of us being related?" I could see her making whatever Punnett squares were called here, trying to figure it out.

"Her first question was when you were born, wondering if you were a missing sister or something." He smiled.

I laughed. "Pretty sure we're not twins."

Though this was weird and a little uncomfortable. Was this a mistake?

"Grace, there you are. You *are* coming to Narif's presentation, aren't you?" Margie hustled over to me, shooting me a scolding look.

"Is it that time already?" I checked my phone. Shit. It was.

"Go on, I don't want you to get in trouble," Creed said.

"I'll see you later. This was fun. Come to pizza." I stood and followed Margie, who was now joined by Tish.

Margie eyed me but didn't say anything. Inside the presentation hall, I found Spencer and sat next to him.

"How is everything going?" Spencer asked me after Narif's presentation. We left the ballroom and found a quiet corner and I took a moment to nestle into his arms.

"It's been interesting. I met an engineering student who applied to one of our programs and is waiting to hear back." I showed Spencer a picture.

He sucked in a breath. "The resemblance is uncanny."

"Yeah. This dimension's me is an alpha dude. Who would have thought? At least this dimension's version of my mom's not part of his family, I couldn't handle that." For a moment I leaned into him, letting his scent wrap around me.

Spencer held me tightly, planting a kiss on my forehead.

"I know that's not true. I'm freaking myself out over nothing, like am I creating an incursion or something by talking to him? But Creed is also really nice," I added.

"Creed?"

"Creed Thorne. Apparently that professor, the one that people keep asking me if he's my dad, is *his* dad. What are you doing next?" I asked.

"Another business meeting. One I need to run to. Would you like to come? It won't be interesting for you, but I've missed you." He gave me a kiss.

"I've missed you, too. But I'm taking a bunch of students out for pizza. I met them last night at the Daedalus Society mixer. You can join us after the meeting, I'm sure they'd love to meet you," I told him.

"You're leaving the hotel?" He gave me a look. "Take a car, make sure you text me the address. Be safe."

"I will." I kissed him. He left and I texted Wes to see how his day was and emailed the fellowship coordinator about Creed.

I ducked into another presentation, then made my way out into the lobby.

"Found a place," Inara told me. "Can we invite others? I have some friends who weren't here today or last night."

She was with Creed and a couple of the people from last night.

"Go for it. I just need to know where we're going," I replied. "Let's go have some pizza."

We'd taken over the entire back patio, which despite the sticky heat, was filled with college and graduate students eating pizza and wings and drinking beer, while talking science.

One of the omegas I'd met yesterday, Russ, came in, waving at us, a young woman with blue hair, an undercut, and a sleeve of tattoos in tow.

"Russ, when you said we were going for pizza you didn't say it was with the science nerd." She rolled her eyes, but waved. "Hey, In*a*."

"Hey, En*id*." Inara grinned. "It's *free* pizza and beer."

"Really, thank Grace," Russ said. "Actually, Enid, I wanted you to meet Dr. Grace Ellington, from Compass BioTek."

The small woman eyed me. "Because they need artists to make murals in their lobby?"

"Because she's like you." Russ grabbed a slice of pizza and took a bite, as he dragged a chair over.

She turned away, scent filling with hurt. "Oh. Russ, it's not like omegas meeting each other. I've explained this to you."

Enid grabbed a cup and filled it with beer from one of the pitchers and downed half.

"I'm sorry," I said softly. "It was my idea. I... I've never met another gamma before."

"Well, now you have," she snapped. "I'm Enid. My parents were Fundies. So, did you have the omega starved or beaten out of you when you wouldn't marry who you were told to before you'd even blossomed?"

I met her gaze, my heart wrenching at the pain in her eyes. "Beaten. And it was because I wanted to be with someone she didn't pick."

Which was sort of true. She really wanted me to marry one of the church boys from our small town. Why anyone would want to marry them was beyond me.

Apparently here Fundies disavowed packs, believing every alpha deserved their own omega and shouldn't have to share—even if it meant mating with teenagers.

It wasn't legal, but it happened.

"Wait, what? I thought gammas were a genetic thing." Inara's jaw dropped.

Enid crumpled. "I'm sorry, I..."

"It's okay. We don't have to talk about it. I'm sorry, I wasn't trying to start anything." I took the pitcher and refilled her glass.

It hadn't truly hit me that most gammas were going to have backstories even more tragic than mine. The idea that I caused her pain made me feel horrible.

"It's fine, it's just... fuck."

"Sorry, Enid," Russ squeezed her hand.

Inara frowned. "I don't understand."

"And that's why I don't do this." Enid chugged her beer and left for inside.

Inara stood to follow.

Russ shook his head. "Give her a moment. I fucked up."

"Sometimes a genetic switch is thrown, creating a gamma, but more often it's circumstance," Creed said softly. "War, famine, extreme poverty, very violent situations, asshole parents."

I waited a moment then excused myself. Enid was in the bathroom.

"Are you okay? I'm sorry. It was selfish of me to ask him to bring you." I asked softly as she fixed her hair in the mirror.

"I don't mean to be a bitch. It's been a day, and I shouldn't take it out on you, but..." Enid sighed. "It's hard."

"It is. I spent most of my PhD in therapy." To have your parents *know* what you were and then willfully take it from you? How awful.

"You escaped Fundies, too?" She eyed me curiously through the mirror as she redid her lipstick.

"My parents didn't believe in designations." It was the truth, just the wrong truth.

"Equalists. Just as bad but without the floral dresses. Russ knows I don't like being around female omegas—even his science friends. They get all sad when they find out I'm a gamma and I don't need their bullshit." She rolled her eyes.

I nodded. "I feel like I don't act or react the way people expect because I don't know better. Growing up, I didn't know there were different designations. Then you add in the bizarro gamma responses..."

"Tell me about it." A smile cracked her lips. "I threw a bucket of paint on a client who startled me today."

"I hit a shooter with a chair and gave everyone in the fancy restaurant a heart attack." I laughed.

"Fuck, that was you? In the green dress? I saw that on social media." She turned to study me.

"Yep. Interrupted my birthday dinner. How dare they?" I snorted.

Enid stood close to me. She frowned. "Wait, you have an alpha. Alphas? I smell mates."

"Yeah. I have two mates, and," my head ducked. "Maybe a third."

"Oh." Her look went thoughtful. "And your mate's pack... they're okay with you?" Enid shifted uncomfortably. "I always thought... I mean... what alpha..." She looked away. "I didn't want to be shot up with drugs and mated at thirteen, but that doesn't mean I didn't ever want a mate..."

"Mine want me." My voice went soft as my heart wrenched.

She sighed. "Well, that gives me hope."

The door opened and Inara popped her head in. "Everyone okay?"

"We're fine, Ina," Enid reassured. "I guess we should stop hiding and come back out."

We rejoined our table.

Russ was talking to Creed. "Are you going back to Natty tonight? Finals are soon?"

"Yeah, next week. There are no classes this week. I'm staying with Ina tonight. I was thinking of bugging my sister tomorrow, since Research Circle's not far by train," Creed said.

"Bug your sister? Just one?" Inara laughed as she sat back down. "Not get a home cooked meal or hug your parents? Verity goes to Briar University. Creed's home is walking distance."

"Oh, is that where you both went for undergrad?" I asked, having no idea where that was.

Enid sat back down by Russ, and he put an arm around her.

"We went to Marquess, but the campuses are adjoining," she told me. "Once upon a time, Marquess was for alphas and Briar was for betas. But now they're both for everyone."

"And omegas couldn't go to university at all. So glad that's not true anymore." Russ grimaced.

We ate and talked and gradually Enid relaxed. My phone buzzed.

Spencer

> **Done. May I join your pizza social?**

Inara grinned. "Who's that?"

"Spencer wants to know if he can come by." I couldn't help but smile.

"*Please* have him come by," Russ said.

"Is Spencer Thanukos your alpha? I've seen the way he's with you." Inara's voice went sing-song.

"He's my mates' packmate." But I grinned. Hard.

I nodded and we laughed. This was nice. They were nice. Maybe I'd make some science friends after all.

Chapter Thirty-One

Brennan

"Thank you. It's a pleasure doing business with you." I shook hands with the man who'd been at odds with my mother for *months* over selling his building.

A building I'd put an offer on a couple days ago and was now closing on.

"Thank you. Are you sure you want to forgo the usual inspections and closing?" The alpha frowned.

"I'm sure. This will make a great building for my foundation," I told him. I wanted to close quickly so my mother couldn't find a way to stop the sale.

He picked up his briefcase. "You know, I nearly didn't call you back, based on your last name. But my pack and I stayed at one of your hotels last year and it was incredible. It's not that I have an issue with her project. It wasn't me being precious about this building–it's more of a pain than a legacy anyway. I won't be sad if you tear it down or even use it as leverage. I just detest bullies and well, I needed to sell it at a certain price, and I won't be called *selfish* for looking out for my pack. Not all of us own lots of buildings."

"It's never selfish to look out for your pack, and I'm so sorry she did that." I shook his hand again and left his office. The building had been in his family for a long time. His pack was aging, and they were selling things off both so that they could retire and to put away some money for their children and grandchildren.

That part of State Street was historic enough that my mom could rally people around 'bringing community back to State Street' but not so historic that she couldn't rip nearly everything down and offer lowball prices. The project took up two city blocks, and was going to be a mixed office, retail, entertainment, and housing complex with green space and gardens–a *live, work, and play* project and her most ambitious development yet.

Now I owned the last building that she needed. While I would absolutely make it the Thanukos Foundation Building, put our office at the top, and rent out what wasn't being leased already, this building was really a chess piece.

But she didn't need to know that.

I got on my motorcycle to go back to my office. The investigator that Terrance had originally referred me to when I'd wanted to research Grace was now researching Ian Murphy. We also had some very interesting information on him that was sent to the lawyer licensing board.

Our pack lawyer had already sent Ian several letters which had been ignored. The next step was to take legal action. Not against my mother, but *him*. It probably wouldn't end well for his career, and I felt bad about it. But what he was helping her do was wrong.

Wes had also found my accounts and changed all the passwords so that my mother couldn't try to hide anything from me. We'd also filed a lien against what she'd acquired to make my inheritances less liquid. I'm sure Wes had done some other things as well.

I came back to my office. Terrance immediately came in and sat down.

"You bought it." His brow furrowed.

"My pack bought it, not the company. I'm having the sign at the top changed tomorrow." I grinned.

"How can something be funny and terrifying at the same time?" Terrance rubbed his chin.

"You've met my family. How is everything going with the estate project? We got a new team in there, right?" I asked, checking my email.

"Yep. Someone already tried to threaten the garden team and were run out with shovels," he laughed.

We'd ended up flying in a team from one of our hotels to do the gardens, and we were bringing in a restoration crew from out of state. Sure, it was a little extra money but knowing that these people couldn't be bought or threatened by my mother was worth it.

"We've also checked everything backward and forward; and shored up our suppliers, we're good," I added.

"I'm sorry, you can't go in there," my assistant said to someone.

"Like fuck I can't. Brennan Brannigan Morris, how dare you?" My mother strode into my office, brushing past her.

"You are going to have to be more specific, Mother. Also, I have asked you to make an appointment." I made my tone bored as I looked through my emails. Should I ban her from the building?

"Terrance, leave," my mother demanded.

Terence's look grew bored. "It really depends on what this is about. I have a right to be here if it involves our company. Also, what would people think if they knew that you were threatening single mothers with getting their children kicked out of daycare unless they gave our project issues?"

"What? As a working mom, I would never." Her look was pure innocence.

Yeah, that was a common ploy of hers. I'd already taken measures to make sure she couldn't get Riley kicked out of Hadley Hall.

"Government phone lines are recorded, Siobhan, and the historical office is part of the government." His look growing fierce, he played the recording.

Wow, I didn't know he had that. This was why he was my business partner. It's not like a lifetime of associating with my family hadn't shown him a lot of her tricks.

She remained unfussed. "You probably got that from those hackers in my son's pack of deviants. No one will believe it's real."

"I obtained it legally. Look, Siobhan, if you have issues with your son, that's one thing. But if you continue to go after this company, you won't be happy with the results." Terrance stood and met her gaze.

My mother bristled at the challenge. "Are you threatening me?"

"Stop the corporate espionage. Your petty grievances with your son have no place in business," he snapped, the room filling with alpha dominance.

"Why are you here, Mother?" I added. Yes, I should just get her blocked completely from the building. I shouldn't meet her at her office or home, either—neutral locations only.

"You cost me a lawyer," she snapped.

Did I dare ask her to be more specific?

"Katie *quit* because you encouraged her. Quit. My own child *left* the business because of *you*," she yelled, knocking a bunch of things off my desk.

Ah, so this was about my sister. My mom had torn up her letter of resignation, which included a generous two weeks' notice. So, Katie cleaned out her office, went down to HR with a new letter, turned in her credentials and laptop, and quit on the spot.

"Katie quit because she got a great opportunity, not because of me," I retorted, grabbing my laptop. "She's very talented and has a right to change jobs."

"I don't believe you." My mother knocked over a chair.

"Mother, you need to stop before I call security." I put my hand near the button under the desk that summoned security. Also, I could see my assistant hovering in the doorway, on the phone.

"I'm guessing that you were the one who told her to withhold my grandbaby from me if I don't *treat her better?* I have given *everything* for you four, and now I'm being punished. I'm the victim here, not the villain." She reached out and slapped me.

I growled. "Don't."

Fuck. While she'd hit me before, it was always in private. Terrance was *in the room.* Usually, she was more careful. I pushed the security button.

Or had Katie threatening to withhold her child sent her to her breaking point?

"Mother, you need to leave. Katie is an adult. She can change jobs. It's her right to keep her baby from you if she wants. Terrance is correct, the corporate espionage stops. Wes found the bugs you had hidden, by the way." Which I'm sure she knew. They hadn't been in my office but they were around. Wes had scoured our offices with his bug-finding device yesterday.

"Again with the wild accusations. And you've been terrorizing Ian, too. He's been like an uncle to you," she yelled.

"Terrorizing? I'm tired of you keeping what belongs to me away from me as punishment. Not to mention taking scholarships from omegas was absolutely retribution for me going to the hospital with an injured packmate instead of staying at the gala. I'm tired of it. I'm an adult with my own pack and I just want to be left alone." As much as I wanted to yell or shake her, I kept my voice low and remained seated.

"If you act like an adult then you'll get treated like one!" She took a step forward.

"How has anything I've done been less than adult?" I pointed out.

Her nostrils flared. "How about this temper tantrum your pack is having?"

"You mean choosing a pack name? That's pretty normal, Mother. Katie and Liam have both chosen names for their packs. Yes, I fired the housekeeper because we didn't like how she cleans. Also, very normal," I told her.

"Ma'am, you need to leave." Security flooded my office.

"This is my son's office. I can be here," she snapped.

The Morris company didn't own this building. I was *very* careful about that.

"Mother, I think it's best for you to go," I told her.

She slapped the hand of one of the guards. "Don't touch me." My mother turned to me. "You won't get away with this. Why are you punishing me?"

They crowded her out of my office.

"Well, that was unusual." Terrance frowned. "Trap? Or did Katie threatening to keep away her baby make her go off?"

"Both are possible." I texted our pack lawyer about what happened.

"I didn't know Katie was pregnant—or got a new job. Good for her." Terrance nodded. "I'm going to make sure that your mother leaves."

"Thank you." I went out to the reception area. My assistant was trembling.

"Sorry, I tried to stop her, I really did." Shayla was a beta a couple of years out of university.

"I know. Hey, none of this was your fault. I'm sorry if she scared you," I apologized.

"I got it recorded. I sent it to you. It's not nice when parents hit their kids. Or make a mess." She eyed the items strewn across the floor of my office.

"No, it's not. And thank you for that." So that's what she was doing.

Going back into my office, I cleaned everything up, then filled out the paperwork to have my mother banned from the building.

I let Katie know what had happened.

"Sorry about that," Katie told me. "Yeah, as soon as I mentioned going no-contact and not letting her see the baby, she went unhinged. Even though a moment before that she told me I was irresponsible for getting pregnant and was going to ruin my career. Hey, sorry to cut this short, but I've got to go."

"Okay, oh, and thanks for the tip," I added.

"Who me?" She laughed. "Oh, when she figures that one out."

I ended the call. A sigh escaped my lips. Jett wasn't working today, and I didn't have any meetings. I texted him.

Me

> **Still at the gym?**

Jett

> **On my way home. Why?**

Me

> **I'm going to cut out for the day. Want to go do something?**

Jett

> **That sounds great. Want to go to the market and pick up stuff to make something for dinner?**

Me

That sounds good to me.

Grabbing my laptop and things, I left my office.

"I'm leaving for the day. Feel free to leave early," I told Shayla.

Going down to the parking garage, I got on my motorcycle, ready to leave this day behind.

Chapter Thirty-Two

Jett

I walked through the outdoor market with Brennan, his arm around my waist, as we browsed the produce stalls. Right now, there was a bit of a lull since it was after lunch but before people came to buy things for dinner. At least here in the produce area.

The market had many sections, including spices, produce, meat, clothes, and hot foods. It was a combination of stalls and shops. The head spa I liked to go to after rough days at work was here. The noodle shop I'd taken Grace to was here as well.

"What are you feeling like?" I asked as I looked at the bok choy. That would make a good side dish for whatever Brennan wanted.

"Oooh, can we get that meat? The kind that you put the sauce on and grill?" Brennan's eyes lit up.

Fortunately, I spoke Brennan and knew what he was talking about. "Of course we can. Though I need to get some more spices so that I can make the sauce. We're short on a few things anyway."

I got the bok choy and some other vegetables to grill alongside the meat and we went to the area of the market where I bought most of our spices. We'd get the meat last.

As we browsed in my favorite spice stall, my phone buzzed.

Spencer had sent a photo of Grace on a patio eating pizza with a bunch of people. She was laughing and looked *happy*. Something I hadn't seen much of since the Temporal Authority had taken her.

The guy she sat next to made me pause. The tall, blond guy looked eerily like her.

I showed it to Brennan as Spencer called me.

"Spence, what am I looking at?" I asked, as I started gathering what we needed spice-wise.

"Grace's new friend that she met at the symposium. Creed Thorne. When Brennan had Grace investigated, did he get a genscan?" Spencer asked.

"Let me ask." I turned to Brennan. "Spencer wants to know if you ever got a genscan on Grace."

Brennan shook his head. "I thought about it. But never did."

"Bren was going to but never did." I put more small bags of spices into my basket. I'd pour them in our jars at home. Evan had this huge collection of antique spice jars, most of them from his mother. Sometimes he dragged me to antique sales to find more.

"Can you have a genscan done immediately?" Spencer asked me.

"Um, sure. But *why?* Isn't Grace, you know, not from around here?" I replied, lowering my voice.

He wanted a what?

"The resemblance is interesting. I found the father online, but I can't find his designation."

"You're talking about the guy in the photo? Yes, the resemblance is uncanny, but isn't that just this world's Grace? What do you mean about the dad? Share your thoughts with the class, Spence," I added as I put the last spice I needed from this shop in the basket.

Brennan shot me a puzzled look. I handed the basket to him so he could pay for it

"What if there are no designations on Grace's world because they're illegal—and have been for so long, it's nearly forgotten?" Spencer started.

"What?" Yeah, this was above my pay grade.

Putting an arm around my waist, Brennan returned with our spices and a frown.

"Hold on. I need to get Bren on this," I said as we left the stall.

Getting my earbuds out of my pocket, I handed one to Bren and used the other so that we could both hear and speak to Spencer.

"Now, where are you going with this? Yes, this guy looks like Grace, but what does this have to do with the guy's dad and getting Grace a genscan?" I asked as we found a place to sit.

"My father was sent to temporal prison for his work with a smuggling ring relocating omegas," he said softly. "He'd get them from other worlds where omegas were illegal, then use the Omega Protection Program to set them up with new lives here. It's a long-shot, but considering there is a chemistry professor here that looks enough like Grace for people to ask her about him—and this young man she met today is his son—it makes me wonder if perhaps he was one of those omegas, and she was a child that got left behind. Maybe omegas are not illegal in her world, but are forgotten?"

"Wouldn't it be quite the coincidence for her to end up here?" Brennan said.

"Not at all," Spencer replied. "Her being allowed to stay has bothered me. As has something the agent told her. If her father was brought here for safety, wouldn't it make sense to bring his omega child here? That's assuming he's an omega."

That was an interesting theory. Spencer had also sent some photos of the dad. Yeah, that was also quite the resemblance. But still...

"I'll do the genscan, but I don't think this chemistry professor is her father. Also, just because there might be a genetic similarity doesn't mean they're actually related. So many things are so very similar between our worlds that it would make sense that there might be genetic ones, too. I mean, this piano piece she played for me the other day is eerily like one here. So are some movie and book premises," Brennan said.

"True. It's just very strange watching them." He sighed. "I suppose it's a coincidence and not an interdimensional conspiracy."

"You're watching them?" I asked. Yeah, alphas were stalkers.

"I was coming from a meeting and about to join them. It's a student gathering we're hosting. Seeing the two of them together made me pause... and worry. I care so much for her, and I don't want to see her hurt." Spencer's voice went rough.

"I get it. I'm all for being safe. Especially if this guy's appearance makes Grace feel a kinship to him. I wouldn't want him to take advantage of her," I replied, thinking of all the ways that this could go wrong.

"Absolutely," Brennan added. "But I'm just not sure this is an interdimensional conspiracy. Oh, I bought the building, also my mother stopped by my office." Brennan filled him in on what happened, and the things the investigator had uncovered.

"I think it's time to sue her for your inheritance and go no-contact," Spencer told him. "So far she hasn't moved against my business. But I don't like her treating Brennan this way."

Yeah, I didn't either. He'd told me what happened, and it made my blood boil.

"I appreciate your support. I'm suing the lawyer tomorrow," Brennan commented. "Also, you're going into Carolina tomorrow for meetings, right?"

"Yes, I'll be in Research Circle for a meeting and Grace is going to tour some facilities there," he confirmed. "Did you need something?"

"Actually, yes. If you have time there's a distillery that I'd love a case from. Grace might like it there. They don't ship. I can send you the information?" Brennan asked.

"I'll take a look. If I have time, I'll try my best," Spencer replied.

"Thank you. Anyway, we'll run the test and I'll let you know what we find. Have fun," Brennan said.

"Thank you for doing that," Spencer told us.

Brennan ended the call and handed me my phone and my earbuds.

"We're going to run a genscan on her? Weird but harmless. But she's not here." Most of the tests used cheek swabs.

Brennan stood. "We'll do a test with all the blonde hair that's everywhere. She probably has a hairbrush in Evan's bathroom. Sometimes with Spencer it's better to let him just mad-genius things while he figures it out. Testing her is harmless."

"True." I took his hand and stood. "You're asking them to bring back bourbon?"

"It's that bourbon that we were given at Christmas from one of my managers," he told me.

"Oh. I remember that." We started walking again. "Do you need anything else before we get the meat?" I asked.

He thought for a moment. "Can we get some of that tea you buy for my headaches."

"Sure." I led him to the tea shop and ordered his tea in Mandarin. Brennan sometimes got headaches, a reminder of his accident.

As she blended it, I looked at all the jars. Hmmm. I should probably get some tea for Grace. Maybe she'd like it better than the stuff Evan kept trying to give her.

I asked for that as well.

Brennan looked up from his phone. "What else are you getting?"

"Something for Grace. I'm glad Evan's trying to make her eat better but there has to be a tea she likes more than what Evan gets from the Center. She's always making faces as she drinks it," I replied.

"Oh, that's thoughtful."

We paid for the tea and left the shop, Brennan carrying everything. Threading my arm through his, we walked toward the area with the butchers.

Delicious smells filled the air as some musicians played. I loved this place more than the grocery store, and I was happy Brennan liked to come with me.

"Oh, those are the things you like." Brennan stopped at a booth and bought me candied fruit on a stick, and one of plain fruit for him. "Here you go, Dear."

"Awww, thank you, Honey." I kissed him. "Oh, you should let everyone know we're making dinner."

Taking a bite of my fruit, the crisp sugar coating cracked, giving way to a ripe strawberry.

"I will." Brennan texted the group chat. "We'll get the meat and go home, unless there's anything else you need? While it's marinating we'll see what we need to do to get the test sent off."

"Sounds like a plan to me," I replied as I bit into another strawberry.

A genscan on someone from another world. Sure. We'd indulge Spencer. It's not like it would find anyone anyway.

Chapter Thirty-Three

Spencer

I ended the call. My attention returned to a large group of students on the patio of the pizza place, which was near the research university I'd spoken at yesterday. I heard Grace before I saw her, that joyous laugh of hers tinkling like bells.

Grace spoke animatedly to some young people. My decision to bring her was resolute–this whole time, she'd been *happy*. Something that had been all too fleeting since she'd come back from the Temporal Authority.

I texted Riley.

Me

Can you tell if a record is fake?

Riley

Usually. What do you need?

I sent her Creed's father's bio.

Shortly thereafter I got a text from Brennan with information for a farm and bourbon distillery not that far from where I'd be tomorrow. I looked it up. Huh. Grace *would* probably love to visit.

I approached the small fence separating the patio from the parking lot. A bunch of the young people stopped talking and looked at me. A young woman tapped Grace on the shoulder. My good doctor turned. Her entire face brightened, a smile breaking out which made my heart warm.

"Well, this looks more fun than any party we've been invited to," I told her.

"Come join us." Grace waved me over. "I saved you a slice."

I went around through the restaurant and joined them on the patio, having a cold slice of pizza and a warm glass of beer as she introduced me to a large number of young people. Many of which were eager to meet me and tell me all about their studies.

"This is Creed," Grace finally introduced. "He goes to engineering school at Natty and is graduating soon. He's applied to work with us."

Yes, this was a young alpha. Not a particularly large or fierce one in appearance, but I could sense it under the surface.

National University of Science and Technology was a premier institution and him being in their graduate engineering program spoke volumes.

The tall and slim young man looked so very much like my good doctor. Some of their mannerisms were similar as well. Creed, too, told me about his work as others headed out and Grace settled the bill.

Finally, I squeezed Grace's hand. "I'm so sorry to tear you away, but we should make an appearance at a couple parties."

"Go have fun, it's getting late," a young woman that worked for PIIP said.

Grace waved and wished everyone left safe drives as I called a car.

"I'm sorry, did I make us late? I was having a good time," she apologized as we left the restaurant.

"Not at all." I took her arm as we waited for the car. "After we stop by where we're expected, we can do whatever you wish."

"Another moonlit walk on the beach sounds nice." She smiled as the car drove up.

I helped her inside. "My good doctor, I can't think of anything better."

In the hotel room, I sat at my laptop, putting out a couple of fires and sending some emails. Grace was in the bedroom talking to Evan and Wes. We'd gone to the parties, had a late dinner at an ocean-front bistro, then gone for a long walk along the water under the moonlight.

A perfect evening. My phone beeped.

Riley

If the record's fake, I'll eat a dinosaur dick.

Oh. Well, it would be quite the coincidence for Grace's father to be one of the male omegas my father resettled.

Me

Thank you. What's his designation?

Riley

Oh, I probably should. I sent Evan a text.

"Is everything okay?" Grace asked, coming out and slipping onto my lap, which always felt so deliciously right. She was only wearing one of *my* button-downs and tights. Her eyes rested on mine, as they got that look in them they often held when I wore my glasses. I wasn't sure why she thought they were sexy.

But I'd take it.

"Everything's fine. I just had a theory dashed." I shrugged.

"Oh, I'm sorry." She leaned up and gave me a kiss. "Which one?"

"I was curious if Creed's father was one of the omegas that my father resettled. That perhaps he came from your world and that's why you were permitted to stay." I shrugged. "But it probably isn't."

Grace frowned. "I can't even wrap my head around that theory."

"It is an uncanny resemblance—you and Creed," I pointed out, hoping my curiosity didn't hurt her fragile heart.

"True. But genetics are weird. Also, designations aren't illegal where I am. They simply don't exist. If for some reason my bio-dad had been illegal and was sent here, that would mean there would have been a possibility that my mom might have known what I was.

After spending an evening with a gamma that escaped a Fundie colony after they *beat the omega out of her*, as she so eloquently put it, I'd rather think my mom was just a regular asshole and not the extra special variety." Grace leaned her head on my chest. "Not that I still understand how I could be an omega in a world where they don't exist."

"True. Pardon me for prying. I was just curious." I planted a kiss on her head.

She looked up at me. "No worries. At another point in my life, I'd probably be curious and full of theories, too. Creed's nice, and I hope he gets the job. But I don't know if I'd ever want to meet his parents or all that. Spending time thinking about what my life would have looked like had I grown up in another world probably isn't very healthy."

"Absolutely. How are Wes and Evan? Are you doing all right? If you miss them too terribly, we can head back early," I offered.

Tomorrow was the last official day of the conference. We were planning on spending the day at the beach Friday, then heading back on Saturday. While I was thoroughly enjoying having her all to myself, I understood if it was too ambitious to expect her to be away from her mates for so long.

After all, while I cared deeply about her, she wasn't my mate yet.

"They're fine, and I do miss them, but not enough to want to go back early." She snuggled deeper into my arms, relief sluicing over me.

"I confess, it's nice having you to myself. But if you need–"

"You're enough. Promise." Her lips closed over mine, soft, sweet, and tasting faintly of chocolate.

Her words were everything I never knew I needed to hear.

"I'm having a great time," she assured. "And it is nice, having you to *myself*. We're going to have more of this aren't we?"

"Of course." I nodded. "We'll have plenty of time to travel together both for business and pleasure."

"Good. Especially if Bren has his way and we're the face of the pack." Grace gave me another kiss.

"Do you have an issue with that? It's fine if you do. I'll stand up for you." I didn't have an issue with it. It was an elegant solution. However, I worried that she agreed only to keep the peace.

Grace shook her head. "Me, have a problem with wearing pretty dresses and hanging off your arm all night? Not at all."

"I'm so very glad." I planted a kiss on her temple. "For Friday, I've gotten us a cabana at the hotel beach, so we can just lie by the ocean all day. Is there anything else you wish to do? To see?" Not that there were many places of note to take her here.

"This is perfect."

"There's a farm and distillery not far from where we'll be tomorrow. How long will your field trip be? Perhaps you can take a car to me, then we can go have a picnic and get Brennan some bourbon. It has good reviews and looks beautiful," I offered.

It was nice that she was making friends and connections. While I had no interest in seeing the construction of a giant super collider with the potential to cause a black hole, I could understand her own curiosity. Especially in regard to the simulator project.

I pulled up the farm on my laptop and we perused photos and menus.

"I would love to go on a date with you. Bourbon tasting and a sunset picnic by a pond sounds nice, especially if I'm with you." She shot me another one of her heart-melting smiles.

I held her while I finished my emails, her head resting on my chest, her eyes closed, as I occasionally tangled my hand in her hair. Finally, I finished my emails, confirmed my schedule for tomorrow, and closed my laptop.

"All done. What would you like to do now? Maybe use the hot tub on the balcony?" My dick was rock hard and I'm sure she felt that.

"Mmmm. That sounds nice. But first, I have ideas." She unbuttoned the shirt, and it fell to the ground. Grace wore no bra and no panties, but she had on a lace garter belt which held up her stockings.

I sucked in a breath. "Do you mean that, Baby Girl?"

Her look went sly as she carefully moved my laptop and draped herself over the desk, bare ass waggling at me. "Oh yes, I do... *Daddy.*"

A pleased growl rumbled in my chest.

"My beautiful, sweet, *good* doctor." I kissed the back of her neck, then trailed kisses down her back as my hand caressed her damp pussy.

"That feels amazing," she whispered.

Languidly, I kissed every inch of her bare back and ass as I continued to touch and stroke her.

"Come for me, Baby Girl." Stroking her hair with my free hand, my other hand teased her clit.

Her body trembled as a happy noise escaped her lips. Her peach scent was heavy with arousal.

"Are you ready for my cock?" Taking off my belt, I removed my pants and briefs.

"Please?" It was a near whine.

Not to deny my sweet Grace anything, I plunged into her, bracing myself against the desk with one hand and continued to stroke her hair with the other.

"You feel so delightfully perfect around my cock," I thrust in and out. "And yes, you look ravishing bent over the desk in only garters."

I brought her back to orgasm. As she came around me, I pushed all the way inside of her, knotting us tightly together, flooding her. Oh, how I loved this feeling.

"So perfect, so beautiful," I crooned, continuing to stroke and kiss her back. Gathering her up, I brought us over to the couch and cuddled her until my knot deflated.

I kissed her nose. "Better now?"

"Always. Magic dicks are the best." She grinned. "Now, let's go in the hot tub."

Chapter Thirty-Four

Grace

"**Y**ou ask a lot of questions, Sugar. Are you doing your dissertation on super collider construction?" one of the people leading the tour of the CeCe at the Research Circle Collaborative asked.

"Just curious." Nope, I was just trying to render them unnecessary for all but the most specialized projects.

Still, the construction site was fascinating and was the culmination of Dr. Alfonso's tour of the Collaborative. It was interesting to see the types of interdisciplinary projects they were doing.

Dr. Mariano rounded everyone up, which included her students, some of the fellows and interns from PIIP, myself, and a few others.

"Okay, back on the bus. Next stop, Marquess University to see the particle visualizer and some other things," Dr. Mariano announced, as we got on the little rented bus that had brought us here from the train station.

I was excited about the visualizer, since it definitely had some promising implications.

Oh, this was where Marquess was? I hadn't realized that. Should I text Creed? After all, he was going to see his sister at the adjoining school. Maybe we could grab a coffee before I met up with Spencer?

Yesterday was so much fun. At the same time, I wasn't sure if I should meet with Creed again, for the same reasons I'd told Spencer.

Still...

I texted Creed anyway.

Me

> Off to Marquess to see the visualizer. Maybe we can meet for coffee? I understand if you're too busy.

The area was so pretty. I could see the charms of studying here, in addition to the sheer amount of things being developed in what was essentially a giant research park.

Creed

> Didn't realize your field trip was here. Is it okay if my sister Verity comes for coffee, too, if she doesn't have class?

Me

> Sure, why not.

When we arrived on campus, we were welcomed and got a tour of their science facilities, which were beautiful and state of the art. I noticed a couple professors staring at me, but if Creed had gone here, I could understand.

When we got to the visualizer, I was fascinated. It was meant to predict and visualize particle reactions, complete with animations.

While it wasn't meant to replace a super collider, and they were dealing with simple experiments, this... this could possibly be the basis for what we wanted to do. I couldn't help but text Blaise and Deb in my excitement.

We finished our tour and Dr. Mariano came back over to me. "We're going to go to the cafeteria for a late lunch then see a rocketry demonstration. Did you want to come with us?"

"I'm actually going to meet someone for coffee then join Spencer. But thanks for the ride here—and including me on your tour." I'd made lots of notes.

"I want a tour when you're ready with whatever it is you're building." She grinned.

"Absolutely." I left the science building and found Creed waiting on the steps.

"Have fun?" Creed stood. Today he was just wearing shorts and a T-shirt, his blond hair in his eyes a bit.

"I did. Where to?" I asked.

"Campus coffee shop."

I looked around as we walked. "It's so beautiful here."

"It really is. But then I've spent a lot of time on these two campuses. Hazards of having professors for parents," he laughed.

"Are all your parents professors?" I asked as I followed him across campus, not really knowing where I was going.

He shook his head. "Just Mom and Dad. She's head of the chemistry department here at Marquess. Dad teaches organic chemistry at Briar. Mumsy works for a chemical company. Baba used to be a professor but now works in pharmaceuticals. Mama's a translator and professional wrangler of children. Harry has a restaurant."

"Mom, Dad, Mumsy, Baba, Mama, and *Harry?*" I grinned. Right, families with lots of parents would mean lots of parent names.

Oooh, what would my guys call themselves? Oh my god, there'd be so many dad jokes, wouldn't there?

Creed laughed. "Harry's a newer addition to the pack. But the littles call him *Daddy*. What about your parents? Oh, wait, that wasn't so good was it. Sorry." His voice went soft as he looked at his phone.

"My dad owns a hardware store. We all worked there. I don't even think my parents went to college. My mom was very young when I was born." I shrugged. "Me going to college was never not an option, though."

His smile went rueful. "I think my parents were a little disappointed that I went to engineering school instead of a PhD program."

"I'm sure they'll be proud of you regardless. Where are we going?" I looked around, as the path grew more fairy-forest-like.

"We're taking the fairy gate to Briar to meet Verity. Wait, backtrack a minute, I thought you said that you didn't know your dad?" he asked.

"The dad who raised me has the hardware store. I didn't know he wasn't my biological dad until I was getting my PhD. That secret died with my mom." That had been a tough conversation to have with him.

"You didn't want to try a genscan and see if you could find him?" He opened a little wrought iron gate, with a sign that said *Briar University.*

"Why? I don't care why he ran out on us. If he has a new family, I don't want to be reminded of what I missed out on." Very real tears pricked my eyes. I'd never know who he was. And I was fine with it.

This was also exactly what I'd told my therapist when she'd asked if I wanted to take a DNA test to try to find him.

"Hey, it's okay." He went to put an arm around me and froze. "Sorry. I have to keep reminding myself that you're not my sister."

"It's okay." I sighed as we walked through a rose garden. "I look that much like them?"

"You do. Mercy has brown hair but has a lot of your features. Hope's a blondie and probably going to be a little thing like you. But then I was a little thing and look at me now." His smile went baleful.

I was missing something. We walked through an area filled with some sort of lily. It was similar to the basic *Easter Lily* I knew but smaller and with multiple flowers on a single stem. A beautiful aroma drifted through the garden.

Stopping, I smelled them. "These are amazing."

Taking a picture, I sent it to Evan and Brennan.

Me

> I like how these smell. Can we have them in the estate garden?

Evan

> Omega lilies are always a good choice.

Brennan

> There's lots of them at the estate. They probably haven't bloomed yet.

Creed was smiling at me. "My sister bred these."

"That's what your sister does in plant genetics? Breeds flowers? I love it. Flowers make people happy." This garden was beautiful.

He nodded as he led us out of the garden. "They do. And that's what she does—she makes happy flowers. The parents think it's frivolous. But not all discoveries need to change the world. Sometimes they only need to touch one person."

That was profound.

"Did they think you would be an omega?" I asked softly. "Sorry if that's a weird question."

Briar had a very different feel than Marquess. It was just as pretty, but cozier.

"Yeah, they did. I tested as an alpha in middle school, but they thought it was wrong, which happens sometimes. Growing up, I was never big or muscular and I had a thing for stuffies. Mumsy is quite the statuesque woman. I shot up but never filled out. It was a surprise to everyone when I *actually* became alpha. Me included. Dad wanted nothing more than an omega child, and so far, it's been alphas all around. Though the younger ones are too little to test, and I'm pretty sure one of them is a beta," he explained.

"Oh." Right, that was a very real thing here–expecting to become a certain designation and becoming something else. Did people throw fits when they were disappointed about their children's designations the way they sometimes did at gender reveals?

He shrugged as he led me through the campus. "It is what it is."

The coffee shop he led me to was airy and full of plants. Students filled the outdoor patio, studying, chatting, and enjoying the afternoon.

We stood in line and got our coffees, along with a chai latte for Verity, who was on her way.

"How long are you here?" Creed grabbed us a table inside.

"We go home Saturday," I told him, taking a sip of my coffee. "Tomorrow we're going to go to the beach." I couldn't wait.

"That sounds fun." He waved at someone behind me.

A young woman with golden skin, long dark hair, and blue-green eyes bounced over to us. Tall, willowy, and lithe, her cute outfit and confident demeanor made me think of some of the popular rich girls at my university. The sort that joined sororities and had fancy cars.

"Is that for me? Thanks." Verity grabbed the other cup, took a long drink, then plopped down into a chair.

My heart twinged. Once I got to middle school I hadn't had that sort of relationship with my brothers.

"Verity, this is Dr. Grace Ellington. She has been traipsing about the Circle looking at super colliders." Creed gave me a big grin, his tone teasing. "Grace, this is my super-annoying little sister who prefers plants to people."

"Plants can't talk back," she joked. "Hi." Her hands clapped together, then went to her mouth, as she looked from Creed to me and back again, a huge grin on her face. "Oh my. Wow. This... this... oh my."

Creed chuckled. "I know."

Verity checked the time on her phone. "Dad's got a lecture in a bit. We should go sit in the back and see how long it takes for him to notice. Has she met Hale? We should all go to Mercy's skate smash game–her team's really far in the finals. Then maybe have dinner at Harry's?"

She was practically bouncing.

"Ver, that's not why she's here. She's from the PIIP conference. Ina introduced us as a possible job connection." Creed's voice got a little stern as he put his hand over hers.

"Oh." Verity looked puzzled.

I realized that like Creed, she was an alpha and smelled of driftwood and sea salt.

"Thanks for the offer, but I can't stay all that long. I've got a hot date," I explained.

Creed took a sip of coffee and grinned. "Ah, yes, because you're being courted. Where are you going?"

"We're going to tour a farm that's a bourbon distillery and have a sunset picnic. I'm excited." My shoulders wiggled happily.

A hand went to Verity's heart. "You're being courted. Oh, that's so sweet. I think I know where you're talking about. It's popular for weddings. Now, is he a physicist too? You're at the conference together, or did he just come to keep you company?"

"I'm a theoretical mathematician, and I work for his company. He surprised me with the trip because I wanted to see the particle cutter over at PIIP." My head ducked a little. "I thought it was pretty romantic."

"It is. Show Verity a picture of him." Creed's grin widened.

I gave him a look as I found the picture of Spence and I from the science dinner. "That's Spencer."

"That dress," she breathed. "That's a Vecci from their new collection. And he's... wait, is that..." Verity exhaled. "You're being courted by *Spencer Thanukos?*"

"I am." My shoulders danced again. "I also work for Compass BioTek." Might as well lay it out.

Verity looked at her brother. "Why would Ina want you to meet someone from Compass BioTek? Are you trying to give the parents a heart attack?"

Creed's look went impassive. "Graduation is *soon,* and I want to get my own job, not work for Strauss. Compass BioTek is a top company hiring people in my field. They're doing great things and treat their employees well."

"You applied for the job. I... good for you... but there will be fallout if you get it and take it. It's also far away." Verity winced. "Our parents don't like Compass BioTek. You work there? Did you walk into his office and there was sizzle? Sorry, I read too many boss romances." She giggled.

"Me, too." I laughed. "Have you read *Assistant to the Boss?* We're reading it for book club and so far it's great. Very spicy, but fantastic." Maybe I'd finish it tomorrow while lying on the beach.

"Is that the one with the omega boss and the alpha assistant?" Her eyes gleamed. "It's in the pile for after I finish this project I'm working on. You're in a smutty book club? Yes, please."

"I haven't gone to a meeting yet, but it sounded like a fun way to make some friends since I'm new in town."

"I've got a couple of good titles to suggest," she said. "Can I text them to you?"

"Sure." I didn't see any issue with Verity having my number. She seemed nice.

"So, how *did* you meet? Courted by the billionaire. There's a novel right there." Verity giggled.

"I think I've read that one," I laughed. "He's packmates with my mates. The first time we met I was standing in the kitchen, in PJs, arguing with one of the other alphas." I pulled up the picture from my birthday. "There's my mate Wes, and my mate Evan, and that's Evan's little sister Riley, she's part of the pack, too. Then there's Jett, Brennan, and of course, Spencer."

"I'm so happy for you. You have two mates in the pack? Are they physicists? Why didn't they come?" She looked around. "I'm a little nervous about you being here without anyone."

I waved that off. "I'm fine. While my mate Wes works with me, he's in cybersecurity and has work to do. Evan's an advocate for the Omega Center. And Spencer is nearby at a meeting, he's just not on campus."

"Evan, that giant one, is *not* an alpha?" Verity asked, studying the picture.

"Nope, he's an omega."

Verity fanned herself with her hand. "That teddy bear of a man is an omega? How do I get me a giant omega hunk? Mmm mmmm mmmmmmm. I had no idea they made them in extra-large and I do like my guys taller than me. Please tell me that he has a younger brother?"

Creed snorted. "Verity has a thing for big guys. And yeah, I didn't know they made them that big either."

Oh? Omegas tended to be on the small side, guys included, while most alpha females were not. I could see how Evan's size might make him especially tasty. Also, Verity was taller than any of the alpha females I'd met so far. She was probably six-foot without her heels.

"He's the only boy. But, yeah." My grin went dopey. "While I love Wes with all my heart, Evan was everything I never knew I needed."

And Spencer was everything I never knew I wanted.

"Cybersecurity? How did *you* meet? He came to fix your computer on your first day at work?" Verity asked. "Or did you have a one night stand in a bar and realized the next day that he was your new supervisor–Oooh, or did you yell at him in the parking lot?"

I laughed because I loved all those tropes. "I just started at Compass a few weeks ago. Spence got me the job after I moved here to be with Wes. I've actually known Wes since I was ten."

"Ten?" Her hand went to her heart. "Friends to lovers? Wait, no, that would be childhood love, right? Playground?"

"The park–I told him I was going to marry him the first time I met him." I grinned.

"That's so romantic. Wait, you told him you were getting married when you were ten? Are you scent matches? I've heard that scent matches can happen before you ever awaken." Her hands waved around as she talked.

I nodded. "We are."

"Awww. But why are you just coming to be with their pack now? I'm guessing you recently finished your PhD. Could you not get into a program in your field near them?" she pressed.

"It's a complicated story." I sighed.

"Sorry, not trying to pry. It's tough getting into a PhD program. It's just that I find stories of scent matches fascinating, given I grew up with the story of Dad and Mumsy colliding at a conference." She grinned.

"Really? A chemistry one?" I giggled. *Finding chemistry at a chemistry conference.* I'd read that.

Creed nodded. "Yep. Mom, Mumsy, and Baba were all PhD students and really good friends. They'd talked about forming a pack but–"

"Baba met Mama. She was an undergrad at their school. He was in love with her and wanted to marry her. But Mom and Mumsy didn't really like her because she was a beta, and *just* a French literature major. I know. Insufferable, right?" Verity laughed. "Baba was debating whether he wanted to marry Mama or form a pack with his besties."

"Meanwhile," Creed continued, "Mumsy was doing a presentation at the conference and just generally in a bad mood. Dad was an undergrad at another university. He was nervous because he was also part of a presentation."

"They literally collided in the hall. Mumsy's stuff went everywhere, and Dad apologized and helped her pick it up even though she was telling him off. Then they looked at each other and froze. Because, boom." Verity clapped her hands together. "They knew."

Creed nodded. "Mumsy was *pissed.* She was considering moving back to England after she finished her PhD if they weren't going to form a pack. Mom was mad because she had this whole idea in her head about her, Mumsy, and Baba going to the Center and filling out an application to be matched with an omega. She doesn't like it when her plans go off the rails."

"Mama was also at the conference, though she was there with Baba just for fun, and she *adored* Dad. By the end of the conference, Mumsy had come around to the fact that she'd found her omega. Mom was attracted to him, too. They decided that even if Baba didn't want to be part of their pack, they'd start one, since you only needed three people in their state. So, they brought Dad to his apartment, packed him up and took him back to theirs–even though they lived across the country," Verity said.

"Wasn't he still getting his degree?" I tried to fathom knowing that fast and making such a decision like that so quickly.

"Oh, he was. But those alpha instincts when you first meet your omega can hit you *hard*, and Mom and Mumsy wouldn't let him out of their sight. They can also be obstinate and overbearing–and it's always Mom's way or the causeway. Dad was so besotted that he just went along with everything. So, even though they'd only known each other a few days, Dad gave up everything and moved in with them, and transferred universities," Creed added.

"It was intense and a bit of a mess. Because Dad just picked up and *left*, with just a few texts and emails. Mama was actually the one who did things like help Dad formally transfer universities with minimal credit loss." Verity laughed. "Eventually, because Mama and Dad had such a friendship, and Baba and Mama were going forward with being married, Mom and Mumsy came to terms with it and the five of them formed a pack."

I finished off my coffee. "As nice as it is that they found their mates, this sounds like an anecdote for why the Center should be involved in these things."

Wow. To meet your mate and it be so intense that you dropped everything, including your classes, and *moved*? That was wild.

"Yep. When we were little, they kept it light and cute. We're told the whole story when we're older so that we understand how not to fuck everything up," Verity added.

Creed nodded. "It was a huge mess. A lot of things might have gone smoother had they taken time to actually get to know each other before mating. So many things got dropped in the whirl-wind, too. The biggest thing was Dad's girlfriend."

My belly turned. He'd had a girlfriend? Poor girl.

"This was where an advocate might have been helpful—and where the story gets sad," Creed continued. "They lived together. She was away when Mom and Mumsy moved him out. Dad was so caught up in emotions and hormones that he literally just texted *Found my alphas, bye.* He left no forwarding address. When she tried to get ahold of Dad, Mom and Mumsy got possessive and kept them apart. They got him a new phone number, had him change his email, take down his social media, and basically he cut himself off from everyone but his immediate family."

My gut wrenched. "He ghosted her. He had a live-in girlfriend, found his pack, and just dropped her with nothing but a *text.* That's not right. I mean, couldn't she have been part of it, too?"

"It's not right and that is not how it's supposed to go," Verity interjected. "This is why the parents tell us this part—so we're not assholes like they were. Because it gets worse. When she tried to see Dad, the moms called the police. When she tried to come on campus they had her dragged off. They got a restraining order. She did trash Mom's car, but to be fair, they were so possessive that they wouldn't even let her talk to Dad. Other than that single text, they never had a conversation. He never saw her letters or read her emails and texts or heard her voicemails."

"Shit. She just wanted closure," I whispered. How awful. I was so glad that me appearing hadn't caused that sort of tragedy with Wes and Evan.

"Yeah. Months later, she found his new phone number and left a frantic message about being in trouble and needing him to keep something for her. But Mom talked him out of calling her back," Creed said. "Not long after he found out that his ex-girlfriend died.

And... and that she'd been persistent because she'd been trying to tell Dad that she was pregnant."

The bottom fell out of my stomach. "What happened?"

The baby.

"I'm not sure," Creed replied. "But that something she wanted him to keep was the baby. After discovering what had happened, Dad was crushed—and mad at Mom and Mumsy, who realized that they'd fucked up, badly. Especially Mom, who did most of it, but Mumsy didn't stop it. Dad was so upset that he actually went to file to have the mate bonds dissolved. The Center stepped in, and with some heavy-duty counseling, they eventually made it work."

"For years Dad searched for the baby, hoping he could fix their massive fuckup. He never found her." Verity's shoulders slumped.

"Wow." I exhaled heavily. "That *is* a massive fuckup. Though I'm glad he never stopped looking for her." More than my dad ever did.

That poor baby. I wished that she had a happy, wonderful life. Hopefully, he never found her, because that story would fuck her up. They were all idiots, and I was surprised that he was able to forgive his mates.

Verity frowned. "He only knew two things about her, her birth date, and that her name was *Grace*. Dad has a thing for virtue names, and I guess he and his girlfriend had talked about it. They were apparently pretty serious, like wanting to bond, but waiting a little because they were only twenty and her alpha hadn't awakened yet. It's a little late, but it happens sometimes."

Shit.

"I... I'm not the girl you're looking for, Verity. I'm not your missing Grace." All these emotions whirled inside of me and part of me wanted to run out of the coffee shop.

My phone buzzed.

Are you okay?

I took a deep breath and replied.

Just hearing a sad story. Love you.

"Okay," Creed said before Verity could say anything. "You might be our cousin though. Dad's from a very omega-heavy family and one of his brothers had an epic slut era. Given how fertile male omegas are, he *has* had a few kids pop up from his misspent youth. If you're ever ready, we'll introduce you. He's a good guy, and his pack is pretty interesting."

Yeah, not the cousin either.

Still, it was eerie, and the parallels brought up emotions I thought I'd worked through.

Verity frowned but nodded slowly. "Given how alike Dad's brothers look, and how strong omega genes can be, that could be an explanation of why you look like Creed's identical twin, who just happens to be a woman."

"Kids tend to look like their omega parent?" My head cocked.

"Not always, but it's pretty common. It's a genetic survival instinct. Once upon a time, when things were more savage, children in packs who looked like their omega parent were more likely to survive, because they were treated better by the others in the pack. Especially those who weren't their biological parent, who might otherwise be hardwired to prefer their own offspring," Verity told me. "Dad's kids all look like some variation of Dad."

"So, if Evan and I have a baby they'll look like him." My hand went to my heart. I possibly wanted a baby Evan one day.

"I don't know a lot about two-omega children, but I think it might go either way? I do know that the likelihood of that child being an omega is very high," Verity said. "Especially if the omegas had an omega for a parent themselves."

I shook my head. "I'm not an omega though."

"No?" Verity's eyebrows knitted.

"She's a gamma," Creed said softly.

"Well, this is a party. Hey, asshole, didn't know you were in town. Shouldn't you be studying for finals?" A guy with long brown hair, lighter than Verity's, with a wave to it, and eyes as blue as Creed's, strode over to us. He wore tight jeans, a band T-shirt, and cowboy boots.

"Hale." Creed stood and hugged him. "I was visiting Ina at PIIP, so I came to harass Verity. Most of my finals are papers and presentations anyway."

"Right, because you and Ina are not a thing?" Hale smirked. He looked almost exactly like Creed, only with sharper features, and long dark hair. He was also broader, with a more typical alpha body type, and smelled of pluots. Like Creed and Verity, he had a southern drawl.

Creed rolled his eyes. "You know how the parents feel about us dating people."

Oh. Yeah, I could see how they might after all that.

"Yet you applied to Compass BioTek for a job?" Verity teased. Then she froze. "Oh, I didn't mean to say that out loud. Sorry."

"You did what?" Hale pulled up a chair. His eyes fell on me. "Holy fuckballs. We found Creed's double. Told you you'd make a pretty girl."

Creed play-smacked him. "Shut up. Dr. Ellington, this is my asshole brother Hale. He's studying o-chem here, which makes him a giant suck-up. Hale, this is Dr. Ellington. She's a friend of Ina's and was over at Marquess touring the physics department."

It was interesting how he kept saying that. But I wouldn't mind actually being friends with Inara.

"Did you actually apply to Compass BioTek? Mom will shit a pumpkin." Hale laughed and grabbed Verity's drink, took a sip, and made a face.

"I'm an adult and I can apply where I want," Creed retorted.

Hale eyed me. "Friend of Ina's? Okay, we'll roll with that. Has she met Dad yet? Fuck, Mom's going to shit two pumpkins. But Mama and Harry will love you. Mumsy's British, so you'll think she hates you, but I think she'll like you well enough. No idea what Baba will think. Your PhD is in physics?"

"Math. And that's not why I'm here." I looked at my phone. "I should probably go. Where's the car pickup station here? I'll call a ride to where Spence's meeting is."

"This is not the missing sister? She looks like how I'd think the missing sister would." Hale frowned.

"Nope. Not me. Do you all know about her?" My heart broke a little for them, to be hoping their big sister was out there some-where. At least they were welcoming.

"Only us three, though Dare and Mercy will be getting the story soon," Verity said.

Creed stood. "I'll walk you to the rideshare stop. It's on the other side of campus. Is he okay with you calling a car? Do you know what service to use?"

"I do." I stood. There was a special service for omegas that only had beta drivers.

"Maybe you should use my car and take her," Verity said to Creed.

"I'm fine. Thanks. And good luck on your finals, they're soon, too?"

"That they are. Though Hale and I aren't graduating. Oh, I wish we had more time. You could see my greenhouse," Verity added.

"You're really small. Wait, you're here *alone?*" Hale frowned.

I rolled my eyes. "Will you pushy alphas *stop?*"

It seemed like here in the South they took that whole *omegas should stick close to their alphas* more seriously than in Rockland.

Hale grinned. "Spoken like someone in desperate need of a whole pile of alpha siblings."

"If any of the little ones are omegas I feel so sorry for them," I laughed. Little Hope was going to have a time of it.

Creed tapped on his chin. "None of your brothers are alphas."

"While they acted like alphaholes, nope. My mom didn't like alphas." I don't know why I said that, though it was part of my backstory and true. She *had* reacted viscerally to me mentioning that Wes was an alpha.

"Oh. But you do have that *small midwestern mostly beta town* vibe," Verity said.

"That's about right. While it's been nice meeting everyone, I should go." I grabbed my phone and purse.

"Oh fuck," Hale said, looking behind me. "Sorry, I... I didn't know you were here, or I wouldn't have told Mom and Dad that Creed was at the coffee shop."

"Creed, what a nice surprise! Everything's okay? Shouldn't you be studying?" a man's voice said from behind me. He didn't have the drawl the others did. His accent reminded me a bit of my recent visit to Seaside with Wes.

"Everything's great. I took a study break to visit Ina and thought that I'd pop by," Creed replied.

"You were visiting Ina?" a woman added, voice dripping with disapproval in a way that reminded me of my mom, and I suppressed a shudder.

"She *presented her research* at the PIIP symposium. I took the train down to support her because it's a big deal for her," Creed explained. "Don't worry, I'm studying and getting my work done."

My back was still to those new people, and I didn't want to turn around. But I couldn't leave without doing so.

"Who's your friend?" the man asked. "Are you a student here? I'm Professor Thorne, and this is Dr. Thorne."

I am so sorry, Creed mouthed. *It will be okay.*

With a sigh, Creed turned to his dad. "This is Dr. Ellington. She's friends with Ina and was on a tour of the visualizer over at Marquess. She needs to leave so I'm just going to walk her out."

He's not your dad. He's not your dad. My heart raced and I turned around, even though I didn't want to for so many reasons.

"It's so nice to meet you." My heart lodged in my throat. Professor Thorne looked like Creed, but his features were more angular like Hale's. He was taller than me, but shorter and slighter than his children—or the woman with a protective arm around his waist.

The man smelled of apricots and custard. His suspenders had chemical symbols on them. His blue eyes—not my eyes but very much Creed and Hale's—went wide.

"Dr. Ellington, it's a pleasure to meet you. You... you can't stay? I've got a class soon, but I'd love to... hear your thoughts on the visualizer." The professor's voice shook as he gripped his alpha.

Dr. Thorne's brown eyes narrowed as she turned her sharp gaze on me. She was as tall as Hale, and had his hair, which was up in a sharp knot, which gave her a hawkish look. "I don't know what you think you're doing but you need to leave. Now."

It had that oily tinge. That bitch was trying to alpha bark at me.

I met her gaze even though I wanted to punch her in the tits for her highhandedness. Because she wasn't my mom.

"Excuse me, but I *am* leaving now. I need to meet someone else. I was here touring the visualizer with Dr. Mariano and a group of students." Turning to Creed, I said, "Thanks, but I'll find my own way."

Taking a deep breath, I tried to walk past them, ignoring the heartbroken look on their dad's face. Her hand grabbed my wrist, the one that had previously been injured, yanking me.

"Ow." Pain shot through me as I lost my balance and fell to my knees.

"Mom, stop, please. It's not her, just let her go," Creed pleaded. "You *really* don't want to start anything with her pack."

"Adriana, Honey, I know you're trying to protect me, but there's no need to choose violence." The professor's face crumpled as he moved toward me.

People were watching and I tried to get up, but it was hard with her still gripping me. Ow. Alphas were generally stronger than everyone else and that was going to bruise.

"Of course it's not her. I won't allow some imposter to manipulate my family," Mom retorted, finally letting go of me with a hard shove.

"Oh, it's not?" The professor's voice went soft, his eyes tearing, as he helped me up. "But her eyes, Adriana. She has–"

"Nate, it's not her," Adriana snapped.

His shoulders slumped. "I see. Are you okay? Sorry, overzealous, protective alphas and all that."

Yeah, I lived with three of them, and they weren't like that.

Before I could answer she scowled at me. "Leave before I have campus security escort you out." Adriana added that bark again.

But I had no urge to be compelled by the likes of her.

"I told you that I was leaving. Pushing me, then demanding I leave when I can barely get up on my own is unnecessary. So is speaking to me like that." I gazed at the professor's heartbroken face, my voice softening. "Professor, I hope that you find her, and I hope she forgives you." I looked at Creed, Verity, and Hale, "and I hope she loves you all, and doesn't resent that you got what she didn't."

"Wait, did she just resist Mom's bark and tell her off?" Hale hissed. "She has a death wish?"

"Gammas have death wishes, we know this," Creed whispered back.

Taking a deep breath, I mustered all my strength and self-control and hobbled out of the cafe, people staring. Part of me wanted to talk to him even though he wasn't my dad. But it would probably end with me slapping his mate and that would not be a good thing.

"Are you looking for my brother, Barrett?" The professor followed me.

"I'm so sorry." My voice broke, my back to them. "I wasn't trying to start anything. I didn't think meeting Creed for coffee would be a big deal."

But I didn't turn around. I couldn't. I wasn't his daughter—and I was glad for it, since he seemed to be part of a pack of assholes. Something about his mate's attitude felt a lot like my own mom's and that rankled.

Still, my heart broke for him.

My voice went soft, "And no, I'm not looking for anyone."

Chapter Thirty-Five

Evan

As I ate my lunch I updated my wedding-inspo pin boards so that I could send them to potential wedding planners. Earlier, when Grace was on the train for her *field trip* as she called it, we'd been sending photos back and forth.

Now I was getting pics from Grace of, well, I wasn't sure exactly what it was. But she was *so* excited. I texted Wes.

Me

I have no idea what I'm looking at. I mean I sort of understood the super collider stuff, but I don't even know what this is.

Wes

It's a modeling program. It could be the basis for what they want to do. Wait, you understand super colliders? I mean I do. But that's because I bullshitted my way into a class I had no business taking back

when I was in university so I could help her with her research.

The idea of Wes fast-talking his way into a class solely to impress his dream girlfriend was fucking adorable. He'd done something similar when we were in the military, only it was him finding reasons to interact with me.

Me

Awww. That's sweet.

Hazards of being friends with Spencer.

Wes

Fair. Hey, you're going to meet with a wedding coordinator right?

Me

Yes, but I'm going to wait for Grace. If you have more pictures send them to me.

My phone was flooded with hand-drawn sketches, including the one I'd seen of Grace in that fluffy wedding dress.

Wes

Grace and I had lots of plans. She probably has different dress ideas. I'm pretty much open to anything, I just want to make sure that if she still wants some of our old plans that she's heard.

They had *plans*. Again, fucking adorable. I created a new pin board and started adding them.

Me

> **Of course.**

Wes

> **Do you think Spence is going to bond her?**

Me

> **Well, he is courting her.**

Wes

> **I mean on this trip.**

Huh. Things had been moving pretty fast between them ever since she got back from the Temporal Authority. But things could move rapidly between an alpha and an omega. I saw it all the time.

Me

> **Would you be okay if that happens?**

Wes

> **Yeah. He makes her happy.**

> **All I want is for her to be fucking happy.**

Me

> **Same. You know when they do bond they'll have to have a party, and they won't be waiting a year until the rose garden is in bloom.**

Wes

> **Why are we waiting a year?**

Me

My parents had a May wedding. Also, Bren did buy a venue because I wanted to get married there. It won't be ready for a while.

But if you and Grace want to reenact your childhood ideas and get married sooner, I'm fine with it.

Wes

It's up to her.

Shit, Spence will throw some fancy-ass party, won't he?

Me

Probably.

Actually, I knew of the perfect person to help plan *that* party. Someone who'd not just get along with Grace, but Mrs. K.

Wes

Well, I'm off to another meeting. Eating lunch? Did I do a good job?

Wes had packed me lunch because Grace wasn't here. Brennan did so for me yesterday. While I was fine with making my own lunch, I loved someone packing my lunch for me. Wes even had put a little *I Love You* note in it.

Me

It's perfect. Thank you.

Taking the note, I put it in the box in my drawer I kept all Grace's notes in. It was my *happy box* and filled with notes from clients, pictures, and things they'd made me. The box was a reminder of why I did this job. I hadn't always wanted to be an advocate. Really, I'd taken social work and psychology classes because it was one of the more interesting education options the military offered me, and I wasn't one to turn down free education.

It wasn't until I awakened as an omega and ended up with a desk job in the family mental health clinic *because* of my background, that I realized that I wanted to be a social worker—and an advocate. I'd worked a lot with both, helping to support the families and packs of service members. So, I'd started taking all the classes I needed, then finished up after I got out of the military and began interning at the Omega Center. Once I was licensed, I applied for the advocate training program.

Now, here I was. Claire fully supported me wanting to take Blanket Brigade training while keeping my advocate position, and just going on the emergency roster. I was excited. The training didn't start until fall, so it wouldn't interfere with any of our summer plans, and it would end right before the wedding.

Another reason to hire a wedding planner. I would be *busy*. So would Grace.

Grace. I was still weirded out a little by that guy she met yesterday. Spencer's failed theory about Grace's bio-dad being one of the omegas his father resettled was also odd.

Closing my pinboards, I opened our database and looked up Nate Thorne.

Yep, there he was. He'd have to have been *young* to be Grace's daddy. But omegas did have kids in their early twenties. I couldn't view everything in his file, but I saw some things. Wow, he'd met with his advocate for decades. I scrolled down. Yep, until his advocate retired. While we kept an eye on our omegas for some time, and they were always welcome to re-engage an advocate, having one continuously for decades was unusual. Huh.

Oh, his file showed that at one point, ages ago, he was flagged as a *vulnerable omega*. Okay, that could be part of it?

Though there was nothing here that indicated he was a bad person. No, there were lots of little notes about him being sweet or applauding his volunteer efforts tutoring people in chemistry.

Hmmm. Could I tell if he was part of the Omega Protection Program? Nope. But, really, I shouldn't be able to tell. Which was why I had no luck with what Wes had suggested–which was me trying to see if I could identify any of the omegas Spencer's dad had resettled in an attempt to find a therapist for Grace.

There was also the issue that this was decades ago, and they were probably processed through Centers in Greece, or at least Europe, which made it a little harder.

Sure, I could call in a favor, but how did I even come up with a good explanation?

With a sigh, I went back to working on my case notes from all my client visits this morning. It was Thursday and Riley would be here soon. I got a hit of anxiety from my bond with Grace, followed by sadness.

What was going on? I looked at her location and she was no longer at the university she'd been at, but the one next door.

I texted her.

Me

Are you okay?

Grace

Just hearing a sad story. Love you.

Me

Okay. Love you, too.

Huh. I went back to work but kept getting panic and anxiety from my bond with her.

Carly came in. "Are you okay? You don't look okay."

I rubbed the center of my chest. "I think something is wrong with Grace."

Did Wes feel it? Their bond was stronger, but still kind of fucked. My bond with her wasn't super strong but was more nuanced.

"You can leave. I'll cover you." She opened her lunch box.

"She's away at a conference." A huge burst of sorrow and anguish rolled over me enough to make my eyes tear.

Yeah. Something was wrong.

Taking a deep breath, I called her. "You're not okay. What's wrong, Peaches?"

She sobbed. "I was having coffee with Creed when his dad walked in. The chemistry professor that people think I look like. It wasn't planned. I had zero interest in meeting him. But it was... intense."

Oh. Shit. I looked at her location. *Briar University.* I looked up the professor. Who worked at *Briar University.*

"Yeah, I could see how that can get weird. I checked him out and he doesn't seem like a bad person, but you absolutely have no obligation to meet him. This Creed guy wasn't pushing you to meet him, right?" Maybe I should have Jett run background checks on that entire family.

Yeah. I should. I texted Jett.

> **Can you background check that Nate Thorne guy's entire pack, please? Mates and adult children, especially that Creed guy who befriended Grace. Things are getting weird.**

Jett

Of course. Love you.

Me

Thank you. Love you, too.

"His alpha yelled at me, grabbed me, and threw me to the ground. But I'm going to find the front of campus and catch a ride to meet Spence and go try bourbon and have a picnic on a farm," she added while I was texting.

"Did you just say some alpha *grabbed* you?" Fuck.

"I'm okay. Apparently Creed might actually have a sister my age out there somewhere because his parents were colossal assholes when they formed their pack. Anyhow, I'm okay. Because they're not my parents. Though Creed is really nice. I'll call you later?" Her voice still shook, though the panic I'd been getting through the bond had subsided.

"Grace, it's not okay for someone's alpha to push you. Where's Spencer?" I frowned at my phone. Of course, she probably didn't realize the huge issues at hand here.

"I'm going to go to him now, and I'll tell him what happened," she told me.

"Good. Text Wes, too. Please? Hey, Creed might have a sister your age?" I went back into Nate Thorne's record. Creed was listed as the oldest.

"So, they say. This is a lot." Her voice broke.

"I know. Go find Spence. Call Wes if you need him. This is what alphas are for, Peaches. I love you."

"I miss you." Her voice became small.

I sent her all the love I could through the bond. "I miss you, too. But we'll see you Saturday."

"Love you." She ended the call.

Carly looked startled. "Someone *grabbed* her?"

"We're having a really weird situation. Grace doesn't know her bio-dad, and she ran into someone at a conference who looks like her and has a missing sister." Which was the absolute truth.

"Maybe she should get a genscan?" Carly took a bite of her sandwich.

"We're doing that." Well, Brennan was. He'd had me get her brush yesterday so that he could submit the test because Spencer had asked him to.

All of this was so weird. I trusted Riley's verdict that his record was real. But we were missing something.

"Where was her alpha?" Carly frowned. "Is she with Wes? She's not alone, right?"

"She's with Spencer. He was at a meeting down the street, and she was having coffee with someone. Grace is also very kind, and I don't want her to get taken advantage of because she feels a connection to someone because he looks like her. Here. Do you see it?" I showed Carly the picture of Grace and Creed that she'd sent me yesterday.

"Wow. Grace makes a very pretty dude." Carly laughed.

"Yeah, especially if you like beanpole alphas," I agreed. Though I wasn't drawn to him like I was Grace.

"Oh, congrats on getting accepted to Blanket Brigade training. Claire recommended me, but I think we're going to try for another baby during my next heat." She grinned as she finished her sandwich.

Awww. Brennan had told me that Katie was expecting and Lexi and Lana were trying, too. Yeah, give me all the sister-pack babies to stave off baby fever.

"I'm so happy for you." My phone buzzed. I got a picture of Riley in the lobby.

Riley

Feed me, you doofus.

Me

I'm in the office. I'll be right there.

I'd finish the case notes later.

A moment later, the door opened, and Riley came in. She plopped down at an empty desk and took out her laptop.

"Hi, Carly. Hold that thought, Evan. I have to cut a bitch." Riley started typing.

"Do I want to know? Don't do anything illegal on a government server please?" I might as well try to finish my notes.

"What am I, an amateur?" Riley rolled her eyes, gum popping. "Grace called and asked for my help. I'm just hacking the footage from the cafe where that alpha dickhead laid hands on Grace so that she can file a report with campus police."

"That is a good idea," Carly told her. One of her mates was a government hacker and he, Wes, and Riley had epic conversations sometimes.

As Riley worked, I finished my notes, and Carly ate her lunch and texted her mates.

Finally, Riley put away her laptop and stood. "Mission accomplished. Feed me."

"I think your valiant efforts also deserve ice cream." I packed up my stuff.

Riley grinned. "Sounds good to me."

Chapter Thirty-Six

Grace

I ended the call, wishing Evan could talk longer but it was Thursday. He probably had things to finish so that he could meet up with Riley. I had *no idea* where I was on campus.

Riley. I texted her and asked her about getting the footage from the cafe.

Overwhelmed, I slumped on a bench and texted Wes.

A sob escaped my lips. That woman *hurt* me.

"Hey, it's okay." Creed sat down on the bench next to me. "Can I hug you?"

I nodded and let him hug me.

"Come on. Verity said I could use her car. I'll drive you to your alpha. Where is he?" Creed asked.

"It's fine. He's not far. He's at..." I checked my phone, "Strauss Chemicals?"

"It just so happens, I know how to get there. I did an internship there during undergrad," Creed told me.

"I told you to leave," a female voice snapped.

"Leave me alone. I already had an asshole parent, thank you very much," I retorted, looking up. Adriana Thorne scowled at me, her scent spicy with anger, making my own anger flare.

Professor Thorne was nowhere to be seen, but then I think he had to go teach a class.

"I. Am. Not. Her. But I'm curious why you think I'm not? I'm guessing you know that she is actually dead and thought it would be better for your mate to look for her all these years instead of telling him the truth? Because you got to *you're not her* pretty quick," I added.

"Do not presume to know what happened," Adriana growled.

"If you'll excuse me, I really do have some place to go. Unless you're going to push me again? That's assault right? There were lots of witnesses, possibly cameras?" I goaded, standing. She crossed a line. I'd done nothing to her.

Creed stood and frowned. "Why *do* you think it's not her, Mom? I mean, you don't even know how old Dr. Ellington is."

"It doesn't matter. Because she's not—and she's too old to be Barrett's, so she must have read about Zain and is after our money," she snapped. "She's probably not even a real blonde."

Who was Zain?

I laughed. "I don't need your money. Creed, let's blow this place."

Creed frowned at his mom and put an arm around my shoulders. "Yeah, let's get you to your alpha."

I half expected her to order us not to leave.

Instead, she huffed off in the other direction. "I'll have your career," she yelled.

"Try me." I flipped her off.

Creed sighed as he led me someplace. "Sorry. I know this is a sore spot for the family, but I wasn't expecting her to *hurt* you–even to protect my dad. While the yelling and threats are spot on when she feels we're in danger, grabbing you isn't. Are you all right? I can take you to the Center clinic, there's one down the street."

"I'm fine." Actually, my knees hurt, so did my wrist. "I can't wait for her to figure out what pack I'm in and where I work. That's what, three pumpkins?"

"Probably. Don't hate Hale. He's a reckless asshole, but not an intentional one. He didn't mention you, he just told Dad that he was having coffee with me. Apparently, it's not unusual for Dad to get a cup of tea before this lecture." Creed sighed again as a parking lot came into view.

"Are you sure it's not a problem to drive me?" I asked him, not wanting to be a bother.

"No." He shook his head.

For a moment we drove in silence. I texted Spencer.

Me

On my way. I'll wait for you in the lobby.

"Is there a reason why *you* don't think you're our Grace?" he finally asked.

Because I'm not from your world.

"Does it matter? Also, my adolescence was a shitshow. I don't need another." I sighed.

"You said your mom hated alphas. You've also known yours since childhood. Is that how things got... complicated with your relationship?" He kept his eyes on the road.

"Yeah." I sighed. "I probably shouldn't have said what I did to your mom."

He shook his head. "You mess with gammas at your own peril—and Mom knows that."

Riley texted me back with the footage. That was fast.

Riley

You're welcome.

Me

Thank you.

I'd look at it later.

"Who's Zain?" I finally asked.

"Baba. He recently made a major discovery. His success brought family members to us expecting help," he explained.

It made sense to me. We pulled into an underground parking garage.

"Thanks for the ride. You don't have to walk me in. I can function on my own," I told him.

"It's fine. I've got time." He led me upstairs and into the lobby.

I plopped down in the waiting area and texted Spencer.

Me

Waiting for you in the lobby. Take your time.

"Don't hate me because Mom can be an overprotective bitch?" he said softly. "I'd like to keep in touch with you."

I should say *no*. But I couldn't.

"Okay. If you get the job and they disown you, please reach out to me for help. As someone who had that happen to them, it's a genuine offer," I told him.

"Thank you."

"So... you and Ina?" I smirked.

"For all my teasing, we're actually just really good friends—and happy to be. My parents seem to think that alphas and omegas can't just be friends." He rolled his eyes.

"Yeah, I get it." Or in my case it was being friends with guys. "Why do you keep introducing me as Ina's friend? I don't care, but I'm curious."

"Ina's friends with everyone. Also, you're both in Daedalus and everyone knows the science omegas stick together—especially in their respective fields. It just makes sense to introduce you like that," he explained.

"Okay."

We sat there for a while and talked. Finally, a clipped British voice came from across the lobby.

"Creed, is everything all right? Someone said my children were in the lobby?" A statuesque blonde in an expensive red suit strode toward us, heels clacking on the floor.

"Shit." Creed sighed. "Mumsy works here as a chemical engineer. That's why I had the internship."

Of course she did. Because this was turning out to be a shit day. That picnic better be worth it.

"I didn't know you were coming. It's been quite the day here. That Greek man showed up, throwing everything into chaos. Like we don't have business of our own to do? I'm not even sure why he's here." Her look was more annoyed than angry or malicious. Then her eyes focused on me. "Who are you?"

"Hi, Mum. Everything's fine. This is Dr. Ellington, Ina's friend. She was visiting Marquess to see the physics department and now is waiting for her alpha who has a meeting here. I gave her a ride." Creed shrugged. "Dr. Ellington, this is Dr. Thorne."

"Pippa. Charmed." Her nostrils flared. "I'll get the tea." She turned and left.

"Mumsy is British, tea fixes everything," Creed said.

"Have you ever been? It's one of the places I've always wanted to go," I told him.

"Many times. Spent summers there as a kid. I almost went to Uni there, but..." He sighed. "It was just better to go to Marquess, though I did study abroad in England for a year."

"I always wanted to study abroad," I said softly. That had been part of my plan that never happened.

Pippa came back over, holding three cups of tea. "There we are."

"Thank you." I took mine and sipped it.

"You and your alpha are looking for work? What are your fields?" Pippa asked, taking a seat in the nearby armchair.

"I'm a theoretical mathematician. Actually, I just started a job. I'm attending the PIIP Symposium and took a field trip here to see a few things. Hmm, I'm not sure what his meeting is about," I replied.

"Oh, that sort of math, yes I can see how you and Ina might get on." She chuckled. "Met in omega science club, I presume? Did you attend Uni around here then?"

"No, I didn't. But I'm part of Daedalus," I told her.

She nodded. "My mate runs the Marquess-Briar campus chapter. He loves it." Pippa turned to Creed. "How *did* her presentation go? It looked fantastic when I read over it."

Creed's look softened. "You proofed it for her? Mum always proofread our papers in undergrad. Mum, it went so well."

"That's really nice," I replied. My mom would never do that.

"I'm glad." She took a sip of tea then turned to me. "And you... you're Nate's or Barrett's? What are you hoping to accomplish from this visit?" Pippa said matter-of-factly.

"Neither and nothing. Not why I'm here and I'm beginning to regret meeting Creed for coffee today." My shoulders slumped.

"Also, according to Dr. Thorne, I'm not Nate's and I'm too old to be Barrett's. Not that I'm either."

Pippa's eyebrows rose. "No, you're not too old actually. We know this. Barrett's only a year younger and fully awakened as an omega at sixteen."

"I'm glad you took the time to meet up with Verity, Hale, and I," Creed said. "I'm sorry Mom got aggressive. Dad's been texting me. He wants to talk to you." He turned to Pippa. "We were having coffee on campus and Mom and Dad showed up unexpectedly."

"You met Nate?" Pippa frowned.

My hands went up in surrender. "Not on purpose. I'm sorry. It wasn't my intention to upset anyone. I didn't even know that's where he taught. I wasn't trying to start anything. Please understand, I wasn't looking. I'm not his, I'm not Barrett's, I'm no one's." My voice cracked and I looked away.

"That's for the best," Pippa stated.

My phone buzzed.

Spencer

I'll be down soon.

"Adriana got aggressive? You have to understand, she is quite protective." Pippa took another sip of tea.

"I live with three alphas and they're not like that." I frowned and rubbed my arm absently.

"Well, of course not. They're yours. But they'd do anything to protect you, I'm sure."

"But I did nothing wrong. I was *leaving*." Tears pricked my eyes.

"Alphas protect. There's a reason why for so long alphas just did as they pleased," Pippa retorted.

My throat swelled and I looked away. "So, it's my fault then. For just sitting there having a coffee, then trying to be on my way? It's not like I tried to meet him."

Yet more social nuances I just didn't understand.

"Mom crossed a line–even for her," Creed said softly.

Pippa nostrils flared and she looked toward the elevator, a concerned look on her face.

"Pip? I am so glad you're down here. I was just coming to find you." Nate threw himself in his mate's arms without a glance at anyone.

"I'm right here, Love." She pressed her lips to his blond head which showed the slightest bit of grey. "Rough day for you to come all the way here. Don't you have a lecture?"

What did I do? I sat there, frozen.

"I had my TA take over. There was an... incident. There's this woman who was on campus for some tour. I... I think it's her. I mean Adriana says she's not, the woman says she's not, but at the very least she's another one of Barrett's? I know the other times it wasn't her, and I shouldn't get my hopes up, especially after all these years. But maybe..." His body shook as his fruity scent grew salty with sadness. "She looks *just like* Creed. It's eerie."

That it was.

I'll go, I mouthed to Creed, trying to quietly slip away before he noticed me.

Nate turned around, and his blue eyes widened at the sight of me. "Dr. Ellington? Please, just a word."

Shit. Now everyone was going to be angrier than they already were. *Other times?* I didn't want to cause more emotional damage to the professor.

"I wasn't trying to upset you, Professor. I'm sorry for the trouble I caused." My voice shook and my knees trembled.

The professor did look an awful lot like me–not quite like Creed, but close enough that I understood why people asked if he was my father.

"You did nothing wrong. I just want to talk—and I apologize for my alpha," he told me.

The elevator doors opened, and Spencer came out. I waved to him, relief washing over me.

"Grace." Spencer closed the space between us in a few short strides, and I launched myself into his arms.

"Fuck," Pippa said softly.

"Mom shouldn't start anything with her pack, seriously," Creed said.

"Your name is Grace?" Nate's voice broke. "How old are you? What's your mother's name?"

"Oh my," Spencer said softly as I buried my face in his shoulder, his arms tight around me.

I looked up at Spencer, the tears starting to flow. "Let's go. I can't do this."

No, I didn't want any of this. I didn't want to hurt anyone. All I had wanted was some coffee.

"Professor, please excuse us. We have someplace to be, apologies," Spencer said. "It's nice to see you again, Creed."

The professor sucked in a breath. "Wait, you're..."

"Another reason why I'm not yours. I also work for Compass BioTek," I said, back still to them. "Apparently they don't like you or your company much, Spence."

Spencer shrugged. "It happens." He kissed me gently. "Shall we go have our picnic?"

"Please." I let go of him but tried to keep my back to the professor and Pippa. "I'm so sorry, Professor."

Creed gave me a hug. "I'll text you later. Have fun at the farm."

I let Spencer lead me out of the front of the building.

"Wait, Grace, please," the professor pleaded.

Spencer helped me into a waiting car, and I pressed my face into him, so I didn't have to look.

For a long while, he rubbed my back and purred for me.

"Will you tell me what happened?" he finally asked, putting the privacy screen between us and the driver up in the big, comfortable car.

I told him about my day; the tour of the CeCe, the potential of the visualizer, then meeting Creed, Verity, and Hale, why they thought I was their sister, and how Nate and Adriana Thorne had shown up—and Adriana's harsh reaction.

"She what? An alpha *laid hands on you* and you didn't immediately call me?" There was no anger on his face or in his voice, just concern, but I flinched, nevertheless.

"At the time I was just trying to get out of there and I didn't want to bother you." My voice shook.

He bundled me to him. "Darling, you are never, ever, a bother. Never hesitate to call me or come to me or interrupt me. I don't care who I'm meeting with."

I nodded, though the idea of interrupting him in a meeting made me squirm.

"Did you tell Wes at least?" he asked

"No. Though I told Evan, and promised him that I'd tell you as soon as I saw you. The story of how Nate met his mates sounds like a cautionary tale in a Center ad," I said.

"Indeed. How awful for that young woman and her child," Spencer said. "Imagine if Luc and the integration team were there to mediate it all for them?"

I nodded. "That immediately makes me not like any of them—even the professor. He and his girlfriend were serious enough to have chosen baby names—and then to just ghost her? At least they acknowledged their mistakes, but still, that's a lot."

And I was so glad Evan and I clicked.

Spencer kept rubbing my back. "It is. But I'm worried about the fact that some alpha felt she could put her hands on you. Are you injured, should we go to the hospital?"

"I think I'm fine. But there might be some bruises." I rolled up the sleeve of my pink blouse to reveal the bruises.

Spencer sucked in a breath.

I handed him my phone. "Take a photo? Riley hacked the cafe cameras and got footage."

He took the photo. "You wish to press charges? No one will blame you if you do. At the very least we need to file a report."

"I don't know," I admitted. "I just feel like proof is good? Also, I didn't like her threatening my career." Finishing my tale, I added about her chasing me across campus and how I told her to fuck off.

Spencer wrapped me in his arms. "I'm sorry, I shouldn't have let you go alone."

"Stop that." I poked him in the chest. "I'm an adult and capable of doing things on my own."

"Yes, I know, my good doctor. You are beyond capable." He touched his forehead to mine. "Still, I'll stay with you for the duration of our trip."

I snuggled back into him. "I like the sound of that. I don't know why this is affecting me so badly. I'm not from this world. He's not my dad. And oh my god, Spencer, while my father most likely abandoned my mom and I, because I feel like she would have told me if he died, I'm not sure I could handle that level of assholery. Also, the likelihood that one of the alphas knew the girlfriend was pregnant is high if she continued trying to get to him after the first few months—or that his family knew. It would make sense that if she couldn't get ahold of Nate she might go to his family. Considering how Adriana was so adamant that I wasn't Nate's Grace, I wonder what she knows about the fate of the baby. Not to mention the idea that he has a Grace, that there's a me in this world someplace..."

"If the other alphas saw her in person, they'd know she was pregnant by scent, even if she wasn't showing. It really is quite the puzzle." He started kneading my shoulders with his strong hands. "His record isn't fake, not to mention he has a family identity that would be hard to create. Several brothers, parents, grandparents, all with social media and history. I think Evan was looking him up in the Center computer, too."

I sighed. "I feel bad for that girl with her mother dead and her dad and his family being what they are. At least he never stopped looking for her and acknowledged that they fucked up. But still..."

Closing my eyes, I sank into Spencer's touch. How much time did we have before we got there?

"Is the pull really that much? To abandon your whole life for someone you just met who could very well be an ax murderer? There's so much I still don't understand." I had been willing to try to travel to another world, but that was different.

"I know." His arms wrapped around me. "Today has been so much for you emotionally, and I can see how you'd resonate with and be affected by all this. But we'll leave soon, and you won't have to see them again. We can even leave tonight if you wish."

"I'm looking forward to the beach. Maybe I want to stay in touch with Creed. Is that weird?" I asked.

"He seems like a good man. But I can also make sure he isn't hired if you want me to."

I shook my head. "Just leave it. If he gets hired, great, and if he doesn't, oh well. But please don't mess with his career."

"As you wish." Spencer checked his phone. "We still have a few moments before we get there. What do you need?"

What did I need? "Hold me?"

Spencer gave me a kiss and snuggled me into him as I laid my head on his chest. "It would be my pleasure."

Chapter Thirty-Seven

Spencer

My phone rang and I gave Grace a kiss, grabbed my glass, then stepped back from the tasting bar in the old restored barn at the farm and distillery Brennan had suggested.

"Wes, I'm so very sorry for allowing her to be injured. I should have canceled my meetings and gone with her when she decided to leave the conference hotel." My voice went rough. "I let my own bias against super colliders cloud my judgment and convinced myself that being in the same town was enough."

Guilt coated me. The bruises on her wrist made me angry. Some alpha felt that it was okay to *push her*, and I wasn't there to protect her. Because I'd put my meetings, my comfort first.

"Are you done?" Wes snorted. "Spence, you didn't *allow* her to be injured. Grace is an adult. One who wasn't raised like us and would absolutely resent any actions we'd take that she might see as us attempting to quell her independence. She doesn't think you failed her in any way and that, my friend, is what's important here."

I watched as she sipped the contents of her glass. True. "I should have been there."

"You were down the street. No one blames you. Is *she* okay? What is she doing right now?"

I looked back over at the tasting bar in time to see her nod and point to a bottle.

"I do believe she's buying more overpriced bourbon than we could possibly need." The converted barn was rustic, charming, and filled with liquor to try, food to taste, and items to buy. Soft music filled the room, and a late afternoon breeze wafted in from the open doors.

"You're bourbon tasting? Not wine tasting?" He laughed.

I took a sip. It wasn't bad. I didn't have an issue with bourbon or whiskey, I simply preferred red wine.

"Brennan likes this place and asked us to get him some. I figured that Grace would enjoy the chance to see the animals, tour the distillery, and have a sunset picnic," I replied. "She isn't all right emotionally. It has her more shaken than she wants to admit. I'm not sure what's going on here–there are too many coincidences."

"Genetics are weird. I mean, this just proves there's a multiverse and there's another Grace."

No.

"As I have told you before, while there *is* a multiverse, *we are not in it.* If he's not one of the omegas my father protected, then who is he?" I wondered.

We were missing something.

"An asshole, obviously," Wes snorted. "But yeah, I saw the video of what happened in the coffee shop. While that alpha grabbing her made me angry, the professor weirded me out. So did some of the kids. Jett's doing background checks on them."

"She's unsure if she wants to press charges, but we did upload the video and file an incident report with campus police," I told him. "While she says she's physically fine, I worry, and have half a mind to have a doctor come to the hotel."

I was so glad that not only did Grace have the foresight to ask Riley to get the footage, but that Riley had been able to do so quickly. Jett getting background checks wasn't a bad thing either. I hope we got that genscan soon.

"I know you're taking good care of her," Wes assured. "Every time I hear from her she sounds so happy."

"For the most part she has been quite happy–making friends and contacts, and learning new things." This trip had been productive for me as well. Like the meeting at Strauss. One of their chemicals was just what we needed for a new quicktest. Not to mention my speaking engagements help raise money for my company's after-school science programs.

Still, she'd been injured, and I hadn't even known. Had Wes? Evan felt her strongly. But then omegas who were bonded to each other usually did.

That was the real reason why, once, packs were discouraged from taking multiple omegas. Not because of omega jealousy, or fairness given the ratio of omegas to alphas, as they wanted us to believe. It was because of *alpha* jealousy at how omegas could feel and love each other so deeply. Not everyone saw it as a beautiful thing.

Personally, I loved how Grace and Evan made each other happy.

If I'd been bonded to her today...

"She does miss you," I told Wes.

"I know. I miss her, too. But I'll see her soon enough–and I'm glad you get to have your romantic trip to the science fair." He chuckled.

"We're having a lovely time." Those dinners, those walks on the beach, they were everything.

"I'll let you go, have fun. If you're planning on bonding with her, go for it. She's already yours, you know. You're doing fine, Spence." Wes ended the call.

I rejoined Grace, wrapping my arm around her. Giving me a brilliant smile, she melted into me, fitting so perfectly.

"So, what are we getting? A case of everything?" I teased, accepting a new glass.

"Did you want a case of everything? Because we can do that, sir." The young woman on the other side of the counter grinned.

"I got two cases of the stuff Bren likes, and a case of this." Grace held up a bottle of peach bourbon.

The woman behind the counter poured some from an open bottle and gave me a glass. I took a sip and winced at the sweetness.

"Do we need an entire case?" I asked her. They probably only sold it by the case.

"Yes. I also made a custom case—two bottles for each of you based on what I think you'd like. Except for Riley. They had bottles from the year she was born, and we'll save them for when she's old enough to drink it." Grace looked quite pleased with herself.

"You made a case for us, that sounds delightful." I gave her a squeeze. If anything, it would be entertaining. "Why don't we pay for the four cases you bought, arrange for them to be sent to the hotel, and go have our picnic."

"This was such a great idea," Grace sighed, laying against me, as the sun set, painting the sky with pinks and oranges.

"It really was." We sat on a blue checkered blanket under a light-festooned tree by a creek, the remains of our picnic feast around us. The food was surprisingly good.

The company had been even better.

I leaned down and stole a kiss, warm and sweet.

"Mmmm, I want another." She pressed her lips to mine.

Oh, I couldn't wait to get her back to the hotel.

If I was certain that we had privacy here, I wouldn't wait. But just because I couldn't see anyone didn't mean they weren't there, ready to take pictures our pack didn't need to be public. I was already certain other guests at the farm had taken photos of us. Though Grace making me feed baby goats wasn't incriminating.

Yet it bothered me.

It never had before. It was part of being in the public eye. My father always tried to shield me from it. It was part of why he'd become an academic. But the moment two teenagers formed a pharmaceutical company and landed national and international contracts, Elaris and I became media targets.

Elaris loved it and knew how to use it strategically and artfully. I just accepted it and tried not to ever do anything that I wouldn't want my mother to see on the evening news.

Somehow everything had changed.

It was one thing if I was at a conference, dinner, or meeting for work. However, I wasn't. I was with Grace, sharing a private moment. Seeing her face light up as she pet horses then tossed hay at me. Chasing her across a garden and then catching her and twirling her around. Holding her as the sun set.

Those moments were for me alone.

The bugs were out in full force, and I swatted one on my arm—I'd taken off my suit jacket and rolled up my sleeves.

"Shall we go before we get eaten?" I asked her.

"I suppose. Let's go in the hot tub when we return to the hotel?" She started cleaning everything up and putting it back into the picnic basket.

"Oh definitely. Perhaps wear that swimsuit you wore yesterday? The yellow polka dot one?"

It was a ridiculously tiny bikini, that for some reason she found amusing.

Grace grinned. "If you insist."

I grabbed the basket, and she got the blanket. Arm in arm, we returned to the barn to turn in our picnic items. The sun had fully set, but the parking lot was busy, since they had outdoor dining in the evening.

"I don't know who you are or what you think you're doing, but you need to stay away from my family," a female voice commanded.

A sharp-featured woman, probably in her early fifties, marched over to us, her brown eyes narrowing in the dim parking lot light. There was something a bit familiar about her. Like I'd run into her before at a conference or meeting. Which was entirely probable.

"Why are you here, *Dr. Ellington*, if that's even your name?" she sneered.

"I'm here for the PIIP Conference, *Dr. Thorne*." Grace rolled her eyes. "Who do you think *I* am? What did you do to the professor's poor daughter that you are so sure that I'm not her? Though I'm not. I'm not the professor's. I'm not Barrett's. All I am is a mathematician who made the mistake of having coffee with someone I met at a conference. Apologies for existing."

Grace did raise a good point. Why did Dr. Thorne immediately assume that this Grace wasn't the Grace her mate was looking for?

Of course, I could put together a small list—one that didn't put Dr. Thorne in a very good light.

"How dare you," she snarled, anger crossing her face. "You're not her. You can't be."

"I *know*," Grace snapped back. "I'm not here to make claims to your family. Believe me, the more I learn about you the more I fear for the professor's Grace."

"Please leave us, Dr. Thorne. As you can see, we're nowhere near your family. We're just enjoying our evening, and I'd advise you to go home and do the same." I stepped in front of Grace, shielding.

I made my voice hard, filling it with alpha authority, though it wasn't quite a bark. Yet. While she was an alpha, I was easily more dominant than her. Part of me wanted to hit her for daring to lay a hand on my mate, but we didn't need photos of that, either.

"Who the fuck are you?" Dr. Thorne blinked as if just truly noticing me.

"I'm Spencer Thanukos, one of Grace's alphas. Please, leave us be, Dr. Thorne. We've done nothing to you," I warned.

"Fuck. You're not her. You can't be." She turned and ran into the parking lot, getting out her phone. "You didn't tell me she was mated to Spencer Fucking Thanukos."

I pulled Grace into my arms as the car arrived.

"Are you all right?" I asked, helping her inside.

"I have no idea what that was," she frowned, leaning into me. "I'm so tired. It's been a day."

"Then rest, Darling." As she dozed in my arms, I texted someone that I used for background checks, trying to figure out why Dr. Thorne bothered me. If she was in chemistry, she probably wouldn't have been one of my father's students. Perhaps I had her as a professor or teaching assistant at some point? I also texted Brennan to see if the genscan came back.

Brennan

Not yet. But my mom is on the rampage because the media picked up on the foundation getting rid of scholarships for vulnerable omegas.

Me

Pity if the footage of her slapping you–or being escorted out of your office made the news as well.

Brennan

Ian Murphy is being served tomorrow. So that will be interesting. I'm not sure she knows about the building yet.

Me

So far she hasn't seemed to be bothering my business.

Brennan

Good.

Oh, there was a really nice picture of you and Grace going for a walk on the beach on the entertainment news.

Brennan attached a shot.

Me

That's not news.

Though it was a very beautiful photo.

Brennan

> You're an eligible bachelor that now looks to be off the market. To some, it is.

Me

> I was never eligible or on the market.

It made me want to growl.

Me

> The farm was a nice recommendation. We had a lovely picnic and got two cases of your bourbon, along with other things.

> What do you use peach bourbon for? Frozen drinks?

Brennan

> That might make a nice marinade or sauce.

> Thanks, man. I hope you're having fun, and that the picture Grace sent to the group chat of you with straw on your head doesn't hit the news.

I checked the group chat and Grace had filled it up with sweet pictures. None of which I'd be embarrassed for my mother to see.

My publicist *had* emailed me, asking if things were getting serious with Grace and if I wanted to address the media. My mother also texted me.

Mother

> Who's the woman?

Ah, yes, I should probably let her know that things with Grace were serious.

Me

> I hope your travels went well. Grace is a mathematician, and we are quite serious. Evan and Riley both adore her. Maybe you can meet her soon.

Mother

> Finally. Happy for you. Bring Evan. I miss that boy. If he likes her...

She was happy for me? I didn't know how much I needed to hear that.

Me

> Oh, he does. I hope you will, too. She bakes.

My mom did have a sweet tooth.

Mother

> Should I send an omega lily? Maybe she can keep it alive.

It was a custom in my part of the world to gift newly-mated omegas a pot of omega lilies. The idea was that it helped make a peaceful home, since the smell made people happy.

She'd sent Evan one, but it got put in a box when they'd moved and died. Grace could probably keep it alive. They were quite lovely.

Me

> You'll be invited when we have our party. You can bring it yourself.

"Who are you texting?" Grace asked sleepily.

"My mother. I'm telling her about you," I replied.

"Awww." She grinned.

We got back to the hotel and Grace disappeared into the bedroom, coming back out in that yellow bikini before I'd even gotten situated.

"Hot tub. Now." She tugged on my tie, pulling me to her, giving me a fierce kiss.

"As you wish, my good doctor." I changed and found her in the balcony hot tub. She had a beer in her hand and a glass of wine for me.

I'd just gotten in when she curled onto my lap.

"I've got you." I held her as she sobbed into my arms. "Apologies for not being there to protect you."

"That's not why I'm upset. I hope you know that. I'm just emotionally overwhelmed and confused." She stared up at me with her big, blue-grey eyes.

"How can I help? What do you need?" I asked.

"First we're going to enjoy our drinks, and the view, then we can go to bed and enjoy each other." Her head rested on my shoulder. "Sounds good?"

"Perfect." I took a sip of wine. It was a good one and I was curious if she'd chosen it herself or asked room service to pick for her.

The hot tub was relaxing and just what I needed, along with some good wine, and my delightful companion.

"Earlier, you said that you were one of my alphas." Her voice went soft as she took a sip of beer.

"I am one of your alphas." My tone went possessive. "I haven't marked you yet but I'm very much yours."

Maybe I should bond with her sooner rather than later. That way I could feel her if she was in trouble. Wes wasn't the only one who worried that he couldn't protect his mate.

"I know. I like hearing it." She smiled. "I think when you bite me, I'd like it to be here." Taking my head, she pushed it gently to the crook of her neck. "Right where everyone could see."

My teeth ached as the thought of sinking into her creamy flesh and leaving a permanent mark.

Go for it, Wes had said.

Why wait?

"Here?" I sucked on the spot, making her gasp as my hand slid under the bottom of her yellow bikini.

A whimper escaped her lips. "Please, Alpha."

Bite her. It's right there. My desire to bond with her extended far beyond just wanting to protect her and be connected to her.

"I'll bite you tonight if you wish, but not here in the hot tub." Just in case anyone was watching us.

"No?" Her lower lip quivered a little.

"I will mark you, Darling. It will look so beautiful. When we finish our drinks, we'll shower, go to bed, and how did you put it? *Enjoy each other?*" I kissed her neck, trying to reassure her so she didn't get upset and think she was being rejected. It happened sometimes with omegas.

"Okay." She looked out past the balcony and sighed. "I guess we don't need anyone to take pictures of us boning in the hot tub."

I laughed. "No, we don't."

Chapter Thirty-Eight

Grace

"You really are the best hair brusher," I sighed as I sat on the large bed, in a soft hotel robe, as Spencer brushed my hair. After the hot tub, we'd taken a shower.

I hadn't missed what he'd said about bonding with me tonight if I wanted it. Also, I hadn't missed my whine, my body's reaction, when he hadn't immediately impaled me with his cock and sunk his teeth into me.

Okay, I hadn't expected him to.

But something in me *had*. Probably the part of me that was always thinking of dicks. Mmmm. Dicks. While I was cozy and snuggly in my robe, Spencer was bare-ass naked.

I'd panic texted Evan who assured me that it was normal and if I wanted to bond with Spencer now, then I should do it–and if I wanted to wait, to tell Spencer, and he would wait.

Obviously, what happened today had unnerved Spencer. Wes, too, to some extent, and we'd video chatted for a bit while Spencer was working.

Though today had unnerved me, too, in so many ways.

Did I want to bond with Spencer?

Yes. Like I said in the hot tub, he was my alpha.

Did I want to bond with Spencer today?

"You're thinking awfully hard, Darling." Spencer kissed my temple.

"Do you want to bond with me tonight because you truly want to bond with me, or because you feel guilty because something happened and you couldn't sense me? There's nothing wrong with either, I just want to know." There was probably some past trauma with not being there when Elaris died wrapped up in it, too.

"I would like you right here in my heart for so many reasons. Knowing when you need me is only a very small part of it. It does not need to be tonight. We can wait as long as you'd like. But I'm happy to do so tonight if you wish." He kissed me again. This time his kisses trailed down my face to my neck. His hand took mine and put it over his heart.

My body shivered as he kissed the same part of my neck he'd kissed in the hot tub when we'd talked of bonding.

Yes. I wanted to bond with him. It went beyond settling something inside myself.

"Yes, I... I'd like that very much. I love you, Spence." Bumping his forehead with mine, I attacked his lips.

"I love you, too, Darling." He kissed me back like his soul was starving. Gently, his hands removed my robe, he set it on the chair by the bed and put the hairbrush on the nightstand. He turned off all the lights but a low, soft one.

Pulling down the covers he positioned me in the center of the bed, like I was a princess. "I think I'd like to enjoy you now."

"Mmmm, I'm yours to enjoy, *Alpha*." I gave him a coy smile.

His lips crashed with mine as his hands caressed my body, reassuring me, comforting me, making my core melt into goo.

Those sweet, soft lips of his left my lips and trailed down my neck again. This time, he didn't suck on that spot. No, his lips just brushed it in promise as his lips continued down my body. They went over my breast, across my stomach, down my inner thighs.

I sighed in pleasure as he kissed my clit. Two fingers slipped inside of me. My hands tangled in his hair, my body bucking in pleasure as he lavished me with hungry kisses.

Mmmm, enjoy me, Daddy.

"Spencer," I called as an orgasm shivered through my body.

But he didn't stop. No, those lips, those fingers, continued, playing me like a piano, until another orgasm crashed through me.

While I loved the attention, I ached for a nice thick cock.

"Please, please be inside me, Alpha," I whispered, as once again, his tongue caressed me.

"Absolutely, Darling." His fingers slipped out of me. But he kissed me again, this time, trailed *up* my body.

Again, they teased that place on my neck like butterfly wings before fastening against mine. His fit body straddled me. Eyes meeting mine, he slowly, almost maddeningly so, slid his hard cock inside me, stopping right at his inflated knot.

A happy noise escaped my lips. This felt right. Before coming here, never did I think I'd want to have such a connection with multiple people. Yet it felt so perfect, so right. Like I deserved love from more than one person.

Like I finally belonged somewhere.

Like I was made for this.

"I love being inside you," Spencer whispered, forehead meeting mine as he thrust in and out of me.

"You make me feel so good," I sighed, my hands running over his back.

His tongue traced my neck, tracing that spot before sucking on it, hard, in a way that made sheer and unbridled need claw from my chest and up my throat, coming out in a whine that was pure want.

"Do you mean that, my good doctor? Do you still want me to bite you? My teeth ache to sink into you and make you mine. But I can wait if you've reconsidered." His lips brushed my ear.

"Please, please, Alpha, make me yours." Need consumed me, rivaling what I'd recalled feeling back in the nest during Evan's heat.

"Oh, I will. I'll knot you and make you mine, my sweet baby girl," he cooed as he brought me to yet another peak. As my body shuddered, he thrust all the way in, knotting me.

I gasped, needing that knot like oxygen.

His lips fastened on that spot, sucking hard as he rocked against me. "Mine," he whispered.

Spencer's teeth sunk into me. It didn't hurt, but it felt a little prickly, as minty lightning shot through me and his leather scent intensified. It felt different than when Evan had done it–and when Wes had so very long ago in our dreams.

That minty lightening zinged straight to my heart, turning warm...

... and there he was. Love. Awe. Relief. And just a hint of worry.

I sent all my love back, surfacing enough to remember that this was a huge step for him.

"There you are," he breathed, wrapping his arms around me and rolling us so he was on his back, and I was on top of him. Spencer threw the covers over us as I snuggled into him.

So much love flowed through me, as did a little tug from Evan as if to say *I felt that.* I sent love to him and Wes, and got it back from them.

Yep, there I was, and there I'd stay. With my amazing guys. Right where I belonged.

Chapter Thirty-Nine

Spencer

There she was. It wasn't just my alpha settling at the act of claiming her. It felt so amazingly right. Just like her.

Never had I thought I'd find someone to love like this again. Yet here she was.

Here we were.

I held her tightly, lavishing attention on the mark until my knot deflated enough to slip out. She started kissing my neck and I felt something through the bond, a want and yearning. Her peachy scent went sweet with arousal and need.

"What do you need, Darling?" I kissed the top of her head.

"Please?" She nipped at my neck.

Ah, yes. She could bond someone back.

"Mark me anywhere on my body that you'd like," I told her, running my hand over her back.

Her eyes met mine, flickering with mischief. "Oh, anywhere because it doesn't leave a permanent mark?"

"No, because my body is yours," I assured her. "I'll get it tattooed if you want." My inner alpha liked that idea, letting all the *bathroom bitches* know that I belonged to someone.

"Evan was talking about it, too. I think you should go together." Grace giggled, delight bubbling through the bond.

My hand rested on her ass. "That sounds like a nice activity. I don't have any tattoos."

"Mmmm. As fun as it would be to bite you on your cock, I think I'd like to mark you right here." She gnawed on my shoulder. "I like shoulders better."

I suppose they were meatier? "My body is yours to bite."

"Okay." Eyes gleaming, she stroked my cock, bringing it to life, and slid it inside her, riding me.

"Mmmm, I like this." Grace bounced up and down.

"Ride me, Baby Girl." I put my hands on her hips.

Grace continued to ride me, eyes closing as she took my hands off her hips, entangling her fingers in mine. Her pussy muscles kept clamping down on my cock.

"I'm not going to last with you doing that." My knot was ready to be inside her again. "Take me all the way if you want."

"Oh, I will." She slid all the way, taking my knot, as I shot warm cum inside her. Leaning forward, she kissed my shoulder, then bit down on it.

"Harder. You need to draw blood."

She bit down harder. I gasped, not in pain, but due to the warmth, the sparks. My alpha relished in it.

The connection I already felt with her deepened and rounded out in a way I'd never experienced.

Drawing in a sharp breath, I nuzzled my face in her neck as she lapped at my shoulder.

Yes. I would protect her always and forever.

Chapter Forty

Evan

While I had to be at the Center early tomorrow, I couldn't sleep. Brennan was working things out on the piano and Jett was at the boxing gym.

So, I went in search of Wes who was in his office, working. Though I wasn't sure if it was work for Spencer or work for Brennan. There was a whole lot going on right now with the Queen Mum and Brennan worried about both us and his business getting attacked.

Also, I'd gotten a really weird message today at work from someone claiming to be Rose's bio-dad. He said that he'd just found out that his ex-wife was in jail and wanted permission to contact her. While I knew her stepfather was her stepfather, and there was a bio-dad in her record and the names matched, I was wary. Why now? What if this was part of whatever plot was going on?

Not that I knew what it was about. Those guys had stopped bothering Rose. Detective Esposito had gone silent. The uncle was in jail awaiting his trial for both everything at the school and the restaurant. Though I was a little afraid that someone would spring him and he'd run.

Wes was in his office, looking delicious, hunched over his laptop, shirtless.

He looked over at me. "Are you just going to watch me from the doorway?"

"No, I'll watch you from right here." I plopped down in the beanbag next to his desk that was there for precisely this reason.

"And there you are, looking so cute." He gave me a hungry gaze.

"Wanna do something about it? Like snuggle me on the couch and watch a home decorating show? I can't sleep," I told him.

"Worrying about Grace?" He closed his laptop.

"An alpha hurting her is worrisome." But it was more like curiosity if she was actually going to bond Spencer tonight or not. It had been a bit since we'd texted. "I also miss her so fucking much," I added.

"Me, too. But she'll be back on Saturday." He helped me up.

"True." I made sure I had nothing going on Sunday so that I could give her *all* of my attention. I'd even gotten a new candle and bubble bath.

Wes and I made some popcorn and settled onto the couch. I turned on my favorite home decorating show.

I squirmed because while I hadn't felt a bite, they were definitely doing something.

Wes pulled me closer. "What's wrong?"

"Do you feel Grace when she's with someone?" I leaned into him, getting a good hint of his laundry scent.

"While I do feel her more now, I um, try to block all that out. Same with you. Not because I don't want you with other people, it just um, gets distracting sometimes." He kissed my temple. "Wait, can you not? I don't know how your bond might be different."

"Part of it is that I don't want to." I grinned sheepishly. Yeah, it was a bit like voyeurism, but I liked it and she, too, had the ability to block me out. Though she wasn't very good at it yet.

"I see." Wes grinned back.

"But it's also harder," I told him. "I don't think it's an us thing, it's a her thing."

Right now, she was enjoying herself *very* much.

"Okay. I'm sure there's a video on it." Wes laughed.

There was a whole unit on regulating bonds.

We continued watching the show then...

My bond with her sizzled. "Fuck."

"I felt that. Wow, that man is fast, but I did tell him to go for it." Wes rubbed his chest.

"Awww, you did? I'm proud of you." I kissed him. Wes was handling all of this so well. Sometimes it was hard for alphas to share, even with their packmates.

Love from Grace wrapped around me through the bond.

"I talked to her about it earlier," I admitted. "She was trying to work out if she wanted to do it now or later."

There he was, just a whisper of Spencer. Just like I'd gotten hints of Grace through my bond with Wes before the two of us had bonded.

Wes rubbed his chest. "Welp, everyone's in there now somehow."

"Yes, they are." I sent love back.

My cock strained against my shorts. Leaning in, I kissed Wes, long and deep. Part of it was that I was fucking turned on by whatever was happening with Grace and Spencer.

Part of it was wanting to reassure Wes in case any of this made him feel insecure. Her bonding Spencer would take nothing away from what she and Wes had, or what I had with her.

Not to mention I was so fucking happy for my best friend, and I could feel flickers of joy.

Straddling Wes, I continued to make out with him, show and popcorn forgotten.

Something else shot through the bond. More sizzle, more love, more lust.

"She just bit him back." Mmmm. I nipped at his shoulder. My other hand slipped under his waistband to grip his cock.

"Omega, I think we should move this to the bedroom," Wes growled.

We were in for a long night. And I wanted it. *Yes, pump all the love through the bond, Peaches.*

I kissed him. "I think that's a great idea, Alpha."

Sure, I had work in the morning. Oh well. Fortunately, at the Omega Center, being tired because you were up late with your alpha was a common and accepted excuse.

Chapter Forty-One

Grace

"This is the life." I snuggled into Spencer on the double beach lounger in the private cabana he'd reserved for us on the hotel beach. It was very spacious and like our own private beach tent with loungers, tables and chairs, and a kiosk to order food. An ocean breeze came in through the open cloth doors.

Yes. I could get used to this.

I had a fruity frozen drink, a view of the beach, and Spencer.

Life was good.

If the whole pack was here, it would be even better. But I'd see them tomorrow.

"That it is, my good doctor." He ran his tongue across the bite mark on the right side of my neck, where it met my shoulder.

The place where last night he'd marked me. Bonded with me. A shiver of pleasure ran through my body, as did a hum of happiness and contentment from Spencer. My bond with Spencer felt different than my bonds with Wes and Evan. Not just in intensity, but the *way* it felt. Spencer's felt silky, comforting yet indulgent, Evan's felt like hot chocolate on a cold day, and Wes, well, he just felt like home.

I ran my tongue across the bite on his shoulder. My phone buzzed and I lazily glanced at it.

Evan

I'm so tired today. Thanks for that.

Evan sent a silly picture of himself.

Me

Sorry, not sorry.

Wes and Evan had felt that last night–and acted on it.

Evan

Me neither. I'm excited for you, and when I see you tomorrow I'll show you exactly how happy I am.

I laughed and Spencer gave me a quizzical look.

"It's Evan. Being Evan," I replied.

Spencer grinned. "Ah, yes. I suppose as soon as we get home I won't see you for the rest of the weekend."

"Probably." I took another sip of my drink. "This is perfect. Are... are you doing okay?"

While I knew Spencer cared for me enough to bond with me, I worried a little about him, and how being bonded to someone again would affect him.

Spencer kissed my temple. "I feel better than I have in a very long time. Is this enough for you for today, just laying here on the beach?"

"Maybe, I'll finish my sandcastle." I eyed my partially built sandcastle. "I might also go back in the water. Perhaps I'll get all the way in this time."

Today I wore a red bikini, and I also had a long, sheer red and gold coverup. My wrist ached a little and bruises still dotted my forearm where Adriana had gripped me. There was a bruise on one of my knees as well.

"We could go out to dinner tonight, if you wish," he offered, his hand brushing up and down my bare thigh. "I'll have the concierge recommend something?"

"That sounds nice. I think I'll want some lunch soon. But I'm happy just eating here in the cabana." Maybe after lunch I'd read more of my book.

Spencer smiled. "Perfect."

"Excuse me, but I'm looking for Grace Ellington." A man in an unfamiliar black uniform with a badge I'd never seen filled the doorway of the cabana, blocking my view of the ocean.

Now what?

Spencer sat up and glared at him. "Can I help you?"

The strange man flashed a badge. "I'm from the Office of Designation Management, and I'm here for Grace Ellington."

"I'm her alpha, how can I help you?" Tension lined his face as I saw him palm his phone as he stood and went to the doorway.

Office of Designation Management? I didn't know what that was. The worry I got from Spencer meant that it wasn't a good thing.

"We're here to take Grace in for testing," he said. "I have the paperwork right here."

He showed Spencer a tablet. The guy wasn't alone. I wasn't sure if they were alphas or deltas but they were large and spoke with authority.

"I see. Well, give us a moment to change and we'll grab a car and meet you there." Spencer's tone went brusque.

Something was wrong. I texted Evan and Wes.

Me

> **What is the Office of Designation Management and why do they want to test me?**

"That won't be necessary. We'll transport her," the unnamed man countered, voice clipped and commanding.

Evan replied immediately.

Evan

> **Nothing good. Text Mrs. Beekman now. Spence is with you?**

Me

Yes.

"I'm her alpha, I'll accompany her," Spencer stated, authority leaking from his vice.

The man peered at his tablet. "Are you Wes Lawson?"

I texted Mrs. Beekman. Evan messaged again.

Evan

> **They test for illegal designations. You have rights under the rules for omegas. I'll watch your location so I can figure out where you're being taken and get the local Center to send someone.**

That made my belly tight.

"Spencer Thanukos. We only registered the bond this morning," Spencer said.

Wes texted as well.

Wes

> **Shit. That doesn't sound good. Do what Evan says. I'm on it. Love you.**

I felt a burst of love from Wes though the bond.

"Well, that's nice, but the only alpha I see here is Wes Lawson." The man shrugged.

"I'm also her packmate. She's a gamma, and has the right to be accompanied," Spencer insisted.

He checked his tablet and shrugged. "No pack listed."

"I insist," Spencer growled.

"If it's not listed, you can't come with her. You're welcome to go on your own and wait, but they're not going to let you stay inside if it's not in the system," the man replied.

Fear coursed through me. I had to go alone?

Me

They won't let Spencer come with me.

I sent that to Evan, Wes, and Mrs. Beekman.

"Grace, you need to come with me. We have two choices, you can walk out nice and quiet, or my partner can stun and cuff you," the man told me.

Still not knowing what's going on, I looked at Spencer, concern shooting through all of my bonds.

"She'll go and cooperate fully," Spencer said, sending me comfort and reassurance.

I would? But the one guy had a scary looking taser.

"Go on, Darling, I'll follow." Spencer picked up my flip flops and put them on my feet. "All you can do is cooperate. I'll be right there."

Tears pricked my eyes. "I don't understand."

"Oh, you wouldn't, now, would you. We don't have time for me to explain, but it's serious. I'll take care of it. Promise." His voice was soft as he helped me up off the lounge chair.

I stuffed my phone in the pocket of my coverup.

He gave me a kiss. "Be brave, be respectful, and I'll be *right there.* I love you."

"I love you, too." It was hard not to panic because I didn't know what was going on.

"Come on, let's go," the man said, his partner flanking me as they escorted me through the lobby and out to the parking lot to a van that said *Office of Designation Management.* People watched and whispered.

Spencer kept up with us. "Are you certain that I can't accompany her? I'll be Wes Lawson."

The one with the handcuffs pushed me into the van as the other gave Spencer the side-eye and climbed into the driver's seat. The door closed and the other got in. There was a screen between me and them. I pressed my hand against the window as we drove off.

Tears trickled down my face. I curled into the corner of the empty van and got out my phone, trying to position myself so that they didn't see.

Mrs. Beekman

On it. Do you know why?

Me

No, but they had documentation. I didn't see it, just my alpha.

Mrs. Beekman

They didn't let anyone from your pack come with you?

Me

I'm on a business trip with Spencer. Our mate registration is too new.

I don't understand what is happening.

Mrs. Beekman

You and Spencer bonded? Congratulations. They're testing you for illegal designations. Which is strange because your full genetic workup is available in your medical file. Cooperate with them and I'll see what I can do. You have a right to have someone from the Center present.

Me

Thank you.

I read through Evan's text.

Evan

They'll first test you for illegal designations. Given you'll come up negative, they'll then run a second, lengthier test looking to see if you're a genetic carrier. If it's found you are a carrier, request that they take you to a Center immediately.

Me

I will. Thanks.

Nothing. This meant nothing. Fear filled me as I curled into a ball, opening myself up to the reassurances of my mates so I didn't completely spiral.

"Fuck. Why are we testing Spencer Thanukos' omega? This better not blow up," one of the officers in the front said, rolling down his window.

"Not our place to question orders. Someone called in a tip I think? Am I supposed to know who that guy is? Also, omegas can still be carriers. I don't smell omega. I think she's just small," the one driving said.

"She's mated, you dingus," the other replied.

I texted this to Evan.

Me

> Someone called in a tip? I still don't know what's happening.

Evan

> They somehow must have gotten a court order to force you to be tested. Usually, they need pretty solid evidence to keep people from being unnecessarily rounded up.

Me

> What if I'm an illegal designation? We still don't know how things work in my world. Don't they execute illegal designations?

Was I going to die? A sob ripped from my throat. Now both of the front windows were down.

Evan

> You're not an illegal designation. If for some reason they say you are, respectfully demand a retest in a secondary facility, someone from the Center, and one of your alphas.

> **I love you and I wish that I was there.**

> **They'll probably take your phone.
> Spencer is on his way.**

"Hey, you don't have a phone, do you?" the one with a taser barked.

I blinked, tucking it into the pocket of my coverup. "I'm wearing a bikini."

We drove for a very long time, and I snuck peeks at my phone but didn't text unless I had to, just taking in all the reassurances that I could. The group chat lit up, including notes to me to cooperate and hang in there.

Someone thought I was an illegal designation? Maybe this was where I was discovered to have no designation at all. What happened then? Was it illegal to have no designation?

The building they brought me to had a big fence and guards. It also looked grey and unwelcoming. They brought me into a lobby where a couple of sad and worried people sat, then through several sets of locked doors and past more guards. The whole bleak place reeked of despair and desperation.

Finally, they shoved me into what looked like a large exam room with several beds and lots of equipment. It was completely empty, and unlike the ones at the Center or the hospital, not cozy at all.

"Sit. Give me the phone." The one who drove held out his hand.

"Phone?" I blinked, pretending to be innocent.

"Give me the phone or I'll have you searched," he demanded.

With a sigh, I handed it to him.

"Thank you. Just cooperate and it will be fine," he said.

"What if it's not." My knees shook.

He sighed and shut the door as he muttered, "Sometimes I hate this job."

Immediately, I found the bathroom, since that had been a long drive. Afterwards, I curled onto one of the exam beds, wishing I had a blanket.

What if I really was one? Would they let me see the guys before I died? Also, what was this about being a carrier? I understood the concept, but what happened to them?

I wasn't even sure exactly which designations were illegal and why.

Head on my knees, I started to cry. I felt comfort being pushed through the bond, but I still sobbed because I was scared, over-whelmed, and alone.

No good ever came of that.

The door opened. "You're Grace Ellington?"

"Can you tell me what's happening?" I continued to sob into my knees, wishing Spencer, or any of my guys were here.

"You're here to be tested. It's all routine. Can you confirm some information for me?" It sounded rote and unemotional. She wore a nurse's uniform. First, she scanned my face with a little box, she then pulled a machine over to me.

The nurse handed me a tissue and asked me a bunch of questions. Some of my answers didn't make her very happy. According to the records Evan had created for me my parents were betas, also deceased.

"I have a right to have someone from the Center be present," I mumbled, finally remembering what I'd been told.

"If the first test confirms that you're an omega, then yes," she replied.

"Is my alpha here? Can't he come in?" My chest shook as she ran some diagnostics on me with the machine.

"For this first test I just need a swab," she said, taking a giant cotton swab and rubbing it against the inside of my cheek.

"You sit tight." She left, the door locking behind her.

Where was I going to go?

Chapter Forty-Two

Spencer

Heart in my throat, it took all of my willpower not to chase after the Office of Designation Management van as it drove away from the hotel *with my mate.* Her panic seared through me and my heart stopped as I remembered the last time I'd felt panic like that so deeply in my soul.

It was the moment Elaris died in a car crash on her way to the airport after a conference. I hadn't come with her because I'd stayed behind to handle some negotiations.

Not that I would have been able to stop the wreck had I been with her.

Still, once again, I was helpless while the woman I loved panicked.

My phone buzzed with texts on the group chat, reminding me that I had to keep it together–at the very least so that I didn't overwhelm Grace with *my* fear. I had a mate bond again and needed to get back in the habit of being mindful of my emotions.

As I walked back to the cabana I let the pack know everything. While I had every intention of going to her, I needed a plan. Also, pants.

My phone rang. Wes. "I'm so sorry that she was taken."

"It's not your fault. How can I help? Evan's attempting to get an advocate to her. Bren's calling the pack lawyer. Jett's trying to get those background checks," Wes said.

"The documentation seemed to be in order, but what do I know? One of the big issues is that right now, you're the only one legally connected to her. I can't even have a say as a pack member because she's not actually part of the pack. No judgment, because we could never anticipate this, just facts." At the cabana, I quickly stuffed our things into the beach bags.

"You're going to her anyway, right? Do you need me to fly out?" Wes asked.

"I'll be on my way momentarily. I'll stand in the parking lot if I have to. Right now, stay in Rockland, though feel free to leave the office," I replied, making one last sweep, the unfinished sand castle visible through the door sending pangs through my heart.

"I can get on the next flight," he offered, voice shaking.

Shouldering the bag, I set off for our villa. "We might need your, um, particular skills, and that would be easier if you weren't on a plane."

"Oh. That makes sense. Yeah, if I'm doing that I should probably leave the office." His voice stopped wavering.

"Don't worry about work today, just focus on her," I stated.

"Got it. What do you need?"

I thought for a moment. "A copy of the court order. I especially want to know why her and why now. Also, ask Bren if the genscan came in."

Unlocking the villa door, I threw the bag on the couch. I headed straight for the bedroom, which still smelled strongly of our love-making.

I'll get you, Grace. I promise.

"Why *did* we have a genscan run on Grace?" Confusion flowed through Wes' voice.

I took a suit out of the closet. Appearances had power.

"The resemblance between Creed and Grace is odd. Even though I don't think that the professor was one of my father's omegas, we're missing something," I replied.

"Yeah, someone thinking Grace is an *illegal designation* is both strange and worrisome. Bren's calling, I'll be in touch. We'll get her, Spence." Wes ended the call.

That we would. Pulling on the suit, I texted Evan.

Me

Do we know where she's being taken?

While I waited for a response, I finished getting dressed. Evan sent an address.

I called a car, then threw some clothes and things for Grace in a bag, considering she was taken in only a bikini.

While waiting for the car, I texted Grace that I loved her, still sensing how scared and confused she was. Grace would have no idea what was going on. She literally never had the assembly in school where the Office of Designation Management did their education talk. Growing up in another world meant she had no reference, no idea what to expect.

"Thank you so much," I told the driver as I got in, then put up the privacy screen between us while I started making discreet inquiries of my own. I needed our mate bond to populate in the system sooner rather than later, so I could be with her.

My phone rang. Brennan.

"What did the lawyer say?" I asked.

"I think this is my fault, and I'm so sorry," Brennan blurted.

I helped myself to a glass of wine from the car's bar. "What are you talking about? I'm the one who asked you to run the genscan. That's where this is coming from? Something strange popped up, causing her record to be flagged?"

"I'm pretty sure it's my mother's doing." Brennan sighed.

"Your *mother*? I know she's on the rampage, but why would Siobhan do something like that?" I frowned as I took a sip of wine. It was subpar but fine given the circumstances.

Brennan exhaled sharply. "Retaliation? Ian Murphy, her lawyer, was served today."

"You think she might have called in a tip on Grace as retaliation?" I wasn't sure about that.

"My mom probably knows that Grace's record is a fake, because she knows everything. Knowing someone has a fake record is often enough for them to be tested," he reminded me.

"True. What did Grace's genscan say?" Honestly, I wondered if it was someone associated with Nate's pack. Adriana Thorne's surety bothered me.

"I don't know. I saw the notification this morning but haven't checked yet. Do you think that's what's caused them to take her for testing? Things have been a little hectic this morning beyond Grace. Hold on," he said. "Shit. I... I have no words. It says Nathaniel Thorne, that professor, is her father."

I sucked in air through my teeth as my mind reeled at the possibilities, the probabilities.

"How? How, Spence? You're the genius? *How?*" Bren prodded.

"We're missing something. Unless his backstory is that good and Nate really is one of the resettled omegas? Who does it say for mother?" I polished off the glass and poured myself another.

"The record is *locked*." Brennan sounded like he was moving. There were muffled voices.

My belly sank. "Locked records aren't good."

"The lawyer is on the other line, I'll call you right back," Brennan said.

Taking another sip of wine as I stared out the window at the trees, I mulled this over. Nate Thorne was her father and her mother's record was locked. What had her mother done to warrant that? Records weren't locked for no reason.

This got stranger and stranger.

I helped myself to some snacks and tried to distract myself from Grace's anxiety by replying to emails, following up on things, checking in at work, and responding to the group chat.

Evan

> **Mrs. Beekman is in touch with the local Center. They're aware of what's going on and are dispatching someone.**

Finally, the phone rang again.

"What did the lawyer say?" I asked Brennan.

"The documentation is valid. Also, the Office of Designation Management is trying to get a judge to unlock Grace's maternal record," Brennan told me.

"Can we somehow delay the order until Wes hacks the record, so that we know what we're dealing with?" I asked.

There were muffled voices.

"Yeah, whatever you need," Wes' voice interjected over the line.

"Grace's mother's record is locked. Can you hack the record and tell us why? Also, any luck on the court order?" I asked. "Knowledge is power."

"Still working on it, trying not to get arrested," he responded. "Here, Bren wants you."

"Okay, what should I say to the lawyer that's not weird?" Brennan asked.

"I'll handle that. What else did she say?" I prodded, wondering if a third glass of wine would settle my nerves or make things worse, as I tried to send more reassurance to Grace.

"The lawyer said it was important for you to show up there. They might not let you wait inside until the bond registration populates in the system. But them knowing that she has someone waiting will help. Hey, I forgot to tell you congratulations," he added.

I rubbed my chest. "Thank you. I know it was a little soon, but..."

"I'm glad she has you," Brennan told me, voice a little wistful. "The lawyer reiterated full cooperation, being respectful, and that there really wasn't much we could do other than hope."

"That's what I thought. But thank you so much. Wes invaded your office?" I asked. Probably better than him alone at the house.

"Yes. Jett and Riley are here, too. I wanted us all together. Evan's still at the Center. He says that he can monitor the situation better from there, especially once the advocate arrives," he added.

Riley was there. Okay.

"Keep me updated on what Wes finds," I replied.

The guards opened the doors, and I walked through the sensors, into the small, dreary lobby of the bleak Office of Designation Management office, which had been a bit of a drive. I should have looked to see if it was on the path of a train, but everything was better in hindsight. Given how few illegal designations there actually were percentage wise, the testing centers were spread much thinner than Omega Centers. A lot of what they did was investigation and education.

Her fear still shot through me.

"Can I help you?" The man behind the desk eyed my suit. Fear and sadness hung heavily in the air.

"Yes, my mate is here for testing. Grace Ellington," I told him, trying to hold myself steady and send her all my love.

He typed on his computer. "You're Wes Lawson?"

"Spencer."

Frowning at the screen he kept typing. "Sorry, I can't find you, so I can't confirm or deny anything. You'll have to wait in the parking lot."

"Please note that I'm here and waiting." I went back out into the parking lot.

While a mate bond registration usually populated in the public record within the day, I needed it *now*.

I opened my contacts. Ah, yes, he owed me a favor.

I'd cash in every favor ever owed to me if it got her back to us safely.

Chapter Forty-Three

Wes

I ended Spencer's call and took Brennan's. "Bren?"

"Hey, Evan's staying at work because he can monitor things better there, but the rest of us should all centralize someplace," he told me. "Home or my office?"

"Spencer's having me hack the government. Where do you want me to be?" I set my status to away and shot my team an email that Spencer was pulling me for an off-site project.

"Hmmm. Here. I'd rather my office be raided than home. I'll see you there."

I caught up on the group chat and sent Grace some reassuring words. I texted Riley.

Me

Is anyone getting you?

Riley

> **Why?**

Me

> **Wanna hack the government with me?**

Riley

> **Instead of a literature test? Please?**

> **What's going on?**

Me

> **Grace has been taken by the Office of Designation Management. I'll tell you more when I get you.**

Riley

> **Fucking shit.**

> **I'm in class so you have to go to the office and ask for me. I can't just leave and get in your car.**

Yeah, I knew how school worked.

Me

> **See you soon.**

I detached my laptop from my work setup, and put it in my bag, along with a few other things. Locking my office, I left.

Grace's panic was hard to tamp down but that also meant she was alive. Fuck. The Office of Designation Management had my mate. Part of me wanted to drive to the airport and fly to her. But Spencer had a point.

I got Riley from school, and we stopped at the dorms for her to get her other laptop, then drove to Brennan's office.

"I'm so happy to get out of the test, but were you supposed to get me?" Riley texted someone.

"Bren said to centralize. Spencer said to hack the government." I shrugged. Riley was pack and could help me.

I was going to need all the help I could get.

"You know, we could do this faster." Riley threw a rubber band at me.

"Let's not get arrested." Right now, I was trying to figure out what was going on. Riley was trying to unlock Grace's mom's record in the genscan Brennan had gotten on her.

Which was fucking weird. I knew all about Grace's mom.

"Please don't get arrested," Brennan sighed. He'd been on the phone a lot with the pack lawyers.

I looked at what I'd found so far. Mind blown.

Brennan's phone rang. He grimaced. "Do I even?"

Jett shrugged. "Would you rather her show up?"

"She's banned." He sighed again. "What do you want, Mother?"

Just what we needed. I kept working, Brennan's scent going sour.

"Mother, I don't want to hear it. What you and Ian are doing is not okay," he snapped. "No. Give me access to everything now, and I'll drop it." He grunted. "Yeah, I know you tied everything up. I'll take the building. Might be better than the press you'll get if I have to force a sale. They're already pretty upset about you cutting the scholarships."

I kept digging, Brennan kept snapping at his mother.

Okay, who had this number that called in the tip? My fingers danced across the screen? Oh.

"Do you even hear yourself? I'm an adult and I'm allowed to do all these things. Why don't you go bully someone who cares." Brennan ended the call. "Fuck me."

"Eww. Not here." Riley made a face. "Sweet baby cheeses, I'm trying to unlock a file, you know."

Jett shook his head. "Not sure how I feel about this."

"I'm the best, fucker." She rolled her eyes.

"Good job for standing up to your mom, Bren." I looked at Jett. "Do you have the background checks on the Thornes yet, Jett?"

"So far I have ones for Creed, Verity, and Hale, who are the adult children in the house, as well as Nate and Harry. Still waiting on the others. Want me to send them?" Jett asked.

"Yeah. I need the one for the alpha that hurt her, ASAP." I kept working.

"Why?" Jett asked. "What did you find?"

My phone rang. Spencer. I answered. "Spence, you're on speaker."

"Hey, I'm there. They won't let me sit inside, but they know that I'm here. I talked to the judge, and he's resisting giving them the court order to unseal the record until we give the go ahead. How are you doing?" Spencer asked.

"The tip was called in anonymously. They cited duplicate records, that Grace Ellington was someone called Grace Silvers, and they thought she might be the child of a fugitive. This Grace only has the barest record, like infant medical records without the genetic registration, like the hospital would make when a child is born. The mother in Grace Silver's file is locked, the father is Nathaniel Thorne. The genscan attached itself to that record. Her birthday is exact except for the year," I told him.

He sucked in a breath. "Yes, because Evan had her birthdate changed to make her a year older."

"Yes. Grace Silvers' record is tagged as a *misfiled child,* cited as a possible duplicate of someone named Cassidy Silvers," I said. "Whose mother's record is also locked, father unknown, who has the same birthdate and also the barest of baby records. Though she is marked as a homebirth where Grace has a hospital listed."

Cassidy *was* Grace's middle name. This was weird.

"Misfiled child? That could mean a number of things. Who's Cassidy?" Spencer asked.

Jett was on his phone, probably seeing what his contacts had.

"Don't know. I managed to figure out what phone number the tip came from and traced it to Adriana Thorne," I added. "We don't have her background check yet."

"Shit. Why? Why was she so convinced this wasn't Nate's Grace?" Spencer said.

"That's the alpha that fucking grabbed her, right?" Riley asked.

"Yes," Spencer replied. "Thank you. Good work I'll call back when I have more info." He ended the call.

"Wait, so one of the alphas of Grace's bio-dad called in a tip, not my mother?" Brennan frowned. "We're fucking missing something."

"This entire thing is so strange," Jett agreed.

According to the background checks Jett got on the Thorne family, the kids were all fine, other than Hale looking like a chaotic mess. Nate and Harry were also upstanding people.

I texted Evan, not liking that he wasn't here with us, but understanding what a resource he was.

Me

Are you doing okay?

Evan

I'm still feeling her a lot. The person the local Center is sending her will be there soon. I'm okay here for now.

Me

The moment you need to leave, leave. We're still at Bren's office. Can I call?

Evan

Give me a second to hide in the closet.

Which was where they took personal phone calls.

I called him. "Hey, Babe."

"Hey. So, what's up?"

I told him everything we'd found so far.

"Shit. So, I sat down and really poked at Nate's record with the Center–at least the parts I have access to. Around the time Grace would have been a baby, Nate filed for an un-bonding but rescinded it. There's a note that it was rescinded for the right reasons, but his file was tagged as *vulnerable omega*, and he was monitored very closely, with mandatory pack counseling for years. Then, he met with his advocate until he retired, just a few years ago. This means something big happened in his pack, early on," Evan told me.

"Wow."

Nate had filed for an un-bonding? What had happened there?

"Wes, I need your help," Riley called.

"I've got to go. We'll keep you up to date. Love you." I ended the call and sent lots of love through the bond to both of them.

I went over to Riley. "Okay, let's do this."

We were running out of time, and I still didn't have a fucking clue what was going on other than some fucker had *intentionally* put my Grace in danger.

Chapter Forty-Four

Grace

I sat in silence in the sterile room, a little chilly in only my bikini and coverup. Spencer reached out through the bond, and I took it, wrapping myself in it.

Eventually, voices echoed down the hall through the door.

"Just put them together. Oh, come on, what are they going to do? Build a blanket fort?" a man's voice grumbled as he stopped in front of the door.

Was that an option? I could go for that right now. Also, a snack.

The door opened and the guard said, "Take a seat, the nurse will be with you shortly."

I looked up to see a bewildered, blond man in khakis, a button down, and suspenders with molecular diagrams on them. The door closed and locked behind him.

"Professor?" I frowned. Why was Nate Thorne here?

"Grace. I thought I saw Spencer Thanukos pacing in the parking lot. Are you all right?" The professor came over to me, worry in his blue eyes.

A dam broke inside me. "I don't know what's going on," I sobbed.

"It's okay to be scared," he said softly. "Getting dragged into the Office of Designation Management is frightening indeed."

The door opened and the nurse walked in. "Grace, this whole process will go much better if you just tell me about your mother."

"She's dead." Not that the information would do them any good.

"Is it not in her file?" Nate frowned.

"Not her birth mother–that record is locked. The court order to unlock it hasn't gone through yet. You'll get out much faster if you just cooperate," the nurse said. She turned to Nate. "You're her biological father, correct?"

"The professor isn't my father," I blurted.

Hurt crossed his face and his scent soured.

What did I do? It wasn't like I could tell them the truth.

Guilt welled up inside me. "*I'm* the reason you're here? I'm so sorry, professor."

The nurse frowned at him. "You're not Nathaniel Thorne?"

"I am," Nate nodded. "I have a daughter named Grace... somewhere. I haven't been able to find her. Records got messed up and I've been searching since she was a baby. This Grace, while a Grace to be proud of, is exactly a year too old. Might be my brother's though. And don't worry, we'll be okay," he reassured me, with a fatherly look.

A bewildered look crossed the nurse's face.

The professor knew how old I was? But then, he was probably curious. *Exactly* a year too old? What was going on here? Especially since Spencer *didn't* think Nate was one of the omega refugees his dad helped.

Evan *had* made me a year older when my record was created...

"I can tell you about my Grace's biological mother, if that would help? Her name was Thora Silvers." He gave the nurse her birth date and a bunch of other information.

Thora Silvers. Not my mother's name. I exhaled in relief.

"Designation?" the nurse asked.

"Alpha. Most likely. She was a bit of a late bloomer and hadn't awakened yet. But then we were only twenty when she got pregnant." His look went wistful, then he finished answering her questions. The nurse did the same diagnostics on him that she did on me, took a swab from him, frowned at me one last time, then left.

You could get pregnant without your designation being apparent? *What?* At least I hadn't gotten dream pregnant. That would have been hard to explain.

"You met her in high school?" I asked him as the door locked us in once again.

"University. As firsties. She was a piano performance major. Thora had the most beautiful blue-grey eyes and a sharp wit."

"She liked Volkov?" I joked. Piano major? Yeah, not my mom. She couldn't even play.

"Oh, she hated him. Kirkokov, too. She liked the powerful pieces, not the technical ones. I loved to hear her play," he sighed. "That's how we met. I liked to study in empty practice rooms in the music building because I enjoyed the music."

"I play a little," I admitted. "Mostly I play Volkov too fast to annoy my packmate."

He laughed. "Annoying packmates is fun. I love to annoy Zain by putting dishes away in the wrong places. Also, Adriana doesn't like how I fold the sheets."

"Bren hates the way I load the dishwasher," I replied.

"Thora hated dishwashers. When we moved in together, I always had to run it when she wasn't around. We were waiting for her to awaken so we could mate." His head bowed, anguish on his face.

His scent went salty, and tears filled his eyes.

"It's the thing I regret most in life. How I wish I could fix it. I've had to live with the fact I can't ever reverse what I did. It... it kills me. Every single day I think of her, I think of what I did to her and Grace, and how even when I find Grace I'll never be able to make it better. I honestly wouldn't blame her if she never wanted to know me or my packmates–though I'd hope she'd try to get to know some of the children. Maybe?" He sniffed.

The pain rolling off him broke my heart.

"I've been told the story," I said softly, my hand brushing his shoulder to comfort him. "I'm glad that you never stopped looking for your Grace, and that you acknowledge you screwed up. Creed and Verity told me because they were trying to convince me that I was your Grace, I think."

He nodded. "Can you blame them? You and Creed look like twins."

"It is eerie. But genetics are weird. Um, why couldn't Thora just be part of your new pack? I get that Pippa was your scent match, but not all mates are. Only one of mine is. Was it because she was an alpha and the other women didn't know her? Because she was a piano major? Sorry if I'm prying, I'm trying to understand." It seemed like the obvious solution.

"Because we're idiots." He raked a hand through his blond hair. "It honestly didn't dawn on me, and well, Adriana did a very good job of convincing me that Thora was a stalker. I think it was alpha possessiveness that drove her to do it. They wouldn't have gotten along, and Thora being a piano major would only be a part of it. Thora didn't play well with other alphas. But, we should have given it a chance. At the very least we could have shared our child."

Huh. Adriana seemed to be the real problem here.

"Are you safe?" I murmured. "Adriana seems like a piece of work, and if you need help, my mate Evan is an advocate at the Omega Center. We can get you help, and keep you and the kids safe."

His look softened. "I'm not being abused, promise. You probably wonder why I stayed. In the beginning it was because of Pip. I *love* Pip with my entire soul. It took a lot of work and therapy. I met with my advocate and therapist regularly for decades until they both retired."

"As long as you're safe." I frowned.

"I am. I apologize for Adriana harming you and yelling at you. She still has anger issues and does take the protective alpha thing too seriously sometimes. But that doesn't give her leave to harm you." The professor frowned and shook his head.

"Do you love Adriana?" I was so confused by their pack.

"I care for her enough that I repaired our relationship and stayed with the pack for over two and a half decades. I've children with her and enjoy her company," he explained. "I get something different from each of my packmates and it's not always romantic love."

I understood that. "Not to change the subject but why would a record be locked?"

His head tilted. "She must have done something very bad or gotten involved with terrible people for them to not want it to populate in your file when you were genscanned."

"I never did a genscan," I frowned. Maybe it was a test I'd gotten along the way?

The bigger question was why would a record on *my* file, my very fake file, be *locked* and why in the world did they think that Nate was my dad? Unless there really was an alternate me here? But then wouldn't that have been apparent when I arrived here, and they kept scanning my face and having me press a finger to that little box?

"I honestly don't know what happened that caused Thora to be in trouble, and what led to her death. They never gave me that information. But, oh, that sister of hers, it wouldn't surprise me if once again, she'd brought her into something shady," Nate added. "Or that her sister tried to blame it on Thora entirely."

"Huh." Things were getting weirder and weirder. My brain–and heart–couldn't take it.

He nodded at my neck. "That mark looks brand new, are you okay? It must be hard being apart from him so soon."

"It is, and..." I closed my eyes, reaching out and getting so much anxiety and panic from my guys. "We were supposed to spend the day at the beach. I was building a sand castle."

"I do like the beach," he told me. "I grew up on the Northeastern coast."

"Oh, I went to Seaside recently with my mate Wes." I grinned, remembering how much fun that was.

"There's a pier there, right?" he asked.

I nodded. "With a sky swing and funnel cake and games. He won me a stuffed rabbit."

"As he should," he agreed.

The door opened and the nurse walked back in. "Good news, neither of you have illegal designations. Nathaniel, you're con-firmed omega, and Grace, you're confirmed gamma. As is your right, someone from the Center is on her way. Now, let's take some blood so we can do the second test."

"You're a gamma?" He went quiet, still sitting next to me as the nurse took a large vial of his blood. No Compass BioTek tests here apparently.

I nodded.

"You grew up in care?" His voice was tentative.

I was guessing he meant foster care. "I had a family. But they're gone now."

"Oh, so sorry to hear that."

"I don't really miss them." Well, sometimes I missed my dad and grandma.

Nate looked horrified.

"Everything was fine when I was small. It wasn't until I got older when the conflicts between me and my mom really got bad. Then I was off on my own and all that." I brushed it off, not wanting him to feel bad. It wasn't his fault that my teenage years were shitty.

The nurse came over to me and tried to take my blood, but my filmy cover up was not cooperating.

"I know it's cold in here, but please take it off?" she asked.

"Fine." Without a thought I shrugged it off.

"Grace, what happened?" Nate's voice went strangled.

Oh, shit. "It's old."

The nurse took my blood and peeked over at my scars. "Oh, you're that type of gamma."

"Yeah." I guess. I put my coverup back on as soon as she finished and left.

The professor's eyes fell on the bruises on my arm.

"Adriana did that yesterday? I'm sorry about that," he said quietly.

My chest shook. "I wasn't trying to start anything."

"I know. Tell me about you?" he pleaded. "How many mates do you have? How did you meet Spencer Thanukos? Also, you said one of your mates is an advocate?"

"Um, sure," I shrugged. He probably needed the distraction—and so did I.

I told him about my guys, leaving out things like my past, though I did talk about my PhD and my job. Given, I was pretty sure he was convinced I was his Grace, I shouldn't lead him on. But talking distracted me from what was happening.

"A PhD in math, that's wonderful." He beamed. "It took me forever to get mine. We moved around a bit as everyone got established in their careers, and had kids, and all that. Do you like where you work?" His voice grew tentative.

"I do. We're going to accomplish some really interesting things."

The door opened and a middle-aged omega holding a duffle bag, and a tablet came in. She wore a hot pink polo shirt that said *Omega Center Crisis Response Team.*

"Hi. I'm Lark and I'm from the Omega Center." She looked at me. "You're Grace?"

"I am." Did she have snacks in that bag?

"And this is your father?" She peered at the tablet, her glasses sliding down her nose.

I shook my head. "He's no–" The words trailed off as I saw Nate flinch. "I can't be your Grace, Professor."

Tears pricked my eyes. I didn't ask for daddy drama.

His head bowed. "I... I understand. What I did is unforgivable–and I can only imagine what growing up was like for you. I won't push for a relationship, though I'm here if you ever want one. Will you stay in touch with Creed and Verity at least?"

Lark just stood there, blinking. Sadness wafted off Nate and he looked like his puppy had been kicked.

"You misunderstand," I took a deep breath, getting another hit of hurt through his fruity, creamy scent. He smelled like the apricot custard tarts from the bakery I'd worked at.

I sighed, trying to figure out how to say this.

"Professor, I think it's great that you are trying to make things right. I'm just not her. I'm sorry. It's just not possible. I don't know why they think that you're my dad and I'm sorry to give you false hope–and I'm sorry you got dragged here because of me." Tears rolled down my face, because I didn't want to hurt him. I just wasn't from this world.

"It's okay, Grace. But why can't you be her?" he pleaded.

"My mom's name wasn't Thora, and she couldn't play the piano for shit. She didn't even go to college." I sniffed. "I'm also a year too old. Um, I'm going to use the restroom."

Getting off the exam bed, I made my way over to the little bathroom. Leaning against the door, I cried into my arms, wishing my mates were here with me.

Chapter Forty-Five

Spencer

In the shade of the parking lot of the Office of Designation Management testing center, I answered emails, kept in touch with the pack, and did everything I could to keep my mind off what could be happening inside. My phone buzzed.

Perfect.

After I finished up, the guards let me back into the lobby. The same man sat there at the desk.

He gave me a look. "If it's not in the system, I can't tell you anything."

"Check again for me? Please. Her name is Grace Ellington. Mine is Spencer."

"Sure." He typed on the terminal. "Yeah, there's a Spencer here. Spencer..." He gave me a look, eyebrows arching, then his eyes went back to the screen. "Today? Congrats man. Well, I mean, I hope?" He pushed a box to me. "I need verification."

I pressed my finger to it.

He looked at his screen. "Got it. You can wait in the lobby, or outside. Here, let me get you her phone."

Taking out a bin, he found a clear envelope with her name on it and handed it to me.

"Thank you." Pocketing the phone, I looked for a seat and saw Pippa Thorne, sitting stiff and white-knuckled in the corner.

Why was Nate's alpha here?

Finding a seat, I continued to stay in contact with the pack.

A middle-aged omega in a hot pink Center polo, carrying an enormous duffle, entered and spoke softly with the man at the front. She then sat down near the door, looking at her tablet.

Me

> **Center sent someone from the Blanket Brigade. Is that protocol?**

Wes

> **I don't care as long as someone is there with her.**

Evan

> **Yes, if someone's available, otherwise they'll just send an advocate. I'm glad someone made it.**

A man with three crying children came in with guards. The little one in his arms looked a lot like Grace, her hair in two little curly ponytails. They were all escorted through the doors into the main part of the building, but not before the man exchanged looks with Pippa.

What was happening?

"You, you had something to do with this." Adriana Thorne, the woman who threatened and grabbed Grace, stormed over to me.

Seriously? *She* called in the tip. But I wasn't going to let her know I knew that.

"What is your problem with my mate, Adriana? She's done nothing to you." I squared my shoulders and gave her a cool look, keeping my voice low and even.

"They've brought my *mate* and the children in because of you," she yelled.

"Me? What did I do? I have no issue with the children or your mate. Again, what is your problem with *my* mate? Why are you so certain that she's not Nate's child even with the genscan? What do you know?" I prodded, taking a deep breath, trying to maintain a cool facade.

Adriana growled at me. "Why are you targeting me now?"

Pippa joined us and looked alarmed. "There's a genscan confirming that she's Nate's child?"

"Indeed." I gave Pippa a look.

"I see. It would have been better if she were Barrett's." Pippa sighed.

The guards present in the lobby watched us. One had his hand on a stunner.

"She's not either. She's faking," Adriana snapped.

"Adriana, sit down before you make things worse," Pippa directed.

"Easy for you to say. They only have one of your children. They have two of mine," Adriana retorted, scowling. "It's Spencer's fault."

They had their children and Nate? I was so confused.

"It is?" Pippa frowned. "Nate's my mate, too."

"Why are you even here?" Adriana shrieked at me.

One of the guards came over, hand on his taser. "Please lower your voices or take it outside," he told Adriana.

Adriana growled. "They have my mate and children."

Pippa tried to take Adriana's arm. "Sit down."

"They have my mate, as well, Adriana. I have no idea why. We know nothing about the parents listed in Grace's genscan, on either side. Could you tell me anything about that?" I prodded, voice still low and even, without a hint of bark. The urge to shake her was strong.

"Why do you think I know anything? Besides, this is all your doing," she shouted.

Before I could react, her fist connected with my face.

Guards descended, throwing her to the ground. I remained very still, hoping her actions didn't get me thrown out.

"She's a bit distraught," Pippa told them in half-hearted defense.

"Everyone here is. But we have a *no-violence* rule," the guard said, gripping Adriana and walking to the door.

"My children," Adriana yelled.

"You can wait for them outside," they told her, kicking her out.

Pippa shook her head. "Adriana is... spirited, especially when defending her pack."

Adriana was hiding something.

"Spirited? Like when she laid hands on my mate? I'm sorry that they have your children, but I don't know why you think it's my fault. They're not allowing them to have a parent?" I frowned. Or were they with Nate and Grace?

"Two of the children are legal adults, and they're all together. Harry's with them now, but I'm not sure how long they'll let him." Without another word she sat down.

Pain and sadness made me almost double over. I took a few deep breaths trying to compose myself, sending everything I could to Grace.

I wanted to break down the door.

My phone rang. Wes. I stepped back out into the parking lot. "Wes?"

"Yeah, so, Riley and I hacked the locked maternal record. Spencer, I don't even know what I'm looking at. How the fuck did Grace get to her world if both her parents are from *here*? Her biological mom's record isn't faked. But here's the thing, Thora isn't Grace's mom's name," Wes said.

There were typing sounds.

"Also, according to this, Grace's biological mom is *dead*. She passed away when Grace was a newborn. The Cassidy thing is weird. I didn't hack the locked maternal file, though. Both the Grace and Cassidy records just fall off after babyhood, like they never again went to a doctor or were enrolled in school or anything. They just disappeared."

All that tracked with what Grace told me about Nate and his missing Grace. Though yes, that part with Cassidy was strange.

"Was Thora a university student? Piano major?" I asked.

"Yeah."

"How did she die?" I was glad I didn't see Adriana in the parking lot.

"Oh fuck," Wes said. "The record was locked because Thora Silvers wasn't just implicated in a federal crime, she's apparently a sigma."

Chapter Forty-Six

Grace

Finally, I washed my face and with a deep breath, went back into the exam room, where the professor and Lark spoke softly.

"It's going to be okay, Grace. It seems like there's lots of big feelings here," Lark said. "I'm sure the stress of all this isn't helping. I have blankets and fuzzy socks." She started rummaging through her duffle bag which sat on an empty exam bed.

Right, because like dicks and cuddles, blankets solved all sorts of problems in this world. Lark pulled out blankets and fuzzy socks in bright colors and busy prints along with some candy bars.

She gave us an apologetic look. "Sorry. I usually work with teenagers."

"I'll take this one. It's cold in here. Thank you. My mate's an advocate and works a lot with teenagers, too. He can throw amazing pizza parties on zero budget." I wrapped a black blanket with neon stars around me.

"I'm sure he can." She laughed, then her eyes fell on my bruised arm. "I've got to ask you some questions, for intake purposes." Lark patted the table.

"Okay." I couldn't meet the professor's eyes as I took a seat.

Voice quiet, she asked me some basic questions, then got into ones I'd heard many times before. *Do I feel safe with my mate? Do I have a place of my own in the house? Do I want to return to them, or would I like to be taken elsewhere?*

Nate got up and went to the bathroom.

"Nate gave me the short version. While you're allowed to have lots of feelings, try not to hurt his? He's trying very hard to be very respectful of yours." Lark's voice was soft.

"I just don't understand." I started to sob.

"Oh, Hun. I have the genscan right here. Do you want to see it? Will that help? You're a scientist, aren't you?" she asked, tapping on the screen of the tablet.

"Mathematician." I blinked. "My genetic workup in my file tells me who I'm related to?"

"No, that's different. Basically, this workup is cross-referenced with a greater database to find extended family. It's something you have to opt into." Nate stood behind us. "Sorry, hazards of living with Verity."

"I didn't do a genscan." My lower lip quivered.

"Maybe your mates did it? Possibly after seeing me yesterday? I could see an overprotective mate doing that out of worry." The professor got close enough to see the screen.

"Oh. Or me meeting Creed. The resemblance sort of freaked some of the guys out–and Bren, he, well, he always thinks people are getting close to the pack for the wrong reasons." My chest shuddered. "Not that you are, but well, you've met one of my mates. Adriana did accuse me of going after your pack's money, so you probably understand?"

Nate nodded. "I'm so sorry she did that, but yes, after meeting Spencer, I'm pretty sure that's not why you're in town."

"No. I just came for the symposium." My voice came out ragged.

"I know." He patted my shoulder awkwardly, then grabbed a candy bar.

My belly growled, reminding me it was past lunch. I took a candy bar and gobbled it while Lark showed me a different screen, which was populated with Nate's name, along with a bunch of other stuff. Another box said *file locked.*

All I could do was shove the rest of the candy in my mouth and stare at the screen. None of this made any sense.

My head spun and bile rose in my throat. Swallowing hard, I rested my head on my knees, wrapping the blankets tighter. *3.14 15926535*

"It's going to be okay, Hun," Lark said.

8979323846

How? The computer said I had a *dad.* Nate was my *dad?* How? How was that even possible?

"Grace, are you all right? What are you mumbling?" Lark asked.

"*Pi*, I think," Nate replied. He sat down next to me.

2643383279

I kept going through the numbers, willing myself to calm down.

"How many places do you know?" The professor finally said when I'd stopped, though I hadn't looked up from my knees.

"More than Spencer. We had a contest." My voice was muffled by my blanketed knees. I looked at him.

How did I ask if the professor was from a parallel world without asking if he was from a parallel world? That's all that made sense. After all, I couldn't be from here.

Could I?

"You... you didn't leave me behind right? Like you went into protection and left me?" My voice shook.

"You're not making any sense, Grace. I looked for you, so hard, I promise." He wrapped another blanket around me.

"Okay." I guess that was a *no.*

Nate looked at Lark. "Is there any way that they'd let her alpha in here? She's newly mated and so scared."

She tapped on her screen. "Not an alpha. Maybe someone else in her pack... oh, you're not registered with a pack?"

"Not yet. We're still getting it sorted." I could use Evan right now.

"Oh, I see," Lark replied.

"I'm still not really sure why we're even here. Thora was a late-blooming alpha. I could almost believe her sister was a sigma, but not Thora." He shook his head and took a bite of chocolate.

"Thora is the mother? The one blocked?" Lark said. "The paperwork said that Grace was suspected of having a fake record and a parent with an illegal designation. I suppose with one parent blocked, they brought you in as well in order to rule that out?"

"I believe so," he said.

"Her name wasn't Thora." I peeked up at him.

"I absolutely believe that whoever raised you wasn't Thora," Nate told me. "I would believe you thinking that the people who raised you were your birth parents. Thora's mom said that she put you in care after something happened to her alpha and son and she couldn't take care of you anymore. She said that the records must have gotten messed up when you entered the system. Given the record just *stopped,* I always wondered if you ended up baby trafficked. It wouldn't surprise me if Thora's sister sold you."

Holy shit *what?*

"Grace, I know this is a lot for you to take in. But it's on the genscan. They're seldom wrong," Lark said.

His voice shook a little. "Whatever you were told about me probably wasn't true. That's what this is about, right? You were told something that makes it hard to believe it's me. Did they tell you that I was a bad person? Did they tell you that I was *dead?*"

"By the time I knew that my dad wasn't my biological father, I wasn't talking to my mom. He didn't know who my bio-dad was and my mom and I never had that conversation before she died. Even though I never looked that much like her, it was pretty obvious she was my mom. We have the same eyes and stuff." My body trembled again, and I squeezed my eyes shut.

It would probably be better to stop questioning and figure it out with my guys later before I said something weird.

"It's just a lot." My chest trembled.

"It is, Hun. I'll leave your advocate a note to find you a therapist. I have some chips and cookies if anyone is still hungry," she offered. "Also, some juice pouches."

Yeah, we were way over poor Lark's paygrade.

I took the offered chips and absently started eating them. "Not to change the subject, but I really don't understand this testing situation. We're being tested as *carriers?* If we carry the gene for the illegal designations, without actually having it ourselves, we could still pass it on?"

"Yes," Nate replied. "Verity could explain all this so much better."

I started to shake again. "Will they kill us if we're carriers? I can't believe they do that to people who had the audacity to be born with the wrong designation."

Now I could better understand why Elaris wanted to come up with an alternative.

"It's sad, but they don't do it lightly," Lark assured. "But your designation is fine—and they don't terminate carriers anymore. But... it might mean that you won't be able to have genetic children so that you can't pass the gene on."

"I'm not sure that's much better." I was starting to rethink my opinions of this world.

"The percentage of people with illegal designations is miniscule," Lark assured.

If it's so small, why were they so worried about it? I pinched the bridge of my nose with my thumb and forefinger.

"I'm still really confused. Like I don't even know what designations are illegal and why." I frowned. Lark gave me a look. I shrugged. "I missed that unit in school. My mom didn't like me to go to those."

"There's a lot to unpack there," she said softly.

"My mate Evan tells me that all the time." I sighed.

"Sigmas are violent and destructive to the order of things. And as for the others, you know what, I'll send a video to your Center account." She tapped on her tablet.

"An alpha gunned down my birthday dinner. I have trouble believing that an *entire designation* is bad." I just wasn't getting this. Things like this were probably what led to interdimensional underground people-smuggling rings.

"This is one of those things that people tend to have very polarizing views on, so we don't talk about it in public," Nate said.

I nodded. "I'm starting to get that."

"Did you just say that an alpha *gunned down* your birthday dinner?" the professor asked.

"We were fine. It had to do with Evan's job." I shrugged.

The nurse came back in. "Grace, dear, can you please just tell me what you know about your birth mother? If you do, we might be able to let the other children go. Nathaniel, your children are here. I can bring you the small ones. Also, we can bring you your mate, Harry."

"The children are here?" Nate looked stricken. "Which ones?"

The nurse looked at the tablet. "Creed, Hale, Mercy, Pax, Tru, and Hope."

"All the ones I'm biologically related to." The air whooshed out of him.

"What?" My chest shuddered.

"None of this is your fault, Grace," Lark soothed. "Since your mother's record is locked, they're ruling out illegal genetics on your father's side."

"The young ones, are they with their siblings or separated? Is someone with them?" His scent grew sour with anxiety.

"They're all together," she told him. "Your mate Harry is with them."

"Harry's here." Relief crossed his face.

"Look, her name wasn't Thora Silvers. Her name was Rosalind Ellington. I don't know her last name before she got married. She never told me. She couldn't play piano for shit. She was one of those people that no one ever believed did wrong—especially once she started preaching with the church." I met the nurses' gaze. "Does that help?"

It wouldn't though.

The nurse looked at her tablet and frowned. "Not without an additional name." She looked at the professor.

"Grace, would you like to meet Harry?" The professor's voice went hesitant. "I... I think you'd like him." He looked to the nurse. "Could you bring Harry after he comforts the children? Just for a few moments? We're not quite ready for the little ones."

Lark shot me a look. One that clearly said *See, he's trying to respect your feelings.*

"I'd love to meet Harry," I replied, even though I wasn't so sure.

"I can do that." The nurse left.

"Harry and I are married and he's only with me. Pip adores him though. She was there when I saw him for the first time. I made a total idiot of myself." Nate chuckled.

I recalled what Creed and Verity said about Harry. "He has a restaurant."

"He does. He's a molecular gastronomist. The youngest three are mine and Harry's. We call them *the littles* because they're so much younger than everyone else. My sister carried the twins, and his sister carried Hope. It's a bit odd having kids both in graduate programs and preschool," he explained.

"Yeah, I can see that." That was quite the age gap.

"You said that your mother's name is Rosalind?" He turned to Lark. "May I see your tablet? I want to show Grace a picture of Thora."

"Um, sure." She handed it to him.

He typed for a moment then turned it to me. The headline was about a piano competition. An older teenager with dark blonde hair and blue-grey eyes stood there, smiling, holding a trophy.

I sucked in a sharp breath. That was my mother.

Yet it wasn't. There was something about her smile, her eyes. She was too joyful.

The teenager wasn't alone. There was a man and woman who were obviously her parents with her, two brothers... and another teenager, who looked *exactly* like her.

But not quite.

The look in her eyes was shrewd and calculating. Her expression was almost jealous of the teen with the trophy. Almost.

To most it looked like she was happy for her. But I knew that look—the one that outwardly looked socially acceptable, when the feelings within were not.

It was the same expression she wore telling people at church how proud she was of me for my grades, then berating me for *embarrassing* her with all my advanced classes. The look she used to convince a member of the church who was a psychiatrist to give me meds that made it hard to think, all in the name of my own good, of course.

Most people bought it. The ones that didn't were avoided.

The room spun and I grabbed my head, squishing my eyes tight as I started to recite *Pi* again. If this was all true, then how the hell did I end up in my world, *with that woman?*

"Rosalind Silvers is Thora's identical twin," the professor said softly. "She disappeared around the time Thora died. The police came looking for her. Said she was dangerous but wouldn't say why. Just like we never knew how and why Thora died."

"Oh. When I look up Rosalind Silvers, the record is blocked with a message saying she's a dangerous fugitive and to..." Lark's voice shook. "To alert the Office of Designation Management. If they're identical twins, I could see why they might be having record issues."

"Indeed. Hmmm. Identical twins nearly always have identical designations–and as I've said before, I would absolutely believe Rosalind being a sigma. Thora had no idea, I'm sure. It's not like they test for it without cause. Sometimes people never know," he explained.

"Sigmas often test as alphas when young," Lark said.

"Are you saying that Thora is my birth mom, but I was somehow raised by her identical twin who pretended to be my mom?" I tried to make sense of all this.

Somehow the woman I thought was *my mother* took me to *another world.*

I needed Spencer so that I could figure out what was happening.

"That's all that makes sense to me. If Rosalind was on the run, she might have thought it would be easier to hide with a child by changing her profile," Nate told me. "Sorry, Harry likes true crime dramas."

"That makes a lot of sense. But shouldn't I have had a record? Shouldn't I have come up on the face-scanny thing?"

"You do have a record under *Grace Theodosia Silvers.* That's how I knew your name and birth date. But they usually don't add the genetic profile of babies when they're first born, especially back then," Nate told me. "The genscan automatically attached itself to that record, based on your name, birthday, and *me,* because I'm listed as your father. The record you grew up with was faked, I'm sure. Especially since you're listed as being a year older, but the same month and year."

"Grace *Theodosia?*" I started giggling, because this was all too weird. "It's Grace *Cassidy.*"

He frowned. "Oh, Cassidy was a name that Rosalind liked. But I'm surprised that she even kept your first name and birth day and month. That was a little sloppy and I'm surprised I never found you. I... I did look."

"I believe you." My mind–and heart–raced. No, Rosalind could be sloppy because somehow she ended up in a *different world.* How did she even do that?

Unless...

Spencer's dad and Dr. K took in illegal omegas. What if in return someone helped them smuggle illegal designations out and somehow Rosalind was one of them?

I *really* needed to talk to Spencer.

But if Rosalind was from this world and she was the one who raised me...

"Professor?" My chest grew tight. "Rosalind knew who you were, didn't she? She would know you're an omega? And that you were my dad and there'd be a chance I'd be like you?"

"Unfortunately, I knew Rosalind very well. We didn't get along, and I'm sure she knew that I was your father. Thora's parents knew I'd gotten her pregnant and left her. Her mother was *never* any help in finding you," he replied. "Told me that it served me right. I always wondered why she wouldn't care about finding her grandchild. But if she knew that you were actually with Rosalind, well, that explains it."

"She knew." Panic seized me as my body shook. Memories came back to me. Every time my mother scolded me for making a burrow or a blanket fort. Every time I was punished for too many stuffies. She knew that there was a possibility of what I could become.

When she found out about Wes, she knew that I could end up being an omega and had somehow found an alpha.

Not just any alpha, my soulmate.

This also meant that me being good at math had nothing to do with embarrassing her. Me wanting to travel to other worlds using math *wasn't* delusional.

No. It was a direct threat to her existence.

Also, she might have an actual reason to hate alphas.

"She knew." I wrapped my arms around my knees and started to sob.

"Grace, sweetie. Oh…" Worry filled the professor's scent. "I'll give you all the space you need after we get out of here, but please, let me hold you now."

His arms wrapped around me, and I sobbed into his shoulder.

"I've got you. I've got you. What are you trying to tell me?" Nate said softly.

"There's a recent note in Grace's file stating she was raised beta and only recently discovered that she was a gamma," Lark said softly.

Nate sucked in a breath, arms wrapped tightly around me as he rocked us back and forth.

I kept crying into his shoulder, thinking of all the times I huddled under the bed with only my pillow, of all the times I was grounded for too many blankets.

Of her knowing what me dreaming of Wes actually meant.

And her knowing that he could be *real.*

"I've never really believed everyone about this gamma stuff, I mean how could I be an omega?" I sobbed, trying to work it all out in my head.

The reality crashed down on me. I'd been born an omega, and not only did wilderness camp rob me of so many things, it *halted* a genetic process that was quite possibly close to being finished. No wonder my body was so screwed up.

"She did that, is that what you mean?" The professor held me tighter.

"Yes." It came out as one big sob. She knew. She knew that Wes was real and had me convinced he wasn't.

Just like she knew that my theories about travel between worlds were possible.

"I'm sorry. I'm so sorry she did that. I'm so sorry that I didn't find you sooner. I looked for you and I never stopped looking. I promise." His voice broke.

"It's not your fault. You never would have found us," I whispered, letting him hold me as love shot through the bond.

But how did we get there in the first place?

Chapter Forty-Seven

Evan

"Evan, is everything okay, you seem distracted," my boss Claire said as I hurried back to the office after teaching a class.

"Um, yeah, there's a lot going on." I sighed. "I might need to leave early today."

It had been difficult feeling Grace's panic, Wes' fear, and Brennan and Jett's concern, and trying to function as normal.

"Come on." She pulled me into the care closet. It was a place where we usually went to have private conversations and phone calls.

The shelves in the small room were filled with clothes, bedding, backpacks, housewares, and so many other things an omega might need.

She leaned against a shelf. "What is wrong?"

I sighed. "Grace has been taken in by the Office of Designation Management. But she's not here, she's out of town. Mrs. Beekman is on it, and someone from the local Center has been sent to her, but it's fucking scary, Claire."

"Oh shit." Her brows furrowed. "Why? Sorry, none of my business."

"We're not really sure. It might have to do with her bio-dad." Well, I wasn't sure. Wes and Riley had probably figured it out by now.

"You can leave if you need to," she told me.

"I have one meeting I need to take, then I'll probably leave. I don't know if we're going there to be with Grace or not, but our head alpha is rounding everyone up." Not to mention I could really use a hug.

She nodded. "That's fair. You're not on this weekend anyway. Can you reschedule this meeting?"

"It shouldn't take long." It was with Rose's bio-dad. I'd already pumped Rose for information and done my own research. Now I needed to corroborate his story, and make sure his intentions were good, before I let Rose know that he wanted to see her.

We left the closet. A couple of people were in the office, eating lunch or working. I took my laptop and found an unused intake room. Ironically, this was the same one Rose had been in when I'd first met her and looked like a little living room.

Opening my laptop, I navigated to the video meeting room. Oh, he was already waiting for me.

I started the meeting and a man in a cowboy hat with red hair and Rose's eyes stared back at me. Behind him were ropes, trophies, books, and pictures. A tiny cow sat on his lap.

"Um, hi. I'm Colt Sterling." He waved awkwardly. "Oh, this is Jess. She's not feeling good today." Colt pet the cow on the head.

"Hi, I'm Evan, Rose's advocate. I'm curious as to why you're reaching out now after all those years of silence." I eyed him. Rose told me a very different story than the one in his email.

He shrugged. "I've tried reaching out to Iris a few times after she turned eighteen, but she wants nothing to do with me. I found out that their mom is in jail, and what happened to Rose, and I got worried about her. I mean I've always been worried about Rose and Iris, but…"

"Yet you haven't seen them since they were babies?" My eyes narrowed.

"I know from my very brief conversations with Iris that what my ex told them and what actually happened are very different." Colt rubbed his forehead. "I got Kira pregnant with Iris when we were in our last year of high school. We married. I studied agriculture. She took community college classes for teaching. Then Rose came along. One day, I was at a rodeo and met my pack. I was so excited to come home and tell Kira and the girls. But…"

A heavy sigh escaped his lips.

"She wasn't excited?" This was different from what Rose told me, but similar to the divorce records.

"I thought she would be. The pack knew all about her and the girls. Sure, we'd need to move. But it would be nice for the girls to live on a ranch and get Kira away from her good-for-nothing brother. Who is apparently also in jail. Instead, she picked up the girls and disappeared in the middle of the night. It took me years to find her. By then she'd met her new husband and poisoned the girls against me. She divorced me and moved back by her brother. She told everyone that I abandoned them and ran off with an omega—and Iris believes her. I didn't abandon them. I didn't refuse to see them or support them. Please believe me when I say that I love them and want nothing more than to be with them. I want to help support them, as long as her brother doesn't have access to the money." He sighed again.

Now the stories came together. Also, this bit about her brother was interesting.

"How did you find out that she was in jail?" I was curious.

"My parents don't live in that town anymore, but I have friends and a sibling who do. I do my best to look out for the girls from afar," he replied.

"Do you? How so?" I asked.

"My friend owns the diner Iris works at. When her car broke down and she didn't have enough for repairs, I paid the rest and the mechanic, another friend, told her that he found a cheaper way to fix it. I always anonymously buy raffle tickets or whatever Rose is selling for cheer. You see, I try to do what I can. It's hard when Kira always sends back the cards or gifts I'd send the girls."

Yeah, Rose and Iris were told that their alpha dad abandoned them and their beta mother because he found his pack and omega and refused to see them. But according to their pack records, they didn't find an omega until a couple years later.

There was also a record of the cops being called by Kira's brother because Colt tried to see the girls. No violence, he was just asked to leave town–and did–and never came back. He also tried to get custody, or at least visitation, multiple times, and each time the case was just sort of shut down. Which was curious because from my research Pack Sterling could care for those girls just fine.

Wouldn't Kira at least want child support? But then it was a lot easier to paint him as a 'bad alpha' if he didn't. There were few alphas in the very beta area they lived in. Her brother was one... as were the bad dudes interested in Rose.

"Is Rose okay? Her being a ward of the Center is troubling, but I'd rather it be that than her uncle. Never met the step-dad but from my understanding he's a good guy and treats the girls well," Colt added.

"What do you think of your ex-wife's brother?" I changed the subject.

"When we were married he was the source of most of our arguments. She gave him all of our money on more than one occasion. He always said she could do better than some bull rider like me. He's been in and out of jail since he was in high school and has a habit of owing money to the wrong people. I didn't like the idea that he had a hand in raising the girls–another reason why I was excited for them to meet everyone and move. And probably the reason why she didn't want to stay with me. Not that she said anything other than *we'll talk about it in the morning*. Only in the morning she wasn't there. I wasn't going to leave her. They were going to love her and the girls. Just like I don't know why I couldn't get visits other than somehow she got the ear of the judge." He looked so sad as he absently pet the cow.

That's probably exactly what happened. Those small, predominantly-beta towns were tight. Colt had fed right into that *Don't date an alpha, he'll just leave you for an omega* stereotype.

"Again, why now? Does this have anything to do with Rose being an omega?" I prodded, needed to protect her.

"Kira's in jail. They're struggling badly. I can't figure out how to help them without alerting Kira's brother. We're not rich, but we have enough to share with the girls. Rose could come to live with us, if she wants. I think she'd love it there. We have horses, cows, and lots of land. It's really pretty. But if she's happy at that omega school you have her in, I support that. Education's important. If she'll let me, then I'd just like to do whatever I can to make her life a little easier. Maybe she'll have a way that I could help Iris, too." Again, he looked so sad. So forlorn.

Okay, I liked that answer.

"Do you know why Kira's in jail?" I asked.

"Someone told me child abuse. While she turned them against me, I couldn't see her hitting them. Her brother, but not her." Colt frowned.

Yeah, he checked out. Everything he said matched my research.

So, I told him everything. From Rose coming into the Center to be matched at sixteen, to Rose' uncle breaking the gates at the school and trying to gun me down.

"Oh fuck. My poor little Rosebud." His knuckles went white. "I can't believe Kira would do that. But it probably was never her idea in the first place. She tends to do everything he tells her, even without him barking her to get his way. I'm sorry he did that to you."

"We can't prove that it was her uncle's idea. But considering he sees himself as head of the family, being an alpha, Rose mating with a rich pack could help everyone," I replied. Though that other pack's interest in Rose worried me.

Colt nodded. "Let me know what I can do. I'm coming down to Rockland in a couple of weeks and I'd love to see her. Maybe we can arrange a meeting? Or could I at least talk to her? I'm trying to do everything proper, especially since just reaching out to Iris didn't go well."

"I appreciate that, and I'll talk to her." I was meeting with her next week anyway. "As for Iris, she's incredibly parentified and stressed, and using that to guilt Rose. If you have any friends with job opportunities that could get her out of that town, that might be the way to go."

"I'll see what I can do." He nodded.

We talked a little longer. Though I kept getting anguish from Grace and it just tore me up inside. I felt so fucking helpless.

"Well, I have to go. The farrier is coming soon. I've made mistakes, but I love Rose. I don't want to uproot her life, just support her however I can. Iris too, if she ever lets me." With a wave, Colt ended the meeting.

Well, that was interesting. I made a bunch of notes. Yeah, when I met with Rose we'd have a little talk about her dad and go from there.

I checked my phone and saw a bunch of texts. But first, I'd finish up here so I could go join my pack.

And hopefully by then Grace would be safe.

Chapter Forty-Eight

Jett

"Thora Silvers has Grace's eyes and was a piano prodigy." I turned the computer around to show Brennan a photo of a very young woman.

"Oh, I see it," Brennan said. "There weren't as many similarities between Thora and Grace as Grace and Nate, but yes, I can see it in the eyes and smile."

"This is wild," Wes breathed. "Not only was Thora a sigma, but her dad and one of her brothers were executed for being sigmas. She also had an identical twin who was suspected of also being a sigma, and her name was... fuck. Rosalind is Grace's mom's name."

"So, somehow Grace and her mom's identical twin got to Grace's world?" I frowned. "I can't even fathom that."

This whole thing was a massive mind-fuck. Like the plot twist where this Adriana person had a history with an organization that liked to terrorize scientific companies, even though she was a chemistry professor. Spencer's old company was on that list.

My belly rumbled. I hoped the food Brennan ordered from the bar at the top of the building would come soon.

"Maybe we should just go to them? I can book us a flight." Brennan got on my laptop.

"Wait, let me see where the jet is." Wes started typing.

Riley looked up from her laptop. "What jet? Our Jett is right here."

Spencer had a *jet*?

"The Compass BioTek jet that we use for work. There's an app that we use for booking. Spencer took Grace on it both for safety and because it's a work trip." Wes looked up. "Yeah, the jet's here… he sent it back today. Oh, he must have done that in case he needed to bring us out in a hurry."

"Spencer has a jet? Why didn't I know this?" Brennan asked.

"It's technically the company's." Wes was texting. "Spencer says to hold off for the moment."

"Okay, but maybe we should get Evan?" Brennan rubbed his chest.

"That's a good idea," I agreed. Sure, Evan was really helpful over at the Center, but I'd like him to be with us. Brennan and Wes might be a little more settled as well.

There was a knock on the door.

"Come in," Brennan called.

Oooh, was our food here? Yeah, I know, there was a whole lot more to worry about than my stomach, but I could focus better if I had something to eat.

"Hey Sport, can we talk?" Frank Morris, Brennan's dad, walked in. His brow furrowed. "Is everything okay?"

"Nothing I want to talk to you about," Brennan snapped as tension flowed through our bond.

His hands went up. "Hey, I'm on your side."

"Riley, did you know there's a free soda machine?" Wes stood. "Let's get some."

Riley huffed. "Fine. Jett, you coming?"

I looked at Brennan sending him all my love and support. "I'll stay here. Get me something good."

No, I wasn't going to leave Brennan alone with his dad. Not only did I want to show my support, but everything happening had frayed him and I didn't want my husband to snap.

Wes and Riley left but didn't close the door.

"What, Dad?" Brennan sighed. "I'm not dropping the case against Mother's lawyer. I should have done this years ago, but I kept trying to go about it the right way, stupidly thinking that she'd change her mind. It's also not just about money. I'm sick of being treated like a child, and sick of fearing that she's once again going to try ruining my life because I disobeyed her."

"I know. I'm not here to ask you to stop," Frank said quietly.

"You're not?" Brennan frowned.

He wasn't? I didn't have any issue with Frank other than that I thought he should stand up for his son more. He was pretty fun to watch sports with.

Frank shook his head and sat down. "I'm pulling everything that was entrusted to Ian that's from my side and giving it to you. I'm sorry. I didn't know I could do that until Katie told me this morning. She looked it up or something."

Wow.

"Thank you." Brennan looked surprised.

That surprised me, too. My husband had been fighting for this for so long.

"Also, while I knew that there were things tied up that your mother didn't want to liquidate, I was under the impression that you'd been given other things. I let her handle all that, and well,

Ian's loyal to her not me and won't tell me anything." Frank sighed.

"I can see that. And I appreciate it," Brennan replied.

Brennan and his dad didn't have a bad relationship, they just didn't have much to talk about other than rugby and the foundation. Sometimes I wondered if Frank was disappointed that none of his children went on to play professional rugby.

"I don't like being called Sport," Brennan blurted.

"Oh. You don't?" His look went concerned. "Sorry, Sport, I mean, Bren. I've been calling you that for so long, I never realized it. I... I'll try not to."

"I'd like that." Brennan looked a little bewildered.

"I'll have the documents sent over." Frank's eyes flickered over me and the laptops. "Can I help with anything? Or are you conducting espionage?"

"It's about Grace. But we've got it," I told him.

Frank's look stayed worried. "Okay. I like Grace. I know I tend to let your mother take charge, but I'm on your side, Bren. I always have been."

Yeah, he was. It just wasn't always enough against the Queen Mum.

"Even though I technically own your foundation building?" Brennan retorted.

"We can go back to operating out of your mother's company building. For the record, I was against buying the building with your money. I was against cutting the scholarships, too. But she said that if we didn't cut those, we'd have to cut the summer sports programs due to the drop in donations. I figured that you'd start your own foundation or get Spencer's company to do it. All my money is tied up, so I couldn't save the programs on my own. I... I love those programs," he confessed.

"I know." Brennan's voice went rough.

I squeezed Brennan's hand. Before the accident, he'd helped his dad coach youth rugby.

"We saved the scholarships," I added.

Relief flooded his dad's face. "I'm glad. I'm proud of you, Sp–, I mean, Bren. You have a great pack, a successful company, wonderful mates, and you have your integrity. It's all I could ever want for you."

"You're proud of me?" Surprise filled Brennan's voice.

"So proud. Honestly, out of all my kids, you have accomplished the most with the least amount of help. I marvel at your strength. While I know the dinners aren't your favorite, I like showing you off to my friends. Especially the obnoxious ones. *Oh, your son works for who? My son owns luxury hotels all over the world*," he told him.

"It's always the same party at the same place," Brennan grumbled.

"I know. If I have to go to the High Tower one more time..." Frank sighed, then stood. "Anyhow, I'm here, Bren, okay?"

"Okay."

With one last look at me, Frank left. I wrapped my arms around Brennan, comforting my mate.

"Do you think he'll really give you what's yours from his side?" I wanted to believe Frank. But I also didn't want to see Brennan hurt because it was some trick of the Queen Mum's.

Brennan nodded slowly. "It would be a start."

"He said he was proud of you," I added. My phone buzzed.

Evan

Wrapping up. I'm on my way.

"He did. Wow, Katie was right." He texted someone, probably his sister.

"Can we come in now? We have the food." Wes came in and put the food on the meeting table and moved his and Riley's laptops.

Riley dumped a bunch of drinks on the table.

"Evan said he'll come over soon," I added, glad we got some food for him.

"Good." Brennan looked relieved.

"I think after we eat and Evan arrives, we should pack our shit and take the jet regardless of what Spencer says," Wes said as he dug into his burger. "I'm not sure what else we can do from here and we know where they're staying. We can always go to the hotel and wait for them."

"I mean, there are things that I want to do to this Adriana person." Riley took a loud drink of lime soda.

"Me, too," I agreed, grabbing an energy drink.

"Perhaps later, once Grace is safe. Um, the sister pack wants to form an alliance," Brennan added, looking at his phone.

"I mean we already sort of have one?" I shrugged.

"I like them. Do you think they'll let me babysit? I'd be a good babysitter." Riley shoveled more food in her mouth.

"Yeah, I mean why wouldn't we have an alliance with them?" Wes nodded. "I think you'd be a good babysitter, too, Ri."

"I'll let her know that we'll form an alliance." Brennan texted her.

We continued to eat our burgers and fries. Well, Brennan had onion rings.

"So, are we going to Grace?" I asked. "I think we've done all we can here. Spencer shouldn't have to deal with everything alone."

Brennan looked at Wes. "You're right. Wes, go ahead and steal the jet or whatever. Grace is one of us, and we should be there for her."

Chapter Forty-Nine

Grace

My entire existence had been dumped upside down, as I continued to sob into the professor's shoulder. If he was my dad, then I was from this world, and everything they'd been telling me about being a gamma, an omega whose body was *forced to stop developing*, was true.

I was from this world.

And somehow ended up in another.

With my biological mother's identical twin.

The woman I'd called *mom* knew. Everything she did to me was *intentional*, which made it all the more devastating.

Especially since I'm sure she wasn't trying to stop me from becoming an omega for altruistic purposes. Like the fact that I obviously didn't belong in that world and might develop some interesting biology.

Was that why I hardly went to actual doctors once I hit my teens and instead saw church people with questionable business practices or her friends who sold essential oils?

Nate's hand ran up and down my blanket-covered back. "Go ahead and cry, Grace. Just go ahead and cry."

The door opened, but I didn't look up.

"She really needs her alpha," the professor said softly. "Also, I'm pretty sure Thora Silvers is her mother. The Rosalind that Grace mentioned previously is most likely Rosalind Silvers, Thora's identical twin. There might be some mix-up in the records."

"Noted," the nurse said. "Grace, are you sure that your birthdate is correct?"

Shit. "Um, it might be a year off."

"Nate, I'm so glad that you're all right," a male voice said. "We're all so worried. Some of the children are here. I just came from them. They're really scared, especially the little ones. The nurse said that you didn't want them in here with you? What could be more important than the children?" Hurt dripped from his accented voice.

"I didn't want them here *this second*, Harry," the professor said quietly. "I wanted to talk to you first. Also, another child has had her world upended, and she needs a breath. Creed, Mercy, and Hale will take care of the littles for the moment."

His concern for my comfort made me cry harder.

"Oh. Is this... so she's the one?" Harry said softly. "We know this for certain?"

"A genscan has been run and yes. We also know that Grace has been lied to about her parentage, things in her record are probably fake, and I'm not even sure I want to know what she's been told about me. Considering that she came here for a conference and not to find me, it's a lot for her." The professor stroked my hair in a way that reminded me of my dad.

"I just wanted to see the particle cutter," I sobbed. How badly could this backfire for me, considering Rosalind wasn't in my file and I hadn't exactly stayed with my backstory?

"I bet the particle cutter was really amazing. How was the simulator that Marquess has? And the CeCe they're building over at the Collaborative? I heard Ina's presentation was really good," he soothed. "I may have pumped the children for information. Creed didn't give me much, but Verity sang like a siren. I confess that this morning I listened to the first two chapters of the book she said you were reading. Very spicy."

Lifting my head, I looked at him through tear stained eyes. "It's for book club. I was going to finish it today, on the beach."

He started reading the book? Damnit. What did I even do?

"Grace, this is my husband Harry. Harry, this is Dr. Grace Ellington," Nate said gently.

"Hi," I sniffed, taking the tissues Lark handed me. A very handsome, lithe man, a little taller than Nate, stood there. His trendy glasses slid down his light brown nose. He had a very trim dark beard and mustache, and short, dark, curly hair.

He also was much younger than Nate, probably not much older than Spencer. Also, not an alpha. Beta maybe. I was still trying to figure out all the smells in this world.

Harry smiled. "Hi."

"Is anyone else here?" the professor asked.

"Pippa's in the waiting room. Esme's at home in case we need to get Dare or Chance. Verity's at the lab. Zain's running interference. Adriana, well, she was here but she punched someone and has been exiled to the parking lot," Harry explained.

"Adriana punched someone?" Nate kept running his hand through my hair as I sobbed.

"According to Pip, Adriana yelled at some guy in the lobby, they had words, she punched him, then was thrown out," Harry said.

"I think he was famous. But you know I don't know these things. Yeah, they let me see Pip really quickly before coming to you."

Spencer. Adriana punched Spencer. That wouldn't end well.

"How many kids does your family have?" I recalled that there were a lot of kids in the photo Creed had shown me.

"Nine," the professor said. "You make ten. The other three are Zain and Esme's. Oh. Twins run on both sides of your family. Fraternal on my side, identical on your mother's. I don't have a twin, but I have two sets of fraternal twin siblings. My family is also very omega-heavy. Most of my brothers and sisters are omegas."

"Twins." I sucked in a breath. "I will take identical twin girls that look like my mate Evan. Or those fraternal twins that have different daddies, then I can get Evan and Wes their kids in one pregnancy." Little girl Evans. They'd get away with *everything*.

"And save the identical twins for Spencer? Because that's what the world needs," the professor joked.

"Why do you hate Spencer?" I leaned my head back down on his shoulder, wanting to hear if his explanation was different from what Creed told me.

"It's not that we hate Spencer. Adriana and Pip disagree with his politics. His previous company was very... vocal on the way some things are done," Nate said.

My head popped up. "You mean that your mates are against developing a pharmaceutical to keep illegal designations from being executed? From where I stand in this moment, I don't see an issue."

"Like I said before, it's a polarizing topic, and they're just not sure for-profit companies should be involved."

"But Compass BioTek has no such stance, and that other company was long ago." I frowned. "I researched them before taking the job. They're helping people—and Spencer keeps it private so that he can have scruples. If it was public, sure they'd make more money, but it would be at the cost of the people."

Nate nodded. "It's–"

"Snobbery." Harry rolled his eyes. "Personally, I would much rather have one of their quicktests or easyscans. I guess you work for Compass BioTek?"

"I do. So do my mates Wes and Spencer."

"Spencer *owns* Compass BioTek, and I suspect that's who Adriana punched. Which is not a good thing." The professor sighed.

"Well, that could make the holidays interesting," Harry replied. I froze.

"I don't think we're there yet," Nate said quietly. "And we might not ever be."

"I can't believe they brought in the children," I sniffed. "I'm so sorry. Also, who called in the tip? Because even if my mates ran the genscan, they wouldn't do that–and well, Thora's record is locked." I rubbed my head. "This makes my brain hurt."

Nate's scent turned bitter. "Someone called in a tip?"

"That's what I was told." I sniffed.

The nurse came back in. "Grace, the court order came through and the record has been unlocked. Identical twin records are sometimes hard to get sorted, but we've got it untangled. Your birth mother was Thora Silvers. She was executed for being a sigma, as was one of her brothers and her father. Her identical twin, Rosalind, is wanted, not just for being a known sigma, but for a federal heist. You were raised by her? Someone will want to speak to you."

Thora Silvers was my mother? Shit. She was actually my mother. Nate was my dad. This was my world. Somehow.

How? How did this happen?

"As far as I know she's dead. Can I have my alpha now?" I tried to force back the tornado of emotions inside me.

"Neither of you are carriers, so you may go. Your mates have your phones and are waiting in the lobby." She turned to Nate.

"Given your other children don't share Grace's mother, they'll be released as well." The nurse looked at Lark. "Thank you, I think you're done here."

It took a moment, and I exhaled sharply. "Not a carrier, that's one good thing about today."

I mean, I guess finding out that I was from this world and who my biological parents were could be a good thing? Or not.

Yeah, I needed that therapist.

"Thora was executed for being a sigma. I... I never knew that," Nate said softly. "They just said she died. I... I was such an idiot back then."

"Don't beat yourself up too much." Harry squeezed his shoulder.

"Yeah, please don't," I said quietly, still trying to keep my emotions in check, instead wrapping myself in love from my bonds. "Here, do you want the blankets back?" I asked Lark.

"You can keep them," Lark said, zipping up her duffle bag. She handed Nate a bunch of candy bars. "For the children. It was nice meeting both of you. Keep communication open between you and I'd suggest some family therapy."

"I don't need two blankets." I scooted off the table. "Would one of the little ones like it?"

"Probably," Harry said, taking the offered pink blanket. "Not that we need more. Their room looks like a home for wayward blankets."

"Grace, I'm so sorry we met under these circumstances. But I'm glad I finally found you. I'll give you space, but I'm here if you ever want to talk. Also, as I said before, I hope you'll stay in touch with Creed and Verity," the professor said as the nurse herded us into the hall.

I nodded.

"Dad! Daddy!" Little feet and voices came down the hallway and my heart wrenched.

"Nate's a really good man," Harry said softly, as three small children attacked the professor. "He's been looking for you a long time and truly regrets what happened. Adriana can be a bitch, and you don't have to forgive her. But if you can find it in your heart to forgive Nate, it would mean everything to him–even if you just have a birthday call and holiday card relationship, maybe grab lunch when you're in town for work. He'll take whatever you give him, and I implore you to give him something. Anything."

"I... I could probably handle that." I gulped, tears pricking my eyes as Nate hoisted a tiny blonde girl that looked like little me in his arms. Hope. I might not be able to handle much more. But I could at least try that? Maybe?

Harry's eyes flickered over Hope, as he took the hands of a little boy and girl, a little older than her, who favored him in hair, their skin a very light brown. The girl claimed the blanket, her eyes blue.

"Dad, are you okay?" Creed came barreling down the hall in a cloud of alpha concern. He stopped short. "Grace. Why are you here?

"It's my fault you're here, and I'm sorry." Tears streamed down my face as guilt ate at me.

"Hey, you got me out of an exam, I'm not mad." Hale threw an arm around me. "Dad, is she the missing sister?"

"Yes, but be *gentle*. I'd like her to, you know, *want* to see us sometimes." Anxiety tinged the professor's scent.

"Oh. Verity was right. It *is* girl Creed," a teenage girl who had Adriana's body type, Nate's face, and light brown hair, joined us. Her hair was in tight dutch braids and her shirt read *Capitol Crushers*. She looked like she'd fit right in with the kids at Riley's school.

This had to be Mercy.

"Hi, Mercy," I said softly. "My name is Grace." I looked at Nate. "Where did Theodosia come from?"

Nate smirked. "You play the piano and don't know who Theodosia is?"

I'd have to ask Brennan. Was that her favorite composer?

"We have another sister?" the little girl holding Harry's hand asked. She looked maybe kindergarten-aged while the tiny one, Hope, looked maybe two or three.

The little boy grinned at me. "She does look like girl Creed. But shorter."

"You are so very small." Hale rested his arm on my head.

Nate stopped. "Everyone, this is Grace. She's your biggest sister—she's even older than Creed. Her mom wasn't in our pack, so she was raised... elsewhere. She's a grown up and has a PhD, a job, a pack, and mates." His scent went salty with sadness. "This is Pax," he indicated the little boy, "Tru," the little girl holding Harry's hand waved, "and Hope. I think you know everyone else?"

Hope looked up at me, thumb in her mouth, blue eyes wide. The blue ribbons in her hair matched her dress.

My heart broke. I wasn't even sure why.

"Don't cry." Tru took my hand. "There's a lot of us. But we're nice."

"It's been a rough day," I said softly, letting her hold it.

"Why are you wearing a bikini?" Pax asked.

"I was at the beach with my mate." I shrugged.

"Did you..." Creed grinned, eyeing my neck. "Oooh. I'm telling Verity and Ina as soon as I get my phone back."

"Yes." My head ducked, cheeks warming. "Wait, how many pumpkins is this?"

Creed laughed. "Not sure. Two maybe?"

"Who's her mate? What am I missing?" Hale asked.

"Should I get *everyone* summer internships?" I joked.

Creed snorted. "Dad, we're all going to work with Grace for the summer, okay?"

Nate rubbed his face with his hand as we approached the double locked doors. "You can have that conversation with the other parents yourself."

"Where do you work? Someplace fun?" Mercy asked.

"You do know she was at the PIIP Conference recruiting for their internship program?" Creed goaded.

"She works for Compass BioTek, but, *mate*?" Hale asked.

A guard unlocked the double doors. We walked into the small lobby. I immediately saw Pippa, who looked as unrumpled as yesterday.

"My good doctor." Spencer rushed to me and gathered me into his arms. He'd changed into a suit.

Letting go of Tru's hand, I started to sob. "I'm okay, I'm okay."

"Darling, I've got you." He squeezed me tight.

"She's mated to Spencer Thanukos, the guy who *owns* Compass BioTek," Creed said.

"Everyone is okay?" Pippa asked. She held up a bag. "I have everyone's phones."

Creed picked up Tru. "We're okay, Mum."

"I want to talk to the parents for a moment," the nurse said.

"Give me the phones and I'll pass them out," Mercy asked, rushing to grab the bag.

"Here, distribute these." The professor gave Hale the candy bars and Hope.

I clung to Spencer like a koala, as Hale divided the candy and Mercy passed out the phones.

"Hi, Spencer," Creed said quietly. "This is Tru, Hale, Hope, Mercy, and Pax. This is Spencer–he's one of Grace's mates."

"They brought in *all* your siblings?" Spencer asked softly, still holding me tight.

"We're missing three," Creed replied.

"I have nine siblings." My eyes closed as I tried to drown myself in his leathery scent.

Nine. So many siblings.

"I've got your phone, shall we go?" Spencer asked, still holding me. "I also have some clothes for you, if you'd like to change?"

"Maybe in the car? I just want to go." I needed to figure out what the hell had happened.

"You're going?" Tru's voice went small.

"I'm sure we'll see Grace again." Creed's look went pleading and I nodded slightly.

Hope was still sucking her thumb, but her other chubby little hand waved. I tentatively waved back.

"I'll call a car," Spencer said, trying to hold me and use his phone at the same time as we left the building. "Are you okay?"

"I'm not an illegal designation, nor am I a carrier. And now I officially vote for trying to figure out Elaris' research." My voice was muffled as I kept my face in his neck.

If they could turn betas into *omegas* couldn't they make sigmas something else?

"Also, I found out some weird shit. Like the professor is really my dad, and yeah, I need to talk to you about all that," I added.

Spencer nodded. "I saw that. I have questions."

"Yeah, I have theories. Also, Thora, my birth mother, had an identical twin." My eyes squeezed shut. *She knew.* The betrayal cut me like a hot knife.

He kissed the top of my head and sat us down on a bench. I reached up and put my hand gently on the bruise on his face.

"Adriana *hit* you?" Anger welled up inside me. That fucking bitch.

"I'll be fine. She didn't hit me hard." He covered my hand with his.

"You can't actually be her." Adriana strode over to me, expression panicked. "Rosalind promised me that she'd take you away and that you'd never, ever look for him or come back. That she'd take pains to make sure that you'd never be found."

Fuck. I hadn't seen that coming.

"You *gave* me to Rosalind? Do you know what she did to me?" I started to sob. It was one thing to convince the professor not to return Thora's call, it was another to *give* me away.

"You talked to Rosalind?" The professor stood there, Hope in his arms, looking stricken.

"Well, yes. Thora had the audacity to list you as the father on her birth record. They literally dropped the baby off, so I took her to the baby shelter, and they took her to the Silvers. One day, Rosalind called and said that their mother couldn't take care of the baby, but if I gave her money, she'd make the baby disappear and we'd never have to deal with her again. No support payments. No visit schedule. Rosalind even had an alternate identity created for her so it would be as if she never existed." Adriana shrugged.

"Well, that's where the Cassidy record came from," Spencer said softly.

Who was Cassidy? Aside from my middle name.

"You *WHAT*? You never thought to *ask me*? You had *my child* in *our home* and never thought to ask me what I wanted to do with her? You watched as I searched for Grace, knowing that you gave her away. You even went with me to meet girls we thought were her. How dare you?" Nate's voice broke, apricot scent a combination of anger and sadness.

"They're fucking variants—a family of unstable hidden sigmas. Not to mention Thora's twin and brother were *criminals*. Why would we want that in our home?" Adriana said in total seriousness.

"Adriana, you're head alpha, not monarch," Pippa said, voice thick with condemnation.

"You weren't keen on Thora," Adriana pushed.

"You didn't *know* Thora," the professor retorted.

"Did you call in the tip?" I prodded, trying to make sense of everything.

She must not have known that Thora's record was locked–or what would happen because of it.

"Creed, let's get the littles in my car," Harry directed, taking Hope from Nate. "They don't need to hear this."

Pippa growled at Adriana. "Did you put our mate and children in danger by calling in a tip on Grace? Last night we decided that we weren't going to do anything until we'd contacted a family lawyer, gotten proof, and figured out what Grace wanted."

"I don't want anything from you, I promise," I said honestly.

"I had no idea they'd take the children or Nate," Adriana back-tracked.

"Mom did what now?" Mercy stood there, frowning, not fol-lowing the others.

"I protected this family, like always." She got in Spencer's face. "And I won't let you ruin everything I've built. You need to stop. I had nothing to do with it."

"With what?" the professor pushed. "Adriana, what did you do now?"

"Adriana, get in your car, now, before you say something even more idiotic than you have already," Pippa growled.

"Mercy, you're with me," Adriana ordered.

"No, she's not," the professor snapped back. "You... you gave my baby away. You subjected my children to something terrifying after we agreed to take no immediate action. I had it under control. I was going to have lunch with her and talk it out when I went to that conference at Rock Tech over the summer."

Oh. He had a plan? I would have agreed to that.

"I *protected* you, Nate. And I still protect you. I have always put you first, this family first. You never would have accomplished everything you have if they were in the picture," Adriana yelled.

"I'll never know because you robbed me of that *choice*," Nate yelled back.

"Mercy, get in Harry's car. It'll be tight." Pippa put an arm around Mercy, shielding her from Adriana with her body. "Adriana, get in your car now, so help me," she growled, oozing dominance.

Adriana looked at the professor. "Nate–"

"Don't talk to him. Get. In. Your. Car. Adriana," Pippa barked.

The professor stood there in front of me, looking forlorn, as Adriana stalked off to her car. Mercy gave her dad a hug, he whispered something to her, then she ran off to Harry's SUV.

I stood and gave Nate a tentative hug. "I'll text you later. Can I get your number from Creed?"

"Yes. I'd like that so much. Maybe we could still have that lunch?" His head bowed. "I... I didn't–"

"I know. Let me know when you're in Rockland." My heart broke. I'd try to see if I could salvage something with him. Harry's suggestion of the occasional call and lunch seemed doable. Maybe some texts.

Pippa put an arm around her mate. "Let's go home, Love. It'll be okay."

A car drove up, and Spencer stood, looking relieved.

We climbed in and he immediately put up the privacy shield. I curled into him.

"I've got you." Spencer held me tight.

"That was batshit crazy," I said softly, resting my head on his chest. "I can barely comprehend what happened, without factoring in that Adriana not only called in the tip but *gave* me to Rosalind and kept it a secret from her mate for all these years."

Adriana sold me to Rosalind. Shit.

"What's a variant?" I blinked.

"The illegal designations are variations, offshoots, of the alpha designation. It's not considered polite." Spencer handed me my phone.

"Oh, okay."

"Who *is* Rosalind?" He sent a text.

"The woman who raised me that I thought was my mom but was actually the identical twin of my biological mother," I said softly. Yeah, not calling her *Mom* anymore. "I have theories."

He curled me into him. "I've got you."

"She was from *here*. I don't know how she escaped to the world I grew up in. But she did. And she knew. It was so much easier to deal with what she did to me because I thought she didn't know, but she did." Another sob escaped my lips.

Her knowing exactly what I was, what I was doing, and who and what Wes was, made it all the more unforgivable.

"Who knew what, Darling?" Spencer stroked my hair.

"Rosalind. Taking away my blankets, not letting me nest in the laundry, punishing me for too many stuffies, sending me to that camp, it all hits so differently knowing that she knew my father was an omega so there was a chance that I could be one too." I buried my face into his chest.

His hands ran up and down my back, soothing me.

"Did she do it on purpose? Did she know that sending me to that place would actually *stop* it? I mean, I had a heart attack from the electroshock. I was close to being eighteen when she sent me there. That's what did it right? How badly did that mess me up?" The sobs came harder and harder.

I felt love shoot through the bond, but it didn't slow my tears. Spencer's leather scent wrapped around me as his purr filled the car.

His phone rang. "I've got her. There have been some upsetting revelations."

That was an understatement.

I took the phone. "Hello?"

"You're out?" Wes asked.

"Yeah, I am... I..." While I was with Spencer, I wanted Wes and Evan, too.

"Oooh, I feel that. We're coming to you, okay?" Wes assured, sending love though the bond. "I'll love you to the end of the universe. I'll be there as soon as I can."

Yes, please. I needed them. My mates. My pack.

I was from *here*. Shit.

Chapter Fifty

Spencer

After she ended the call with Wes, Grace continued to sob against my chest, setting off every alpha instinct I had to calm my mate and make her happy.

My mind also spun, trying to process everything that had happened back there in the parking lot. *I had nothing to do with it.* Adriana had just admitted that Elaris' accident might have been murder. I'd have the professionals look into it later. First, I had to attend to Grace.

"Tell me everything, Darling?" I needed to figure this out.

Grace told me what happened. None of this did anything to diffuse my simmering anger. How could they?

"This at least solves *why* Rosalind didn't want me to be good at math. She knew that the mathematical theories were *real*. And if I managed to get back..." Grace grimaced. "I mean, I understand not wanting to tell me the truth, but there had to be better ways than hurting me."

And *making her forget her mate.* A horrible, terrible thing.

"She's gone, and you're here with us where you belong," I soothed. Now *that* was the type of brutal behavior that caused wars and genocides. The sort that condemned entire designations.

But not all were like that. The bit of information Wes dug up on Thora Silvers led me to believe she was just an ordinary young woman. If you looked at the data, most sigmas, or omicrons, for that matter, really weren't that different temperament-wise from alphas. Society *accepted* alpha temperaments—violence, possessiveness, and anger issues included.

Not to mention there were alphas who did very bad things. It wasn't like getting rid of certain designations eliminated all the horrible things in the world.

Maybe it truly was time to revisit Elaris' research and find someone willing to take it on.

"Who's Cassidy?" she asked.

"It's a record with similar information to yours that was flagged as a possible duplicate. I am guessing that after Adriana sold you to Rosalind, she had a fake record made for you. If she was on the run from the law, and couldn't assume your mother's identity, a child would at least change her profile," I told her. "She took the money, you, and ran. Yet then somehow ended up in your world. I haven't heard of naturally occurring portals accidentally taking people to other worlds, so it would be deliberate. But *how?*"

"All I can think of is that somehow your dad and Dr. K actually sent some sigmas to other worlds, and Rosalind and I were part of that?" she sniffed.

"That was my thought as well." I could also see my father and Dr. K prioritizing families, considering both had children themselves.

Poor, sweet Grace. That woman had known Grace could become an omega. She probably saw, and smelled, the signs—and *squashed them*. Brutally and painfully.

I texted Wes to see what he could find out about Rosalind and if he could discover a connection to my father or Dr. K. While we'd found the missing piece, we'd uncovered an entire new puzzle.

Grace had mentioned that there were all sorts of worlds. If my father was taking sigmas and putting them in worlds they might be unsuitable for, well, then I could see how the Temporal Authority might get a little upset.

"I'm right here," I assured Grace, kissing her forehead, her cheeks, her lips, her jaw, her neck, while running my hands up and down her mostly naked body, grounding her, covering her in my scent, making sure she knew that I was here and would care for her.

"Drink some water?" I handed her a bottle of water and cleaned my hands with a packet of wipes. Because I knew what was coming.

Also, I needed to reassure myself that she was here, with me, and I would make everything okay. Somehow.

"I want..." Her sob turned to a whine, as her ass, only clad in a bikini bottom, ground against me, though she did drink half the bottle of water.

I checked to make sure the privacy window was up.

"Tell me what you need, Baby Girl?" I breathed in her ear as I pressed my thigh into her. "Tell me or give me permission to give you what you need."

Nipping her pulse, I worked my way down to her bite mark and lavished it with attention.

A shudder ran through her body and her scent spiked with sweet desire and arousal. Purring, I undid her top.

"He can't see us, but he can hear us if you're loud. Now tell me what you need," I instructed.

"You," she moaned, taking my lips with hers. Her scent poured down my throat as I took it in like a man dying of thirst.

"Then I'll give it to you," I breathed, sucking on her neck as I removed the rest of her clothes, leaving them on the floor of the car.

What I wanted was to rail her long and hard, over and over, as my sweet darling screamed my name. That would have to wait. First things first.

Positioning her so her back was to the seat, I held her in my arms. I caressed her naked body with my mouth, my hands, finally thrusting two fingers, curling them inside her in just the right place to make her squeal.

A happy squeal ripped from her lips. I covered them with my own.

"Shhh," I murmured, as I pumped my fingers, thumb finding her clit. "Come as much as you need, but quietly."

The anxiety and tension in her body melted away as she rode my fingers, her lips feasting on mine, the air filling with the scent of her peaches, my leather, and both of our arousals–along with those sweet caramel wisps that appeared when she was especially wanting her alpha. *Fuck me, Alpha.*

Oh, darling, I will.

My fingers continue to glide and rub her to her peak, my lips swallowing her sweet cry as the orgasm took her.

"You look so beautiful when you come," I praised, stroking her through the aftershocks.

"I want you inside me," she murmured, arching her back.

"Oh, I will. I'll absolutely knot you, then let you nap on my cock all the way back to the hotel," I told her, meeting her eyes, cupping her face with my hand.

I leaned in for a kiss, then nipped the bond mark ever so gently, making her jump.

"But first I'm going to taste you." Settling her on the seat, I sank down so that I was on the floor in front of her–with the perfect view of her sweet pussy. Leaning in, I flicked her clit with my tongue.

A whimper escaped her lips. "Please, Alpha."

"You're so wet for me," I crooned, tasting her again, deeper this time, as two fingers went back to work.

Continuing to eat her like dessert, she rode my hand, moaning with pleasure, dripping with wetness as she contracted around me. I pushed another finger into her passage, stretching her, curling them to make her squirm just so, my other hand toying with her nipple, kneading it gently.

"Oh, yes, Alpha, more," she groaned, eyes closed, her hands tangling in my hair.

"More? Mmmm." I nipped her clit with my teeth, to distract her as I worked a fourth finger into her, moving them in and out of her pussy as I continued to suck on her clit, focusing on bringing her pleasure, making her come.

Happy noises filled the car.

"That feels so good," she moaned.

Taking my fingers, I dug the tips into that spot that I knew would make her come. Another moan escaped her lips as she rewarded me by spasming around my hand, bliss covering her face.

"Come again for me," I whispered into her clit, as I stroked her insides over and over.

"There, right there." Her body bucked, spasming with orgasm.

"So good. Show me how good you can take me," I breathed, devouring her juices, which had taken on an even sweeter flavor than usual.

Taking advantage of her wetness, I began working my thumb into her pussy, watching closely for any signs of pain or fear. Her back arched. The only look on her face was that of sheer and utter desire.

"Don't stop, Alpha, please," she begged again, one hand still in my hair.

"I'm just getting started," I assured, as I slowly eased my knuckles through her entrance, while teasing her clit with my tongue, my free hand moving down her body, settling around her hip.

Her pussy clamped down on my hand as I worked it in.

"Yes, yes," she groaned.

"Take a deep breath, Darling," I told her, giving her clit another nip, my hand on her hip clamping down. Slowly, gently, I curled the hand inside her into a ball. I brought my fisted hand down just enough to trigger those muscles near the entrance of her pussy, the ones that craved a knot.

"Alpha," she gasped, as it hit just the right spot, body trembling, as liquid gushed out of her, running down my arm.

"You take my fist so good." A primal growl rumbled low and deep in my throat, as I moved my fist back in fully, taking it as deep as I could. My knuckles softly rubbed her insides, then went down to that spot and back again, claiming her with my hand. *Mine.*

"I love you," she whispered.

"I love you, too." I pumped faster and faster, adding the occasional twist when the heel of my hand hit her entrance. Orgasm after orgasm washed over her. Slick, or something very close to it gushed out of her as she surrendered completely to me.

Mine.

More happy noises filled the car. My dick strained against my pants. Yet another orgasm wrecked her. This time, instead of continuing to work my fist inside her, I stopped moving. Opening my fist, and holding still, I sat up slightly to bring her to me until her body stopped trembling.

Her lips attacked mine. As I kissed her, I made my hand as small as I could, slowly easing it out of her.

A needy whine slipped from her lips when my hand finally pulled free.

"Do you need more?" I asked her, moving my lips to her throat as I wiped my dripping hand on the edge of her coverup.

"Knot me, please, I need you, Alpha," she begged.

"You have me. I'm all yours." Unzipping my pants, I repositioned her so that she was now also kneeling on the floor of the limo, me behind her.

I placed her hips at the edge of the seat, and her hands on the top of the seat back. My hands ran down her body. My lips traced patterns on her neck and her shoulders, as she moaned. Finally, one hand wrapped her hips, as the other guided myself into her, sliding in with no resistance. I groaned, seating myself inside her with one stroke.

"Oh, yes," she sighed happily, her ass wiggling slightly.

Giving that sweet ass a squeeze, I pinned her to the seat with my body and fucked her in smooth, firm strokes that bottomed out each time. Fucking her the way I needed to fuck her; fucking her the way she needed to be fucked.

My hand moved down to stroke her clit, as I murmured to her how good and perfect she was.

She whimpered again. "Knot me, please?"

Sliding nearly all the way out, I push into her fast, not just bottoming out, but pushing my swollen knot all the way in, in one hard stroke. Grace exhaled sharply. But I didn't stop.

"Come for me, Baby Girl. You're being so good, one more time," I urged, continuing to move while knotted to her, one hand rolling her clit, as her body tensed, readying for another orgasm.

"Daddy," she cried softly, another orgasm taking her.

Such sweet words. I loved it when she called me that. My hot heat spurted into her, satiating my need to cum inside my baby girl who always took me so perfectly.

"Good girl." Clamping my teeth down on her bond mark, I growled again.

For a moment we just stayed there, hearts pounding. Her arms slipped off the seat. I kissed them and rubbed them. Still knotted together, I settled us back into the seat, her curling against me, completely naked. Grabbing the blanket she'd come out with, I covered her with it.

"Do you feel better now?" I purred. Certainly, I did.

I'd need to tip the driver well. Also, I'd probably be billed a de-scenting fee, but it was well worth it.

"So much better." She kissed my shoulder.

We snuggled a bit, as I continued to rub her arms, her shoulders, and tell her what a good job she did, and how much I loved her.

"Drink a little more water?" I finally asked, offering her the bottle from earlier.

After she finished it, she closed her eyes and dozed on my chest. Getting my phone, I checked the group chat and sighed, given they were well on their way.

Grace would love to see them, and well, I did send my jet to them. I changed the hotel reservation to check out Sunday instead of tomorrow, then dove into my email.

There was some information about Adriana. Pictures of her with protest signs outside a hall where Elaris was speaking. Social media posts of her organizing rallies.

While Adriana wasn't the leader of a thinly-veiled hate group that protested any science they didn't personally approve of, she'd been heavily involved in the protest efforts against Elaris.

I had nothing to do with it. But she'd known.

Elaris didn't deserve to die simply because she wanted to make the world a better place.

A safer place.

After all, the entire reason that Elaris started trying to compound better suppressants was because one of her friends had been attacked by another student. One who really should have been on the blockers offered to young alphas as they learned to control their anger and hormones.

The young man said he didn't like the side effects, even though they were much milder than the side effects the omegas who took blockers and suppressants dealt with every day.

And unlike alphas, for many of these omegas, not taking suppressants or blockers because of side effects wasn't an option.

Something alphas took for granted. For some, not being on medications like this made them a public hazard.

Elaris made something better. She sought my help, and together we came to a solution. We registered it, tested it, formed our company and brought it to market.

Before we even finished university.

I pressed a kiss to Grace's head. Yes, Elaris would have loved her so much. Grace and Elaris together would have revolutionized the world.

Grace and I could still change the world, but it wouldn't be quite the same.

Perhaps the world didn't deserve the future that Elaris wanted for them.

Still, it was time to see if I couldn't make some inquiries and find a new generation of young scientists that might be able to come up with solutions.

Finally, we drew closer to the hotel. I peppered Grace's face with tiny kisses.

"Are we almost there?" she asked, sleepily.

"Yes. You should probably wear clothes." I cleaned her up and helped her get dressed in the clothes I'd brought her, tossing the swimsuit and coverup into the bag.

"Are you hungry? I'm guessing that you'd like a shower or a bath?" I added.

"And more of you." She pulled me to her by my tie and locked her lips to mine. "Thank you for taking such good care of me."

"I will give you everything," I breathed, getting lost in her eyes. "Just to warn you, the rest of the pack is on their way."

"Wes told me. Do we have a little time?" Her look went coy.

Getting out of the car, I scooped her into my arms and snagged the bag. Waving at the driver, I walked her toward the hotel entrance. She felt so right in my arms. All of me tightened because I needed to ground myself in her again. And again.

I gave her a deep kiss, a promise that I would give her anything and everything. "Darling, we have all the time you need."

Chapter Fifty-One

Jett

"Will you stop squirming?" Riley elbowed her brother as the three of us sat on the couch in the small jet on our way to Grace and Spencer.

How did we not know Spencer had a jet? Okay, it was the company's jet and usually used for company business, which was why Wes knew about it. But still...

At least Grace was okay. Shit, it had been a fucking day. If anything happened to her it would destroy the pack. Every single one of us cared for her in our own way. Even Brennan.

And me?

Yeah, I wanted some more alone time with Grace. Even if it was just her riding behind me on my motorcycle.

Though I'd take more movie nights with her and Evan. Also, I hadn't taken her to karaoke yet.

"Um, sorry." Evan squeezed his eyes shut, took a deep breath.

He got up from the couch and moved back to one of the rows to sit with Wes.

Wes pulled Evan into his arms. He looked like that guilt monster was on him again. Yeah, Wes needed to get over that. Literally, that was the point of packs.

Also, Spencer and Grace had mated. Good for them. But I wasn't even sure how they could have just been lying on the beach. I was a beta and when Brennan and I mated we had sex for *days*.

Same with when we'd mated Evan.

"Why *are* you so squirmy?" Riley watched as Evan tried and failed to get comfortable in the overstuffed airplane seat next to Wes.

"Spence's jet has no bedroom." I grinned at Riley. We'd been trying to watch an action movie with Evan while Wes and Brennan worked.

The couch faced an entertainment center with a pop out TV. Two more seats, which swiveled, were beyond the couch. After that, there was a small galley filled with snacks and a bathroom. Apparently, there was no flight attendant today.

Behind us was an area with rows of seats and tables, which was where Wes and Brennan were working.

"Some of the seats do fold out into beds, as does the couch," Wes replied.

Evan squeaked, as he buried his face in Wes' shoulder. "Yeah, I vote for a pack jet with a bedroom or two."

"Sounds good to me." I mean, I could get used to this. Also, Brennan hated flying. A pack jet would probably make his business trips easier.

"I don't get it." Riley blinked.

"Do you really want to know?" Brennan looked up from his laptop, as he worked on the other side of the aisle from Wes at a fold-down table.

"Grace must be getting *railed*. And he can't block it out." I paused the movie, enjoying teasing him just a little. Because there was nothing like trying to arrest someone and then feeling Evan getting busy through the bond.

"You can feel things through mate bonds," Brennan explained diplomatically. "While you can tamp them down, so others don't feel them or you don't feel others, strong emotions leak through, especially if you're close physically. Many times, it's a good thing–like sensing when your mate is sad or in danger. But when you're in a meeting and your mates are, um, not, it can pose a challenge." He gave me and Evan looks.

Riley started laughing, then stopped. "Do Evan and Grace even have a bond with each other?"

Evan held up two fingers.

"They're bonded through me, and to each other," Wes replied, rubbing Evan's back.

"Omegas can do that?" Riley asked.

"They can bond with each other, yes. It's just not legally binding like a bond between an omega and alpha," I replied.

Riley nodded. "Can I bond with someone? Because I want an omega with big tits and hair past her ass."

"Are we really having this discussion?" Evan moaned.

I was here for this discussion. It was much better than thinking about all the favors I owed Cam and Lexi back at the station for everything we'd done today.

"You're a sex educator, do you want to lead it, Evan?" Brennan goaded. "Riley, I really appreciate you being comfortable enough with us to ask us questions like this. As far as I can tell, alphas can bond thetas. Then, you can bond an omega through an alpha. Like how Jett and Evan are bonded through me."

"Oh. I can have a pack and mates and all that right? Even though I'm a theta?" For a moment her voice went small.

"Yes," Evan assured. "While thetas have a tendency to be loners, that doesn't mean they don't have mates."

Riley gave him the side-eye.

"He's right. I know a few, and while I think only one has a pack, they're all mated, mostly to betas, because thetas don't like to be told what to do. But I suppose if you have the right alphas, the right people, you could absolutely have a pack and thrive in it," Brennan assured her. "You're doing okay with us."

"There are packs without alphas," I added. Such as all-beta packs, and the occasional omega pod, which was an all-omega pack.

She thought about it for a moment. "Yeah, okay. I'd just need a backhouse, but why not? Hey, what's my superpower as a theta?"

"Superpower?" Wes asked as Evan buried his face in his shoulder.

I mean, *I* could feel that Grace was getting all the sex, so I could only imagine what Evan and Wes were feeling.

"You know, Alphas have knots or locks, omegas are sex gods, betas are generous lovers. What are thetas?" Riley prodded.

"I'm a professional and can answer this," Evan mumbled over and over as if trying to gear himself up for it.

Again, I was here for this conversation.

"I've got this, Evan," Brennan started. "According to the paper I read, thetas generally have no gag reflex, they also are really good at a type of circular breathing that allows them to breath while their mouth is, um, full."

"You've read papers about thetas?" Riley slurped her soda again.

He had. I'd looked over some of them, too.

"Of course. With two new designations in the pack, I've been doing all the research I can. There's a lot more on thetas than gammas. Do I even want to know why the military would have an interest in the gamma danger response?" Brennan looked at us.

"Gammas in battle sounds like chaos," I replied. Though that could be just what some black ops team needed to disrupt governments and shit. No wait, that's what they used kappas for.

Riley frowned, hard. "How is having no gag reflex a superpower?"

I tried not to laugh as Evan looked uncomfortable.

"It's like what female alphas can do, but *more*," Brennan replied tentatively.

Riley set down her soda, grabbed her phone, and frowned.

"Yeah, I'd be careful what group chat you ask that in." I stole her phone.

"Just tell me." She knocked her shoulder into mine and took it back.

Fine.

"Blowjobs," I replied.

I knew she knew what those were. Not just from her friends. Evan did have general sex and relationship talks with her, but I could understand how a conversation about thetas being particularly talented at blowjobs could get uncomfortable.

"Um, I can send you an educational video. You could also talk to Grace," Evan said, looking a bit uncomfortable. "I'm sure she'd love to chat with you about all sorts of things."

"Okay, still not sure how that works, but whatever." Her eyes rolled.

"Again, thank you for being comfortable enough to discuss things like this with us," Brennan told her. "You can talk to any of us about anything–even your brother. Though I understand that you might want to speak with certain people about specific things. One thing I have never doubted about Grace is her care for you. I think she'd speak with you about anything you'd like. That being said, don't feel like you have to. We can find other people for you to talk to–Katie or Lexi or your sisters for example."

Riley snorted. "Yeah, not talking about blowjobs with my sisters–or yours. I like Grace. While I'm glad she and Spencer are going to change the world with their computer program, I can see her teaching high school. Don't know what her mom was thinking, wanting her to teach kindergarten. I'm envisioning the gamma danger reaction in that sort of environment."

"Oh shit, I didn't even consider that," I replied, thinking of the chaos small children could bring.

Riley gave her brother a look. "You know, I don't care if you go in the bathroom and join the sky sex club or whatever. Don't get blue balls on my account, you prudes."

Wow, really? Usually, her favorite sport was cockblocking.

I howled with laughter. "Evan's already part of the sky sex club."

Evan's hand went over his face. Yeah, this was too much fun.

"This is why I live at school." She tackled me.

For a moment we grappled on the couch. Finally, she grabbed the remote and turned the movie back on.

I grabbed some more sodas and candy to try to keep Riley entertained so one of the alphas could sneak off with Evan and settle him.

My phone buzzed. It was Cam, from work, along with some information I'd requested.

Cam

You owe me so much.

Oh, I knew it. Between her and Lexi I'd had shifts covered, background checks pulled, and so many other little things.

But Grace was safe. And that was worth it.

Chapter Fifty-Two

Wes

The limo pulled into the luxury waterfront resort. The sprawling property was landscaped to the hilt, bedecked with palm trees and fountains, and we hadn't even pulled up to the main building yet.

"Bren, can you buy this place? It's nice." Riley looked out the window as a family walked through the parking lot, hand in hand, probably to find dinner, since the sun was starting to set.

Brennan shook his head. "This isn't my kind of property. Though if Grace is going to be spending any time here, it might be worth looking to see if there's something local that would be suitable. Or just get us a small place."

"That's a good idea," I replied.

"I'm guessing she will." Riley shrugged. "Given you know, they're trying to make a fake super collider, and PIIP does a shit-ton of work with them. Not to mention the military and research implications."

"So, you're assigning yourself to that project?" I asked. "I could really use you in my department."

"That project? No, it's boring as sausage on a Tuesday. But I'll come up with a better one. What about her beach house? That could be here," Riley said.

Why was sausage on a Tuesday boring? I wasn't sure I wanted to know.

"Um, I told Spence he could pick." Bren looked at me. "That's okay?"

"It's fine. You know it's going to be a villa overseas or something, right?" I replied. Grace deserved it.

"We did get Evan a forest mansion." Brennan shrugged.

We pulled up to the front of the columned white building, with awnings, a revolving door, and uniformed bellhops with brass carts.

The five of us got out and went inside the lavish, airy lobby with lounge areas nicer than our living room, a cart of tea and snacks, tasteful art work, and a fucking fish pond.

Brennan checked his phone, then looked at the map on one of the walls. "He's in villa four. He gave me the access code."

Riley came over to us with a handful of colorful sandwich cookies. "We're *on the beach*. We're not leaving tomorrow right?"

"Sunday," I assured, taking one of her cookies.

"Rude." She rolled her eyes at me then stuffed the remaining two in her mouth.

"He thought it might be fun for us to spend the day on the beach as a pack tomorrow, since Grace's beach day got cut short," I replied.

Brennan led us outside where we were met with a swimming pool filled with families and children on one side, and a restaurant patio with fairy lights and live music on the other. The ocean lay straight ahead. We followed him down a lushly landscaped path, past the pool bar, a fire pit with children roasting marshmallows, and an area with oversized outside games filled with teenagers.

Spencer booked a *family* resort. Huh.

We passed a waterfall and what looked like an adult-only pool with a swim-up bar. It really was beautifully landscaped.

"I need a picture." Riley grabbed her brother and pulled him over to the waterfall.

"I'll take it," Jett offered.

"Are you doing okay?" Brennan asked me softly as Evan and Riley shoved each other in front of the waterfall.

"Yeah. I mean, once again, Spencer was there to comfort her and I wasn't. But it's better him than no one," I replied. "I'm also glad they bonded."

And I meant it. I really just wanted her to be happy, to have everything.

Especially since her shitty childhood just got shittier. Fuck. How could her mom make her forget me when she *knew what it meant?*

"It's okay to be a little jealous sometimes. It's what you do with that jealousy that matters," Brennan replied.

"It was a little hard on the plane when things got intense. But I also know he's just taking care of her. I'm sure she's a wreck and will need all the dick for a while. There will be enough for me later," I replied.

"Later? You mean in five minutes when we get there?" His eyebrows rose. "You know, I get a little jealous of Evan and Grace. What they have is so easy between them."

"I'm so relieved by that." I watched Riley and Evan make silly faces. "Grace seems to think we can tell Evan *no.*"

Brennan snorted. "Yeah, no more than we can tell her *no.*"

"You couldn't?" I eyed him curiously. "I see the way she looks at you—and no, I don't have an issue if you ever act on it."

"What are you talking about?" Brennan asked, following Evan, Jett, and Riley as Riley took off someplace.

"You *can* have an intimate relationship without bonding with her as long as you're open about it," I told him as we walked into an area filled with little cottages with ocean views. Must be the villas. Some of them had hot tubs.

His eyebrows rose. "It doesn't usually work that way. Eventually they want bites."

"Grace didn't grow up here. It doesn't mean the same thing to her." I shrugged.

"True. I..." He sighed. "I don't know."

"That's fair. Not trying to push everyone together. I'm just throwing it out there if you want to try and see if anything comes of it," I replied. I knew from experience that it didn't always work and that was okay.

"She's probably just curious. They usually are once they know I have a ladder piercing." He shrugged.

I rolled my eyes. "Which has been in her ass. One of the most fucking beautiful things I've ever seen."

"She was high on pheromones. We were in the nest. I was also beyond fucking gentle. In the bedroom I'm not gentle. That's what she needs. Gentleness. She's a fragile little butterfly." His hands shoved in his pockets, a look that was almost disappointment on his face.

Oh, was that why he called her that? To remind himself to be careful with her?

"For now," I replied.

While she was a fragile little butterfly, she also had a core of steel. She always had.

"Oh, there's villa four," Riley said from somewhere up ahead. "They're so fucking cute. And like as big as my grandma's."

We joined them as we approached what looked like a cute little two-story house with a hot tub on the top balcony, and a grill and fire pit on the patio.

"We're roasting marshmallows after dinner. Which I hope is soon because I'm hungry," Riley stated as Brennan let us in.

Excitement thrummed through me as I entered...

An empty living room. My heart fell. Oh. She was probably sleeping–I felt contentment, not pleasure.

Riley read from a note. *"Taking a shower. I marked the rooms. There's food in the fridge. Though we can go out to eat or order in if you want. Marshmallow roasting later? Love you. Grace."*

A door opened, and Grace, in a bathrobe, with wet hair, ran out and wrapped her arms around me. "Wes. Wes, you're here."

My heart filled right back up again. "Of course I am, Peaches. I'm here. I'm right fucking here."

"Boo-Bear," she whispered.

"Yes. I'm right here." I kissed her long and deep, sending all my love to her, vaguely aware that Spencer and Brennan were talking and Evan was tugging on me, wanting a turn.

Mine.

Evan finally pulled her away from me to him and kissed her so long that Jett coughed. He gave Jett a look then kissed Grace again.

"Peaches. I'm so glad you're safe," Evan whispered, voice rough.

"Um, my turn." Riley shoved him so she could get a hug. She hugged Grace hard.

"Come here, Babydoll." Jett squeezed her and lifted her off the ground. He kissed the top of her head.

She looked at Brennan and bit her lower lip. "Hi. Thanks for coming."

"Always." Brennan wrapped his arms around her.

"Well, my heart just melted," Jett whispered with a chuckle.

She was safe. Though I could see it in her face, feel in through the bond, that she was still shaken from her ordeal. But then if I'd gotten dragged to the registry and feared for my life, I'd be rattled, too.

"Feed me, you fuckers," Riley complained.

"What do you want? To go out? To order in?" Spencer offered.

"Quick while they're distracted," Grace whispered, tugging my hand and leading me to a door that was marked with a note that said *Wes*. "I labeled the rooms. Jett and Bren, and Riley are upstairs. I figured Evan and I would stay with you. Spencer's in the other downstairs room."

She wanted just me? *Yes, please.*

"We'll let Evan join in later." I locked the door. Right now, I needed all of her. Alone.

"I missed you so much." She kissed me like she was trying to ingest my soul.

"I've missed you, too. What does my Princess Peaches need?" I picked her up and tossed her on the fluffy bed, in the fancy, well-appointed room.

"You, Alpha." Her lips seized mine, kissing me as if she were starving as she fumbled for the buttons on my shirt, arousal filling the room.

She needed *me*. That made me so fucking happy.

"You have me." I took the bathrobe off her, revealing her still damp, naked flesh. Spreading her legs, I licked her length. "Oh, I missed this. I missed you."

I had my Grace naked and under me. I'd make her come, have her beg for my knot, then fill her until both of us were content.

Noises of delight tumbled out of her pretty little mouth.

"Shhh," I whispered, worried that if she was too loud someone would find us.

I tasted her again, allowing her peachy sweetness to satiate my alpha soul. Mine.

"Come for me," I breathed. My tongue declared my love for her on her clit while my fingers pumped in and out of her.

Her desire for me, her love for me, and her relief that I was here flowed through the bond with a strength I'd never felt before.

She loved me. Needed me. *Wanted me.*

That settled me more than any knot.

Though I was absolutely knotting her.

"Wes," Grace cried as an orgasm shot through her. "I need you inside me. Knot me, Alpha, *please.*"

"How could I deny that?" I looked up at her, sending all my love, desire, and relief back.

She was *okay.* It could have been bad, but she was fine and here.

I patted her ass. "Present for your alpha, Princess Peaches."

"Yes, Alpha," she breathed, her scent heavy with arousal, as she got on her knees, ass in the air.

"Good girl." I stroked her ass.

Hands on her hips, I got behind her and sunk into her warmth.

"Mmmm, that's it, you feel so good," she moaned as I started to thrust.

"That's my line." I peppered her back with kisses, one of my hands moving to toy with her clit.

"I missed you," she whispered as I brought us both closer to her peak.

"I'm here."

"But I need your knot," Grace whined.

"You have it." I was just about there. I thrust a few more times, then seated myself all the way inside, knotting her and filling her with my cum.

A happy shudder shook her body as she hummed contentedly.

I rolled us so we were on the bed, me spooning her, continuing to kiss her, and fill the bond with love, relishing in the adoration that she sent back.

We were complete once again.

Hopefully it would take Evan a while to figure out that we were gone. Because in this moment, she was mine and mine alone.

Chapter Fifty-Three

Evan

I gave the closed door of the room with Wes' name on it the side-eye as we came back into the living room. Riley had dragged all of us out to eat at the hotel's waterfront restaurant, then we'd gone for a walk on the beach and explored the hotel.

Well, all of us but Grace and Wes. Right now, the bond was quiet, but it hadn't been for most of the time that we were gone.

Spencer put a hand on my shoulder. "Are you okay?"

"Just jealous that I didn't lock her in a room first." I shot the door another look like I'd sprout laser vision and be able to open it.

He chuckled. "I sort of thought you would."

"Hey, congratulations on bonding with her." I gave my best friend a hug.

"Thank you. She makes me so happy." Spencer's eyes grew misty.

"Good. You deserve all the happiness." I hugged him again.

"And I deserve marshmallows." Riley bounded over holding two marshmallow-roasting kits.

Spencer nodded. "I'll start up the fire pit."

"Good. I'll get Grace." Riley shoved the marshmallows in my hands.

"You might want to let them have some time," Spencer told her.

Riley snorted. "I did." She went over to the door and pounded on it. "GRACE! Marshmallow time. You said we could roast them later and it's later."

There was a muffled sound, and Riley came back over with a smug look. "Grace is coming."

Jett laughed. "So, she's coming, and she'll join us?"

"What?" Riley's face screwed up and she smacked him. "Sweet baby cheeses. This is why I live at school."

Though soon she'd be home for summer.

"There's beer in the fridge. Also, Brennan, we got your bourbon. It's in the kitchen," Spencer told him, nodding to the open kitchen facing the living room and office areas, the living room opening up onto the porch.

Brennan appraised the *four* boxes. "Ah, yes, Grace went on a bourbon buying spree. Should we open a bottle of the one I like or the peach one she got."

I came up behind him and wrapped my arms around his waist. "Peaches. I want peaches."

"We know," Jett laughed.

Yeah, he and Brennan got my annoyance all through dinner and our walk.

Spencer went outside to turn on the fire pit. Brennan opened a bottle of bourbon and grabbed some glasses. Riley took the marshmallow kits from me and got a soda from the fridge.

I just stood there, glaring at the door. How dare Wes sneak off with her without me?

Spencer came back in and wrapped an arm around me. "Come on, she'll be out soon. I know she missed you so much."

"Did she?" I knew she did, but I was feeling cantankerous.

"She did."

It was a really nice patio with a grill by the table and chairs, more chairs and couches around the fire pit. While it wasn't *on* the beach, we could see it—and other villas. A pack grilling waved at us.

Brennan handed out glasses of bourbon.

Riley opened one of the kits, which had everything you needed to roast marshmallows, including the sticks.

I sipped my bourbon. "Oooh, that is sweet."

"Oh, it is." Brennan winced. "But I could see her adding this to that barbeque sauce she makes."

"That was the idea. Well, that and making peach bourbon slushies." Grace came out, hair wet, wearing Wes' shorts and one of my shirts. "Hi." She kissed me.

I dragged her to one of the couches, and sat her on my lap, savoring her peachiness. "Hi, Peaches."

"Here you go." Brennan handed her a glass, then sat down with Jett on the other couch.

"Thanks."

"Hey, is there any food? Are we grilling?" Wes came out, shirtless.

"You missed dinner." I gave him a look, eyes narrowing.

"Are you hungry, Darling? I'll order you something," Spencer told Grace.

Grace nodded and made like she was going to get up, but I held her tighter.

"Do you want anything in particular or should I choose something?" Spencer kissed her head.

She thought for a moment. "Mashed potatoes."

"Of course. Would anyone like something? Wes, would you like to see the menu?"

"Please." Wes followed him inside.

Riley passed out sticks and marshmallows.

"Sorry. I just…" Grace's voice was soft as she held her marshmallow on a stick over the fire.

"I know. The ire's not directed at you." I kissed her temple. "It's not even ire, more like annoyance. I wanted to get to you first."

Wes and Spencer came back out. Spencer took the chair opposite Riley, Wes joined us on the couch, putting an arm around us both.

"Sorry we missed dinner, Babe." Wes kissed me.

"It's okay, Babe. The food was really good though." I leaned into him, still roasting my marshmallow.

Jett's caught fire. "Shit." He blew out the flames. "Still good." With a grin, he popped it in his mouth.

I patiently toasted mine, trying to get it all gooey and golden.

Grace's fell off her stick, and her lower lip quivered.

"Here, have mine. I think it's done." I carefully took the hot marshmallow off the stick and fed it to her.

"Thank you."

I licked marshmallow off her face.

"Unsanitary." Riley threw me two marshmallows.

Grace and I roasted our marshmallows.

Spencer disappeared and came back with a cart laden with food. He set two covered dishes on the table, along with a meat and cheese board, a bucket of beer and sodas, and a bottle of wine.

"Oooh, I'll take one of those." Jett grabbed a beer.

Spencer tossed Riley a bag of chips, poured himself a glass of wine, and sat at the table. "My good doctor, come eat. Wes, food."

Giving me a kiss, she got up and went over to the table. Spencer pulled her onto his lap, without spilling his wine.

She giggled. "Are you going to feed me?"

"Yes." Putting down his glass of wine, he uncovered the plate.

Wes sat next to them. "I'm so hungry."

While those two ate, or rather, Wes ate while Spencer fed Grace salmon and mashed potatoes, we snacked, drank, and roasted all the marshmallows.

Finally, we all ended up back around the fire pit, Grace laying on top of Wes and I on one of the patio couches.

"Spencer, you're golfing in the morning, right?" Grace asked sleepily.

"I am. Afterward, we can all have breakfast, then go to the beach. I took the liberty of reserving a cabana again." Spencer sipped his wine.

"Perfect. I still need to finish my book for book club," she replied.

I scooped Grace up. "I'm going to put her to bed before she falls asleep on me."

"Okay. Good night. I love you, Spence, see you in the morning. Night everyone." Grace waved as I carried her back to the room with Wes' name on it.

"Mine." I tossed her on the bed and blew on her belly, making her giggle.

"Oh, yes, sir. I'm all yours." Her look went smoldering.

I kissed her. "Have I told you lately that I love it when you call me *sir*?"

Rolling off the bed, I went to lock Wes *out,* as he strode in. I glared.

Wes looked hurt.

"Awww, sorry, Babe." I kissed him. "I just want a turn, too."

"I... I want you both, please?" Grace whined. "Evan, you can lock me in your room when we get home, but tonight I need you both."

How could I deny that? And, well, the three of us were good together.

I dive bombed her, making her laugh again.

"Tonight's all about you." I kissed her neck as Wes joined us on the bed. "Wanna be the filling in a sandwich?" My cock strained against my pants.

"Mmmm, yes, please." Her scent went sweet with arousal.

"Anything you want," I told her, gazing into her eyes. "Anything you want."

Chapter Fifty-Four

Grace

Evan snored on one side of me, the other side of the bed empty. The curtains moved in the breeze coming in from the ocean. Getting up, I went to the bathroom, took a quick shower, and brushed my teeth and hair. My body ached from last night–and yesterday–but in a good way, because my soul and heart were all filled up.

Pulling on one of Wes' shirts and a pair of drawstring shorts, since my clothes were all in a different bedroom, I padded out to the main area. The living room was quiet, but the smell of coffee wafted from the kitchen area as I entered it. Grabbing a mug from the rack by the pot, I poured myself a cup and added creamer and sugar.

"Good morning, Grace." Brennan sat at the glass kitchen table working on his laptop, a cup of coffee at his side.

"Morning." I leaned against the counter and took a long swig of the hot brew.

When Spence had said that everyone was on their way I hadn't expected *everyone*. Coming out of the shower yesterday to see that all five of them flew here, just to make sure that I was okay, had warmed me to my very soul.

"Spencer's golfing, but where's everyone else?" I asked, looking around.

"Jett went for a jog and Wes is swimming laps. I think Riley's still sleeping," he told me.

"So's Evan." I drained half the cup, then added more coffee. Plopping into the chair next to Brennan at the table, I sighed as I took another sip.

Brennan looked over and closed his laptop. "Are you okay? We were worried. Yesterday must have been really scary for you."

"It was. I had no idea what I was going into, what to expect. I... I was so afraid." All these emotions swirled inside me, ones I was able to keep at bay because I was too busy being loved. But now, awake and still, the reality of what happened yesterday settled inside me, smothering me like a too-heavy blanket.

I could have died for reasons I didn't even understand.

"I've got you." Brennan pulled my upper body to him.

I rested my head on his shoulder as I started to cry. Sob after sob wracked my body as Brennan's hand ran up and down the back of my neck, as I started to finally process everything.

"We're all right here. Wes should be back soon, but I'm not above texting Jett to drag Wes' ass out of the pool, or asking Spencer to leave his golf game. Why is that man even golfing?" Disapproval tinged his voice.

"Because I said that I was fine if he did. It's a pretty important game that has been planned for weeks. They're brokering a big contract that's going to lead to a bunch of jobs." My voice choked with tears as my head continued to rest on his shoulder.

Spencer and I originally planned on flying home after a post-golf lunch.

Brennan's phone buzzed. With his free hand he texted something.

"I'm fine," I mumbled into his shoulder. That was probably one of them asking the group chat if I was okay.

"I know you think you're fine, you always do. It's okay to not be. If I was pulled away for testing I'd be unsettled. Not to mention everything else that's happened to you," he said softly, playing with the hair at the nape of my neck.

"It's just that I can't wrap my head around the whole genocide thing," I sniffed. "Or not letting carriers have kids." Remembering Lark's attitude, I looked up at him. "Or how polarizing it is. My health class didn't cover this. Executing people for their genetics is frowned upon where I'm from."

"Oh. Yes, you literally didn't have that assembly. One of the things they do is talk about people from those designations that have done horrible things throughout history to help put it in context. But you don't know the history here, so that wouldn't mean anything to you. We're talking about everything from killing millions of people because of where they were born, to bombing skyscrapers, to using the charisma of their dynamic to perpetuate hate," he explained. "It's the idea of sacrificing one for the many."

"It doesn't mean they *all* have to die. They killed Thora," I started to sob. "She hadn't even done anything. She was a pianist. I didn't even get to know her." I was going to cling to what the professor said about her being good, smart, and funny. Especially since the woman who raised me was none of those things.

Brennan rubbed my neck. "I'm so sorry. She played the piano like you?"

"That's what the professor said," I sniffled. "He showed me a picture of her with a trophy. Who's Theodosia? That's apparently my middle name. When I asked the professor about it, he laughed and was like *You play the piano and don't know who she is?*"

In hindsight, that sort of hurt. I didn't like being laughed at like that. But then he had no idea where I'd grown up.

"Well, that wasn't nice. Theodosia was an omega that masqueraded as a beta in Golden France and became a renowned composer and pianist that played for leaders all across Europe. She was known not only as a prolific composer, but as a prolific lover. Many of them were patrons who helped her to keep her secret. It was only after she died that the truth came out. This was a time when omegas had very little freedom and it angered people that an omega dared do such a thing and they tried to erase her."

"Omegas couldn't create art?" In the few conversations I'd had with adult omegas, who'd grown up knowing they were omegas, they'd all studied the arts. Kilroy's mom played in the symphony.

"Oh, they could. They've always been encouraged to learn music, dancing, painting, and such. It's being serious about it. *Contributing* to their field the way she did. Not to mention all the unchaperoned trips and concerts. Oh, and not finding an alpha and having lots of babies." He grinned. "So scandalous. Even worse, she gave omegas *hope*. She's considered an inspiration for omegas who want careers."

"That sounds like a good namesake. Are her pieces nice?" I asked.

"They're very lovely to listen to—but a bitch to play. While in theory they're not as technical as say, Volkov or Kirkokov, it's all in the execution, which takes skill and maturity. Nothing sours a recital quicker than a beginner trying to play one of her pieces. We can find some if you'd like, either to listen to or play," he soothed.

"I'd like that. Apparently Thora didn't like Volkov. I... I do."

"And that's fine. You're right, science should be able to find a better way. They just have to get past the fear of the people first."

"I suppose if I had the historical context I could grapple with it better. I don't even know what it means to be a sigma or whatever." I put my face back into the crook of his neck and inhaled his pine scent.

His hands ran up and down my back in a way that was relaxing. "It's a lot I'm sure, discovering you're from a family with illegal designations."

"That doesn't change anything, right?" Fear shot through me. "You're not going to kick me out of the house."

"Never." His head leaned on mine, his pine scent continuing to envelop me. "And not just because the house would revolt."

His words soothed me and my body relaxed into him.

"You found your bio-dad, too. That's a lot for what was supposed to be a work trip," he added.

"A bio-dad who, while apologetic for the shitty things that went down when I was a baby, is from a pack of colossal assholes. I have *nine* siblings. And I'm from here. That means she knew I was omega." I started to sob. "I used to make burrows in *laundry* when I was a toddler. You know who smells like laundry?"

Brennan held me tighter. "Fuck. She probably did. Given your mate bond with Wes actually worked, you were probably so fucking close to awakening, too, if you hadn't already. She could probably smell it."

Oh shit. Sobs wracked my body as I continued to cry. Finally, they slowed.

"It's okay, Little Butterfly. I have you. You're okay," he whispered.

"I'm sorry to cry all over you. Again," I sniffed, face buried in his shoulder.

"Never apologize for needing comfort from someone in the pack, Grace. That's what we're here for." Jett scooped me out of my seat and onto his lap, so we both leaned into Brennan.

"Thank you for coming." I snuggled into Jett. I'd missed him, too.

"If it was one of us, you'd do the same," Brennan told me, fingers tangling in my hair as my head rested on his muscular chest.

"Wow, you're wearing Wes' clothes," Jett teased.

I scratched my nose with my middle finger. "You can't get on me for wearing Evan's stuff then tease me when I don't."

"You're from here. That is fucking trippy," Jett said.

"It just makes everything worse."

It felt so good to be in their arms. For a few moments I just let them comfort me.

"Everything's going okay with work, Jett?" I asked. "You didn't miss a boxing tournament or anything?"

"Not this weekend, and everything's fine," Jett assured.

I looked at Brennan. "Is the Queen Mum still on the rampage?"

"Well, she hasn't figured out that I bought the building she needs yet. But she did figure out that my dad signed some of my assets over to me." Brennan rolled his eyes.

"I'm so glad that your dad actually followed through and sent the documents. I think he actually cares for you." Jett squeezed his shoulder.

Brennan nodded. "I think so, too. I've gotten some upset texts from my mother's lawyer telling me that I just don't understand."

"Mmmm, I'll still slap her if you need me to," I offered.

"Thank you." Brennan stroked my hair.

"Well, this is fucking adorable." Evan came into the kitchen in a T-shirt and shorts. He leaned in and gave me a kiss tasting of toothpaste, then kissed Brennan and Jett.

"I..." I looked up at him. Even though he didn't seem mad, Evan had never seen his guys comforting me like this. As I got to know them better, I could understand why Evan was with them, why Wes and Spencer formed a pack with them.

"Grace." Evan's nose touched mine. "Relax. You can snuggle my guys."

I got a hint of arousal in his lemonade scent.

"Absolutely." Jett nuzzled my cheek, amber scent flaring.

Desire surged between my thighs, and I smelled Evan's perfume. Jett hardened underneath me. My mind flashed back to Evan's heat, when Jett and Evan took me between them over and over again. I wouldn't mind that right now. Especially if Brennan let me suck–

What was I even thinking? Why was I so needy?

But the scents of pine, amber, and lemonade wrapped me in a hazy, sexy blanket.

"Should we take this upstairs? That's where your room is, right?" Evan's voice went husky.

"Fuck of the morning to you. What's for breakfast?" Riley strode into the kitchen.

Disappointment zinged through me as I sat up. Snuggle time was over–as was any prospect of sexy cuddles. "Good morning. Let's order some food."

"Maybe later?" Jett whispered in my ear as I crawled off his lap.

Later? My pussy clenched at the thought. *Down girl.* Would I really have sex with them? Was I even ready for Brennan? Sure, I liked looking at him, he had been very kind to me, but was I?

But Jett, yes. Yeah, I'd let Jett and Evan take me...

...as I sucked Brennan's cock.

Yeah, I'd fuck Brennan. Or nap on his dick.

Pushing my lusty thoughts aside, Riley helped me order food from the console in the kitchen. Jett and Brennan disappeared.

"Hey, Peaches." Wes came in wrapped in a towel. "I'm going to shower. Are we ordering breakfast or going out?"

"We already ordered for you," Riley told him.

I made more coffee and was pouring a cup for Wes when Spencer came in.

"Did everything go okay?" I asked Spencer.

"The contract has been signed." Spencer gave me a kiss. "Should we order breakfast?"

"Already did." Riley rolled her eyes and put Wes' cup at his place.

"Excellent. I'll be right there." Spencer kissed me again and left.

There was a knock on the door.

"FOOD, FUCKERS," Riley yelled as she ran to the door. A moment later, she pushed the cart in, and we set everything out on the table.

I made sure everyone had coffee and juice. Riley had ordered herself the fanciest hot chocolate that I'd ever seen. I'd gotten myself a latte.

"Oooh. I want to keep this tiny syrup pitcher." Riley put it by her plate of waffles.

There was thumping down the stairs.

Jett slid into the kitchen. "I am so hungry."

Everyone came in and we all sat around the table. I was between Wes and Spencer.

"Can you tell us what the fuck happened, Grace?" Riley asked, cutting into her waffles, smothered with chocolate, bananas, and whipped cream.

"Yeah," I sighed, taking a bite of fruit. I started with meeting Creed, going through the events at the university and farm, then yesterday at the testing center, telling them not just about testing, but being in the exam room *with* the professor and everything he told me—and the events in the parking lot.

"That's a lot." Wes squeezed my shoulder.

"It is. So, not only am I apparently from here, but one of the professor's alphas *sold me* to my mom's evil twin who somehow smuggled me to another world." I sighed. Spencer placed a hand on my bare thigh.

"But how did she get there?" Riley asked. "It's not like it's easy."

"The obvious answer is that somehow my father and Dr. K managed to use their network or tech to send them elsewhere," Spencer replied. "They had originally wanted to send our illegal designations away in return for taking in omegas from other worlds, it just didn't work out the way they'd planned."

"Makes sense. If these designations are illegal in most places it might be hard to find places to put them, and the network thought it was too much trouble or something." Riley took another bite of waffle.

"That's what I was wondering. If we got mostly male omegas because many worlds didn't want them, then how difficult would it be to find a home for sigmas and omicrons? That could be why you ended up in a world without designations at all. Especially since unlike alphas and omegas, sigmas and omicrons don't have discernible anatomical changes. That's often how sigma and omicron males are found. They test as alphas as children, then fail to get knots, though their scents are usually *very* close, even without chemical help, and their builds and other abilities are about the same. They even have pheromones that operate similarly but aren't as potent," Spencer explained.

Huh. I continued to make inroads in my veggie omelet.

Riley swiped a piece of Evan's bacon. "Makes sense to me."

"Hey, that's mine," Evan tried to swipe it back.

"You know what they say about snoozers and losers." Riley shoved it in her mouth.

"I'll see if I can figure anything out, but I think it's safe to assume that Rosalind was somehow smuggled, either pretending that Grace was hers, or masquerading as Thora," Spencer said. "While I was told it didn't work out the way they wanted, that doesn't mean they didn't get some to other worlds. Just not very many, I'm guessing."

"Rosalind could be very charming when she wanted, so I can see her spinning a nice sob story. I mean that's how she got my dad. He met a pretty, young, down-and-out single mom with her infant. Took her in, gave her a home, married her, and had more babies. Though I'd be interested in how Rosalind even found the underground network to send her over in the first place. I wonder what her major was," I added, in case she'd somehow been one of Dr. Thanukos' students or something.

"On it." Brennan speared a potato with his fork.

"Me, too. I called in a favor to see what I could find as well, given Rosalind's criminal record," Jett told me, taking a sip of coffee.

"That would be good, especially because I'd like to know what sort of trouble Thora was in when she called the professor and wanted him to keep me," I replied, trying to figure out the full story.

"Yeah, that sounds like the law was after her, then somehow she ended up in a testing facility," Jett told me.

"Can someone explain what the illegal designations are and why?" I asked, taking a sip of my latte.

"Sigmas commit crimes to punish people—think eco terrorists and mass shooters. They don't want to be part of the system, and generally think it's bullshit," Riley replied. "Omicrons are charming, and think that the rules don't apply to them. They want to take over the world and fix it and aren't afraid to use violence." She looked at Spencer. "That's right? I looked it up. I won't get that assembly until next year."

Spencer nodded. "It is. Both are very smart designations, too, and passionate about their work. One thing about omicrons is that early on they found their homes in religion and philosophy and often used their belief systems to get others to execute their visions."

I frowned. Hmmm.

"One of the reasons why people were against Elaris' research on the illegal designations was because she wanted to include the phi designation as well. A phi is a cross between a sigma and a kappa," Spencer added.

"I don't know what a kappa is." I ate another bite.

"Kappas are fun and adventurous thrill-seekers who make exceedingly bad choices. They're not illegal, but they're almost non-existent. Sometimes the military uses them in disruption-oriented operations," Jett explained.

Oh. Okay. Kappas disrupting governments with chaos. I'd watch that movie.

"A phi is basically a chaotic psychopath," Jett added. "While they can be a loner like sigmas, they can also be fun like kappas, and even charismatic like an omicron. They can get violent and aggressive, and unlike the others, can hide among alphas, because they have a bulb that can pass as a slightly-deformed knot. They're also often selfish. The running theory is that phis aren't organic variations, that they were somehow created or bred at some point, probably for military purposes, and it went horribly terribly wrong."

Wes nodded. "I could see that."

"So, you could just hide your designation?" I ate some fruit. It was nice fruit, too, not just melons.

"Once you're tested in middle school you might not ever be tested again if there's no need for it. There are ways to alter your scent if you need to," Brennan told me.

"It's a lot harder to find illegal female designations without a test, because alpha females just have extra pussy muscles, which is less noticeable than a knot," Spencer added.

"Hey, digammas aren't illegal, right? They were mentioned in literature class during our poetry unit." Riley took a sip of hot chocolate.

Evan shook his head. "No. While it doesn't always end well for them, they're not illegal."

Wes blinked. "I don't even know what that is."

"It's the reverse of Grace—an alpha whose environment was so awful, or their trauma was so great, that their bodies halted the process of becoming alphas," Evan said.

"Do I even want to know what that would be like?" Brennan shuddered.

Evan shook his head. "No, you do not."

"I feel so bad for them." I put my hand to my heart.

So many designations. Wow. Yeah, I had some homework.

"Back to what happened with the Thorne Family. I have all the background checks. They're all pretty normal, other than a few small arrests for Adriana for being involved in some fringe scientist group," Jett told me. "Well, Hale is pretty reckless, but he's done nothing truly bad."

"Huh. I wonder if Adriana knew that I was sent elsewhere and that's why she was so adamant I wasn't the Grace they were looking for," I said to Spencer. "She could very well have had science friends that worked with your dad and Dr. K. But both yesterday in the parking lot and at the farm she blamed *you*. Though it does seem weird that Adriana would trust Rosalind, but whatever."

Spencer nodded. "Yes, trusting Rosalind does seem like an unstable plan. Adriana... that fringe science group she's part of protested the company I had with Elaris. Do you remember when I told you that sometimes I wondered if her death was an accident?"

I gasped. "When she said that she had nothing to do with it."

"Yes. I suppose she somehow thinks I'm getting my revenge by introducing you to your father?" He shrugged.

"That feels like a stretch on her part," Brennan said.

"Adriana strikes me as the type of person that always needs to place blame on someone," I replied. I'd encountered them many times, especially at church.

"What are we doing to her?" Riley asked, flexing her fingers.

"Adriana? I think that we should turn everything over to the authorities–if that's all right with you," Spencer added to me. "I'm not saying that we need to press charges, but the authorities should have this information."

I thought about it for a moment, and as much as I didn't want to cause grief for the professor and his family, giving the information to the authorities seemed wise–especially if it led to justice for Elaris. "I'm fine with that."

"Great. So can we go to the beach now?" Riley asked, finishing her juice.

"As soon as we're done eating." Spencer turned to me. "What do you say? Should we give our beach day a do-over?"

"Yes," I told him, draining my latte. "This time I'm going to finish my sandcastle."

Chapter Fifty-Five

Jett

Brennan had brought me to some very nice resorts over the years—ones he owned, ones we wanted to check out for research purposes, and ones we just wanted to visit.

But this one made me homesick for the massive family vacations we'd take every few years when I was growing up because my grandmother and aunties wanted to visit a tropical beach.

Today, this part of the beach wasn't packed, but most of the cabanas dotting the beach were occupied. People also laid on chaise lounges, as kids frolicked in the water and played in the sand.

Wes, Spencer, and Riley played flying disc, the ocean waves lapping at their feet.

Grace had asked me to help her build a sandcastle, but it quickly turned into us burying Brennan in the sand.

Yeah, that was something I never thought I'd say. But here Brennan was, making Grace happy by being up to his neck in sand.

She laughed, as she patted the sand around him. That yellow bikini she had on made me want to tear off her coverup and little beach skirt, and pin her to the chaise lounge in the cabana Spencer had rented for us.

"How do I look?" Brennan asked, unable to move.

"Perfect, Honey." I kissed his nose.

Grace giggled as she took a photo with her phone. "Perfect." She stood. "Well, that was fun. I'm going to go read inside the cabana. I'm getting too much sun. Don't want a sunburn!"

With a wiggle of her ass, she went into the cabana.

"Did she just bury me in the sand and leave me?" Brennan blinked.

"I've got you, Honey." Giving him a kiss, I unburied him. "You were so patient. I'm proud of you."

He thought for a moment. "I'd always wondered what it would be like. I don't think I want to do that again."

"You made her happy." I helped him up. Sand covered his body.

"I'm going to jump in and wash the sand off. Thank you, Dear." Brennan gave me a kiss then ran straight into the ocean.

Grace was inside the cabana on a lounge chair reading on the book reader that Spencer got her, sipping a drink. She'd taken off her little beach skirt and cover up, laying on some towels over the double chaise lounge.

She didn't look sunburned. I'm pretty sure she actually came in here because she was reading something spicy and didn't want us to smell how turned on she was by it.

As a beta, I couldn't smell the more nuanced scent changes, so the fact her sweet arousal filled the cabana only confirmed my suspicions. Though her three mates should be feeling this.

Her breath caught in her chest. Eyes closing, she laid back and put her hand to her throat.

"Good girl," she whispered as her thighs rubbed together.

It made me remember our time in the nest.

"What are you doing, Grace?" I asked.

I straddled her on the chaise lounge, one knee on each side of her, no part of my body touching her. Desire for her, to make her aroused like that, to say that to her, consumed me.

Her eyes opened, and her look said *caught*.

"Reading." Her scent flared.

I smirked. "Read it to me."

It wasn't a request. I was easygoing by nature, so I was easy to dismiss as neutral, not dominant. But there was a lot more under the surface than I let on.

"Out loud?" Her eyes flickered toward the doorway.

"Do you have another way?" I helped myself to some of the hand cleaner that sat on the little table next to us in between the sunscreen, her phone, and her drink.

Before she could answer, I leaned forward, putting my hands on both sides of her, caging her on the chaise. As I did, I watched her carefully. Since I couldn't catch more nuanced scents I relied a lot on body language.

Every part of her screamed that she didn't mind this *at all*. Not to mention someone would come running at her distress.

"Read to me, Grace." I met her eyes. Those beautiful blue-grey eyes reminded me of the ocean back in Bayside where I grew up.

She held up her e-reader and started to read aloud. "*His large hand wrapped around my throat, pushing me to the wall. Emerald eyes glimmered with dominance as he smiled coyly. A scent reminiscent of a thunderstorm encompassed me, going straight to my pussy. His forehead touched mine as my insides burned with desire. He licked his kissable lips as I stilled under his grasp, his gaze. Only two words escaped his lips as his grip tightened around my neck. "Good Girl." Two words and everything I'd built myself up to be melted into a puddle on my office floor. Two words and I was his.*"

Her legs rubbed together again as her peachy scent enveloped me.

My face got very close, and I nuzzled my cheek against hers like I had this morning in the villa. Which had been amazing until Riley interrupted us.

"Good girl," I told her.

Her chest shuddered and her eyes blew out with desire.

"Do you like it when I call you that?" I murmured nipping her ear. But I knew the answer.

She nodded.

Yes, little-miss-praise-kink *loved* to be told that she was a good girl.

"Do you want me to call you that again?" My lips caressed her temple.

"Please?"

"You're so good, aren't you." My lips brushed her jaw. "Has Wes even noticed that you have a massive praise kink? I know Spencer has."

"I don't know what that is." Her thighs rubbed together again.

"It means that you like to be told how good and perfect you are. You're just so good, aren't you? Such a good girl." I nibbled on her neck as her desire flared.

I felt Evan as he entered the cabana, his sweet lemonade joining her peaches.

Biting her lower lip, her eyes darted to the doorway. Yes, she was new to all this.

"Eyes on me, Peaches," I ordered. "Evan can be jealous when I don't let him watch, or make him watch and not touch, but he's not going to object if you want to be with me. Neither are any of the others."

Like the good girl she was, she looked at me.

"You wouldn't let Evan watch? Or watch but not touch?" Her breathy voice was a near-pant.

"Sometimes I don't want to share. Now, is this what you want, Babydoll?" Shifting my weight, I took my hands off the top of the chaise; one closing very gently around her throat, just like it had in the nest during Evan's heat.

Just like in the passage of that book she just read me.

"Oh yes." A shudder shot through her body.

I settled my weight on her, still straddling her, one hand around her neck. Again, I looked her over, looking for any sign she wasn't enjoying herself.

"Look at you, responding to my touch like that. So perfect. My hand looks beautiful around your throat." Leaning forward, I nibbled on her pulse on her neck.

"So beautiful," Evan agreed.

My free hand moved her book reader to the table. I got curiosity from Brennan through the bond, and I sent reassurance back. Later, I'd tell him all about it, but I also let him know he was welcome to join us through the bond-code we developed.

"Do you want me to do that to you?" I whispered in her ear. "Shove you against the wall, my hand around your throat, telling you what a good girl you are as I impale you over and over with my cock."

Yes, I could give her all that… and so much more.

My hand tightened ever so slightly, as I ground myself into her, only her thin yellow polka dot bikini between us. My lips brushed across her neck, my hand tightened just a little more.

Her eyes went half-lidded.

"Fuck, I can feel how wet you are through your bikini." I slipped my hand underneath the fabric, swiping her. Oh, yes, she was so wet.

She creamed at my attention, a quiet moan escaping her lips.

"What a good girl you are, getting all nice and ready for me." Slowly, I brought my fingers to my lips, tasting her peachy goodness. "So sweet. Suck."

I put my finger in her mouth. She sucked on it like it was my dick. Which was rock hard.

I groaned. "Close the curtain, Baby."

The cabana went dark, with just the small light from the fan illuminating everything. Evan rejoined us, want pouring through the bond.

"Stay right there," I ordered when he moved to join us. "Peaches and I are having story time. Eyes on me, Babydoll. Don't look at him. Look at me. And *only* me."

My hand tightened around her throat a little more, then relaxed again.

The cabana's walls were made of cloth, so I couldn't quite re-enact the scene. But if she wanted me, well, I'd certainly give it to her.

"There's no nice hard wall, but this will work. If this is what you want? After all, I did make you a promise earlier, and I'm happy to make good on that now." I ground against her again. I could offer her things, too.

She nodded, eyes still on me.

"You have to use your words." I squeezed gently again.

"Yes, please," she breathed.

"Good girl. Safeword?" I asked, wondering if she had one.

"Trampoline."

"Perfect. If my hand is too tight, tap my shoulder twice. If you want me to stop and can't get out the word, tap my shoulder three times. Understood?" My eyes stayed locked on hers, making her understand that while I was in charge, she had a say.

"Understood."

I was already shirtless, so I only had to strip off my swim trunks, which had palm trees on them. My pierced cock sprung free.

"Show Evan what a good girl you are. How beautifully you take me. How much you want my cum." I repositioned myself then pulled off her yellow bikini bottoms and slid right into that soft wetness with one smooth, forceful motion.

A gasp escaped her lips. I smothered her mouth with mine, sealing in her noises. After all, we were on a crowded beach. I pinned her to the chaise, spearing her with stroke after stroke. I was firm, but not harsh in the slightest.

Her hands traced the dragon tattoo on my back. Looking over, I could see Evan playing with his cock in the dim light... and her watching him.

"Eyes on me," I ordered, squeezing her throat and releasing it again. "Good girl." I kissed her. I kept my eyes on her. "Evan, you don't get to come until I say. Babydoll, I'll make sure you come, but you *have* to ask. Understood?" I continued to thrust into her, keeping her pinned to the chaise.

"Understood." She wrapped her legs around my waist, pulling herself to me.

"Such a good girl," I praised.

One hand slipping under her bikini top, I pinched her nipple hard. She gasped and her body bucked.

"Oh, that's it, you take me so good. Mmmm." I nibbled on her neck, on the opposite side of Spencer's bite.

"I'm getting close," she whispered.

I picked up my pace, rolling her nipples hard between my fingers and sucking on the chords of her neck. She continued to hold onto me with her legs–and I liked that a lot.

"Please, please let me come," she begged.

Oh, what a sweet sound that was. I was ready to cum in that sweet pussy.

"Come for me, Peaches." I bit her nipple through the fabric of her bikini top.

Her pussy spasmed around my cock as an orgasm rushed over her. That pushed me over the edge. I thrust into her deeply as my cum flooded her.

I unwrapped my hand from her neck, still inside her. Also, I was well aware that Evan was struggling to heed my directions. Not out of jealousy, but out of want.

"You take my cum so well. I can't wait to try that up against a wall." My fingers stroked her throat in a possessive gesture.

A little aftershock trembled through her body at my words. Even if she was never ready for everything I could offer her, what we'd have could be so good.

"You took him beautifully," Evan said. "Please, can I come now?" His voice was almost a whine. "Fuck, Peaches, seeing his hand around your throat undoes me."

Yes, it was time to let Evan have a turn. He was more patient now than he was when we first got together, but he still had his limits.

"Evan, for being so patient, you can come inside her. Peaches, get on your knees. Show me how prettily you take our omega." I slid out of her and patted her ass.

She got on all fours on the chaise, my cum dripping out of her.

Evan stood over her, and slammed into her, holding her hips tight. "Sorry, Peaches, but this is going to be quick. I'll make it up to you later."

"Oh, yes, sir," she said softly.

One hand rubbed her clit as he took her hard and fast. I pinched both her nipples through the fabric of her top at the same time as Evan pinched her clit.

My mouth smothering her cry as Evan pounded her one last time and they both came.

"Oh, look at you two. You're so good, and look so amazing together," I praised, stroking both their backs.

I grabbed a towel off one of the other chaises and cleaned them up, continuing to stroke and praise them as I got them put back together.

"Here, both of you should drink some water, it's warm today." I pulled her to the chaise and curled her into me, planting little kisses on her neck and shoulders, as she drank half the bottle.

I handed it to Evan, and he finished it.

"So good." I patted the chaise. Evan laid down with us and the three of us snuggled. I played with her hair and nuzzled Evan's cheek.

Her eyes fell to the fabric that separated us from everyone else. "They all know, don't they?"

"Yep." I planted a kiss on her temple.

"There's absolutely no shame in needing to get impaled on a chaise lounge." Evan ran his fingers up and down her thigh. "I think I want a turn later." He gave me a smoldering glance.

"Absolutely." Yes, I'd do this with him.

Hopefully, I'd get to repeat this with her soon, too.

Chapter Fifty-Six

Grace

Oh my god. I'd just let Jett rail me on a chaise lounge in a cabana on a beach full of people. With two of my mates just outside.

And I liked it a lot.

Being with Jett filled up something inside me, something that I didn't know was empty.

Also, I was very curious as to what it would be like to actually be taken against a wall. Though this had been really nice.

And that hand...

Light flooded the cabana as Brennan slipped in through the cloth doors. Shit. Anxiety shot through me.

"Hey, none of that." Jett lightly bit the lobe of my ear. "Bren would be so impressed with how well you listen, and how pretty you look with my hand around your neck."

Brennan's pine scent flared as he strode over to me, and he took my chin in his hands. "Is that right?"

"Yes, Alpha." Every inch of me trembled. He wore long board shorts and a tight shirt that showed off every muscle and I bit my lower lip wondering what would happen next.

His blue eyes met mine. "Good."

Something shuddered straight through me. *Down girl.* I had three guys and wanted two more? Did I really have to catch them all?

Would it be bad if I did?

Brennan touched his forehead to mine. He smelled like he'd gone for a swim in the ocean. Letting go of my chin, he caressed my cheek.

Then he took Evan's face in his hand. "What about this one?"

"For once, he listened." Jett planted a kiss on Evan's temple.

"Excellent. That's what I like to hear." Brennan rewarded Evan with a kiss. "Everyone's hungry. I'm supposed to order lunch." He went to the tablet on the wall of the cabana where you could order food and drinks. "What do you want?"

Crawling up off my hot man pillow, I joined him to see what I wanted. Anxiety shot through me again. What did Bren think of me letting Jett fuck me on a lounge chair. Was it weird that I wanted a hand wrapped around my throat?

Brennan ruffled my hair with his hand as his body touched mine. "Settle, Grace."

The growl in his voice did the exact opposite.

"I trust Jett to give you what you need–as should you. You obviously need a little extra with what you've been through, and there's no shame in that." His hand rubbed the back of my neck like he had this morning.

The hand stayed there as I entered my selection on the tablet. Even though he didn't purr, the simple act of his hand on the back of my neck like that did something to me.

My pussy muscles twitched. While they'd gotten two delicious cocks, what they hadn't gotten was a nice thick knot.

What was going on? While there were times I wanted Brennan, did he want me? Or was this just caring about me? I was so confused.

"My turn." Evan broke the moment, entering his selection on the tablet.

I used that interruption to duck out of Brennan's grasp. "I'm going to check on Riley."

Slipping out, I blinked at the bright sun. My sunglasses were inside. As was my wrap.

Wes was now being buried in the sand by Riley. Wes. More anxiety shot through me. Wes sent back love and winked. Winked!

Strong arms wrapped around me as Spencer hugged me from behind. Spence. Fuck what did I do?

"Easy, Baby Girl, it's just me," Spencer growled in my ear, pulling me down into the low chair someone had dragged out of the cabana.

I melted into him, putting my face in the crook of his neck and breathing deep. My heart slowed, as the scent of oiled leather filled my lungs.

Why was everyone being so growly?

Spencer licked the bond mark on my neck in a possessive gesture that sent more sparks through me. His fingers traced my cheekbone. "Were you a good girl for Jett?"

His growl made me melt even more, my breath, once again, catching in my chest.

"Yes, Alpha." It was breathy and barely there.

"I'm so glad. He's much stricter than I am, and I'm not saving you from someone else's punishments, Darling." The growl turned to a purr.

I curled into his arms. He continued to hold me tight, covering me with a beach blanket.

"That's it, just settle into my arms right there where you belong," he purred. "Perfect."

His praise and purrs comforted me. Spencer's hand slipped under my bikini bottoms, hidden by the blanket. Fingers slipped inside of me. Burying my head in his shoulder, I let him play with me, *in public*, with only a blanket to conceal us.

I should be scandalized. But it felt so good. So much love and desire slipped through our bond as I inhaled his scent, sweet with his desire.

"That's it, Baby Girl," he whispered, as my body shuddered.

I hid my cries in his neck. Hand slipping out of me, his arms tightened around my body.

"There you go." Spencer kissed my bond mark.

It wasn't a knot. But I did feel better. Maybe after lunch I'd drag someone back to the room with me.

Until then, this was nice. I got cozy in his arms as we watched as Jett, Evan, and Brennan came back out and started playing a game with scoops and a ball. Riley made the sand-buried Wes a mermaid tail.

A little girl in a purple bathing suit ran over to Spence and me. Her brown hair was in two little poofs, and she carried a red bucket full of toys.

Her little light brown freckled face broke out into a grin. Her blue eyes, the professor's eyes, sparkled. "There you are!"

"Hi, Tru." Any other words escaped me and for a moment I had no air. It wasn't that I didn't want to see Tru, it was that I didn't expect it.

What was she doing here?

My belly tightened. Was the professor here? Was this some kind of emotional blackmail? I couldn't look.

"Breathe, darling," Spencer whispered in my ear. He smiled at Tru. "Hi, Tru. It's nice to see you. Who are you here with?"

"Me. Hi." Mercy strode over, wearing one of those sporty bikinis with a sports bra top and boy shorts, showing off her leg muscles and toned arms. Skate smash took major leg power. Like yesterday, her brown hair was in two neat dutch braids, secured with colorful scrunchies. A straw beach bag was slung over her broad shoulder.

I looked up and down the beach, and while it was dotted with people I saw no one I recognized from that pack. No professor. No Creed.

"Do your responsible adults know that you're here?" I asked, easing out of Spencer's lap so I was standing. Mercy was quite a bit taller than me.

Mercy shrugged. "That's why they track our phones. Besides, Tru wanted to see you and I didn't want to be home, so we thought we'd take the train to the beach. It's a beautiful day for it."

That it was. It was sunny and warm with a slight breeze.

"How did you know where I was?" I frowned. "Creed?"

"Creed's phone." She shrugged.

"You use a mirror?" Riley jogged over to us. She wore a cute black swimsuit that would be perfect for Wednesday Addams. Her braids were wrapped around her head in a poofy braid bun.

Mercy shook her head. "He hasn't changed his password in years."

"That works," Riley nodded, as her gaze shifted from Mercy to me and back again. "Wow, just wow."

"This is nothing. You should meet my brother Creed. It's so weird seeing the two of them standing next to each other." Mercy laughed.

Tru's face broke out into a wide, sweet grin. "Grace, I have another sister? One with such pretty hair?"

Riley's hand went to her heart. "Hey, Babycakes. I'm Riley. I wish Grace was my sister. Mine aren't that cool. Grace is mated to my brother."

"This is Tru and Mercy. Mercy is a crusher–Riley's a swing," I introduced.

"Should we build that sandcastle?" Riley offered.

"Sister." Hale came out of nowhere, wearing the tiniest swimsuit. He picked me up and spun me around, laughing. His unbound hair went flying as we turned.

Wes immediately came over to us, Brennan and Jett flanking him, Evan standing by Spencer.

"You're so fucking light." Hale laughed. "I bet you're fun to throw. Catch."

He *tossed* me at Wes, a shriek escaping my lips as I flew across the sand.

Wes dove and caught me. "Got you."

"My turn." Tru laughed.

"Shit," Wes muttered as for a moment he just held me. "You okay?"

"Yeah." I watched Hale toss Tru at Mercy. What the hell?

Hale grinned at Wes. "You play *toss the Grace* all the time, right? Way more fun than flying disc."

Brennan strode over to him. "I'm Brennan, you are?"

"I'm Hale. Grace's favorite brother. I brought Mercy and Tru." Hale grinned. "So, Big Sis, this is your pack? Nice hotel."

I made the introductions. Mercy and Riley were deep in conversation. Tru trotted over to the hole Riley had dug and picked up some of the sand toys.

"I'm sorry to crash your pack beach day, but Tru was crying last night because Creed wouldn't bring her to see you, since he has to get back to Natty for finals and shit. And well, when Mom rolled in drunk this morning, things literally started to fly. Dare took Pax and Chance to the park, Verity took Hope to the arboretum, and Mercy and I took Tru because they don't need to see that shit," Hale told me quietly.

"Oh. I... I'm sorry. I didn't mean to cause problems with your pack." My belly twisted.

Wes put his arm around me, sending me love through the bond.

"This isn't your fault," Hale told me. "Mercy and I don't want to be around Mom right now, anyway. Besides, I want to work on my tan."

"Are you Adriana's? I don't know the whole family tree yet," I said softly.

"Yeah. Creed's Dad and Mumsy's, Mercy and I are Mom and Dad's, Verity, Dare, and Chance are Mama and Baba's, and Tru, Pax, and Hope are Dad and Harry's," he explained. "Well, Dad and Harry had help, but you know what I mean."

So much to remember.

I looked over and saw Mercy and Riley helping Tru build a sandcastle. If they were staying, I should order them some food, since our lunch would be here soon.

"Well, welcome," Brennan said. "It's probably best to get the younger kids away from any fighting."

"Yeah, yesterday was scary enough," Hale replied. "At least the littles didn't really understand. It freaked Mercy out though, since she just had that assembly."

My shoulders rounded. "I'm so sorry."

"It's Mom's fault." Hale made a face. "I don't know why she's so upset. You're an adult, it's not like you'd come live with us."

I'm sure she hoped I had inherited those illegal genetics, and then she'd be rid of me and whatever problems I represented. But I wasn't about to say that.

"I'm glad Dad finally found you, and..." For a moment Hale looked anxious. "He really wants to get to know you. For all the mistakes he made when he was younger, Dad really tries to be a good guy. Also, Harry's made him a whole lot better."

"That's nice to know. I'd like to see him when he comes to Rockland. Maybe I can show him my work," I replied.

Hale laughed. "Oh, you should. If Creed gets the job, you should absolutely hire Mercy and Dare as interns. Might be good for them to get away for the summer."

"That's a thought." Maybe Mercy and Riley could go to skate smash camp together. I still felt awful at the idea of their pack fighting so badly the older ones got the little ones out of the house.

"Come build a sandcastle with us," Riley yelled, waving me over.

"If you'll excuse me." I turned.

"Grace?" Hale's voice went rough. "What happened?"

Right, I wasn't wearing my cover up, so the scars on my back were on display. *The woman your mother gave me to did this.* But I couldn't bring myself to say it. It wasn't his fault.

"It was a long time ago." I squeezed Wes' hand then went over to the girls. "Mercy, Tru, we just ordered lunch, do you want something?"

They told me what they wanted and what to get for Hale, and I went inside the cabana to place the order.

Wes' arms wrapped around me. "Are you okay?"

"Yeah. I should try to get to know my siblings. I just feel awful that everyone is fighting." I finished entering the order on the wall-mounted order tablet.

"Not your fault, Grace. That pack sounds like it has issues." Wes kissed my neck.

"Do packs get divorced?" I frowned, leaning into him. Through the doorway I saw Hale playing flying disc with Jett and Evan. Would the other kids resent me if I was the reason their family broke apart?

"Sometimes. It all depends on how it's formed and who's bonded to whom," Wes said. "My dad just picked us up and left. Given what you told me, the professor probably has legal grounds to un-bond Adriana. They might kick her out, or he could just take the younger ones and move with whatever mates he wants to stay with."

"It's all so much." Closing my eyes, I sighed. The cabana still smelled like sex and anxiousness shot through me.

Wes nuzzled my neck. "Stop. No seriously, Grace. Whatever you, Jett, and Evan got up to in here is fine, as long as it made you all happy."

I rested my head against his bare chest as I tried to quell the urge to push him down on the chaise lounge. "My hormones are raging. I was seriously thirsting for Bren this morning."

His hands tangled in my hair. "You've been through a lot, and your hormones want to be comforted with dick. It's normal. You just bonded Spence, too. Also, I think we all thirst for Bren sometimes. And, you, Princess Peaches," he pressed his lips to the top of my head, "are a people pleaser who seeks attention as approval."

Frowning, I looked up at him. "What do you mean I seek approval?"

"That's not a bad thing, Grace," he soothed. "But yeah, you sort of do."

"I like it when people like me. Wait, you thirst for Bren?" Amusement tinged my voice.

He grinned. "Sometimes. There was a point where Bren and I tried to see if me, him, Jett, and Evan could be a thing together. It didn't work, but that doesn't mean I don't enjoy myself with him sometimes."

"The idea of you two fucking is going to live rent free in my head." My pussy clenched at the thought. Yeah, if we didn't have guests...

Wes kissed me long and deep, his hand squeezing my ass. "Maybe after lunch you can get a headache, and I'll take you back to the villa and take care of you."

"That's a thought." I kissed him back, my arms wrapping around him. Yeah, I'd still like a knot or seven.

Brennan entered the cabana, unfazed by us making out. Brennan and Wes fucking? For the love of baby Jesus, who was the top? Maybe they arm wrestled for it.

"Grace, are you all right?" Brennan asked. "I'll make them leave if you don't want them here. Hale is... a lot."

"It's fine—and I didn't invite them. I did let Creed know we were going to the beach, but that was because his friend wanted me to come to some sort of science brunch and I didn't want to be social," I told him.

Brennan squeezed my shoulder. "I believe you. And even if you did, I understand wanting to get to know your siblings."

My phone buzzed on the table next to my abandoned fruity drink and e-reader. Extracting myself from Wes' arms, I expected it to be the professor looking for his children. Instead, it was filled with threatening texts from a number I didn't recognize. But given they were all variations of *How dare you break up my family?* I could figure it was probably Adriana.

"What's wrong?" Wes took the phone from me and read over them and showed Brennan. "I'm on it."

"Stay with one of us at all times," Brennan said. "If we need to, we'll get a protection order to keep her from you."

I gulped. "Right, because she's confronted me before, she'll do it again."

"You're safe with us." Brennan ruffled my hair.

Wes did something to my phone. "Okay, it's blocked. I'll run the number later, but I'm guessing this is one of the professor's alphas?"

"Adriana probably." My phone rang. Before I could see who it was, Wes answered it on speaker.

"Hello?" His voice was rough and demanding.

"Oh, hello. This is Nate Thorne. I'm calling for Grace. Spencer, is that you?" the professor said over the phone.

"No, this is Wes. You're on speaker. Grace is right here," Wes said, frowning.

"Hi, Professor. Mercy, Tru, and Hale are here at the beach with me and my pack. We're going to have lunch soon. Do you need me to send them back to you after we eat?" I asked.

"They're with you?" His voice filled with hope. "I saw that they were at the beach. That makes sense. Tru is curious and she kept asking Creed and Verity about you last night."

"Well, it will be fun to spend the afternoon with them." *I hope.* I peeked through the doorway again. "Mercy and Riley seem to be getting along well."

"Good. Um, Creed said something yesterday that puzzled me. He said that you were *disowned* by those who raised you for getting a PhD in math?" he asked.

"Um, yeah. She wanted me to be a kindergarten teacher and when I decided to enter a PhD in math instead of moving home after undergrad, she cut me off. When I found out she'd died, I hadn't spoken to her in years because of it." I leaned into Wes. Brennan hadn't left.

"Oh. That strikes me as strange, because Rosalind was at community college getting her certificate in *book keeping.* She was good at math. Both sisters were very smart. I had no idea music was related to math until Thora showed me. Though Rosalind primarily used her math skills for card counting and safe breaking. But still..." The professor's voice drifted off.

"Huh." I nodded.

Well, that solved the mystery of Rosalind's major. And the mystery of why she hadn't wanted me to get a PhD.

"I... I'm sorry to have caused fighting in your family, Professor."

"It's not your fault, Grace. I was calling because I wanted to share a bit of information I learned. Apparently, when you were dropped off with Adriana, Thora wasn't gone yet. She was imprisoned and questioned for a crime that ultimately Rosalind and one of their brothers helped commit. Based on that, I guess she'd called wanting me to keep you because the police were after her. How it went from that to her being executed for an illegal designation, I... I don't know. I never knew that. There are so many gaps. I'm sorry. If I'd only been home when you were brought to us." His voice broke.

"It's okay, Professor." My head rested on Wes' shoulder.

"Professor, it's Wes. Where's Adriana? She's been sending threatening messages to Grace," Wes added.

"Shit. I'm sorry. Save them in case you need them. Zain and Pip threw her out. She's probably sleeping in her office. I... I don't know if things can be saved between us—and this is not your fault. Obviously, I didn't know her as well as I thought," he sighed. "But then things have been fraying between us ever since, never mind, you don't need to know about my relationship problems. Anyhow, enjoy the beach." He ended the call.

Wes took my phone. "I'm saving the texts. What he said was a good idea."

Riley came in. "Um, sandcastle?"

"Yeah, coming. The professor called. I'm coming now." I gave Wes a kiss then went back outside to join in the sandcastle making.

They'd already gotten to work. There was a small pile of shells, rocks, and sticks, and several buckets had been filled with water. An assortment of sand toys were all laid out.

"Hi." Tru grinned. "Creed says you're a math scientist and you work for an important company. Verity says that you fell in love with your scent match when you were little. That's so romantic."

"It sort of is. I dreamed of him, too," I told her, as I took a shovel.

"Which one is he?" Mercy asked as she started to make a big mound of sand.

"Wes," I nodded, as Wes and Brennan came out of the cabana, and I started to dig a moat.

Mercy nodded. "Cute, if you like clean-cut guys next door. He plays rugby? He looks like he plays rugby or lacrosse."

"He played rugby in high school. Bren, too." I nodded toward Brennan.

Spencer came over to us and quietly started helping, moving his leg so he touched mine, which was comforting.

"I like math science. One day I am going to prove Garamoci's Theory of Everything," Tru told me, helping me dig.

Mercy rolled her eyes. "How do you even know what that is? You're *five*. For once, I'd like to live in a normal house where we don't have nights where we only speak another language, and everyone's not something that ends in –tist."

"I like the idea of language nights," Spencer said quietly.

"That could be fun." I turned to Mercy. "What do you want to do? Skate smash, right?"

"Yeah, I want to play for the Capitol Crushers. Or any team really, but they're my favorite. When I retire, I'm going to teach history and coach skate smash at a high school," she told me. "Science and math are fine, but I like history better."

"History can be interesting." Wow. So, she had a plan–and a pretty decent one. Creed made it seem like she had none. Maybe they just didn't listen.

"Capitol Crushers? Respect," Riley nodded, as she poured some water on the sand pile in the middle of the moat. "I like the

Rockland Raiders. Tell me more about this travel league you're in, because that sounds like a lot of fun."

Chapter Fifty-Seven

Wes

I laid on a chaise lounge I'd dragged out of the cabana, drinking a beer and watching as Grace, Tru, Mercy, and Riley finished making a *very* elaborate sand castle now that lunch was over.

Hale and Spencer skimboarded along the shore. Brennan sat nearby, frowning over his phone. Probably more drama with the Queen Mum.

Evan came out of the cabana, a smug look on his face. Grace looked over at him and raised her eyebrows. He grinned, then came over to me, snuggling into my arms, and stealing my beer.

"Feel better now?" I murmured in his ear. He smelled of Jett.

"Oh yeah." Evan sighed, rubbing his ass against me. "I'm still horny though, if you want to escape to the villa."

My hand ran down his bare chest. "Tempting."

"What do I have to do to seal the deal?" Evan eyed the sand castle. "Wow, they have been at that all afternoon."

"Yeah. It's really weird watching them work. The others have some of the same mannerisms as Grace. Like Tru does that thing Grace does where she looks up at you and blinks in a cute way," I replied.

"Grace should have grown up here. It would have been so much better for her. But if she had I wouldn't have ever met you." Worry shot through the bond.

I planted a kiss on Evan's temple and ran my fingers through his hair. "What are you talking about? While sure, I would have found her faster, you and I still would have met. Even before everything happened that caused me to almost fail out of the university, I'd been thinking hard about changing majors. Grace would have been desperate to escape them and to not go to whatever university they teach at. I probably would have gone into the military so I could help support her. Just like you called Spencer as soon as we met, I would have called her and been like, *Peaches, I met this hot guy you're going to love.*"

"Yeah?" Evan kissed me. "I might have had to help you actually steal her from her parents. Because scent match or not, they seem like the kind of family that would lock their teenage omega down."

The image of Evan helping her climb out a window while I manned the getaway car made me chuckle.

"Yep. We'd still have gotten together. We just would have been sharing that bowl of noodles or ice cream cone between the three of us," I grinned, running a hand down his face, remembering our broke days.

"And the moment Spencer met her. Oh yeah." Evan nodded. "She'd be spending every summer interning with him. When we went to Bren's wedding? Fucking fireworks. Bren would have known all about your dream girlfriend. He might have even helped you find her. Most definitely, he would have helped you write bad poetry and talk her parents into letting you take her to the school dance despite the distance. We might even already be forming a pack with Spencer–even if he wasn't ready to be with her, he'd be just as enamored."

"I can see all of that." I ran my hand down his shoulder. "Yeah, there'd still be an us. There just would have been more Grace in it. Helping her with her homework, taking her to campus formals–"

"Making sure she ate more than ramen, day-old baked goods, and coffee." Evan rolled his eyes. "I know my eating habits can be shit, but her talking about what she lived off while getting her PhD gives me hives."

"Yeah. She really could have used us then. But she's got us now." I gave him a lingering kiss. "And I'm so glad that I have you to share her with."

He hummed as he kissed me back.

"Get a room, you doofuses," Riley yelled. She rolled her eyes. "Brothers are dumb. Do your brothers do shit like that?"

Mercy shook her head. "They're not allowed to date. The parents are weird like that."

Evan shook his head and lowered his voice. "Yeah, I'm not sure if growing up as the oldest of *ten* would have been any better for her. The parentification would suck. At least we answered some of our own questions."

Brennan came over to us and I sat up, pulling Evan with me, to make room on the bottom of the chaise for him. He sat down and eyed the guys skimboarding. Jett had joined them and kept falling off, but Spencer looked like he'd been doing it his whole life.

"Is there anything Spencer can't do?" Brennan shook his head.

"Not really. It sort of bugged me when I was a kid," Evan replied. "My mom always said it was because he's a little older, but I think it's just because he's Spencer."

"Sounds about right." I nodded.

"She's having fun, right? Because the moment she's not, or they make her cry, they're going home," Brennan grumped, looking at Grace.

"Awww, it's so fucking sexy when you give a shit." Evan gave him a kiss on the cheek.

"What else am I supposed to do, Love?" He frowned, like this was an honest question. "I'm worried about her. She already went through some shit–and now this? More than ever, we have to fucking protect her."

"Yeah, you're right. The moment she's not okay, we mumble something about dinner reservations and bid them good night," I agreed, looking over at her as she helped Tru decorate the castle with seashells.

"I vote for room service and movies, with hot man pillows," Evan agreed.

"They seem like good kids. Though Hale is like a high-energy puppy with zero obedience training. I'm a little afraid of what small country Mercy and Riley might conquer. But Grace does seem to be having fun." I waved and she blew me a kiss. I blew one back.

"Are we even doing this right?" Brennan frowned. "I don't know how to take care of her."

"What are you talking about?" I shot him a puzzled look. "Yeah, Grace is getting some painful answers to her questions. But she's got us, and all we need to do is just keep loving her and making sure that she knows she's safe and we still want her. All this information doesn't change our feelings for her. She'll just need us to give her lots of snuggles and ice cream."

Taking care of Grace was easy. I wasn't sure why he was stressed.

Evan nodded. "That's really the most important thing." He squeezed Brennan's shoulder. "You're doing great. Just keep being sweet with her like you were today. I think she likes it when you play with her hair and rub the back of her neck."

"Does she?" He looked both anxious and pleased.

Oh. Brennan didn't just give a shit about her, he was half in love with her–and confused as fuck about it.

Brennan and Grace. When Brennan loved, he loved *hard*. And I was here for it.

Chapter Fifty-Eight

Grace

Spencer came over and kissed me on the cheek. "Oh, that sand castle looks spectacular. Make sure that you get some pictures."

The castle was beautiful, decorated with sticks, rocks, and shells, and even had a moat. It was everything I envisioned making a sandcastle would be.

Riley scoffed. "What, do you think we're amateurs? We've already made several videos."

"I'm going to steal Grace." Spencer took my arm, and we walked a little down the beach.

He took a couple of pictures of me, and we snapped some silly selfies.

We walked past what looked like a wedding or mating party or something.

"Hi." I leaned into him. People were watching us, but I didn't care.

"Hi. You know, at some point we're going to have to announce ourselves to the public. Even if it's a photo on social media. Though I'll probably need to give my publicist a few things to say," he told me.

"You have a publicist?" It made sense.

"Yes. Mostly she does things like book my speaking engagements that raise money for Compass BioTek's afterschool programs and keeps the press out of my business." He kissed me.

I nodded. "We can take some cute pictures to post. Your mom knows about us, right?"

"Yes."

"We... we should invite her to our party. We should have one, right?" I remembered what Brennan and Evan had told me.

"I'd love that." He squeezed me to him. "But I don't want to interfere with what Evan's planning."

I laughed. "Never. That's a year away because Brennan had to get the property renovated and the garden blooming. We could have something sooner for just me and you."

"I'd like that. It doesn't have to be large, but a little something would be nice. I'd like you to meet some of my family from Greece," he told me.

"That sounds wonderful." I squeezed his hand, and we walked back toward our cabana.

Sandcastle done, Tru and Mercy were now burying Evan in the sand as Jett and Hale played flying disc some more. Hale didn't seem to stop moving. Ever.

I was getting hungry again, and as much as I yearned for my guys, maybe we should take my siblings out to dinner then see them onto the train home.

"Oh shit," Mercy said softly, looking down the beach. "HALE."

I looked over to see Adriana storming over toward us. Hale ran to meet her, expression cloudy. Jett joined me, phone in hand.

Spencer stayed close to me.

"Why is Mom so mad? I don't understand." Tru's lower lip quivered. "She was *throwing* things this morning. And there was so much yelling yesterday."

I sat down with them. "It's not you. It's me. My mommy was your dad's girlfriend before he ever met her and Mumsy. I think that upsets her a bit, me coming back into his life. It was never my intention to make anyone sad or angry and I'm so sorry that I hurt feelings. I just wanted to know you and your siblings and your dad a bit since I never knew you existed before," I explained.

Yeah, that sounded nice and gentle and not blame-y. Evan nodded as if to tell me I was on the right track.

"We were a surprise?" Her blue eyes blinked.

"The best surprise. I've always wanted sisters and now I have so many!" Okay, I never expected *nine* siblings, but I liked everyone I met so far. Not to mention Tru was *really* into math and I loved it.

"Creed said your real mommy and fake mommy were dead. But you have me and Pax. We're really nice. Creed and Verity are kinda boring, but they're really good at grown-up stuff. Verity makes the *best* snacks and cake pops. Hale and Mercy are more fun. Dare and Chance are annoying. So's Hope, but she's just a baby." Tru rolled her eyes.

"Mom, you really should just go home. We're fine," Hale said, trotting alongside Adriana as she walked toward us, determination in her brown eyes.

Mercy and Riley exchanged glances and Riley stood, grabbing a bucket. "Tru, let's see if we can find any flat rocks."

I stood and blocked Mercy with my body. "Adriana, I think you should leave."

"How did you even find him? You were never supposed to be in his life. That was why she created the other record. She *promised* me that you'd go away and never come back." Adriana's words slurred and she reeked of beer.

Why had Rosalind made a record calling me Cassidy, then called me Grace again in the new world? I'd probably never know. There was so much I'd never know. Though it might have been another way to lure in the dad that raised me. He was a church man and always liked my *good Christian name.*

Evan extracted himself from the sand and stood, positioning himself to protect Mercy, Hale at her side.

"Go home, you're drunk," Mercy replied. "Did you really give Grace *away* without Dad knowing? Who does that?"

"They were *twenty.* Who has kids at twenty?" She rolled her eyes. "Also, what sort of alpha has a *piano* major? Not that she was a real alpha, dirty variant," she spat.

"So much to unpack there," Evan whispered.

"First off, lots of people have kids at twenty," I countered. "Oopsies also happen. Whatever the case, he should have had a choice–as should have Thora. You robbed them both of that, for what, snobbery against fine art degrees?"

I pushed, standing toe-to-toe with her, as anger built inside me. "Do you know what Rosalind did to me? Do you know what it feels like to–" I stopped, seeing Mercy's face. No, she didn't need to hear that story.

"Oh fuck," Hale said softly. Other beach goers were watching us. Some had cameras.

"I was protecting him. That whole family was toxic–and so are you," Adriana shouted.

Spencer stepped in front of me. "Stay away from my mate, Adriana."

"You." Adriana snarled. "This was your doing, wasn't it? How dare you upend my family? I told you. I didn't know they were going to kill her. They were just supposed to scare her."

"Who are *they* and who did they kill?" Mercy said softly. "She said this yesterday and no one knows what she's talking about."

"Some protest group that may have killed Elaris. She and Spencer were mated and had a controversial company together. She died in a car wreck years ago," I replied, seeing Wes and Brennan running toward us.

"Controversial? It was *unethical.*" Adriana's face screwed up in anger.

"How the fuck is wanting to keep people from being executed for something they can't control, unethical." My hands fisted and I really wanted to punch her in the tits.

"Mom, you need to go," Hale demanded as some uniformed security from the hotel made their way toward us.

"How dare you turn my own children against me?" Adriana growled, grabbing something from her pocket. Metal flashed as she darted around Spencer and lunged at me, knife in hand.

"Grace," Wes yelled.

Jett flew at Adriana, as Spencer knocked me out of her way, taking a knife in the side. A sting shot through me as Spencer growled in angst.

"Mom, what did you do?" Mercy screamed as Brennan helped Jett take Adriana down.

"SPENCER!" I caught him in my arms, as we sank into the sand, as pain shot through our bond. "Wes, call an ambulance. She stabbed Spencer."

"I'll call," one of the guards said. "Go get the first aid kit," he told the other.

"Police are already on the way," Spencer croaked in my arms, blood spilling from his side, warm and sticky. "I'll be fine, my good doctor."

"You better be." I held him tight, biting back the mean words that wanted to spill from my lips at Adriana, because all I could see was Mercy sobbing in Hale's arms.

Down the beach, Riley kept trying to distract Tru with rocks.

"Here." Evan ran over with a towel to staunch the bleeding. "Today's not the day to die, old friend."

"I don't plan on it," he said.

"Just hold on," Wes said, joining us and holding my hand.

"Ambulance is on the way," the guard said, gesturing to a lifeguard carrying a first aid kit. Other guards were helping Brennan and Jett with Adriana.

"Hang in there, Spencer. Please?" Tears streamed down my face as the sirens grew louder. I hoped that it was an ambulance.

Tru ran toward us, Riley chasing her.

"Evan, help her, the little one doesn't need to see," I whispered.

With a nod, Evan left me and went to help Riley.

Police flooded the beach, surrounding us, guns out, eliciting screams from other beach goers.

"Hands up, everyone," someone yelled. Police were everywhere. Emergency personnel trekked down the beach holding a stretcher.

"Let me go," Adriana screamed, thrashing against Brennan, Jett, and the security guard. "That man and that bitch are trying to ruin my family."

"That woman stabbed one of my packmates and threatened another," Jett told them.

Spencer groaned and my attention went back to him as the police swarmed Adriana.

"Over here." I waved to the emergency personnel. "Hold on, Spence." I pressed my lips to his head.

Spencer groaned. Pain exploded through me, and I started to scream, vaguely aware of Wes calling my name.

"Adriana Thorne. You are under arrest in conjunction with the death of Elaris Thanukos and the trafficking of Cassidy Silvers," a voice I couldn't see boomed.

But all I could do was crumple to the sand in pain, as everything went black.

...to be continued in DREAM PACK, Into the Parallel Omegaverse, Book Three.

Thank you so much for reading. I hope you enjoyed the second book of Grace's journey. Pick up your copy of DREAM PACK today and read the conclusion to this story of a love so strong that it spans the universe.

Glossary of Select Terms

<u>Designations</u>

Alpha: Larger, faster, and with better senses, they make up about a quarter of the population. Their barks and pheromones can influence people. Male alphas have knots, female alphas have locks. Their scent holds a distinctive note that marks them as alpha. Female alphas can carry children.

Beta: They make up over half of the population and are your average ordinary people. Like the other designations, they can have kids, join or form packs, and an alpha can bond with them.

Gamma: Medical designation for a specific type of 'failed' omegas. While sometimes a genetic switch is thrown, halting development, most of the time it's environmental. Something is so dangerous in their environment that the body declares it unsafe to become an omega and halts a genetic process. Gammas can have many omega traits, but it varies from person to person and is often proportional to how close they were to becoming an omega. Gammas rarely respond to barks, pheromones, or danger the way omegas do. Common causes of gammas are war, famine, extreme poverty, and asshole parents, and not as common as they used to be.

Delta: They have a lot of alpha characteristics–especially in regard to size, speed, and senses. They make excellent soldiers and security. They're rarer than the 'big three' designations (alpha/beta/omega) but much more common than any of the rarer designations.

Digamma: Essentially, digammas are 'failed' alphas. Something is so dangerous in their environment that the body declares it unsafe to become an alpha and halts a genetic process. Exceedingly rare to the point where not much is known about them.

Zeta: Sometimes a genetic anomaly creates a designation that is a cross between an alpha and omega, some of them can even switch between the two. Like gammas, each zeta is a little different. Incredibly rare and coveted.

Kappa: The life of the party, they're usually adrenaline junkies with poor decision-making skills. They're an extremely rare designation because they've almost chaosed themselves out of existence.

Theta: Thetas tend to be misanthropic loners who like to amass wealth. While they do mate and form packs, they often aren't with alphas as they don't like to be told what to do. They wanted to be needed, but don't like to be smothered. They're closer to alphas than betas. A rare designation.

Iota: A rare designation, Iotas don't have scents, they also can't smell other scents and don't respond to barks or pheromones. This can be dangerous because they can't catch the scent-cues other designations can. Because they can't be barked or influenced, some iotas think they're better than other designations. They're closer to betas genetically.

Omicron: Omicrons are charming and charismatic but are conceited and don't think the rules apply to them. They want to take over the world and fix it, and aren't afraid to use violence, which has caused this designation, which is an alpha mutation, to be declared illegal. While they often can pass as alphas, because of their size, strength, and speed, and they smell enough like an alpha, they lack knots/locks. Often, they test as alphas when young.

Rho: Medical designation for a feral alpha.

Sigma: Often loners with anger issues, they tend to commit crimes to punish people. They don't want to be part of the system and generally think it's bullshit. Even though it's an extremely rare designation, and an alpha mutation, they're illegal. While they often can pass as alphas, because of their size, strength, and speed, and that they smell enough like an alpha, they lack knots/locks. Often, they test as alphas when young.

Tau: Medical designation referring to someone who lost their bonded scent match, also known as *soulbroke* and *shadow*.

Phi: A rare super-mutation of alpha and illegal. While they can be a loner like sigmas, they can also be fun like kappas, and even charismatic like an omicron. They can become violent and aggressive. Unlike the others, they can more easily hide among alphas, because males have a bulb that can pass as a slightly-deformed knot and their smell is often undistinguishable. Commonly, they test as alphas when young and have the size/strength/speed of an alpha. It is thought that Phis were created for battle long ago and something went horribly, terribly wrong.

Omega: One of the three main designations, omegas are usually smaller than the other designations and tend to be nurturers and caregivers. They're the most physically compatible with alphas, so they're often sought after as mates, even though they make up less than ten percent of the population. They can and do partner with other designations. Omegas have the same rights as everyone else. They have an extra element to their scent that marks them as such. Omega males are very good at making children, though most omega males can't carry them.

Other Terms

Alpha-Blockers: A type of medication that dulls alpha senses and instincts. It's most commonly prescribed to violent alphas, young alphas who aren't in full control, and criminals. There's a huge stigma around them, so many who should take them, don't.

Awakened/Blossomed: When someone fully comes into their designation after puberty.

Bond Test: A government test used to detect an alpha-omega bond.

Designation: The term used to indicate someone's specific genetic dynamic. The three main designations are alpha, beta, and omega. Other designations exist, including ones that are considered illegal.

Equalist: Someone who believes that designations should not be used/recognized so that everyone can be on equal terms.

Fundie/Fundamental: Someone who believed that packs are about population control and the stripping of rights by the government. They think that every alpha has the right to their own omega, even though it's statistically impossible. They often keep to themselves and usually don't take part in government services or programs or go to hospitals.

Heat: An omegas fertile cycle, which results in wanting sexual attention and satisfaction from their alphas and partners. Female omegas often have four to five heats a year; male omegas have two or three. Heats can last from a couple of days to a week.

Heat Spike: A quick rise in hormones, often right before a heat, which result in temporary heat-like symptoms.

Heat Suppressants: A type of medication some omegas take so that they don't go into heat. Heat suppressants are completely legal, though prolonged use can have side effects.

Mate Bond: The connection that forms when certain designations bite another in a certain way where proteins are released into their bloodstream creating a chemical reaction. Some bonds, like alpha-omega, have legal implications. Not all designations can make or accept bonds.

Mega-push: A street drug that can 'push' betas with certain genetic markers over to being an omega and often used in human trafficking. A legal version is available but highly regulated.

Omega Center: Omega Centers offer services ranging from healthcare and pack matching, to education and housing. Omegas don't have to register with the Center, but once registered can use their free services, including having an advocate–an assigned social worker that guides them through the process and helps them understand all their options.

Oxotipoline/Eazy-E: A sedative commonly used in human trafficking. The designer version, Eazy-E, is sometimes used by sexual predators.

Prick-Test: A simple blood test used to test for the three main designations–alpha, beta, and omega. All children are tested in middle school. The test is mostly accurate, but not always. It doesn't test for rare or illegal designations.

Scent-Blockers: A type of medication omegas take to blend in/function in society. These range from light scent-blockers that simply dull an omega's distinctive scent to heavy duty ones that lock down both omega scent and instincts, enabling them to hide as a beta. All are completely legal, but can be hard for hidden omegas to get. Prolonged use, especially of the heavy-duty blockers, can make them lose their effectiveness and/or cause health issues.

Scent-Match/Soulmate: That perfect match between two people—usually an alpha and omega. They usually know it by smell. Scent-matches are rare and plenty of people have happy and long relationships without being scent-matches. Sometimes scent-matches dream of each other, but that's mostly in books and movies. A scent match can be 'lopsided' when it is not alpha/omega, usually where one becomes an alpha/omega and the other stays a beta. A 'dead match' occurs when a couple would have been a scent match if they had been an alpha and an omega but instead both stayed betas.

Shadow: A term for someone who has lost their bonded scent match, also called *soulbroke*. The medical term is *Tau*.

Spiral: Dangerous drop in omega hormones which can result in unconsciousness, irrational behavior, and/or hospitalization. Often a trauma response.

Textbook Gamma: A gamma that became a gamma due to external conditions such as famine, poverty, war, or asshole parents.

Trevadol: A commonly prescribed anti-depressant. One side effect is that it can mess with the basic prick-test. This isn't considered much of an issue because this drug is for adults, and once the prick-test is given in middle school it isn't usually given again without reason. Some hidden omegas take the drug solely as a precaution because of that specific side effect,

Ultra-Bullet: Super-fast train that can turn an hours-long drive into moments.

Un-Bonding: The chemical process of removing a mate bond. It's governed by an extensive legal process to make sure that it is not abused.

Variant: A derogatory name for someone with an illegal designation.

The Thorne Family

The Parents

- Adriana Thorne (Alpha, *Mom*) — Chemistry Professor; mated to Nate, mother of Hale and Mercy.

- Pippa Thorne (Alpha, *Mumsy*) — Research Chemist; Mated to Nate, mother of Creed.

- Zain Thorne (Alpha, *Baba*) — Research Chemist; Married to Esme, father of Verity, Dare, and Chance.

- Esme Thorne (Beta, *Mama*) — Translator; Married to Zain, mother of Verity, Dare, and Chance.

- Harry Thorne (Beta, *Harry/Daddy*)–Restaurateur; Married to Nate, father of Pax, Tru, and Hope.

- Nate Thorne (Omega, *Dad*) — Organic Chemistry Professor; Mated to Pippa and Adriana, married to Harry, father of Grace, Creed, Hale, Mercy, Pax, Tru, and Hope.

<u>The Kids</u>

- Creed (Alpha)--Engineering student at National University of Science and Technology

- Verity (Alpha)--PhD student in plant genetics at Briar University

- Hale (Alpha)--Undergraduate student in organic chemistry at Briar University

- Dare (Alpha)--High Schooler

- Mercy (Alpha)--High Schooler

- Chance (designation still unknown)--Elementary Schooler

- Pax (designation still unknown)--Small Child

- Tru (designation still unknown)--Small Child

- Hope (designation still unknown)--Small Child

About Jane Handler

Jane Handler is the author of why choose omegaverse romance, including the HockeyVerse series. A hopeless romantic, Jane grew up reading romance and often got them taken away by her teachers for reading during class. Now she writes why choose, romance. When not writing, she's camping, eating sushi, doing laundry, or binge watching TV.